The Eulogist

Liz McKinney-Johnson

This novel is a work of fiction. The characters, incidences, names and places within this book have been totally created by the author's imagination. Any similarities to persons, living or dead, events or locations, are entirely coincidental.

Circle of Light Books, LLC

Regarding: The Eologist

2001 NW Aloclek Drive

Suite #7

Hillsboro, OR 97124

Printed in the United States of America

The Eulogist/Liz McKinney-Johnson -- 1st edition

ISBN: 978-0-9890681-3-0

Dedication

To all those who keep a little part of themselves to themselves.

To my family: Bob Johnson, Angela Johnson, Benjamin Johnson, Lydia Johnson, Anne Adams, and Mike McKinney, thank you for never giving up on me . . . and for allowing me the space and time to pursue something other than laundry. Your love and support mean everything to me. To the memory of my parents: Max and Sally McKinney, thank you for telling me, long before it was fashionable, that I could be and do anything.

ONE

In death we find eloquence.

"I was just another little boy with no hair. They'd brought out everybody and plopped us down on the carpet in the therapy room. Except the kids in the wheelchairs. They were parked in the back. I wasn't so special. At least not until Bippo picked me. He wore big yellow gloves, with big yellow fingers like sponge cakes. He pulled a quarter out of my ear and squeaked a balloon into the shape of a wiener dog."

I pause for effect and look around the room. A redheaded woman in the front pew digs in the pocket of her sweater. She's wearing black, but has smuggled in some illicit color: purple rhinestone buttons, an emerald scarf at her neck, a small orange ruffle at the bottom of her skirt. I wonder if she's a clown. It's against the Clown Creed to wear your make-up or costume to another clown's funeral. Clownish hints of color are okay, I guess. No one seems to mind. She blows her nose into a shredded Kleenex. Another few minutes and there won't be a dry eye in the house.

"He made me happy. Normal happy. He probably never even remembered me. There were so many of us that day. So many kids every day of his life, I imagine. But I remember him. I remember Bippo. He made me laugh at a time when there wasn't very much to laugh about. And what more can you ask of anyone than that?"

I hand the microphone back to the minister and look out at the faces: women with unfortunate haircuts, men with wrinkled foreheads, a random collection of bulky purses, shiny loafers and even tempers. They're just average folks who could be your next-door neighbors, a shirttail relative, that kid who works at the dry cleaner. Their sad eyes fill with pride as they silently plead for me to keep saying nice things. I've touched them and made them believe.

It's a hell of a rush. No wonder those TV preachers go nuts with power.

I have *tried* to find something conventional to do with my spare time. I hate gardening. There's so much dirt and squatting. In college, I lived around the corner from a guy who just stuck plastic flowers into the ground around his house. I think he was mentally challenged, because he also rode one of those giant adult tricycles, but on the gardening front, he had the right idea. I can't golf worth a damn. Most people can't golf worth a damn, but they look great in their matching polo shirts and slacks. I took a pottery class once. After thirteen weeks of study, I created a small, beige coaster. Valiant efforts, but nothing's ever been as appealing as my current pastime. Every morning I read the obituaries. I circle any that sound interesting, and then I show up at the funerals of dearly departed strangers.

Unusual? Sure. But so is square dancing or making mailbox windmills of endlessly sawing lumberjacks. No one has the corner on unusual. Not even me, Charlie Sandors, death groupie.

This morning I've selected Lester Harrison of Park Hills, Illinois.

Our loving father, husband, brother, son and friend passed away on February 11, at the age of 49.

It all started about five years ago when Pete Aldrich in Claims Management dropped dead of a heart attack at his desk. I worked in Insurance Fraud, five cubicles down from Pete. We got the day off for the funeral, but somehow I wrote down the wrong address and ended up across town at a funeral for some guy named Arthur O'Malley.

Lester is survived by wife Marcella, sons Richard and Christian, father George, brother Lyle Harrison, and sisters Lisa Harrison and Linda Harrison Slade.

However, I didn't know that—yet. Running late, I just grabbed a seat up front. Things were well underway before I realized I didn't recognize anyone.

Born in Park Hills on August 21, 1958, Lester graduated from Franklin High School. He was a guitar player and singer, performing in jazz and blues clubs from Chicago to Indianapolis.

I couldn't stand up in the front row and walk out. So, I stayed.

In 1984, he married Marcella Farrendino, also of Park Hills.

After Mr. O'Malley's funeral, we had tea and coffee, some of those mini muffins. About ten minutes into the reception, I realized no one questioned my being there.

Everybody talked amongst themselves, hardly paid any attention to me at all. A chubby lady in a black velvet hat commented to me in the mini muffin line about how sad it all was. I agreed, and that seemed to make her very happy.

Remembrances to the American Lung Association.

It was a great feeling to be companions for the moment, me and the rest of Art's real friends and family. I belonged. Besides, who wants to throw a funeral and then have hardly anybody show up? You're always glad to see another bereaved face in the crowd—whether you recognize it or not.

Family and friends are invited to attend a celebration of Lester's life on Saturday, February 17 at 2:00pm at Montgomery Chapel of Roses, 21st and NE Broadway.

I've been house sitting about a week for a nice lady named Opal. Her son bowls with my client Dennis, and Dennis told him I'm a great house sitter. Fine by me. I've done it lots. I make a couple bucks for simply existing and escape my own lousy apartment for a few days.

Opal's bungalow is decorated circa *Father Knows Best.* There are doilies on every surface. It smells like mothballs, steamed vegetables and her cat, Mr. Tippens. The saving grace is the car I've been told I can use while I'm here: a 1964 blue Corvair Spyder convertible. Opal's the original owner and she's kept it in sweet condition. The leather upholstery is as soft and shiny as the day it was born. Thank God neither the vegetable smell nor Mr. Tippens has invaded the car. I think the Corvair makes an excellent statement for Lester's funeral. It's hip without being kitsch. The same can be said for my black turtleneck and cords with a pea coat. I axed the beret at the last minute. Too cliché.

The parking lot is about half full when I arrive, with plenty of parking spaces near the front. People don't like to park near the front doors at a funeral. They're probably worried if they linger too near the hearse, they could be the next to die. "The ants crawl in, the ants crawl out, the ants play pinochle on your snout."

After that first funeral-by-mistake, I kept thinking about trying another one on purpose. Thinking and thinking and finally, doing. First one, then two, then every week. I liked being part of a group for a few hours, the raw acceptance of it.

I have to admit, apart from this weird hobby nobody knows about, I'm not particularly exciting. I think most people would describe me as "the quiet type," which really means, "kind of a bore." I have not yet been ostracized all the way over into the "scary nerd" category since I don't collect comic books, attend Star Trek conventions, or have a fascination for miniature railroads. At my funerals, I am who I create, and I always create someone way more interesting than me.

I haven't been to the Chapel of Roses before, but the design is identical to a dozen other funeral homes. Dark wainscoting, the paint above a bland yellow-beige. Two faux stained glass windows are stuck to the wall on either side of a tiny stage on which sits a wobbly wooden dais. Padded folding chairs line up in short rows on either side of a narrow center aisle. And there's the faint syrupy scent of air freshener. It's used to cover up other, unmentionable smells. I think it makes it worse, like that mothball reek they use in urinal cakes.

Today, our guest of honor lies up front flanked by sprays of gladiolas and a gleaming Martin 12-string. The casket is solid oak in a rich mahogany finish with bronze corners and accents and full matching handle bars. The family went for the high quality white velvet lining with matching pillow and throw. Very nice. At least three bills.

I had no idea of the variety and excessive cost of caskets before I started going to funerals on a regular basis. It's not something that comes up in general conversation, but it should. Think about trying to make a $3,000 to $4,000 decision ($10,000 and up if you go for the premium copper or bronze Permaseal) when you can't see straight from grief and denial. Most people go way overboard, compensating for what they couldn't give the departed in life by wrapping them up like Christmas presents in death.

Lester looks very peaceful against his Eterna Rest bedding. He was a good-looking guy. A few lines around the eyes, a lot more around the mouth, probably from several decades dragging on cigarettes. There's a tiny horseshoe shaped scar on his right cheek, platinum band on his left hand and a heavy ruby and gold signet on his right. Thick hands with heavy veins. I can't figure out how people with such large fingers play an instrument with such tiny strings. My uncle Dan used to play the mandolin. The guy must have weighed 350 or better. His hands were like two canned hams, but he could go to town on that little thing, fingers flying, notes as distinct as night and day. Amazing.

I'm staring at Lester's hands when a tall, slim woman in a tight black skirt comes up next to me.

"I've never seen him in a suit," she says.

"Not a suit man, that's for sure," I agree. "But he looks good. Don't you think he looks good?"

"I'm Mia, Lester's cousin. I don't think we've met before."

She extends a pale hand. Her fingers are long and thin, like miniature versions of her legs.

"My name's Randy. I used to tend bar at one of the clubs Lester played."

I reach out, but we don't really shake. Her fingers simply slide through mine, and before I can catch them, they waft up to brush her blond bangs behind one ear, revealing a line of tiny silver hoop earrings curving from lobe to cartilage. Several people come up behind us and we move to one side to let them see how good Lester looks.

"Are you here with anyone?" asks Mia.

"No. I just happened to see the funeral notice in the paper. I had no idea it had gotten so bad."

"He went from bad to worse after the holidays," says Mia. "Not many people knew. Les didn't want anyone coming around crying over him."

I chuckle quietly. "What a guy."

Mia's blue eyes blur and she blinks. "Do you want to sit with me? I'm essentially here by myself too. The rest of the family usually steers clear of 'crazy cousin Mia.' I'm surprised you've never heard of me." She dips her head and the bangs fall back over her eyes. Her hair smells like fruit punch. I like fruit punch.

"Les and I talked music not family."

"All the better. It takes a lot of energy to be the black sheep. It'll be nice to sit in anonymity for awhile."

Mia gestures at two empty seats in the middle of a row and we walk over to sit down. Memorial folders lie on each chair. I pick up mine and read through it as other mourners file past good-looking Les. The little chapel is almost full. Good turnout. A promising crowd.

When I started going to strangers' funerals, I was just an observer. And then I discovered how much you can learn about someone between the obituary and that little program they hand out at the service. An entire life whittled down to the highlights. Most of us lead relatively dull lives. A few paragraphs are probably plenty.

"So, Crazy Cousin Mia," I say, leaning towards her. "What is it that makes you the black sheep?"

"Too many things to mention, but primarily, it's the fact I'm an exotic dancer not a concert pianist."

"Uh-huh."

The eulogies fill in the interesting tidbits, the snippets that let you know the real person between the lines of the obituary.

"All us Harrisons are musicians of one stripe or another," Mia continues. "Some, like Lester, are more successful than others, but we all can carry a tune, strum, pick or bang something. My weapon was the piano. I was playing professionally by 10, getting paid for it by 12, hating it by 16, which was the same year I ran away from home to become a dancer."

"Are you good?"

"Excellent. An amazing sense of rhythm I'm told."

She smiles slyly and goes back to reading her program.

You'd be amazed what people will tell you when you act like you're interested. My day job as a freelance insurance fraud investigator is prefect for this. I'm always asking questions, looking for a chink in the claims of accident and misery. It makes you a master interviewer, which is really nothing more than being a good listener. After enough seemingly inane questions, people begin to believe you find them fascinating. Pretty soon they're blabbing away, positive someone finally understands just how great/weird/shitty their lives truly are.

"I can't believe your family would toss you to the wolves just for selecting a unique occupation," I say.

"Some of them have come to grips with it over the years. Les was always open-minded. He didn't care what someone did as long as you were a good person. I'm a good person."

Of course, at funerals, I'm not trying to catch them, I'm trying to keep them from catching me. But the same techniques work, and when you're pretending to have been a good friend of the deceased, it helps to have the real bereaved fill you in on important details, like his favorite beverage, what he drove, and whether or not he was a Bears fan.

"Are your parents here?" I ask Mia.

"Of course."

She gestures several rows up towards a middle-aged woman in a loose-fitting black dress. The woman's head is bowed. Her long graying hair, only slightly contained by a pair of silver barrettes, spills over her face and hangs down into her lap. Her shoulders are shaking gently, which I assume means she is crying. A short, round man in an ill-fitting suit sits next to her with his arm around her shoulders.

"My parents, Dianne and John Harrison. You'd think by the tragic tableau that Mom was the blood relative, but actually my dad was Les' dad's younger brother."

The first time I raised my hand to volunteer a eulogy was John Moller's funeral. I'm not sure what moved me to action; maybe I was seized by the spirit, like those snake charmers. Whatever it was, I summoned the courage to get up and relate a very moving story about what an inspiration John had been to me. About how, as a lowly copy machine repair boy, I'd been in and out of John's office quite a few times, and every time, John had a smile and a kind word of recognition. "Hey man," he would say. "You're not runnin' off a bunch of copies of your bill are ya?" Then he'd laugh that big, ol' laugh of his and clap me on the back. I told John's friends and family that John had made me feel like a real member of the team and inspired me to start my own copy machine repair business.

"It's really not worth trying," Mia whispers.

Her statement makes no sense, until I realize she must have been wondering why I was staring at her father so intently.

"Where's the family resemblance, right?" she asks. "Give it up; my dad and Uncle George do not look like they came from the same litter."

"Wait a minute," I say. "Your uncle's name is *George Harrison*?"

"Les never mentioned that? I'm shocked. It was one of his favorite jokes. He loved to tell people he was the bastard Beatle."

Mia laughs, and when she does, several people in the front row turn around and glare. She stifles her amusement and leans in closer.

"That's Uncle George over there. The one in the front row with all the white hair."

Mia cocks her head in the direction of an impeccably dressed man with tortoise shell half glasses hanging around his neck. He does indeed have a wild amount of pure white hair.

At John Moller's reception, at least a dozen people came up to thank me for giving such an uplifting eulogy. We chatted about John and agreed the world would be a lesser place without him. His sister, Claudia was particularly moved by my sentiments. We talked until the funeral parlor workers started picking up the chairs. Claudia told me all about her big brother. Then she told me all about herself. I told her she had incredible eyes. Claudia was my first funeral fling. But before you label me a total social deviant, you have to understand that just like the funerals themselves, the funeral flings were completely serendipitous. I did not attend John Moller's funeral expecting to deliver a eulogy or expecting to get laid by his sister. Sometimes things just happen. But it was an interesting side benefit with potential for development.

"Your uncle looks like that guy from the Bugs Bunny cartoons. You know, the crazy orchestra conductor."

Mia chuckles again, but much more quietly.

"He *is* a conductor. Retired now."

A man steps from the audience and approaches a small organ on one side of the stage. He glances at maestro Harrison, who nods. The man places his hands on the keys, closes his eyes and begins to play.

"That's Lyle," says Mia. "Lester's brother. You might recognize him if you can look past the suit and tie. He played with Lester off and on over the years."

Organ music fills the little chapel. I watch Lyle rock backward with the force of the crescendos then roll forward as if to protect the keys as the tone softens. His hair is pulled into a tiny ponytail that dips behind the collar of his suit coat, which is a deep parrot green fabric that shimmers amongst the rest of dowdy brown and black flock.

"Were you that good?" I ask Mia.

"I was on my way."

"What a shame you gave it up."

"I suppose, but then, you've never seen me dance."

"I'd like to."

Mia places her hand on my knee and I cover it with my own. We sit silently through the rest of the performance. At the conclusion, Lyle stands and returns to his seat next to his father. No one makes a sound. This is one thing that always bothers me about funeral services. No one claps. It seems rude, and everybody always looks a little uncomfortable.

A minister enters the room through a door behind the dais. His white clerical collar bites into the flesh of his neck, creating an abrupt dividing line between head and torso. He adjusts the microphone, which sends out a few painful blasts of feedback, and looks out at the assembled group. His lips are huge and pink, like cherry puff pastries.

"Thank you all for coming," he says, and I expect crumbs to fly out over the audience. "We have gathered here to remember the life of Lester Harrison. To celebrate the time he spent with us and to rejoice in his new life with our heavenly Father. Let us pray."

Mia withdraws her hand from beneath mine, clasps it with her other and bows her head. I do the same. The minister drones on about life everlasting. I shift my gaze from my shoes to Mia's. Her calves are slender yet muscular. I imagine them in a pair of thigh-high black patent leather boots. I am going to have to deliver one hell of a eulogy if I want to see those legs wrapped around my own.

An *amen* ripples through the crowd and heads bob back up to attention.

"And now," says the minister. "I'd like to ask Lester's family and friends to come up and share their memories and stories."

One by one they approach the podium, nervously at first, and then more eagerly as the crowd warms up. There's a beefy guy in an embroidered biker vest who's slicked back his hair for the occasion, an elderly woman in pearls who was "little Lester's" piano teacher, a stringy young kid, swimming in a white dress shirt with a wide tie. This is the part of the funeral where the veil of solemnity lifts. The assembled crowd is allowed to show emotions other than grief. There are several very funny stories about Lester, and I collect and catalog key details: wild in school, devoted to his family, liked to drink and smoke, loved life on the road, had a soft spot in his heart for animals, had a soft spot in his head for motorcycles, wrote songs that could sweep you away.

The procession of eulogists begins to thin. The minister surveys the crowd and asks if anyone else has something to share. I raise my hand. Mia looks surprised as I stand, smooth my trousers and slide past several pairs of knees to reach the aisle. I hear whispers and murmurs. This is normal. People are trying to figure out who I am. I smile as I walk up to the podium, then I turn to face the expectant crowd.

"My name is Randy McDonald. Lester and I got to know each other during his set breaks back when I used to tend bar. I'm not as talented as all you folks out there, and I'm not used to talking in front of a crowd."

I stop and take a breath. As a bartender, I think I need a tougher personality, a harder edge, even a little vulgarity. I begin again, deepening my voice and stepping in closer to the microphone.

"I bet none of you knew that Lester Harrison saved my life."

A few gasps float up from the audience. I glance at Mia. Her lips are curved into a little "o" shape and her eyes are wide. She crosses her legs and leans forward in her chair.

"He wouldn't have mentioned it to anyone. Les was real proud, maybe even a little obnoxious when it came to his band – and his family."

I stop and smile at the front row.

"But he wasn't one to brag about *his* good deeds. So, now that he's gone, I'll do it for him."

"It was summer. A weeknight and the place was pretty light. Lester was sitting with me at the bar, taking an extended break. Nobody was complaining since it was really too hot to do much of anything. He was telling me about his newest motorcycle, the Indian rebuilt. I was only half listening. I'd done some pretty heavy drugs before my shift and the world was still a little artificial. Les knew I was wiped out and asked what was going on. He said I'd been messed up nearly every night that week. Of course, I told him *he* was crazy, that he was the one fucked up."

With this well-placed profanity, I immediately grab the attention of anyone left not listening.

"I asked him if he didn't have anything better to do than accuse people of being stoned. That's when he hit me. I didn't even see it coming. Nailed me right across the nose. Hurt like Jesus, and he was just sitting there with this big ol' grin on his face. I asked him what the hell he did that for. Actually, I screamed it at him, but he just sat there. Nobody else even bothered turnin' around. It was just too damn hot."

"Finally, Lester took a swallow of a beer and wiped the smile off his face with the back of his hand. He looked right at me and said, 'Listen, shit-for-brains, either get your sorry ass together now or you'll be standin' in this same spot five years from now, staring at some middle-aged barfly's tits, thinkin' you gotta get you some of that.' Then he stood up, walked up front and started back playin' before the rest of the guys even got up on stage."

I look around the room. They are in the palm of my hand, listening to me, believing in me. Attention is addicting.

"I listened to that song and when he finished, I clapped."

I clap for a few seconds to show my audience what I mean.

"I was the only one clapping, but I didn't stop. I kept clapping until I couldn't get any more sound to come out of my hands. Then I walked out of that bar and never went back. I've been clean for two years now and I'm goin' to school. I'm goin' to be a chef. But if Les hadn't busted my chops, I'd still be slingin' juice—more'n likely, I'd be long dead from the shit. So here's to you, Lester."

I start clapping again. A few seconds later Mia joins me, then Lyle, and then George Harrison. Even Mia's mother stops crying and puts her hands together. When the whole room is clapping, I step down, walk out the doors, through the foyer, back out into the parking lot and lean against the Corvair, waiting for Mia.

TWO

My pen is poised over the newspaper. There's a doozy of a funeral notice today. It has wealth. It has fame. It has a very attractive widow. Michael Rudolph, crown prince of the city's medical community, has been killed in a plane crash.

We are all saddened by the sudden and tragic death of Dr. Michael Rudolph, well-known Chicago-area neurosurgeon, medical researcher and philanthropist. His 1972 Piper Cherokee spiraled into the Rock River last Sunday after take-off from Barnett Memorial airport.

The obituary reads like a nomination for the Nobel Prize. I'm surprised he wasn't able to escape by walking across the water.

Dr. Rudolph is known throughout Illinois for his generosity to both the medical community and the general populace, as well as his fierce dedication to Alzheimer's research. Groundbreaking for the Rudolph Research Wing at Lake Community Hospital will go forward as planned, and his estate will continue to fund the clinical testing of a promising new Alzheimer's drug from local company, Nesler Pharmaceuticals.

There's a large picture and two full columns of copy. There's even a news story on the front page of the financial section. This is the funeral big leagues.

Mr. Rudolph is survived by his wife, Lily and his mother, Beatrice J. Rudolph. A memorial service will be held today, Wednesday, February 28, at St. Mark's Cathedral at 11:00am. A private graveside service follows prior to interment in the Rudolph family vault at Lake Shore Memorial Gardens.

I've seen pictures of the Rudolphs in the paper before. Most people are simply born into the world with nothing but the luck of the genetic draw, but a select few arrive carved out of granite in the likenesses of the gods. Michael and Lily Rudolph were the kind of beautiful people you could set down in any situation and they would rise to the top. Raven haired and fine-featured, they were equally gorgeous, equally charming, more like siblings than husband and wife. In the case of truly stunning individuals, I don't buy the old saw that opposites attract; I think a sameness draws them together, a comfortable mirror image.

Michael Rudolph's death was a wrong turn in the fairy tale, yet in some ways his death was as spectacular as his life. The financial page story adds a few grisly details absent from the obituary.

Police and Department of Transportation investigators continue to comb the crash site and do not expect to have a full report for several weeks. Barnett Memorial is a non-towered airport and there were no witnesses on the ground to confirm the situation surrounding the accident. Based on preliminary crash scene evidence, investigators are speculating Rudolph experienced some sort of engine failure shortly after take-off and attempted to turn back to the airport. Experts agree that if Rudolph lost control in the turn, it could have resulted in a spiral from which he would have been unable to recover. Debris at the scene initially indicates Rudolph's plane hit the ground at 100 to 120 mph, suggesting a plunge from 500 to 800 feet.

Funerals notwithstanding, I like to think of myself as a pretty average guy. I'm honest enough to know I'm not traditionally handsome, but I don't think I'm completely unattractive either. About five foot eleven, six feet if I stand up straight, trim, pale skin, very blue eyes. In high school, I perfected a hairstyle that allowed a cascade of black curls to fall across my forehead as I hunched over chemistry calculations. I liked to imagine it as the look of a tortured Irish poet: brooding yet not quite suicidal. There's even been a few co-workers over the years, female co-workers I emphasize, who've said if they looked past the rather disheveled first impression, they could see some definite potential. Not necessarily ringing praise, but I cling to it nonetheless.

Rudolph's wife reported her husband missing late Sunday afternoon when he did not return home for a previously scheduled dinner engagement. A check of the flight plan filed at his home airport of Aurora revealed the remote Barnett as his destination. Civil Air Patrol was dispatched and spotted the wreckage from the air. Emergency vehicles were immediately sent from several points surrounding the airport, but all arrived hours after impact. Rudolph was pronounced dead at the scene from multiple injuries.

My childhood was pretty average too—until our house burned down. When you're a kid, change sneaks up on you. You go along riding your bike, eating pizza, getting dirty. Everything is present tense. More than that, it's instant tense. When something intrudes and spins your world out of balance, it's bewildering. My universe flew apart Thanksgiving Day 1980. I was ten. All my relatives were at our house for the holiday. I didn't question it; I just moved my pillow and blankets onto a sofa and pretended I was camping. My little sister Gina was sleeping with my mom and dad. Various aunts and uncles and cousins and grandparents were strewn around the rest of the house. There were 17 of us altogether. At least that's what they told me, and I'm sure they knew what they were talking about—the dead body counters.

For the next couple of weeks I'm housesitting at a high-rise condo. Roger and Ronnie, the two gay guys who run the Italian bistro around the corner, are on a tour of the Riviera. As Roger, the more flamboyant of the two, described it to me, "Fags in France! Should be fun, Charlie Boy. Too bad you can't come, but then who'd watch the home fires burn?" Staying at their place is like living inside an issue of *Metropolitan Home*. All natural fibers, granite countertops and artfully arranged collections of souvenir ashtrays. They left the fridge packed, with instructions to, "Eat everything in sight." And, I have full use of their red Miata. It's a good gig.

I put a call into work to tell them I'm following up a lead on the Ted LeMoine case, a crafty little accountant who seems to suffer more on-the-job injuries than a longshoreman. As a freelancer, I don't have to account for every minute of my day, but I prefer keeping questions to a minimum. So I explain to my boss, Dennis that I've found a guy who used to work for Ted and is willing to sign a statement saying he'd been in charge of purchasing all Ted's fake medical appliances. I'll likely be gone all day. "Not a problem. Go get 'em, Tiger." Yes, I currently work for an idiot.

Parking around St. Mark's is limited on a good day. This morning there are so many Mercedes and BMWs circling for position it's like a luxury car rally. I consider challenging the Cadillac SUV hugging my bumper to a race, but seeing how my transport is about the size of one of the SUV's custom hubcaps, I instead make a quick right turn and dart down an alley onto a residential side street. There's a tiny spot behind a sleek Porsche 911 into which I squeeze with approximately two-and-a-half inches to spare. As I chirp the Miata's alarm and stroll away, the SUV cruises past, still hunting.

After a week of torrential downpours, it's not raining now. I suppose this has been pre-arranged by the mayor and aldermen. We couldn't have the city's movers and shakers showing up at church like drowned rats. Too bad. I like to see rich people bedraggled. It kind of levels the playing field.

There are various groups of people on the church steps, everyone in black, shaking hands and talking quietly, like clusters of crows pecking at each other's wings. I head inside unnoticed. I've been to St. Mark's several times for funerals. Episcopalian. Not as ornate as the Catholic cathedrals, but still impressive. The ceiling of the sanctuary vaults to a 50-foot rotunda with a magnificent mosaic at the center point depicting Christ's torment in the Garden of Gethsemane. The high, arched windows surrounding the room are leaded rather than stained glass. The morning light falling through is bright and unapologetic.

Growing up, we had this funny little detached garage. One year, over the course of several months, I turned a corner of it into a fort, smuggling in three old pillows, a few ratty blankets, my comic books and some snacks. It was cold that Thanksgiving night when I snuck out there, but it was also much quieter and more fun than a lumpy plaid sofa in a crowded house. I fell asleep as soon as the blankets warmed up against my skin and didn't wake up until the garage windows started shattering. By the time I scrambled outside, flames had swallowed up our house. I heard sirens in the distance. I saw neighbors on their porches. I screamed until a fireman in a rubber coat picked me up and carried me away. At ten years old, I was the only surviving member of my immediate and extended family.

There are ushers at each of three, double-door entrances to the sanctuary of St. Mark's. I select door number two and a portly man with a ruddy nose and pockmarked cheeks solemnly hands me a memorial folder. It's thick gray parchment with gold foil lettering on the front, *Michael Herbert Augustus Jamison Rudolph 1971 – 2007.* Wealthy people can afford more names than the rest of us.

I'm twenty minutes early but the pews are already crowded. I take a seat about three quarters of the way back, next to a family with four young boys in matching navy blazers and red ties. The boys are fidgeting, punching each other and yanking the hymnals in and out of the racks on the backs of the pews. Their mother leans over periodically to shush them and threaten their lives should they not sit still. Their father stares straight ahead, apparently oblivious to the chaos. I smile at the youngest blazer boy next to me, a blond with freckles and dirty fingernails. He looks back at me suspiciously, then turns away and continues slugging his older brother.

I watch the rest of the church fill up with the city's most influential citizens. There are quite a few recognizable faces: media celebrities, politicians, and some people I can't place but who are so good looking, they must be important.

A low, vibrating chord from the organ rolls out over the crowd and we fall silent. Even the blazer boys stop jostling and listen as the huge sound builds in intensity. Church organs have their own spiritual power. The real ones, not the cheesy roller rink/garage band kind, the kind of instrument built right into the structure. The brass pipes of this beast reach almost to the ceiling, some as big as tree trunks. The sound pumping through them is alive, breathing; it bursts out the top and spreads across the room, *Listen to me, listen to me . . . I can save you.*

The ushers leave their posts and collect near the back of the center aisle. The two tallest give their arms to two women who have appeared from nowhere. One woman is small and delicate, in her seventies at least. She leans heavily on the usher's arm, for balance or emotional support or both, making her way down the aisle with tiny, tentative steps. Behind her follows a much younger and taller woman. She barely touches the arm of her escort. She looks left and right, acknowledging people along the way with a nod or a slight smile. I recognize her instantly as Lily Rudolph. I assume the other woman must be the mother, Beatrice.

As she passes my row, Lily turns and looks down the line of concerned faces. Her eyes are dark and calm. She does not appear to have been crying. Her black hair is pulled back, revealing a smooth forehead with arched eyebrows. When she spots the matching blazer boys, her expression softens for an instant. She continues up the aisle, taking her seat in the first pew next to the older woman. The organ stops and the resulting quiet is like the numbing silence of snow.

Way back then, our fire made headlines around the state. It was a gas explosion. The investigators told the reporters it was most likely the flexible copper line into our gas water heater that failed. The entire basement filled up with gas, then the electric motor on the big freezer sparked and the back of the house blew off. Everyone heard about it; everyone knew my name; everyone felt real sorry for me. Several people wanted to adopt me. But there was a lot of paperwork and, ultimately, I think the magnitude of the whole tragedy must have scared folks off. So I was sent to a foster home, and then another, and another. Eventually, everyone forgot I was the famous little fire tyke. I became the fifth wheel in a picture postcard family. I figured out how to adapt my personality to blend into whatever environment I found myself. The rules were simple: Learn to fit in; learn not to stand out.

Lily has just been seated when the priest stands and crosses to the ambo to address the congregation. We stand, there is the mumbling of a prayer, a more distinct *amen* and then we are sitting again. This is a priest from central casting, small and knobby with kind eyes, graying hair and a solemn yet sympathetic expression. He speaks about Michael Rudolph in past and future tense, about all the wonderful things he did and all the plans he'd made for even more wonderful things. People throughout the church are sniffling and dabbing at their eyes. The blazer boys have called a truce and are now trying to make each other laugh. Their mother occasionally whacks them on the knees to silence them, but stifling a laugh in church just makes snot come out your nose, which in turn makes your brothers laugh harder.

The organ starts up again and this time the assembled choir joins in. The rest of us rise and thumb nervously through our hymnals looking for the proper page. Finding it, we try in vain to follow the wildly gyrating notes. Hymns are not written for normal people to sing. Each one has a range of an octave or more with strange grace notes that leave ordinary singers in the vocal dust. On top of that, the lyrics break words into syllables that don't exist so we sputter and spurt like boiling teakettles. I shoot for hitting about every fifth note, like singing along to a song on the radio when you don't really know the words.

The hymn concludes and I know the eulogies are next. There's a definite pattern to funerals, doesn't matter the denomination: prayer, sermon, song, eulogies, benediction, exodus. Breaking this sequence would probably lead to complete social unrest, like sticking Christmas before Halloween.

The priest moves around to the very front of the altar, robes rustling against his wireless microphone.

"Ladies and gentlemen, Mrs. Augustus Rudolph and her daughter-in-law, Lily Rudolph have asked me to thank all of you for being here this morning. It means so much to them to have your support in their time of grief."

So all the amateur psychologists are nodding their heads and saying how obvious it is I ended up with such an unusual hobby. I must be obsessed with death. I must secretly crave the attention and fame I had so fleetingly as a child. I must love my chameleon existence as one of a cast of characters. Maybe. Maybe I'll mow down all my co-workers one day then turn the gun on myself and neighbors will comment about what a quiet guy I was. Maybe. But I think I just like what I do. I'm good at funerals. If I'd been good at bobsledding maybe everything would have been different. Maybe.

"We must remember this is also a time to celebrate a life well lived," the priest continues. "Michael Rudolph was a man of great talent and tenacity, a man who touched us all in one way or another. I know there are many of you with us today who have directly benefited from his talent, his generosity and his optimism. I have a short list of those who have already asked to say a few words, and when they're done, I welcome any and all to come up and share their tributes to this man who was so many things to so many people. To start us off, I'd like to invite Mayor Taylor to come forward."

Our honorable Mayor lumbers to the front of the church where the priest passes him a slim cordless microphone before retreating to a carved throne at the back of the altar. Linus Taylor is a beach ball of a man with a pencil thin mustache and a perpetually shiny forehead. I've always thought he would be a better fit as a circus barker or maybe a hotdog cart vendor. His tribute centers on Michael's accomplishments as a groundbreaking surgeon and researcher.

What little notoriety Park Hills can claim comes from Michael Rudolph's innovative exploration into the causes of and treatments for Alzheimer's. Rudolph's radical success against the insidious disease made him a sought-after speaker and a frequent guest on everything from *Larry King* to *Oprah* to *David Letterman*. It didn't hurt that he was also as handsome as a movie star and an eloquent spokesman for elderly rights. I remember seeing him on TV one night doing an interview with Connie Chung. She was desperately trying to get him to take a stand on Oregon's "Death with Dignity" law that had legalized assisted suicide for the terminally ill. Rudolph kept looping the interview back on itself, demanding to know why Ms. Chung assumed all Alzheimer's patients were terminal. She finally gave up and let him talk.

"If it weren't for Michael Rudolph," Mayor Taylor continues, "Alzheimer's patients all across this great country of ours would be lost in worlds they no longer recognize. Dr. Rudolph's work brought hope and health to thousands. And his generosity brought prestige and prosperity to our city."

Mayor Taylor looks genuinely sad. Several of his chins twitch as he struggles for control.

"We will miss his vision and his spirit."

He holds the microphone aloft as an indication that the next person should rescue him before he begins to weep.

A tall man in an elegant suit hurries down the aisle, collects the microphone from the deteriorating mayor and strides quickly up the steps. His address is followed by that of an equally aristocratic gentleman with no hair and a pronounced lisp. Streams of people flow up to take their turn. Several of the previously unidentified good-looking denizens reveal themselves to indeed be important individuals with amazing stories to tell of Michael's earthly endeavors. Each one builds upon the testimonial of the last until it seems we will have to canonize Michael Rudolph should but one more person attest to the miracles his life had wrought.

During the waves of eulogies, I dutifully study my memorial folder and take notes. The blond blazer boy watches me. He probably thinks I'm doodling, something for which his mother has recently whacked him.

I'm chewing on the end of my pencil. I've never gotten up in front of such a large crowd. What if there's someone here from another funeral? None have ever been for anyone this famous or successful. There couldn't possibly be any crossover. Alzheimer's? I don't think I've been to a funeral for anyone who died of Alzheimer's.

I work out my speech in my head as the other eulogists go on. The coughing and rustling makes it hard to hear some of the more reticent orators but I can tell things are winding down. I stand and the blazer boys gawk as I sneak out of the pew to take my place at the end of the line of speakers. I'm edgy and not quite convinced of my material. The woman in front of me turns and smiles, a sad knowing smile.

I can see Lily and Beatrice Rudolph now, their faces upturned, letting the good words wash over them. The sadly smiling woman is speaking now about her father and his recovery and how Michael Rudolph made it all possible. As she finishes, the priest walks to the front to take the microphone from her. He better not cut me off.

"We have time for one more before we leave for the graveside service. On behalf of the family, our thanks go out to all of you again for sharing this day with us."

"Sir?"

He's holding the microphone out to me. Everyone turns and stares. Lily Rudolph stares. I put out my hand and walk forward. Designated hitter, closing act, anchor leg. I grab the microphone from the priest's hand as we pass, spin on my heels and face the congregation. There it is again. The silence of snow.

"Thank you for letting me say a few final words. My name is Albert Mackey and I'm an old college friend of Michael's from Columbia. We spent more than a few nights up to our elbows in what we used to call 'the three B's' - books, bones and brew."

A small ripple of laughter undulates through the room.

"I'm afraid I'm not nearly as illustrious as my fellow alumnus, and I have to admit Michael and I hadn't even spoken, let alone seen each other, for years. But in the last weeks before his death, we'd been working together quite closely."

Lily Rudolph's eyebrows jump up and she stares at me more intently.

"I earn my living as a writer. Of course unless you're a big fan of medical research journals and pharmaceutical annual reports, you're probably not familiar with my work. But Michael was, and he hunted me down several months ago with a very special project. He wanted me to help him write a book that would explain his theories about aging. Something that would get people thinking about potential instead of assuming getting old was a mental dead end."

I hear whispers ricochet from pew to pew as the mourners begin to grasp the importance of my words.

"To hear him tell it, I think a lot of *other* people wanted him to write this book, and he'd been doing a pretty good job of dragging his feet. But he'd finally gotten it into his head that a book about his research might actually do some good promoting his philosophies about aging. Michael never stopped thinking about ways to get his message out."

"As excited as he was about the general idea, he didn't know how to pull it altogether. That's when he contacted me. He wanted me to look through the material he'd collected, and believe me, he had collected a lot of material. He needed me to help him outline the project. He was concerned it would be too complicated to get across. That's why he kept the whole thing a secret. From everyone. His business associates, his friends, his family, even his beautiful wife. He didn't want anyone to know about it until he was sure there was really a book."

I look directly at Lily Rudolph and smile. She looks back. Her eyebrows have settled back down but her gaze remains cool.

"Unfortunately, we didn't finish before the accident. But, as I was going through my notes this morning before the service, I was pleasantly surprised at the progress we did make. There *is* a story here. What Michael did and what he wanted to do is both significant and inspiring. He accomplished more in his thirty-five years than most of us ever dream of in a lifetime, and he was completely dedicated to his cause. He told me once, he would willingly trade five years of mindless youth for just one extra month with the wisdom and perspective of age. It made him so angry to see society give up on the very people who had the most to offer. He believed *all* senior citizens deserved the clarity of mind to tell their life stories, and we needed the good sense to listen. It's a crime Michael didn't get the chance to experience his own golden years. Which is why I'm up here today. To reveal this secret to Michael's wife, his mother and all of you. To let you know Michael's story will be told and we'll all be better because of it."

I glance again at Lily Rudolph. She is still looking at me, but curiously now, like a little bird. I hear it start near the back and roll up to the front. Applause. People are standing. Deafening applause. Suddenly the priest is next to me, raising his hand in blessing, trying to settle things down.

"May God bless you and keep you. May God make his light shine down upon you and keep you from harm. Thank you all for coming. Amen."

Everyone rises and begins gathering their things to leave. I'm trapped on the altar. The priest takes the microphone out of my hand and clicks it off.

"That was a beautiful speech, son," he says. "I'm so glad someone is going to write a book about Michael. He deserves every word."

He shakes my hand then disappears through a hidden door directly under the feet of crucified Jesus.

I walk down the steps into the crowd and try to make my way up the aisle. The beautiful people stop to shake my hand and whisper their appreciation. I can't go more than a few feet without interruption. Even Mayor Taylor thrusts his chubby hand in my direction.

"Mr. Mackey, Linus Taylor. Very pleased to make your acquaintance. I'm sure you can tell how proud all of us here in Park Hills are of Michael Rudolph. I know you'll do your best to make sure this book of yours does him justice."

He squeezes down hard. My knuckles pop.

"Of course, sir," I say. "Nothing would please me more."

He relaxes his grip and the blood rushes back into my fingertips.

"You call me if you need any details about the town."

He presses a business card into my throbbing palm then excuses himself to crush the hands of more important people in my wake.

A small, round man with an expensive haircut catches my elbow just as the Mayor exits from view. Next to him stands another man, thin and serious.

"Incredible speech," the thin man says. "I'm Howard Stanich and this is my partner, Gavin VanMorten. Nesler Pharmaceuticals. As you know, Michael was working with us to launch the clinical testing phase of our new Alzheimer's drug therapy."

I nod hesitantly.

"We had no idea Michael was working on a book," the round man named Gavin says.

"No one did."

"It's very exciting," Howard continues. "If you'd like to include information about the Nesler research, I'd be more than happy to speak with you."

Someone taps me on the shoulder. I turn. It's Lily Rudolph. She stands slightly apart from a group of beautiful people.

"Mr. Mackey," she begins. "I can't tell you how much it means to me to find out about your work with Michael. We must talk about it soon. May I call you?"

"I'm, uh, I'm traveling quite a bit over the next few weeks. Could I call you?"

"Certainly."

She reaches into her purse and pulls out a slim, gold pen. She holds out her hand to me. What does she want to do? Write her phone number on my hand like we used to do in junior high? I realize I'm still holding the memorial program. I fumble with it for a moment trying to fold it back into its original shape before handing it to her. She takes it and writes a phone number across the top.

"Please call me as soon as possible. This is my private cell number."

"Thank you."

That's all I can think to say. *Thank you.* As if she had just complimented me on my shoes. Thank you.

"Good. Then we'll talk soon."

She hands back the memorial folder, nods to the Nesler Pharmaceuticals men at my side, and leaves with her stunning entourage.

"She's such a brave woman," says Howard. "Lovely and gracious, even under such unfortunate circumstances."

"Excuse me?"

I turn back around. Howard is holding out a business card.

"Please put us on your calling list as well," Howard says. "Michael's work was so important. We're doing our best to keep things moving with the testing, but it will be a challenge without him. He is missed by so many people. You must promise to let us know if we can help in any way."

"Thank you, gentlemen," I say, stuffing the card into my jacket pocket. "I'll be contacting you soon, I'm sure."

I hurry the rest of the way up the aisle. People continue to stop and talk to me as I try to make a break for the doors. This is usually my favorite part, but today I just want to get away. I think I'm in a little too deep. I have to disappear immediately. That's all there is to it. No friends, no fling, no follow-up. Medical writer. What was I thinking? The sum total of my medical experience is trying to catch people with fake neck and back injuries. There's no way can I hold my own against real doctors and scientists.

Outside, the sun has broken through the clouds. I slide on my sunglasses, wishing it was that easy to disappear. I glance behind me before turning down the alley to retrieve the Miata. People still pour out of the church.

I'm not a doctor, but I play one on TV.

THREE

It's been two weeks since the Rudolph funeral and I've been at work every day. Fourteen days. Three-hundred and thirty-six hours. But who's counting.

I haven't been to any new funerals. I haven't called anyone. I haven't done much work either. I did catch that lying little accountant, Ted LeMoine. But it wasn't any of my doing. It turns out Teddy was screwing his secretary at the same time he was carrying on with one of his clients. How he captivates two women is beyond me. The guy wears floral polyester shirts, the kind that pill around the collar after one washing. What's left of his hair is combed straight back over his little head with so much gel he resembles a sea otter. And he's tan, everywhere, at least according to the secretary. She caught him and the client pouring over, or should I say poured over, the books one night in the office, and decided to squeal to me about all his fake injuries as revenge. All's fair in credits and debits I guess.

The bistro boys will be back from the Riviera tomorrow, and I don't have another house-sitting job for several weeks. That's almost an eternity in my little apartment. Lily Rudolph's phone number is tucked away in my desk drawer.

I think the fear of getting caught is starting to mess with me. The other day when I was pulling out of the gas station in the Miata, I could have sworn I saw that chubby Gavin guy from Nesler across the street at an espresso cart. I even circled around the block to double check. It wasn't him, it was another chubby guy in a dark suit, but it could have been him. I could start running into people who recognize me. That would suck.

Does everyone go through the hair-brush-celebrity phase? I really don't think it was just me. I think everyone has, at least once, grabbed a brush and belted out a song into the mirror or accepted an Oscar with humility and a few witty remarks for the press. You imagine how awesome it would be to be famous, people clamoring for your autograph, recognized wherever you go. I bet in real life it's annoying and beyond creepy.

I don't want to be known. I don't want to suffer that double-take moment when someone realizes he's seen you before, but in an entirely different capacity. At its heart, my hobby makes me a liar. People don't like liars. Sometimes I can convince myself I'm simply expanding on the truth, borrowing a few facts to shape an improvised anecdote, one that *could* be true given the right circumstances. But that's just the bureaucratic definition. Strip away the legalese, and I'm a liar. Liar, liar pants on fire . . . that doesn't sound like a very good outcome. Maybe it's time to take up kayaking or skydiving or some other, less dangerous hobby.

A picture of Lily Rudolph is frozen in my brain. Her dark eyes, the trail of freckles over the bridge of her nose, and her feet—tiny feet in black ballerina flats. She took my hand and her fingers were a cool breeze against my sweaty palm. She smiled at me and one side of her mouth curved up a little higher than the other. She wrote down her number and asked me to call. I must have really thrown her for a loop with that crazy story about the book. A nice lady like her doesn't deserve to be led down the primrose path by the likes of me.

"Hey there, big guy."

My boss, Dennis looks at me over the top of my cubicle and the top of his glasses. He's a big, gushy guy, soft and white, like bread dough on the rise. I give him points for trying to reverse this trend; he's always starting some new diet that's going to change his life. The problem is, he can't seem to get past the first week before the Call of the Oreo drags him back to reality. Dennis pushes his glasses up onto his head, like a pair of sporty shades. But they are not sporty shades, they are steel-rimmed aviators from the seventies.

"Hey, Dennis."

"Just wondering what's next for our star investigator."

"Dennis, that LeMoine thing was dumb luck. You want star-quality work, take a look at the file Draper's put together on the Wosnieck case."

"Modesty will get you nowhere, Sandors. Gotta grab for the limelight when you can. Besides, Draper's case is a slam-dunk. For you, I get the true rock crawlers."

Rock crawlers. That's what Dennis calls the people we investigate. He likens them to the slimy bugs that squeeze out from under rocks at night to chomp on your vegetable garden. Sneaky, slippery, something you'd step on given the opportunity. I guess it helps to have a healthy dose of disdain for people you're trying to get arrested.

"Who do we have this time?" I finally ask.

"Hugh Klein. Guy's fallen down more times than a drunk at last call. He's trying to collect double. Medical claim for a back and knee injury and a property claim against the Dunkin' Donuts he went down in front of. Several people saw him fall. He says it was improper sidewalk maintenance."

"Sounds like a classic slip-and-fall, Denn, couldn't Ernie handle it?"

Dennis steps around the wall of the cubicle and whips his glasses from his forehead to punctuate the rest of his lecture.

"Klein's gotten enormous property settlements over the last seven years from Kroger's, West Island Health Systems, and Providence. He's a professional."

The steel frames come dangerously close to whacking my nose on every popping P in his diatribe.

"I need my best people on this one."

With this final appeal to my hubris, Dennis dumps three large file folders on my desk and leaves. Each folder is labeled "Klein, Hugh" and rubber banded to control its bulging contents. There's a date stamp and a case number and a routing slip. No one else's name is on the routing slips, which means it's my baby ... my problem.

I reach into the top drawer for a note pad. There's Michael Rudolph's memorial folder with Lily's private number in loopy handwriting across the top. She's probably forgotten all about me already. Probably *not*. If someone reveals, out of the blue, that he's writing a secret book about your dead husband you're likely to remember. She must be wondering what happened to me. She's probably starting to think I'm a flake. She does not know how very right she is.

Lily Rudolph is not funeral fling material. She is way out of my league. Claudia, Mia, the other women over the years have been much more realistic, easier. More, okay I'll say it, more gullible. That'll get me twelve years in feminist purgatory, but sometimes you gotta call 'em like you see 'em. Something tells me Lily Rudolph can spot genuine cashmere at fifty paces and smell a rat at ten. If she spent any time with me at all, she'd no sooner believe I was Michael's old school chum than I believe Hugh Klein is just clumsy.

This whole situation is ridiculous. Shifting out of character and moving on has always been easy. Clap on. Clap off. If you're not a real person then there aren't any real connections. You just shake hands, a heartfelt hug where appropriate, and you leave. Like Pat Romano's funeral, right before all this insanity. It was perfect. Pat got taken out in a bizarre construction accident. A trench collapsed, burying him under a couple tons of dirt and gravel. He was only twenty-nine and most of the guys in the crowd were that or younger with huge muscles packed inside their wrinkled white dress shirts. Must've closed the gym early so they could all come. They split as soon as the service ended and there wasn't anyone interesting left to talk with except a dusty old woman with a large purse. She stank of tuna casserole and I half suspect was only there to get out of the cold. Nice to meet ya, gotta go.

There have been a couple of times when it was a little harder than usual to shake it off. Jimmy Peters was tough. Cute kid whose father died in a boating accident. He followed me around for the whole reception. Every time I made a break for the door, he was right there with his big, brown eyes boring into my soul. He drew me a picture of a rabbit on one of the dessert napkins. I had to wait until some relative took him to the bathroom to escape. I saw those eyes in my dreams for weeks. But, all in all, it's been nothing I couldn't handle. Nothing I couldn't erase. I do think about my old funeral friends sometimes, wonder what's happened to them. Maybe some of them have had their own funerals by now. I wonder if they ever think about me, about that nice young man who moved in and out of their lives like a summer breeze through the trees. Nah, too poetic. More like a blip on the radar screen. A moving target is almost impossible to hit.

Those loopy numbers stare up at me. I should just call her and make an excuse, any excuse. Then I'll find myself a new funeral and new friends and everything will go back to the way it was.

I'll just pick up the phone and call her.

I'll just organize my paper clips.

I'll just pick up the phone and call her.

I'll just finish reading my computer manual.

I'll just . . .

"Hello, this is Lily."

"Lily, it's Albert. Albert Mackey."

"Mr. Mackey. I thought you'd forgotten about me. Are you done with your travels?"

"Travels?"

"I believe you said you were going to be traveling, but perhaps I'm mistaken."

"Oh, *travels*. We must have a bad connection. I thought you said *trials*, and I haven't had any trials lately. Some tribulations, but no trials."

I make a strange sound somewhere between a laugh and a cough, but at least it stops the words from hurtling out of my mouth.

"I am very anxious to speak with you, Mr. Mackey. I think it's so exciting that Michael was working on a book."

"Please don't call me Mr. Mackey. It reminds me of that guy who designed all of Cher's outfits. Albert's good, or even Al. Some people call me Al."

"I like Albert."

"Albert it is."

There's a bit of a pause, which I think I am supposed to fill but can't.

"When would you like to get together, Albert?"

"Soon, soon."

"I'm free next Tuesday."

"Tuesday's good."

Why don't I just grab a shovel and start digging? Maybe I can slide even deeper into this pile of shit. The call is not going at all the way it supposed to. I'm supposed to be coming up with an excuse to drop my current façade not setting an appointment to see her again.

"Shall we say ten o'clock?"

"Ten works for me."

"You're welcome to come out here to the house, or I'm happy to meet you somewhere. Where are you staying?"

Where am I staying? That's a damn good question. I live in a furnished apartment consisting of two small rooms with a Playskool kitchen along one wall and a bathroom the size of a cereal box. Hardly acceptable lodgings for a successful writer working on a book about Michael Rudolph. I'll be out of Roger and Ronnie's condo by next Tuesday. Where the hell *am* I staying?

"I'm actually at a hotel right now until I can find myself something a little more permanent."

"We have several rentals around town. Nice ones. I'd be happy to see if any of them are vacant. You could stay there. No charge."

"That's completely unnecessary. I'll be fine."

"It's no trouble, really. Besides, I can't find you anywhere in Michael's accounts."

"What?"

"Was he paying you in cash or did you have some other kind of arrangement?"

"We, ah, we hadn't set down anything official yet, it was still preliminary. We needed to figure out the scope of the project."

"Then the least I can do is put you up somewhere until we get things back on track."

"I'm not worried about the money."

"Then you're not much of a businessman. Michael hired you to do a job. I want you to finish it and I certainly plan on continuing to pay you for it."

This woman is really decent. I cannot take advantage of her. Albert Mackey has got to go.

But first, maybe I could have just *one* meeting with her. I'll tell her, face to face, I can't finish the project. That somehow all my notes were destroyed in a freak toaster oven fire. Why can't I stop? You tell yourself not to look at the accident on the freeway, but you slow down, you gawk, you crane your neck for dismembered limbs.

"Well, when you put it *that* way," I hear myself say. "I'd be more than happy to accept your offer of accommodations."

"Great. I'll make the arrangements. Let's meet here on Tuesday and I'll go over all the details. Did you and Michael ever get together at the house? Do you know how to get here?"

"No, I'm sorry, we never met there."

"Do you have a pen? I'll give you directions."

I've made a horrible mistake. This is not how it goes. Who the hell do I think I am, Robert De Niro? I've got four days to concoct a believable identity as a brainy technical writer who had complete access to Michael Rudolph. Brilliant, successful, beloved Michael Rudolph. The tight rope from reality to insanity is becoming dangerously thin. I am 99% sure sane people don't do what I do. Oh sure, everyone pretends to be something they're not sometimes. But it's usually harmless.

Do you water ski?

Are you kidding? I'm wicked good. Love the jumps – really love the jumps.

Awesome. You wanna go with me this weekend?

No.

I'm a step up from that. I'm stomping around in someone else's life, leaving behind a big dirty mess. Who does that? I've made a horrible mistake, but I don't seem to care.

The Internet seems like a good place to start. How the hell do you spell Alzheimer's?

FOUR

The brain is a masterpiece. I think we're too insignificant to even begin to understand its potential. Like a guy who gets a Ducati motorcycle and then uses it to tool around town. Something meant to go one-twenty or better should not be forced to putt along at thirty-five. Michael Rudolph was trying to rev up the brain's speedometer.

The more I find out about him, the more I realize he had no business dying. No wonder everyone is so upset. I certainly haven't been able to identify anyone else who has the imagination, let alone the cranial capacity, to pick up the pieces of his research. Maybe that's too harsh. I'm sure there are plenty of people in the world as smart or even smarter. It's just he was a true visionary. One of those people who can look at unrelated items and put them together into something unique and extraordinary. Admit it. You think regular folks like us could look at a sick cow and a cute milkmaid and come up with the idea for a small pox vaccine. Hell, we'd never get past the milkmaid.

My research is starting to pay off. The company computer system has access to every major database. Insurance companies are a lot like banks. They can find out just about anything on anyone: your contributions, your professional affiliations, your credit rating, where you shop, what you drive, outstanding warrants, your alimony payments, your shoe size. When big money's at stake, privacy takes a holiday.

I've dug up a few things about my two Nesler Pharmaceutical buddies from the funeral. They're an interesting pair. It turns out Howard Stanich is Nesler's top researcher. The guy's got a real pedigree: graduated from Yale with twin degrees in pharmacology and psychology. He can probably tell if your problem is a bad cold or a bad psychosis. He's been with Nesler almost thirty years and has been driving the wheel on the Alzheimer's drug from day one.

Gavin VanMorten seems to be a minor player. It's been hard to find much on him. If you can't unearth anything on someone it usually means he's either an incredibly dull goody-two-shoes or an incredibly crafty piece of shit. A rock crawler. The jury's still out on VanMorten. All I know is he's worked for Nesler for the last five years, since they went public with the Alzheimer's drug. He's not married, not divorced, donates regularly to the British Columbia Killer Whale Adoption Program, and likes to vacation in Branson, Missouri. That last fact alone is enough to scare the crap out of me. Branson is the only place in the known universe where you can see a John Wayne impersonator, the International Ventriloquist of the Year, and a troupe of circus acrobats from China. It's like Las Vegas' loopy stepsister.

I've also found a boatload of information on Alzheimer's itself. I didn't realize how prevalent it is: 4.5 million Americans. It can develop in people as young as their forties, although what they call "late-onset" Alzheimer's is much more common. However, *late* is considered to be anyone older than sixty-five. In today's baby-boomer society, that's right around the corner for a huge number of people. By age eighty-five, there's a nearly 50% chance you'll develop the disease. Those don't sound like terrific odds to me. That's coin-flip territory.

What's most fascinating about Rudolph's research is his success rate. There are case histories on dozens and dozens of people with all levels of memory deterioration, from not being able to remember where they put their car keys to not being able to remember what a car is. The answer, according to Rudolph, was memory expansion.

Think of your brain like one of those old Rolodex business card wheels. When you're young, you only have a few cards to keep track of and can easily flip through all the information. As you age, more and more cards get jammed in until the wheel is so full it can't turn anymore. The newest cards fall out as soon as you try to put them in while the old cards are firmly stuck in the back. This explains why most of us can't remember what on earth we ate for breakfast yesterday but can sing the entire theme song to *Gilligan's Island* at the drop of a hat.

What Michael Rudolph was working to develop was, in essence, an overflow valve, a way to kick open underutilized areas of the brain so all that old information had somewhere to go, freeing up space for new, incoming information. He was positive a certain combination of mental exercise, surgical intervention and drug therapy could open up new pathways in the brain. One controversial element of his theory was what he called "Cranial Calisthenics." Most people subscribe to the belief, *You can't teach an old dog new tricks.* Rudolph preferred the old typing exercise, *The lazy, old dog jumped over the quick brown fox.* He theorized we allow our brains to get lazy over the years. You're getting by, why push it? With a little prodding, he was sure we could teach our brains to get up and jump over new ideas. That prodding came in the form of stem-cell injections. Stem cells can grow into various types of tissue, which means they have the potential to reproduce and replace ailing Alzheimer's cells with healthy cells.

Early results showed amazing transformations. Michael's patients seemed to not only regain their original mental capacity, they were better than before. Smarter. Brain connections were restored and new neurons generated. A few of Michael's talk-show appearances were archived on some network web sites and the interviews of patients he brought with him were astounding. These people were vibrant, energetic and eloquent.

The experts in head trauma and mental retardation had rather strenuous objections to Rudolph's research. They insisted their own experiences showed unbreakable limits to the brain's ability to grow and heal. Rudolph countered that the brains of most Alzheimer's patients were essentially in good physical shape. There were some plaque issues, not unlike the clogged arteries that can lead to heart attacks. But the entire brain wasn't compromised, just some of the connections. You wouldn't total an engine because of a clogged fuel line.

This didn't seem to be a case of a Dr. Frankenstein trying to work with damaged goods. Michael was talking about taking an old, but basically healthy organ and bringing it up to full capacity. He was also completely aware mental jumping jacks weren't the only route. His surgical experience had shown him the brain could be rewired to achieve dramatic results. And we all know various drugs have the ability to vastly alter our thought patterns. Just ask anyone you know who was hanging out in San Francisco around 1967.

Michael had perfected the process of collecting adult stem cells and expanding them in culture. That's where Nesler came in. Their breakthrough was a differentiation drug, which guaranteed the adult stem cells knew they should become the same kind of healthy tissue the Alzheimer's cells used to be. The drug would travel within a powerful immuno-suppression suspension from a surgically implanted reservoir pump in the patient's abdomen, up the spinal column, and directly into the affected area of the brain.

This consistent infusion of chemicals and stem cells into the brain is a key part of Michael's theory, however, I can't get a clear picture of the drug itself. There's some recent media publicity about the initiation of the clinical trials, but those articles center more on the new hospital research wing and generalities about the drug's potential for Alzheimer's patients.

There's no access to the actual test results: Nesler's internal documents are all proprietary. I never realized how competitive the pharmaceutical industry is. A successful new drug can be worth hundreds of millions to the company that patents it, and not just a drug for a serious disease like Alzheimer's. A new hay fever remedy rakes in the same kind of big bucks, maybe more since *everybody* sneezes. These guys keep their research locked up tighter than a lug nut on a rusted out Chevy.

I'm over-simplifying, I know. A lot of Michael's papers and studies are way too technical for me. I figure I'm doing pretty darn good just catching the high points. I need some stuff translated into layman's terms, and I'm counting on being able to get Lily Rudolph to bring me up to speed on several key details without realizing she's doing it.

Tomorrow's meeting with Lily will be a true test of my acting ability. I've done my homework on Columbia. I even looked up a few of the student hangouts from the late '80s when Michael would have been there: *Cannon's*, a classic old bar on Broadway and 107 th, *Augie's*, also on Broadway near 106th, and the noisy, steamy *West End Café* up on 112th. It seems Michael was a bit of a jazz aficionado and liked to drop in to the *West End* to catch tenor saxophonist Willis "Gator Tail" Jackson and the Pazant Brothers playing in the back room behind the big oval bar.

I've laid out a resume of impressive yet little-known technical journals where I've supposedly been working for the past ten or twelve years. And, I've read enough articles about Rudolph to have a respectable arsenal of childhood anecdotes and family connections.

I'm as ready as I'll ever be.

I'm scared shitless.

I arrive early at Lily Rudolph's house. House is not the right word. Normal people have houses. This is an estate, a mansion, la hacienda. There is, of course, a gated entry. The wealthy don't want just anyone driving up to their doors. The Rudolphs aren't ostentatious enough to have a guardhouse, just a small intercom discreetly stashed in an ivy-covered wall. It beeps as my bumper splits an invisible beam.

"Hello," I yell, as if ordering a burger in the drive through. "It's Albert Mackey."

There's no response, but the gate noiselessly swings open. Without a current house-sitting gig, I'm actually driving my own car: a dull gray Ford Taurus I hope to pass off as a rental. I pull through the gate and idle for a minute, staring down the tree-lined driveway, becoming Albert Mackey.

Sometimes I wish I were more like the *Incredible Hulk*. I wish I could abruptly turn chartreuse and bust out of my suit. When I was about thirteen, I developed a character named Bobby to get through Mr. Corrado's P.E. class.

I like to think of myself now as trim, but back then, I was just plain skinny. We were playing dodge ball. I still wonder what life lesson we were supposed to be learning in a game whose object is to hurl a large, rubber ball at your opponent and hit him, possibly hard enough to knock him down. The guys in my class who had paper routes were really good. I was small and quick, so I could hold my own with the dodging. I was, however, pitiful in the hurling category.

"Sandors," Mr. Corrado would shriek from the sidelines, the veins in his wrestler's neck close to bursting. "I want to see some power behind that ball. Unless, of course, you'd rather play badminton with the girls' class."

That would make most everybody laugh. Then a couple of guys would start to leap around waving imaginary rackets and the whole gym would lose it. That's when I called on Bobby. I was already the skins of shirts and skins, so I couldn't rip off my shirt, but in my mind's eye, my muscles bulged, my height surged, and my hair got really messy. Bobby was a bully. A take-no-prisoners, shoot-first-ask-questions-later pillar of power. When I was Bobby, I could hurl. I could knock a kid out of his Keds at twenty feet. It's kind of like those people who can lift up a car in a crisis. Eventually, I could summon Bobby even when I wasn't mad or embarrassed. Sometimes I'd just be walking down the hall and feel like being Bobby, then I'd turn around and slam some kid into a locker.

These days, my transformations are subtler. Albert Mackey is a good guy. He's careful and quiet and respectful. Albert Mackey would never consider doing something that would harm another individual. He couldn't live with himself if he took advantage of a situation. Albert Mackey is a bit of a schmuck. If I'd known I was going to get trapped as Albert, I'd have come up with a better personality. Maybe a quirky habit, like counting the marshmallows in a bowl of Lucky Charms or an interesting hobby, like cage fighting. Given the proper time, I could have developed an entire back-story, complete with evil stepfather and ties to the mob. As it is, Albert is about as boring as I really am.

I press down on the accelerator and roll toward Lily Rudolph's front door. I have a list of names in my pocket. Names of freelance journalists. Folks who are actually capable of writing a book about Michael Rudolph. I figure I have enough basic research notes to pretend something has been started. I'll add to that what I find out today from Lily, and then turn over the whole shootin' match to a real writer. I've rehearsed a short speech for Lily in which I explain I don't have the style to pull off a book. That Michael deserves someone with more skill writing for mainstream readers. I plan to politely thank her for all her time and wish her the best of luck. Have a good life. Then I'll drive back through the gate in my "rented" Taurus and things will go back to normal. I've even selected a nice funeral to attend later this afternoon.

In front of a massive *Gone With The Wind* porch sits a new silver Lexus SUV. I pull up behind it and kill my engine. Grabbing my leather folder of notes, I release the seat belt and step out into the cool morning air. In the distance a lawn mower hums and on the breeze is a hint of its signature perfume blend of gas and grass. The white ionic columns of the porch reach up two stories and support a full-length, corniced roofline. The windows on both levels are as tall as a man, with black shutters flattened to each side like bat wings against the sunny yellow paint. There's a small balcony in the exact center with an ornate wrought iron railing framing multi-paneled French doors. If I didn't know we were in Illinois, I reckon Scarlett should be coming on out right 'bout now.

Thousands of bits of information tumble through my brain like those giant drums of ping-pong balls. B56: Spent summers in Maine. N42: Started geriatric specialty while still in his residency. I22: competitor rower in college. O16: Married Lily five years ago. G36: No kids. BINGO.

"Albert! Did you find us okay?"

Lily Rudolph glides out the front doors and down the stone steps to meet me. She is wearing jeans, a crisp white shirt and blue Converse sneakers with no socks. Her sleeves are casually rolled up to her elbows and a delicate gold necklace glints in the sun, the end of it dropping out of site somewhere behind her second shirt button. She's thinner than I remember from the funeral

"No problem. Good directions."

"Come in, come in. You'll have to excuse my appearance. I've been up to my eyeballs in paperwork this morning and time got away from me. Usually, I at least put on socks to greet my guests."

She smiles and extends her hand. "I'm so glad we're finally able to get together."

"I only wish it was under better circumstances."

Lily's smile droops but she maintains her composure. How had Gavin described her at the funeral? Lovely and gracious. He dark hair is wrapped into a loose ponytail that bounces against her neck as she climbs back up the steps.

"This book is one of the things that keeps me going," she says, turning and motioning me to follow. "Michael's work has to be documented. The more people understand it, the more likely someone will pick up the ball and run with it."

"The Nesler trials are continuing, aren't they?" I ask, trailing behind her as she sweeps through the doors and into a spacious living room with floor-to-ceiling windows, oriental carpets, and furniture that looks too nice to sit on. Lily plops into an overstuffed club chair covered in bright floral tapestry. I guess it is okay to sit. I drop down on the sofa directly opposite her and nonchalantly lean back, but there's a quicksand pit of pillows behind me, and I feel myself being sucked out of sight. I quickly pitch forward, covering the frantic move by reaching out to place my notebook on the coffee table. Lily doesn't seem to notice my furniture faux pas. She kicks off her shoes and pulls up her legs underneath her. Criss-cross, applesauce. That's what Mom used to call it.

"The Nesler trials have a life of their own," she explains. "And the funding is in place for the entire test period. Michael was excited about the drug, but it was always just one part of the picture. But you know that."

I smile.

"So, tell me. What's our next step with the book?"

My spit evaporates and I can feel my tongue start to stick to the roof of my mouth. I suck in my cheeks to swallow and start into my prepared speech.

"I've been thinking quite a lot about that next step," I say, searching for the right tone. "Now that Michael's gone, I see things taking a new direction. Like you said, it's important someone continues his work, and the success of this book could have a lot to do with that. I think you need someone on this project with a stronger style. A bigger name. Someone who could help push it up the best-seller lists."

"What are you talking about?"

"I've brought some names with me. We can talk about them and I could even call a couple for you if you want."

"You don't want to finish it?"

Lily looks at me. She's twisting the gold chain at her neck.

"It's not that I don't *want* to. It's just that I don't think I'm the best person for the job. When Michael was alive, I was feeding off his enthusiasm. That carried right over into my writing. Sometimes it felt like I was simply taking dictation. But now, you need someone who can generate that passion out of thin air. I'm a technical writer, Lily. I write the kind of stuff people read because they have to. You need a professional biographer."

I reach into my shirt pocket and pull out my list. It's a single sheet of paper folded into quarters. I hold it by one corner, as if I've pulled it from a hot oven. Lily keeps twisting that damn gold chain.

"But Michael hired *you*. He must have thought you were the best person for the job. Why else would he go to all that trouble to track you down?"

The gold chain is looped so tightly around her finger it has raised the pendant into view from behind her shirt buttons. A small heart shaped locket knocks against her collarbone.

"I think he wanted someone he could trust to keep the whole thing a secret. He was doing most of the writing himself. I was just correcting his grammar and punctuation."

"Michael hated to write."

"I know," I lie. "But all he had to do was get his thoughts down on paper in whatever stream of consciousness made sense to him. I'd take it from there. I've been trying ever since the funeral, but I can't seem to get going without his jump start."

"If Michael trusted you, then I trust you. I don't want to work with a stranger. No matter how good a writer he is."

"That's nice of you to say, but I know my limitations. I'm a damn good medical writer, but I've got no business tackling a mainstream biography about someone as important as Michael."

Lily's eyes drop into her lap. The gold chain unwinds from her finger and the locket tumbles back into its hiding place.

"I've got people calling me all day, every day," she says, still looking down. "Asking what they can do to help. I tell them I'm fine, that they're so sweet for asking, but *really* I'm fine. I've got plenty of people around to help. Lawyers and accountants and administrators of one kind or another are always swarming around."

She looks up at me. Her eyes are no longer clear. They're tired. Tired and lonely.

"But I'm not fine. Of course, if you tell anyone that, I'll deny it."

She manages a tiny smile. I can tell she's struggling to keep from letting go of even one ounce of composure.

"I'm not at all fine. I can't even visualize what it will be like to have a normal life again. It's like I'm in some kind of purgatory for the living. This book is a way out. A way to be a part of Michael's life again. It wouldn't be the same working with someone who's just doing a job. It wouldn't be personal. You knew him."

I am an asshole. An asshole at a crossroads. Turn to the right. It's a wide-open path. Admit the whole ugly truth. It will be painful, but only for a little while, and I'll never see her again anyway, so who cares if she thinks I'm the biggest shithead to ever darken her door. Turn to the left. Big, bad briar patch. Gnarly, prickly vines twisting every which way. Could be a trap. Think about it, Brer Rabbit. Think before you jump.

"It'll be a lot of work, Lily. I'll need a tremendous amount of your help."

"I don't care. I want it to be a lot of work. I want it to take up every minute of my day."

The list of names is still in my hand. I crumple the paper into a ball and toss it onto the coffee table. Lily smiles.

"Thank you. You won't be sorry," she says. "I promise we can do it. I know we can. It'll be the best book you've ever written."

It'll be the only book I've ever written.

FIVE

I'm settling into my new digs. Lily's put me up in a furnished condo with a view of the lake. She said she knew us "artistic types" liked unconventional spaces. I reminded her I was not artistic but was certainly grateful for the absurdly gracious surroundings.

The unit is a single story with a garage below and nine-foot ceilings above. A trio of large, square windows looks out west across the water. When the sun sets it will burn out your cornea if you don't shut the drapes. When they're closed, their heavy floral pattern reminds me of my grandmother's footstool. She'd sit in her rocker to read *Goodnight Moon* and I'd perch at her feet to listen. It's funny how I can't remember what I wore on my first date or who spoke at my college graduation, but I can remember my grandmother's blue sneakers with the flat white soles and six silver eyelets lacing up to a bow.

There's a sleek granite breakfast bar separating the front room from the small gourmet kitchen. Someone has gone to great pains to coordinate the designer tile backsplash with polished chrome pendant lights and the clear maple floors. It's really quite nice. Too bad I can't cook.

For the last five days, Lily and I have worked every afternoon. She has dozens of notebooks filled with copies of Michael's interviews and articles. Each one has been neatly trimmed and encased in its own plastic sleeve. I used to have a baseball card collection I kept like that—protected in individual vinyl envelopes like those slices of American cheese. Except vinyl melts at 176° F. I imagine at 1200° F, the average temperature of a house inferno, it liquefies.

I've told Lily I'm spending mornings at various research libraries. Her daily routine is so jam-packed with charitable obligations and appearances on behalf of Michael, I'm sure she never gives my absence a second thought. This schedule allows me to make an appearance at the office in the morning, enough time to make a little headway on the Klein case. That's kept Dennis off my back.

It turns out during previous lawsuits Mr. Klein identified himself as a Type 1 diabetic with severe ulcers due to the stress of his injuries. He is, at least temporarily, at a loss to explain why, in his delicate condition, he was leaving the Dunkin' Donuts with a large black coffee and three raisin danish. I've also located two people who were in the doughnut shop that morning and are prepared to testify they saw Mr. Klein lingering outside the window for at least five minutes. One woman swears she saw him drop something. She says she remembers it because she was shocked to see a grown man deliberately littering. If I didn't know what an awful knee injury poor ol' Hugh had sustained, I'd say we have him on the run.

This afternoon Lily is taking me for my first visit to Nesler Pharmaceuticals. She says Howard and Gavin are anxious to talk about the clinical trials. They've called her almost every day since the funeral to inquire about the book. Lily speaks highly of them both. She says Howard is a brilliant scientist. He and Michael talked enzymes the way some guys talk fishing or cars or women. And she thinks Gavin is cute, because he tries so hard to be helpful. Cute, huh? I suppose there are also people who think those little dogs with smashed in faces and an under bite are cute. I can't fault Lily for looking on the bright side; my first instinct is to search for the rotten spot in someone's character. It's a really nasty habit brought on from too many years spent sorting out the goody two shoes from the rock crawlers. It's probably just cynicism. They're probably great guys. Michael wouldn't work with anyone less. Michael would never have worked with me.

Nesler Pharmaceuticals is located in a business park of identical buildings on the outskirts of the city. We snake along a narrow asphalt drive in a maze of random parking lots, finally pulling up in front of a square, concrete building covered in fake stucco. There's a giant number "3" and letter "A" painted on the side. A blue and white Plexiglas sign over the double glass doors identifies Building 3A as the World Headquarters of Nesler Pharmaceuticals. I don't know what I was expecting, but it seems like the world headquarters of something shouldn't need a big directional number painted on it. The lobby consists of two metal chairs, one coffee table, a pale green ficus tree lusting toward the thin light from the doors, and a tall reception desk behind which sits Janet Thompson. I don't know Janet, but the only thing on the shiny wooden surface of the desk is a carved metal nameplate that says, "Janet Thompson." Her face, hair and eyes are deep black, almost blue black. She's young, probably not yet 30, and wears her hair in an elaborate spiral of miniature braids.

Lily approaches Janet's desk and announces our arrival. I sit down in one of the metal chairs and shuffle through the magazines on the coffee table. There are recent issues of *BioPharm*, *Pharmacy Today* and *Pharmaceutical Formulation & Quality* plus a stray copy of *Sports Illustrated*, because there's always a stray copy of *Sports Illustrated*. It's mandatory in all lobbies and waiting rooms.

"Howard and Gavin will be right out," Lily says, joining me in the other metal chair. "They're finishing up a conference call."

"Have you been here often?"

"A few times. Just after Michael started working with them."

"I thought it would be bigger."

"That's because you probably only write about the big boys, like Merck or Glaxo. Nesler's a little fish. At least they are until this new drug comes out."

"I've kind of wondered how they got together," I say. "Michael and I jumped right in to the research part of the relationship. He never told me how he got hooked up with Nesler in the first place."

"They contacted him. Everyone knew about Michael's work. Drug companies were calling him all the time. I don't know exactly what it was about these guys that moved them to the top of the list. Maybe it was because they were local, or their results. They had incredible early results."

My brain snaps to attention. We are entering territory I need information about, but it's dangerous terrain. Step carefully because the trip wires are everywhere. Say enough to keep the conversation rolling, but don't say anything stupid. I don't know anything about the preliminary test phases. That was the stuff I couldn't access during my computer research. If I can keep Lily talking, I can follow her footsteps into the middle of the story. Interview tip number one: state the obvious. Ask the questions as if you know the answers.

"You mean the tests they did prior to working with Michael?"

"Michael was so impressed with them, but you know that. You probably couldn't get him to shut up about it. I heard the stories more than a few times myself."

I smile in agreement. Interview tip number two: do not fear the pause. Don't follow every statement with another question. Let the interviewee fill the gap.

"I actually have a few favorites," Lily continues. "I love the one about the guy who was able to play the piano again. I almost cried the first time Michael told me about him. But I think the best one was that woman who recognized her daughter again after two years. You know the one I'm talking about?"

Interview tip number three: embrace the generality. Details are the job of our source.

There aren't a lot of trade secrets in the world of investigation. It's common sense mostly. But if you ever find yourself in a situation where you need more information than what's readily available, remember that getting back out is always easier than finding a way in. Shove your foot in the door and nudge until they budge.

I nod yes and raise one eyebrow. "That was something."

"Can you even imagine what it would be like to *know* you're losing touch? You can tell there's something wrong but you're not sure what. Like *Alice* tumbling down the well into *Wonderland*. It must be so scary."

Lily turns and stares out the glass doors of the lobby, as if she sees herself tumbling. As if she understands the fall.

"Don't you think fear goes away as they lose their grip on reality?" I ask, hoping to interrupt her thoughts and get her talking about the tests again.

"I don't think so," she says, still looking out the front windows. "It's our first emotion. A baby's cry. That's fear of the unknown as we break through into the world."

Lily turns and looks at me.

"I think fear is the *last* to go."

Her dark eyes are as soft and sad as that very first day I saw her at Michael's memorial. Her hair is loose around her face. I want to reach out and touch it, brush it back gently behind her ears.

A door opens behind the reception desk and Howard Stanich and Gavin VanMorten finally make their appearance.

I haven't seen either man since the service, but they haven't changed in the month that's gone by. Howard is starched and pressed to within an inch of mannequin status. He's dressed in a sleek silver gray suit with a white shirt and pale yellow tie. Gavin, although his brown wool suit is just as nice as Howard's and easily worth a month of my salary, looks rumpled and a little sleepy.

"Mrs. Rudolph, Mr. Mackey."

Howard approaches us like a long, lost friend. He embraces Lily then heartily shakes my hand. Gavin waits in the background, a lopsided smile on his round face.

"I am so very sorry to keep you waiting," Howard continues. "Damn conference calls. They'll monopolize your life if you let them. I thought we'd start today with a quick tour since Mr. Mackey has never seen our facilities."

"Albert. Please call me Albert."

"My pleasure. Would you like to take a look behind the scenes, Albert?"

Howard gestures toward the door through which he and Gavin just entered. I look at Lily. Gavin looks at me.

"Well come on then," Lily says, walking toward the door. Gavin opens it for her and she steps through into the hallway. We follow.

"Which way first, Howard?" Lily asks.

"I think the research pod. That's the most interesting."

Howard leads us down a narrow hallway with black steel doors about every forty feet. Each door has a small red plaque with a number and a letter. Alphanumeric, just like the building. We enter door 17C.

"This is our main research pod," says Howard. "It's the heart of the operation. We call it our B&B, beakers and burners."

He smiles at me. I realize he's made a little joke, probably a rare occurrence for Howard. He strikes me as someone who might find laughter a waste of time. Why laugh when you could spend that minute multiplying four digit numbers in your head? I smile back and glance around the room. It's fairly large, maybe 3,000 square feet with plain white walls and a gray vinyl tile floor. Steel-topped tables fill most of the available space. Each table holds the trappings of experimentation: glass tubes, petri dishes, autoclaves, centrifuges, and dozens of high-tech testing and measurement devices. There are two people in requisite white lab coats working together at one of the tables. They had looked up briefly when we walked in, but are now completely uninterested in our existence. It seems odd that only two people are working in such a big lab. It's too late for everyone to be at lunch.

"Is this where you started your work isolating the amyloid-beta protein plaques?" I ask.

That should sound impressive to Howard. I'd come across a Swiss study in my research that mentioned Nesler's experiments in conjunction with its own. The article, thankfully written in layman's terms for *USA Today*, explained the core theory of how certain proteins called amyloid-beta or AB proteins often clump or tangle in the brains of Alzheimer's patients. This appears to have the same effect on the brain as plaque build-up in our arteries can have on the heart. The reporter quoted the Swiss researcher as crediting Nesler with the discovery of a drug that appeared to be able to distinguish and attack only the clumping AB plaques, leaving intact the longer form of AB that occurs in healthy nerve cells.

Howard nods. He doesn't seem at all impressed by my question. I search for body language and find what I'm looking for. His hands, which had hung in a loose clasp in front of his crotch just a moment before, are now white knuckled.

"If I understand the function of the antibodies created by your vaccine, and please correct me if I'm wrong here, clearing away the plaques seems to reverse symptoms of brain degeneration, creating new nerve connections, and in some cases, even new neurons."

"Well put," Howard says, relaxing his hands and slipping them into his pockets. "Of course there are many people working on the same assumptions. It's a promising area of research right now."

"But I'll bet it's nice to be the first one to the table, and with such positive results. I've read some of your patients test at new intelligence levels."

"It's not as excessive as you might have heard."

Howard's face is smooth as ice. Throw out those bottles of skin cream, forget the Botox; it's much more effective to simply excise all emotion from your personality. Howard's a flippin' fountain of youth.

"The tabloids took some of Michael's television interviews and blew them out of proportion," Howard continues. "We have some dramatic stories to tell, but sometimes the media makes it sound like we're creating geriatric geniuses. That's preposterous of course."

Of course. End of conversation. Really smart folks, like Howard, are masters at directing a conversation. They can stop you dead if you're not careful. And once they've turned off the ignition, they do not like to restart.

"But the limbic system is so complex," I continue. It's like I'm poking Howard with a stick. "Can you really rule out anything?"

He breathes out a silent sigh—through his nose, so the only evidence he's perturbed is a slight pause and the rise and fall of his silk tie.

"We certainly hope our trials continue without complications. Anytime you're working with something that has to cross the blood-brain barrier, you're in uncharted territory."

"If you two are going to continue the neuro-whatever mumbo-jumbo, I'm finding another tour group," Lily says. She is standing behind Howard and her sudden insertion into the conversation startles him. In her heels, Lily is nearly as tall as Howard, and I realize her outfit of tailored linen pants and pale gray sweater set is a perfect match for Howard's suit. They could pose for a Corporate Chic magazine cover. I brush some imaginary lint from my slacks and wish they didn't look so shiny at the knees.

"I'm sorry, Lily, you're right," he says. "I imagine Albert and I could stay here all day discussing the finer points of antibody accumulation, but perhaps we should save that for another time when we won't bore our companions to tears."

Howard turns his back to me and points at the two people in lab coats.

"Sheila and Hiroshi are working on a dosage matrix. It's one of the last operations before we go into testing next month. By then, we should be in the new facility. Don't you think, Lily?"

"You know contractors, Howard. They say next month, they mean three months. I was over there last week and it looked like they'd made progress on the framing, but they haven't started the sheet rock yet."

Gavin, who is standing right next to me, speaks for the first time this afternoon.

"Have you seen the new lab, Albert?"

His voice is louder than it needs to be. There's a lot about Gavin that's a bit much. A little too hefty, a smidge too generous with the cologne, a habit of staring at you with his small green eyes a moment too long.

"No, but I'm looking forward to it. Lily tells me we'll go over there soon. Maybe next week."

"I'm surprised Michael never took you there," says Gavin.

"He showed me the plans. He was very proud of it."

"It will be one of the premier research labs in the country when we're finished," Howard says, taking back control of the conversation. "We're *all* very proud of it. Shall we let these folks get back to their work?"

I didn't notice Sheila and Hiroshi had ever stopped working. I imagine a group of nude showgirls could walk through and receive the same nonchalance. Howard holds the door open and ushers us back into the hallway.

"Most of these other rooms are storage and offices, but I do want you to see the manufacturing pods."

I wonder why they call everything "pods." It reminds me of *Invasion of the Body Snatchers* and I consider asking Howard if they ever check the basement for pods, but I doubt he'd get the joke. Lily is walking next to me down the hallway. She glances up and catches me smiling to myself. She smiles back then quickens her pace to pull even with Howard.

"One of the things we pride ourselves on here at Nesler is our dedication to quality assurance," Howard says.

A cell phone rings.

Howard interrupts himself. "Would you excuse me for just a moment? Gavin, take them through Quality Control and into Manufacturing. I'll be right behind you."

Gavin steps forward and picks up Howard's speech. "We understand each and every pill we manufacture has the potential to make a life or death difference to the person who takes it. We're rigid in our monitoring of all phases of research, testing and manufacturing. If you'll follow me."

We march along behind Gavin. I glance over my shoulder. Howard has walked several feet away from us. His back is turned and he's talking on a small silver cell phone the exact color of his suit. His voice is low and quiet, and with Gavin rambling on about integrity and quality, I can't distinguish what Howard's saying, but I can tell he's extremely tense. Even someone as normally rigid as Howard gives off some physical clues. His shoulders are pulled up almost to his ears and his knees are locked. I bet even his butt cheeks are clenched. Must not be good news.

I turn back around and follow Gavin and Lily around a corner.

The rest of the tour consists of the manufacturing floor, for which we have to don "bunny suits" so as not to contaminate the environment with any of our disgusting human cells. It's like wearing a giant paper napkin.

We finish up back in another alphanumeric hallway, this one with standard wood doors and yellow door plaques. Gavin knocks twice on door 8E then takes us through into a tidy office with floor-to-ceiling bookcases, an oriental carpet and a large oak desk with two leather chairs facing it. The top of the desk is empty except for a brass lamp, a digital clock, a crystal paperweight devoid of any paper-holding duties, and a single file folder. Howard is seated behind the desk.

"I trust the remainder of the tour was a success," he says, standing as we enter the room. "I'm sorry I was unable to catch up to you. With all the details to take care of for the new testing, I'm a slave to my phone. Please, have a seat. Janet is bringing coffee."

Howard indicates the two chairs in front of his desk. I look at Gavin. It's been a long time since I played musical chairs, but I can tell there aren't enough here to go around.

"I have a few things to take care of before the end of the day," Gavin says and nods for me to sit. "So, if you'll excuse me." He reaches out and quickly shakes Lily's hand and then mine. His hand is a little sweaty.

As soon as the door closes behind Gavin, Howard sits down and indicates we should do the same. He slides the file folder over to one side and addresses Lily.

"I thought we could take a few minutes to go over any questions Mr. Mackey, excuse me, Albert might have concerning Michael's work with us."

Lily looks at me. "That's your cue, Albert. What do you need to know?"

Howard smiles at me. His eyes are watery blue, small and very close to the bridge of his nose. All his features are small and sharp. Even his chin comes to a point. When he smiles, nothing crinkles—just like his suit.

The door opens again and Janet Thompson carries in a black lacquered tray with three white coffee mugs. Steam circles above each mug. She sets down the tray on the expanse of empty space that is Howard's desk.

"Thank you, Janet," says Howard.

"There's cream and sugar and I also brought honey. I know Mrs. Rudolph likes honey." Janet smiles shyly.

"You are so right, Janet," says Lily. "Thank you for remembering."

"I think that's everything, Janet. Thank you."

The smile vanishes and Janet wipes her hands across the back of her skirt. Her nails are long and painted in red, black and gold stripes

"Yes, Mr. Stanich. If you need anything else, just call me."

She hurries out.

The room is silent except for the clink of Lily stirring the honey into her coffee.

"So, Albert," Howard says. "Tell us how we can help with this book of yours."

"It's not really my book; it's Michael's book. I'm just trying to pull everything together into coherent pages."

"I'm sure that is a monumental task. Especially now."

Howard looks at Lily.

"I'm sorry, Lily. Is this going to be too difficult for you? If you'd rather Albert and I finish this alone, I'm sure Janet would be happy to keep you company out front."

Lily sets her coffee mug back on the tray. There is an air of cold professionalism about her I haven't seen before, as if someone snapped on a fluorescent light over her head. The angles of her face distort from refined to razor sharp. She stretches forward, ready to pounce on Howard and rip out his throat. This is a profoundly different woman from the one who, just a few hours earlier, spoke with such sweet eloquence about the miracles of Michael's work.

"I'm fine, Howard. As I've told Albert over and over again, this book is what keeps me going. I'm happy to stay. I'm not going to come unglued or anything if that's what you're worried about."

"Of course not," Howard backpedals. "I don't mean to offend you. I'm happy to have you stay. In fact, I'm sure you can add quite a bit to the discussion. I know Michael shared his enthusiasm for this project with you."

"Actually, Howard, I'm the big-picture gal. I give the parties and raise the money. I can quote the case studies that will generate the most astonishment or turn on the tears, but I don't really know a lot about the nuts and bolts."

She retrieves her coffee and relaxes back into the chair, wrapping both hands around the smooth mug.

"Albert was asking me earlier about how you and Michael started working together in the first place," Lily continues. "And I couldn't answer him very well. Perhaps you could."

Howard's small, sharp eyes snap with enthusiasm at this idea.

"We had been following Michael's Alzheimer's work since the early days, long before he became a media celebrity. Nesler had already achieved a modicum of success with a hypertension product as well as our cornerstone product, VeriLethic, which as you may know, is one of the top cardiac medications."

I nod. This was one of the few details I was able to find out about Nesler. It seemed to be their original claim to fame. After my impressive beta amyloid protein speech, this should cement my expertise as a medical writer.

"I covered VeriLethic for a couple of the trades when it came out in '94," I say, uncrossing my legs and leaning forward. "It caused quite a sensation. One of the very first formulations targeted at the geriatric market."

Howard's left eyebrow lifts, but he makes no other show of surprise.

"Yes. Yes it was. It's still popular although some generics are out there now. It positioned us in the field of geriatric pharmacology, which is when we started watching Michael's work. My first thought, foolish as it might have been, was to get him to come to work for us. But by the time we had our product to a point where we could approach him, he had become so well known and successful that he didn't need to work for anyone. So, my next idea was to at least convince him to work *with* us."

"When did you start talking?" I ask.

"It must have been late '99. Turn of the century and all. Everyone was aiming for something to bring out in the new millennium."

"And at that point, you'd already conducted your initial testing phase?"

"Of course. We'd never have gotten Michael to talk with us without those initial results.'

I needed to see those tests. I needed to understand what originally drew Michael's attention. What had he seen in these people that was so astonishing? But both Howard and Lily believed I already knew everything about them. Maybe I could stir up Howard's ego.

"You know," I say, drawing out my words so they sound heavy with importance. "I was just thinking. I only have Michael's perspective on the initial testing. I'm wondering if you have another way of looking at it, something from the company's view. Something that conveys your mission in developing the drug?"

Howard looks at me, but not with pride. His jaw clenches and his blue eyes go flat. It's just an instant. He blinks, which seems to release his features, and his smile takes control again. A big, full smile with lots of teeth.

"I think that's a fine idea," Howard says. "Unfortunately, I don't have an official packet prepared you could take with you today, but I'd be happy to put together something that summarizes case histories and outlines the company's objectives. I appreciate you providing us with a platform to tell our story."

"Michael was adamant this book be about his research, not just about him. More than anything, he wanted people to understand the real story."

"The real story? As opposed to what, Mr. Mackey?"

Howard's big, toothy smile is gone again. So is some of the color in his face. His hands are flat down on his desk, as if he might push himself up and out of his chair at any moment.

"What it's really like to suffer with Alzheimer's," I answer, haltingly, questioningly. "What it's really like to struggle to find a cure. Did I say something wrong, Howard? You look a little tense and you're back to that Mr. Mackey stuff again."

Howard pulls his hands into his lap.

"My apologies. The media has descended upon us since Michael's death. They want to know exactly when the next round of clinical testing starts, when the new lab will be up and running, when the drug will be ready for final FDA approval. I've been unable to give them definitive answers so now they're insinuating I'm evading the questions, that perhaps the whole release is completely off track. No offense to you, Albert, but reporters can be very trying."

"It's what we do best."

"I've had half a dozen calls just today, including the one that interrupted our tour. When they can't get any information out of me, they start calling our board members and then the investors in the lab expansion. As you can imagine, these people do not want to be bothered. I get the calls explaining exactly how much they do not want to be bothered ever again."

"It's true," Lily interrupts. "I've had to deal with some of it myself. Sometimes I get the feeling the media is just waiting for us to fall. Like they want the house that Michael built to collapse."

"The bigger they are?" I suggest.

"The harder they fall," Lily agrees. "Everyone loved Michael, but people still seem to get a weird satisfaction out of watching famous people fail. It's the ultimate, 'I told you so.'"

"Please, Albert," Howard says, standing up and extending his hand. "Please accept my apologies for jumping to conclusions. It's been a bad day, but that's no reason for me to lose my temper. I'm very grateful you're telling the story. The *real* story."

I stand to shake Howard's hand and take this as the signal that our meeting is over. Lily is standing too and Howard comes around the desk to give her the obligatory two-handed clasp. Personal yet businesslike. They walk toward the door discussing lab construction issues. As I step around my chair to follow, my coat brushes a napkin from the coffee service onto the floor. I bend to pick it up and drop it into the nearby wastebasket. As I do, I notice a discarded paper resting at the bottom. It looks like an Internet search results page, "*Medical Writers or Technical Writers - Freelance*" is the page heading.

"Albert," Lily calls from the doorway. "Howard says he can have that report ready for you in a couple of days. I told him to have it sent over to your condo. Is that okay?"

I look up from the wastebasket, wad the napkin and drop it in.

"That would be great," I answer, hurrying over to meet them. As I reach the doorway, I see Gavin coming down the hallway.

"Gavin will see you out. These old buildings are a bit of a rat's maze. I hope we'll hear from you again soon, Albert."

"I'm sure I'll have more questions."

"If you need anything, just call. I'd welcome a friendly phone call."

Howard is smiling again. His teeth are very white and very straight. Everything about him is straight. I bet he's not even rumpled when he gets out of bed in the morning.

"I'll do it. And those reporters who are bothering you? Tell them 'no comment.' We hate it when people do that."

SIX

It's getting harder to make it out of the office early. Yesterday, just as I was putting on my coat to leave, Dennis came in with some statistical report he felt the need to share with me, for about an hour. Then today was Ernie Johnson's birthday. There was a card going around and cake in the lunchroom. Ernie's a nice enough guy. I think he might have been kind of popular when he was young, maybe a football star or something. He still acts as if the world is his locker room. There's a lot of slapping on the hand, the back, even the butt if he's particularly jovial. He likes to tell bad jokes really loud, which he must believe get funnier with age because he'll tell you the same damn joke ten times unless you stop him. There's a collection of baseball caps lining the top of his cubicle, most with team or beer logos but some with funny sayings. My favorite is, "*If I throw a stick, will you leave?*"

I sneak down the stairwell and out through the maintenance offices. This forces me to walk two blocks around the building to get to my car, but does save me from singing *Happy Birthday* to a grown man in a brown suit and Snoopy tie.

As if that wasn't bad enough, I also had to turn down another house-sitting client. Rita McElvoy in accounts payable is going to Hawaii with her family. I house-sat for them last year when they went to Disney World. She was counting on me, she said. She never thought I'd be busy. *Well, think again Rita. Charlie's made plans and they don't include you.* Of course, I didn't say that. I just told her I was already sitting for someone else. And then I apologized again and again and again. She still looked like she was going to cry.

Working two jobs like this is going to kill me. If I don't make some serious headway on the Klein case, Dennis is going to get suspicious. But Lily has the rest of this week and the next planned out, and she is paying me too. That's a flimsy excuse. I'd work for Lily for free. Hell, I'd pay her to let me hang around.

Howard's report is leaning against my front door when I get home for lunch. It's not as big an envelope as I'd expected. Must be the *CliffsNotes* version. I pick it up and unlock the door. The message light on my phone machine is blinking as I walk into the kitchen. Lily was appalled I didn't have a cell phone and insisted I at least get an answering machine. Fine with me. Seeing how Albert Mackey doesn't have any friends or relations, the only person ever on my answering machine is Lily. I punch the message button.

"Albert, it's Lily."

What did I tell you?

"Did you get the report Howard promised? Let me know what you think as soon as you read through it. I'll be at the lab construction site this morning. The local press is getting a walk-through of the progress and guess who's the tour guide? Hey, maybe you should come with me and coach me on my 'no comments.'"

She laughs and even on the tinny phone recording it sounds lovely.

"I'll call as soon as I'm done and shoot over there to meet you. We can discuss how you want to use the new information. See you then."

Click. Beep.

"Hello, Albert, Howard Stanich here. Just confirming the papers were delivered safely. Please call me at your convenience."

Howard has my phone number?

Click. Beep.

"Hi, it's Lily again. It's a little after noon. I'm on my way. Hope you're home when I get there."

Click. Beep.

I look at my watch. 12:20. I must have just missed Lily's last call. She'll probably be here any minute. The place isn't too messy, just a comfortable, *lived in* look. But this outfit has got to go. Something tells me most writers don't conduct research in a suit and tie. I undress while running down the hallway, a skill I perfected in my teenage years that allowed for an extra six minutes of sleep before school.

I'm pulling a sweatshirt over my head when the door bell rings. No time for shoes.

"I am starved," Lily says, striding in and dropping a large, suede shoulder bag on the couch. "And my feet hurt. I think I walked ten miles with those reporters."

She looks very much the society maven in a navy suit with red trim. Her hair is swept up and clipped with a gold and pearl comb. Clusters of red and white stones glitter on each ear. I'm sure they're real rubies and diamonds. She glances at my feet.

"Hey, no fair, you're not wearing any shoes."

She pulls off her navy blue heels and deposits them in the leather bag on the couch.

"Much better."

"How'd it go?" I ask.

"Fine," she says, dropping into a chair at the dining room table. "They ask the same questions every time. How will Michael's death affect the opening of the new laboratories? What's happening with the research now that's Michael's gone? Who will be taking over Michael's work? It's exhausting."

"Did you try 'no comment'?"

She smiles and smoothes a few stray hairs back into place.

"Actually, I forgot. I did try to get them to concentrate on the construction. The project manager was there with me, but I don't think he said more than two words."

"He's probably not as good looking as you."

I regret this statement as soon as it leaves my mouth. I've been fantasizing about Lily from almost the first moment I saw her, but I never planned on admitting it.

I suck back in a gulp of air, as if I can suck the words back in with it. Two thin vertical lines form on Lily's brow. She sits straighter in the chair. And then she smiles. I've seen that smile before. It's a noxious mixture of sadness, kindness and pity. Women use this smile when they're trying to explain a complicated concept to a small child or when they are about to tell a man he is a pathetic oaf.

"I'm sorry," I, the oaf, interrupt. "That didn't come out right. In fact, it sounded down right idiotic. Let's pretend it never happened. Let's pretend instead I said, 'Gee, Lily, I'm sorry you had such a crappy morning. Let's go grab a sandwich and talk about Howard's report.'"

Her eyes register some relief, but the worry is still there in her smile.

"Okay," she says. "I am pretty hungry."

"Lily, please don't take what I said the wrong way. It was just a compliment. I'm not going to hit on you. I would never dream of it. Michael was my friend."

I know I'm rambling, but I can't stop. I want to fill the silence with something until she stops looking at me like that.

"I have way too much respect for you, and if anything I do ever makes you uncomfortable . . . "

"Albert," Lily says, interrupting my scramble for dignity. "It's okay. I believe you. Besides, if you keep going, you'll probably tell me I'm really quite *un*attractive, and then I'll be offended and you'll have to start apologizing all over again."

She smiles and amusement shines through this time.

"Thank you," I say. "I promise not to say anything stupid for the rest of the day. And, I'm buying lunch. Deal?"

"Deal."

Sandwich King is just a few blocks from the hospital. In a world of cookie-cutter fast food joints, it's a welcome beacon of individuality. The place must have originally been retail, because there's a huge plate-glass display window along the front. The Sandwich King folks added red gingham half curtains along the bottom and bright blue shutters across the top, then they painted the building itself neon yellow with orange dinner plate-sized polka dots. The land of Sandwich is a colorful place. There are actually two Sandwich Kings, this one and one downtown by the high school, but this is the original location. I've always liked their logo, which is painted almost life size on the door. It's a tubby, smiling monarch, but rather than the traditional robe, scepter and crown, the Sandwich King sports a bejeweled apron, a spatula held aloft and a bacon, lettuce and tomato club perched jauntily on one side of his cartoon head. My liege.

There are several people in green scrubs at the small tables. One of them, a short, beefy man with thick gray hair and one continuous eyebrow, calls over to Lily as we walk toward the counter.

"Hello, Grayson," Lily says, crossing to the man and taking his outstretched hands in hers. "I'm surprised to see you taking a break."

"Lily," he says. "How are you doing?"

"As well as can be expected, I guess. Each day is a tiny bit better than the last." She gestures in my direction. "Grayson O'Donnell, this is Albert Mackey. He's the man working on Michael's biography."

The man turns and extends both his hands to me. I guess he's not a one-hand-shaker kind of guy. I bring up both my hands and he immediately grabs them, squeezing tightly and hanging on.

"You're the one who spoke at Michael's service. Incredible story, just incredible."

With each adjective, he gives my hands another squeeze to emphasize his point.

"In case you haven't guessed by the fetching green outfit, Grayson's a surgeon. He worked with Michael at the hospital," Lily says. "He's one of the best vascular guys in the business."

Grayson, apparently distracted by Lily's compliment, drops my hands and turns back to her. She tilts her head to one side and smiles at him. Mutual admiration society; but then, who wouldn't love and admire Lily? How could you not?

"You have always been one of my biggest fans, and believe me, I am quite grateful for the attention. But seriously, dear, is there anything at all I can do for you? Anything? Because you know Sarah and I would be happy to help in any way we can."

"I'm fine, really. I've been keeping so busy I've barely had time to think, which is probably a good thing."

"If you ever need to talk, you call me. Promise?

"Promise."

"That's my girl. Now, go get some lunch. The ham and cheese hero is the special today and I can personally vouch for its quality."

"Thank you, Grayson."

"Pleased to meet you, Dr. O'Donnell," I say.

He nods and sits back down to his own lunch.

"He's got an awful lot of energy," I whisper to Lily as we cross to the counter.

"Grayson? He's a delight. He probably just got through with a surgery. Michael used to be the same way. He'd be exhausted, but if things had gone well, he'd also be as hyperactive as a two-year old."

We stand and look up at the menu on the wall. A bored teenager with a nose ring and too much eye makeup waits for our decision.

"Based on Dr. O'Donnell's four-star review, I'm going for the ham and cheese," I say.

"Sounds good," says Lily.

"Two ham and cheese specials," I say to the teen.

"You want the Royal Sauce on the sandwich or on the side?" the teen asks, twirling a pen between two blue fingernails.

"Royal Sauce?"

"It's Sandwich King's secret sauce. Some people like it on their sandwich and some people want it on the side."

"So many options. I'll take it on the sandwich."

"Put mine on the side," Lily says, leaning around me and smiling at the clerk.

"For here or to go?"

"For here," I answer, pulling out my wallet.

"That'll be $11.90. Here's your cups. The beverage bar is over there. Thank you for choosing Sandwich King and have a nice day."

This entire speech is delivered with the exact same inflection on each sentence, as if she's reading something taped to the register. She slams the cash drawer closed and hands me my change. I sneak a peek at the grimy touch screen on the register. There *is* a piece of paper stuck to the front. Like it's too tough to remember, "Have a nice day"? What's the world coming to?

Lily is already at the beverage bar, drawing a cup of Diet Pepsi. I join her.

"Do you suppose the youth of America are destined for insignificance?" I ask, pushing the root beer button.

"Are you talking about the girl at the counter? Cut her some slack. How excited would you be to work at Sandwich King? We can't all be great authors, you know"

"Are *you* a great author?" I ask in mock astonishment.

"Very funny."

"Very true."

Lily rolls her eyes and points to a table for two at the front of restaurant next to the large window.

"How about over there?"

"After you."

We sit at the table only to be immediately interrupted by the crackling sound system. The speakers are so awful, I'm not positive if she called out our number or shouted something in Latin. I go back up to the counter anyway and hand the teenager my receipt. She hands me a tray with two sandwich plates on it. I smile. She chews her gum. We have achieved communication.

"I'm really curious to see Howard's report," Lily says as I get back to the table.

"I haven't even looked at it myself."

I pull the slim envelope out of my briefcase, tear open the top seal and pull out a small sheaf of papers.

"That's it?" Lily says. "What does the cover letter say?"

"It's just a note from Howard," I say, reading from the memo. "Per your request ...executive summary ... call me with questions. The basics."

I turn over the memo and start reading the first page of the summary. It's broken into short paragraphs. The first couple describe the details of phase one and two of Nesler's testing. These are the phases conducted on healthy volunteers. No side effects are noted other than the standard headache, diarrhea and nausea. I house sat for a nursing student once and she told me that on the drug interaction and side effect quizzes, if you answered, "headache, diarrhea and nausea" you were guaranteed to be correct ninety-nine percent of the time.

After this introduction, each paragraph appears to outline a specific participant from the early stages of phase-three testing. There are no names, just age, gender and length of time since initial diagnosis of neurological problems. I flip forward through the other pages, counting paragraphs as I go. There are twenty-four people profiled. The last page covers Nesler's history and mission statement.

"So?" Lily asks.

"I don't think there's anything new. It's just a listing of some of the original phase-three test participants."

I hold up the first page for her to see but she reaches out and grabs the whole thing. She scans through the pages then slaps it down on the table.

"I could have told you this. Is this really what you wanted?"

I'm actually delighted to get anything, but since Lily thinks I already know about these people, it's probably best to feign disappointment.

"I was hoping for more details about the research, maybe even some editorial comments from Howard about specific results. But, they're a big company. They probably don't want me combing through their private papers."

"And why not?" Lily eyes demand an answer. She stabs at the ice in her cup with her straw. "They have everything to gain if you present them as a great company in Michael's biography. Do you want me to talk with Howard again?"

"Not yet. There might be something here I can use. How's your sandwich?"

"Are you trying to change the subject?"

"Not at all. What would you suggest we do about it?"

"I think we should talk with Howard again."

"To be honest with you, Lily, the guy gives me the creeps. I'd just as soon space out my conversations with him a little farther. Which reminds me, did you give him my phone number?"

"I don't think so. Why?"

"He left a message on my answering machine this morning, checking that I'd received the report and asking me to call him with any questions."

"That was nice of him. Why does he give you the creeps?"

"Have you ever noticed how clean and pressed he is all the time?"

"Good grooming makes you nervous?"

"He's so stiff. Like if he bent over he would snap."

Lily smiles and picks up her sandwich. She takes a bite and chews slowly. I watch her lips undulate. I must have been staring because she grabs her napkin and holds it to her mouth as she swallows.

"He's no stiffer than any other CEO I've met," she says. "And I've always thought he was a pretty snappy dresser. If we're trying to pinpoint odd characters at Nesler, I'd be more likely to put Gavin on the top of that list."

"VanMorten? He doesn't seem bright enough to be so high up in the company. What do you know about him?"

"Not much. He hardly says a thing if Howard is around. The longest conversation I've ever had with him was about whales. He seems to know an awful lot about killer whales. I was waiting with him at the lab site one day. I don't know where Howard was, probably on the phone. Anyway, I was making small talk about an article I'd seen in the newspaper, about that whale they shipped from Oregon to Iceland. Remember the one, from the movie?"

"Free Willy?"

"That's the one. There was some story about him being flown half way around the world to be set free. I only mentioned it because I'd seen it in the paper that morning, but Gavin grabbed a hold of the topic and started going on and on. It was very odd."

"Some people have pretty unusual hobbies."

The topic is beginning to make me nervous. I smile at Lily.

"You have a sprout in your teeth," she says.

I clamp my mouth shut and search across my teeth with my tongue. It touches a sprout hair on the right canine. Great.

"Hey, don't sweat it. If I didn't like you, I wouldn't have told you. I'd have let you go through the rest of the day with it wiggling in the breeze."

"Is that supposed to make me feel better?"

I reach in with my pinkie nail and scrape the offending vegetation off my tooth and onto a napkin.

"I once let this girl I worked with go the whole afternoon with a giant piece of spinach covering one of her front teeth," Lily confesses. "She didn't realize it until she went to the bathroom after a big meeting we'd had with the head of our department."

Lily laughs. I like this slightly evil side of her personality.

I reach over and take back Howard's report. It's open to page four and I began reading about a seventy-four-year-old male diagnosed with Alzheimer's disease. His cognitive function had been deteriorating rapidly for twelve months. Brain scans as close as three months apart showed a clear downward spiral. After just three weeks in the Nesler trial, his cognitive function had improved to the point he'd been at three months prior. After five weeks, he had returned to the cognitive function of nearly nine months prior. And after twelve weeks, his cognitive function was higher than when he was first diagnosed. It sounded miraculous. I show the page to Lily.

"Do you remember this guy's story?" I ask, sliding the paper in front of her.

She reads for a few moments and then looks up.

"That sounds like Charles. He's the musician, the pianist. A pretty good one. I think he might have even been a little famous. When he started the Nesler trials, he'd completely forgotten how to play. He still knew what a piano was and what it was for. His children said he'd sit in front of the keys for hours, staring down at them. Then one night, about ten weeks into the trials, his daughter woke up in the middle of night to the sound of a Beethoven sonata. She went downstairs and there was her father at the piano, playing exactly as she remembered him doing so many years before. Tears were streaming down his face but he kept playing and playing. I'm sure Michael must have told you about him."

I nod slowly, as if remembering the actual moment when Michael told me the story.

"Have you ever met any of these people?" I ask.

"No, I've only heard the stories."

"Did Michael meet them all?"

"You know, I don't know. If he did, he never mentioned it to me. I know he helped select the new patients for this next phase of testing. That part is so hard. People are desperate. Drug trials are usually their last hope."

Lily takes another bite of her sandwich and sips a bit of Diet Pepsi. Silence stretches out across our little table. I can hear people at the other tables talking about their days, their plans for the weekend, their lives. Their real lives.

I'm about to take another stab at getting some new information when Lily pipes up.

"Did you know Michael's father, Augie?" She asks, picking the sesame seeds off the crust of her sandwich.

This was tricky. Michael had spoken often in interviews about his own father's struggle with Alzheimer's. I knew it was the source of his dedication to the research, but I didn't know any more about Augustus Rudolph than anyone else who watches Oprah or CNN.

"I met him a couple times during college. Why?"

"Just wondering, I guess. Reading through these stories makes me wonder what would have happened if Augie had been able to be a part of the testing."

She licks her finger and sticks up each fallen sesame seed on her plate then sucks them all off. I want her to do it again.

"He was such an incredible man," she continues. "So smart. Smarter than Michael I think."

"Well, anyone who could put together a fortune like his from scrap metal must have had a pretty good head on his shoulders."

My brain is frantically clicking through data, searching for anything about Michael's father.

"Isn't that the truth?" Lily agrees. "Everything wears out sooner or later. It's the perfect self-sustaining business. Did you know Augie was one of the first to figure out how to make money in recycling? It was his chemistry background. He could tell you what anything was made up of and what it could be broken down into."

I remember seeing several pictures in Lily's living room of a tall, muscular man with white hair and a bushy mustache. In most of the photos, he was in shirtsleeves. No tie. Nothing formal about him. That's it. Brain data hit!

"He always seemed like a regular guy when he visited us at school," I say. "In fact, I never even knew Michael came from money until I saw his dad on TV one night. He was part of some presidential symposium on recycling. He was sitting right next to Ronald Reagan. It was unreal. Michael just shrugged it off, saying something about how his dad didn't like Reagan and he couldn't believe he was sitting there with a straight face."

This tidbit was mostly true. One of the stories I'd pulled up on the Rudolph family was a *New York Times* piece about Augustus Rudolph's strange dichotomy of influence on and revulsion of the Reagan administration.

"He was not fond of Ronnie," Lily agrees. "It's kind of ironic that the same disease ended up killing both of them."

"How bad did it get? At the end, I mean?"

"It was pretty bad."

She stops and looks down again at her plate. Her finger searches across it for imaginary sesame seeds or maybe she's writing something with her finger on its white plastic surface.

"I'm sorry," she says, finally looking back up at me. "I guess I don't like to remember him that way."

"Was he completely gone?"

"No. I almost wish he had been. It would have been awful to have him not know who we were, but I think it would have been better for him if he forgot everything."

"What do you mean?"

"You'd watch him struggle to find the right word, he wouldn't be able finish his thought, he couldn't follow the simplest of directions. Most of the time it bothered us much more than it bothered him, but there were times he'd have flashes of clarity. Some message would make it all the way through his brain, and you could tell he knew something was horribly wrong."

"Is that what you meant about never losing the fear?"

"What?"

She looks at me, quizzically. A what-are-you-nuts expression.

"When we were at Nesler the other day, you said you thought fear was the last thing to go."

"Did I? Maybe that's right."

Lily pauses, picks up her paper napkin and wipes each finger. Quickly but carefully, systematically, like a surgeon.

"Have you ever been lost in the woods?" she asks.

"I'm not really the outdoorsy type."

"I got lost once when I was little. Our family was on a hike and I ran off without them and got all turned around. I remember seeing a tree and thinking it had to be the same tree I'd seen when I'd run off the path, but I looked at it again and I wasn't so sure. At first glance everything looked familiar. I'd look a second time and it would all be wrong. I'd never been so scared. I think that might have been what it was like for Augie. Something would look familiar to him again for an instant and then just as quickly it would morph into something completely foreign."

"You're saying it would have been better for him if he didn't recognize anything?"

"I was perfectly happy running through the woods until I stopped and realized I was lost."

"And you think Augie knew he was lost?"

"Michael told me about one morning, really close to the end, when Augie looked him right in the eye and said, 'Pack my things, I won't be coming back.' At the time, Michael thought it was just nonsense. Augie had been rambling about all kinds of things for days. But later, after he was gone, Michael realized it was the last time his father had looked at him. I mean really looked at him."

As she speaks, Lily stretches and twists her napkin into the shape of a serpent.

"When I go," she says, waving the napkin snake in my direction. "I hope I just get hit by a truck."

"Or an explosion," I offer. "They say a gas explosion can take you out just like that."

I snap my fingers.

SEVEN

"How about a cup of coffee?"

Lily looks down at me as I sit in front of her computer. We're outlining chapters this afternoon, trying to decide what each one will be about, discussing how much space to devote to Michael's childhood, his schooling, research, theories. I find it grueling, mostly because I have to think so hard to maintain the illusion of competence. If I'd known I was going to get myself trapped in an alternate personality, I would have picked something way easier to be, like a shoe salesman or the President. This book writing shit is for the birds. The stress must be showing on my face if Lily thinks I need coffee. I don't believe it will help, but I'm grateful for any interruption.

"That'd be good," I say, taking my hands from the keyboard to roll up my sleeves and poke the tails of my shirt back into my jeans. Perhaps if I look less rumpled, I'll also look less disturbed.

"You keep going. I'll be right back."

I watch her leave the room. It's a nice view. Her short denim skirt pulls across her backside a little as she walks and her pink sweater brushes her waist. If she lifted her arms you'd see skin.

I can't take this much longer. Not only are we starting to get into the actual writing part of this farce, I can't be around Lily without picturing her naked. I'm not sure if she can tell. It's ridiculously obvious to me, but if she knows, she's being awfully gracious about it. Either that or she finds it so pitiful she puts up with me, like some hideous creature she has to visit in the hospital. *Let's chat while I pretend not to notice half your face is mutilated beyond recognition.*

This distraction aside, the larger problem is the fact I will not be able to prolong this researching and outlining stuff much longer. Very, very soon I am going to have to start writing. This will be disastrous. Not difficult, not a challenge, but simply and wholly ruinous. I cannot write. Oh, I can put pen to paper to produce an investigative report denying an insurance claim, but that's not writing. That's stringing words together into sentences.

How about all those eulogies, right? I make those up. They're two, three, four-minute stories born of circumstance. They hang in the air like smoke. People breath them in, enjoy the smell, and then they're gone. Forgotten. No one quotes me. No one checks back to see if what I said made sense. But ... a book, that's serious business. That's tens of thousands of words, lumped into paragraphs, broken into chapters. And this is a real person. A real important person who did real important things. I need more than a cup of coffee. I need caffeine injected directly into my veins with a whiskey chaser.

Lily comes back into the room with two steaming mugs. I'm frozen in the exact position she left me. Hands in my lap, eyes staring past the screen into oblivion, perspiration running down my ribs. Hopefully she can't see that last part.

"Are you okay?" she asks, setting down a mug near my immobile hands. "You look a little pale. I hope you're not coming down with something. I know more people who have some horrible flu thing right now."

"I think I just need a little break." I stretch back in the chair and rub my neck, enjoying the release until I remember how sweaty I am. My shirt is now stuck to my back and my hand is damp.

"Then let's take a break," Lily says. "Get up from that chair and come sit over here."

She grabs my mug and moves it over to a table next to a soft brown chair that resembles a well-worn baseball mitt, like you could collapse inside it with a satisfying thunk.

"This was Michael's favorite chair. It was in his room when he was a kid ... in fact," she leans down and touches the side of one arm. "He wrote his name right here and drew a funny little face. Look."

I get up to walk over to the chair. While she's not looking, I wipe my hand on my butt and tug at the back of my shirt to create a small, drying breeze. Bending down to look over Lily's shoulder at Michael's chair, I catch the scent of vanilla in her hair. She's pointing to some black markings, faded but still visible against the grain of the leather.

"Mikie was here," I read. There's also a silly face with a big nose and spikes for hair. "I bet he got in trouble for that one."

Lily laughs and stands up. I step back quickly in order to avoid her head crashing into my face. But when she turns around to answer me I am still very close. Too close.

She steps away and points to the chair. I sit as directed. She curls into a loveseat opposite me. We're in Michael's office. Not the darkly paneled doctor's study you'd see in the movies, this room is bright and well used. In addition to the chair and sofa we occupy, there's a sprawling desk covered with computer gear, a printer, fax machine, phone, and stacks and stacks of papers and manuals and magazines. Lily cleared off a space for us to work, but it's not much more than a tiny crop circle in a field of confusion. There are bookshelves on every inch of wall space, under the windows, over the door. There's even a small fireplace at one end of the room with books across the mantle and piled like fuel on either side of the screen. Could anyone read this much stuff?

"Have you been sleeping alright?" Lily asks.

I must look puzzled, because she rephrases the question.

"When I have a cold coming on, I can't sleep. That's the first sign. It's all downhill from there."

"I am a little tired. The storms these last few nights have kept me awake."

"Hasn't the wind been incredible? They say another one's coming through tonight. We can call it a day if you want."

"I'll be fine. I just need to sit for a few minutes. This is a great chair."

Lily smiles. She must be picturing Michael sitting in the chair because her eyes look right through me. Maybe that's why she doesn't notice my overt leering; she can't imagine herself with anyone but Michael. I reach for my coffee and the movement breaks her stare. She reluctantly returns to our conversation.

"I've been thinking we could go through Michael's appointment planner on his computer," she says. "We might be able to find some mention about meetings or interviews with the original test participants. Remember you asked me about that? It's been bugging me that I couldn't answer you. I never stopped to notice that a lot of the time I had no idea where Michael was."

She takes a drink of her coffee and stares down into the mug rather than looking at me. I wonder what she sees in the blackness of the coffee. I don't think you can read coffee grounds the way you can tea leaves, and either way, I know you can't tell anything from the liquid that's covering them up. I bet if you look at anything long enough it changes. We're just not clever enough to recognize the minuscule shifts and movement. Everyone notices when they demolish a building. But sometimes, the difference is just an energy shift at the molecular level, just one leaf falling from a tree, leaving a hundred thousand behind.

"Such is the life of a doctor's wife, right?" I ask, trying to lighten the mood. "A phone call away from desertion at all times."

Lily looks up at me and her smile takes an instant to catch up with her eyes. She had to remember to sweep back the curtain. What is it that drives us to be so stoic in the face of death? Where's the tragedy? On television, you always see foreign women in black veils wailing over the coffins of their departed loved ones. Here, everyone puts on a brave front. Looking sad is acceptable, much more than that is undignified. I think there should be more crying.

"I was used to that part," Lily answers. "But when I try to put together a week, sometimes even a day of

Michael's life, there are giant chunks of time I can't account for. I thought maybe if I looked through his schedule it would fall into place."

Outside the windows, shadows stretch forward, trying to hold on to the escaping afternoon. Day and night sometimes remind me of bickering siblings. Technically, it's an equal split, twelve hours for day and twelve hours for night. But I think night is the older brother and usually gets more than his fair share. Day, the little sister, has to whine and cry and struggle to hold on to every single hour she can. The colors in the room dull in the vanishing light and the rustling of our small movements intensifies.

"It's getting gloomy in here, isn't it?"

Lily leans over and clicks on a table lamp. The sudden illumination pushes away the darkness to wait at the edges of the room.

"What did you find?" I ask.

"I haven't looked."

"Why not?"

"I am so lame when it comes to computers. Give me a pen and paper any day. It used to drive Michael crazy that I still balance my checkbook by hand."

"Do you want me to take a look?"

"That would be great."

Lily reaches out to set her mug down on the table in front of her. There it is. Skin. And then it's gone. She's up and over at the desk before I can climb out of the baseball mitt.

I consider myself pretty adept when it comes to wrestling information out of a computer, but who knows what kind of program Michael used for his personal scheduling. However, I am more than happy to try to figure it out. It will divert attention from the task at hand and I'm all for that. I sit back down at the computer and open the Start menu. A pretty standard assortment of programs.

"Did you try Outlook?"

"I didn't try anything."

"I use Outlook's calendar. We may as well start there."

I click the icon and a box pops up asking for the password.

"What's Michael's password?"

Lily steps around me and leans in towards the screen. She reaches out and touches the prompt box with the tips of her fingers.

"How did you do that? How did you get that box to come up?"

"I clicked on the program icon, but it's password protected. Do you know Michael's password?"

"No."

She turns away from the screen and sits on the edge of the desk. She's looking at the floor and her bottom lip is clamped under her front teeth. Body language experts, of whom I consider myself a member, would tell you she is "biting back her words." She is afraid to let her real feelings tumble out. She fears emotional pain more than physical pain. Well, don't we all? Her shoulders slump forward and she hammers on her thighs with two tight fists.

"Stupid, stupid, stupid," she says in rhythm with the pounding.

"Hey, it's all right. I'm sure the password is written down somewhere."

Her head snaps up. She's looking right at me now. Her eyes are sharp and dark, like bullets that could come flying out of their sockets and tear a path through my brain.

"Why would he put a password on his calendar?" Her voice strains out through her teeth. "Who was he afraid of? Me?"

I roll the chair over to her and tentatively put a hand over one of her clenched fists. It doesn't relax. I cover the other one.

"Not you," I say. "I'm sure it wasn't for you. I bet he used the same calendar on the system at the hospital. He probably didn't want people poking around in his personal notes when he was out of the office."

Her hands relax under mine, but she slips them out to catch her head as it falls forward. My palms hover above her bare thighs, desperately wanting to land. Instead I sit back in my chair and place them in my own lap.

"I should know things like this, shouldn't I?" she says, raking her fingers through her hair. "A wife is supposed to know this kind of stuff."

I don't answer. I don't know the answer. I don't know what to say to help her. It's like watching a building burn. You want to run in, but then you'd burn up too. So you stand there, helpless, burning up on the inside instead.

"He didn't trust me," she continues. "I don't mean he didn't love me. I know he loved me. I just don't think he trusted me to understand things. I could handle the parties and the press and the house, but I wasn't supposed to worry about the details of his work. When he'd tell me about things, he'd always stop short of explaining the real focus. I tried to pester him into it a few times, but he always brushed it off as being too boring for me."

I'm listening to her. No, I'm watching her mouth move, watching it form letters, watching the corners turn down and the lips pout. I press my back against the chair because every muscle in my body wants to reach out and kiss her. I try harder to listen.

"I don't think that's so unusual," I say. "I think a lot of husbands just give their wives the highlights. Not being a husband myself, I can't guarantee this, but I am a guy, and I do know that when you've been working all day, the last thing you want to do is come home and relive the whole damn day."

She smiles just a little. "Maybe you're right."

"Of course I'm right," I say, trying to be encouraging. I'm afraid if she gets sad enough to cry, I won't be able to stop myself from wrapping her up in my arms. "All we need to do is figure out his password. Most people use words that mean something to them. And like I said, it's probably written down somewhere."

"I've been wondering about that."

"About where it is?"

"About why you're not a husband."

Whoa. Incoming from left field.

"You know an awful lot about Michael and me, but I don't know very much about you. Is there someone special in the picture?"

Must not vault to conclusions. I'm sure she's just curious. Wouldn't anyone be? I'm curious about it myself. I *should* have someone special by this point in my life. Shouldn't I? I don't know many men who've gotten this far in the game without at least one serious relationship.

Even I am not shallow enough to label any of my funeral flings as serious relationships. I could tell her the truth. That would be a novel idea.

"No one special. I'm not a particularly good catch. Mediocre looking, boring job, no hobbies to speak of."

Okay, mostly the truth.

"I guess I've never run into anyone who could put up with me for any length of time."

"You've probably never given anyone a chance," Lily says, pushing herself off the desk and crossing to the window. She stares outside for a minute then turns back to me. "You're interesting and funny and certainly better than mediocre in the looks department. I could name a dozen girls right off the top of my head who would love to go out with you."

A cartoon balloon pops over my head and whizzes around the room, bouncing off the ceiling and walls. I can hear the escaping air whistling in my ears. As if. Like there was ever a chance in hell. She could name a dozen girls, huh? None of which would be her. Pathetic oaf.

"That's okay," I say. "What would I do with a dozen girls following me around? We'd never get any work done."

Lily leans back and delicately balances on the edge of the windowsill. Framed by the window with the darkness behind her, she looks like a painting. What would it be like to hold her?

"I could say something here about all work and no play," she says. "But I think there's more to you than a dull boy. I think you don't want anyone to know the real Albert."

Yikes! She's hit the nail on the head. Give the lady a Kewpie doll. People are usually more perceptive than they realize. If you go with your gut, ninety-five percent of the time it's right and the other five percent, it's hungry. We simply choose to ignore the message, especially if it's something we don't want to hear. I wonder what Lily would do if she knew interesting, funny, more-than-mediocre Albert Mackey doesn't even exist.

"Very true, Dr. Rudolph," I say in a very bad German accent. "Perhaps I should stretch out on the couch here and you could delve into my fear of spiders."

"Okay, you win," she says, laughing and crossing back over to the computer. "Enough soul searching for today. In fact, enough of everything for today. Let's call it good. Besides, I'm a little worried about you getting back before the storm hits. I'll look around for that password and we'll pick up tomorrow."

"Did Michael have a briefcase or anything that he carried on a regular basis?"

"About the only thing he always had handy was his flight bag. That way he could escape and go flying at a moment's notice."

"That would be a good place to start."

Her eyes cloud.

"We lost it in the crash."

"I'm sorry. I am so sorry. That was such a stupid thing to say."

"You couldn't have known."

"I could have thought for two seconds before speaking."

"It's okay, really."

I stand and grab my coat from the back of the chair. I want to throw it over my head and slink out of the room.

"I know if I just think about it, I can come up with some good places to look for the password," Lily says. I can tell she's trying to dissipate the tension. She's probably also trying to stop pictures of the crash from filling up her brain.

I reach out and put my hand on her shoulder. Gently. A friend comforting a friend.

"Get some sleep," I say. "I know I always think better in the morning."

She reaches up and squeezes my hand. Her skin is soft and warm. Her nails dig into my palm.

"Don't bother to walk me out; it's too nasty out there. I'll see you tomorrow."

She smiles.

"See you tomorrow."

EIGHT

As soon as I step outside, I can tell "nasty" was too mild a description for the weather. The wind blasts rain across my face. Lightning snaps in the distance. Lily's gardener comes up the driveway sheathed completely in rubber and clutching a small chain saw.

"You better get a move on," he shouts over the howling. "The wind's takin' down limbs everywhere. I just cleaned up the end of the driveway. You should be able to get out of here okay, but I heard on the radio earlier that a couple whole trees went down on Highway 39."

"Is there another way into town?" I shout back at the man.

The wind whips the hood from his head. He doesn't bother to pull it back up. He stands for a moment, thinking, the rain forming tributaries along the wrinkles in his cheeks. Ultimately the rivers merge and cascade off the end of his chin. He wipes a hand through the waterfall and points down the driveway.

"Go left out of here, like you're heading toward Franklin Grove. Just follow the signs. You'll eventually pick up 88 and that'll bring you back around to 39."

"Sounds good. Thanks."

Actually, I have no idea what the guy is talking about, but it's pouring out here. With no hat and a windbreaker that is not living up to its name, I'm already as soaked as he is. Vague generalities of direction seem sufficient. I run for my car, yank open the door, chuck my things onto the passenger's seat, then hurl myself into the driver's seat. It's warm and dry inside the steel cocoon. The larger gusts of wind are tough enough to rock the car back and forth. I start the engine and head for the gate. Piles of limbs line the driveway, little sawdust pyramids marking the chainsaw's targets. Sensors under the pavement warn the gate of my approach and it slides open to let me pass. I flip on my blinker to indicate a left turn. Force of habit. No other idiots are out here driving around. No one to notice which way I'm going.

The wipers are on high, frantically trying to hold back the rain. Movie rain.

About a year back, a Hollywood film crew came through Park Hills. It was one of Mayor Taylor's finest moments of civic pride. Not only had he convinced the crew our fair city was the perfect location to shoot a car chase across a bridge, he had also wrangled a part for himself as an extra. There was just one little problem. The Mayor had promised rain. Of course no one can guarantee the weather, but rain in November is a pretty safe bet in our neck of the woods. Except that year. That year, it didn't rain all month. A few threatening clouds, a couple foggy mornings, but not a drop of rain and certainly not a storm, which is what the film crew was really after. They spent several weeks tying up traffic, doing all the non-rain shots they could think of. It was all rigged and ready for the big chase scene. Finally, when they couldn't wait any longer for nature to comply, they plumbed the bridge. They ran huge pipes parallel with the roadway. These fed dozens of smaller vertical pipes each of which had a massive sprinkler head. Everything was painted the same color as the bridge so you couldn't even tell it was there. Then the trucks came, giant tanker trucks of water. They hooked them up, opened the valves, and there it was. Lights, camera, rain. Torrential rain. The perfect illusion.

I don't see any of the gardener's promised signs, but I can't really see much of anything beyond about a twenty-foot radius. There could be herds of wildebeests grazing along the road for all I know. I've passed exactly two cars since I left Lily's. Both going the opposite direction. Maybe that's the sign I'm looking for. *You're going the wrong way.* The rain is tapering off a bit, but the wind is taking up the slack. Suddenly, there it is, an encouraging beacon, a green and white sign of salvation. *Franklin Grove, 36 miles*. I am on the right track.

I press down on the accelerator and confidently plow through the storm. The road to Franklin Grove curves and dips, but I stay the course. In the distance, my headlights reflect off the red of a stop sign. Its lone companion, a flashing red light, signals a new decision to be made. I slow to a stop. My road T's into another road. Across the way, a new sign stands sentry, the flashing light illuminating its proclamation with pulsing regularity. *Turn to the right, Scarboro. Turn the left, Eldena*. No Franklin Grove. I conjure up a map of Illinois in my head and try to remember how all the little towns out here relate. That first sign for Franklin Grove wasn't more than four miles back. Why wouldn't it be listed here? Sometimes I think they deliberately hire the practical jokers to work for the Department of Transportation. There's someone in a nice, warm office somewhere in Springfield, typing up signage orders. "*Wouldn't it be funny,*" he thinks. *"If I put up one sign for Franklin Grove, and then never put up another the whole way there?"* What a riot.

I turn left, if for no other reason than the gardener's original instructions were to "go left." Maybe he meant to go left whenever given the opportunity. Sooner or later there has to be a sign. Ahead the road splits again, this one more of a knife in the road than the proverbial fork. Each side peels off at a clean 90° angle. I go left again. If I don't hit something familiar before too long, I'll eventually just make a giant circle.

There are no street lights out here. I click on the high beams. That helps a little; at least I can anticipate when the road's going to swoop off one way or another. Normally, I like driving at night, buzzing along in my own portable pool of light. There are fewer distractions. Unless something is lit up, it simply blends into the blackness. In the fairy tales you read as a kid, the night is always described as being "cloaked in darkness." That's such a great description, thick and heavy and dark. It can make you feel safe and warm or shadowy and ominous. I think guys should still be able to wear cloaks, like the princes who always rescued the pretty princesses in those same books. Unfortunately, the only people I know who wear cloaks now are middle-aged women with long gray hair and fairy earrings.

The few houses along the road are set back behind protective hedges and trees. Mail and newspaper boxes mark the entrances to graveled driveways. Out here is the realm of the landed gentry, the gentleman farmer, which is one of my favorite oxymorons. You are either a farmer or you are a gentleman. If you're a farmer, you get up at dawn to feed something, plant something or fix something. You know the working end of a two-bottom plow and what a come-a-long is for. If you're a gentleman, you own a five, ten, fifteen acre manicured estate, drive a shiny pickup without a dent in the lift gate, and employ one or more of the aforementioned farmers to handle the dirty work. I could swing in and ask for directions. But, I'm sure I'm almost there. Wherever there is.

The green numbers on my dashboard clock say 6:46. I left Lily's around 5:30. I'm going nowhere fast. The road crests a hill, the backside of which falls off into a long straightaway. I wonder why it is you feel less lost when a road is straight. Maybe curves make it seem like the road itself is trying to figure out which way to go. I let my foot off the accelerator and try to coast down the hill. In high school, a friend and I used to drive out into the country and find big hills like this one. We'd take the car out of gear and see how far we could coast before popping the clutch. It's not the same thrill in an automatic.

Okay. I'm lost. The rain has let up a little bit. The wind hasn't. The straightaway is behind me and I'm back on a serpentine course. I slow down and pull off the road. Maybe if I get out, get a little fresh air, clear my head, and start out again, I'll have a directional epiphany and emerge onto a highway. I turn off the engine, leave the headlights burning, and get out. Outside the car, the wind slices through my coat and cuts my core temperature to zero. I walk around the car and slide down next to the rear passenger door to escape the gusts. Here's a delightful circumstance. Lost, squatting along the side of the road, in a storm. It could be worse. I could be falling in love with a beautiful woman who thinks I'm a successful writer about to immortalize her beloved dead husband in an award-wining best seller.

Directly in front of me is a field. Actually, directly in front of me is a fence, beyond that is a field. It's too dark to tell what's growing in it. Grass or wheat maybe? In the morning, someone will probably drive out here and see what damage has been done by the storm. Maybe the crop will be ruined. They'll have to plow it under and start over. How do they know when to give it up? At what point does everything become so ludicrous you throw up your hands in defeat? Now seems like an opportune time. It doesn't get much more ridiculous than this.

But what if I could pull it off? Put aside for the moment the fact that I can't write worth a damn. Let's concentrate on sheer willpower. It's an interesting study in human nature. You craft an alternate personality for yourself, one that is more interesting and successful and likable than your true personality. People believe this manufactured reality is the true you. If it's working, why not just take on the new, improved personality and phase out the old? People change all the time in more subtle ways. You get rid of an annoying habit, you mature from a belligerent teen into a caring adult, you say nice things to the customers then spit in their soup. Why not on a grand scale? Every once in a while you'll hear about someone who got busted for posing as a physician. That takes guts. Pretending you know how to restore health is way more complex than pretending you know how to punctuate. But it worked; people believe what you feed them. The real question is: do *you* believe? Should you be true to yourself or to the best self you can create? Pretty existential stuff for a lonely guy in a tan coat huddled on the side of the road.

It's starting to rain again. But there's another sound too, distant yet unmistakable. It's the bottom octave hum of a diesel truck engine. I spring up and squint through the billowing curtains of rain. Headlights. A truck wouldn't just be cruising around clear out here. He's got to be on his way to a freeway, to civilization. I run around the

Taurus and jump back in. The headlights in my rear view mirror are close enough now to illuminate the entire car. I start up the engine and slam it into drive as the truck flies past. Jamming my foot down on the accelerator, the wheels spin, kick up mud and rock for an instant, then catch. I fishtail back onto the road and ride the truck's slipstream into town.

Even with the wind and rain hammering the car, I'm feeling pretty damn smug about the whole thing, cruising down the Interstate, just ten miles from Park Hills. Thank you very much, Mr. Freightliner. The radio is running down a list of closures, but none of them sound like they're near the condo. I should be there by 10:00, just a little four-hour detour.

The door to the condo isn't locked. On a day of non-stop stupidity, how appropriate I would have forgotten to lock the door. I step in and flip on the lights. Cabinets and drawers hang open everywhere, the sofa is turned over and the cushions are slashed, there's a blank spot in the entertainment center where the TV used to go, and the refrigerator door is wide open. The place is trashed. I've been robbed. What the fuck have I done to deserve this?

My first instinct is to call Lily. After all, most of this stuff is hers not mine. But it's late; it would only upset her. She can't do anything about it tonight. I slowly turn around, push the front door closed, click the deadbolt into place, and bang my head against the door until the little security peephole starts to drill into my forehead. I roll back around and survey the damage. The TV is obviously gone. I wonder what else they took. I walk room to room. Other than a dinky radio from the bathroom, there doesn't seem to be much missing. Why would you make such a mess to score a used TV and a Samsung clock radio? They must have thought the really good stuff was hidden. Joke's on you, bud.

There's a puddle of orange soda in the middle of the kitchen floor. Now, that's over the top, don't you think? Breaking in and taking my stuff isn't enough? You have to spill sticky soda pop on the floor? Of course, the shit in the toilet was also a nice touch. I can't clean all this up tonight. Maybe elves will come in during the wee hours of the morning and take care of it. I need some sleep.

The crash of shattering glass jolts me awake. For just an instant, before my eyes fly open, I see flames. But there's no heat in the room, only cold and wind and rain, and glass. The picture window facing the lake is gone and there's a tree limb the size of Indiana in the middle of the rug. Rain is blowing in. I reach for the lamp next to the bed. Nothing. It's either broken or, judging by my luck so far, the electricity's out. I jump out of bed. Bad idea. There's glass everywhere. Now there's glass in my feet. I hop the rest of the way across the room, trying to avoid glass I can't see. Really bad idea. I hit the light switch by the door. Nothing. I think I'm bleeding. I drop to my butt in the hallway and gingerly examine the soles of my feet. Extremely bad idea. It's too dark to try to pick out the glass and now I'm stuck down here. How are you supposed to stand up without touching the bottoms of your feet? I try to push myself up by balancing on the sides of my feet. This must be some type of advanced yoga move, because it's not working for me. I roll over onto my knees, and holding my feet up, crawl down the hall into the dining room. Crawling hurts like hell. How do babies do it? It must be the undeveloped joints. They can't possibly feel the same pain currently stinging across both my knee caps or else they'd be up and motoring on those chubby little feet by six months.

I know there's a decorative candle in the middle of the dining room table and matches on the fireplace hearth. If I can just bring these two things together, I can cast a romantic glow onto my bloody feet.

I'm sitting on the hearth digging out glass shards by candlelight when the electricity comes back on, signaled by a sudden whirring of the refrigerator and the reappearance of the security light over the front porch. I lean over and snap on the table lamp. One of the few things the burglars left upright in the living room. My feet look much worse in the harsh glare of an incandescent bulb. Now I know why fancy restaurants use candles. Everything looks better in low light with an elegant drop shadow. A cheap chuck steak resembles filet mignon and your date looks a lot more like Drew Barrymore. That's good for business. Bring out the dessert tray.

Satisfied most of the glass is out, I try standing. It hurts. Oh yeah. It hurts. I roll onto the outside of my feet and hobble into the kitchen like a wounded orangutan. There's a drawer full of kitchen towels I use as bandages to stop the bleeding and cushion my steps. However, now I look less orangutan, more Dickensian street urchin. I should see what the bedroom really holds. Grabbing a broom from the pantry closet, I make my way back down the hallway.

The lights are already on. It's not as bad as I thought. It's worse. The room is soaked. Glass is everywhere. It's amazing one window could disintegrate into so many pieces. I sweep clean a small circle and step inside to get a better view. It doesn't look any better. If I pull down the shower curtain, it might be big enough to stretch across the window. Ample duct tape and I should be able to keep out most of the rain until morning. I won't be sleeping in here tonight, but there's probably not much sleeping time left anyway. The bedside alarm clock is blinking the default 12:00. Beyond the hole that was once my window, the sky is lightening; it's probably about four or five. I continue to sweep a glass-free path across the rug in order to get a closer look at the tree limb. In the proper lighting, I see it's not really the size of Indiana, but it's still big. It's as thick around as my thigh and about six or seven feet long. Nature's javelin.

Outside, the pine trees surrounding the apartment bend and buck in the storm's leftover gusts. I look at my tree limb again. It's not a pine tree limb. I bend down closer to be sure. No way. No needles, no pitch. The bark is mottled gray and covered with lichen. This branch is from an oak tree or something, but there's nothing around here but pines and cedars. The closest I've seen any other kind of tree is at least twenty blocks away in the new Doheny subdivision.

What's a branch from an oak tree doing in the middle of my bedroom?

NINE

I'm wearing my bedroom slippers at work. They are black corduroy with a small band of faux leopard trim across the instep. They were a gift. Since I'm at my desk most of the day, I figure no one will notice. I bandaged my feet with gauze and tape this morning instead of the kitchen towels. The towels were actually more comfortable, but they didn't fit inside the slippers.

When I finally phoned Lily, she was horrified to hear about everything. She said she'd arrange for a property maintenance crew, but warned me there was a lot of damage from the storm, some of it actually worse than mine. Her rental managers had already called to fill her in on other problems around town, including a desperate woman who had a tree from the other side of the street fall across the road like a guillotine, taking out two cars and her entire front porch. There were branches through the ceiling of her living room. I guess I can wait.

I told Lily about my ingenious shower curtain patch job. I'd also cleaned up the basic mess and righted all the furniture. It's amazing how much you can get done when you get up before the break of day. I didn't tell her my suspicions about the foreign branch. I wanted to walk around first and see if I could spot a tree that looked like was missing a branch like mine.

Even with all the chaos in my life, I'm not late to work. In fact, I am early, which means I can pad through the halls to my assigned cubicle without anyone noticing my slippers or my unusual gait. But now, I really have to go to the bathroom. Truth be told, I've had to go for about forty-five minutes. I'm desperate now. I lean as far back in my chair as I can and peek around the corner of my dividing wall. Coast is clear. I get up and head down the hall, trying to maintain a brisk yet nonchalant pace, which is not easy when you are limping like Quasimodo.

I wave to Helen at reception. She waves back. Just a few more feet. Here's the door, and...

"Charlie!"

It's Dennis, coming out of the bathroom. This must be my lucky day.

"Hey, Dennis. What's up?"

"Just what I was coming back to ask you. How's it going with our Mr. Klein?"

"Not bad."

Dennis is looking at my slippers. He seems puzzled. Maybe he's jealous because the black oxfords he's wearing can't possibly be as comfortable.

"Are you wearing slippers, Charlie?"

"Yes I am, Dennis."

"You don't always wear slippers to work, do you?"

Now that sounds a little condescending. Give me a break. Like he's some kind of freakin' fashion icon? I don't comment when he wears those stupid seersucker blazers in the summer.

"No I don't. I had a little accident last night during the storm. Lost a window to a tree branch and I'm afraid I cut up the bottoms of my feet pretty bad on all the glass."

"Uh huh," says Dennis, half listening.

I can tell when Dennis is only paying attention to every third word I'm saying. His watery brown eyes flick from me to a vanishing point beyond my left ear. As if he's looking for something, anything more interesting than me. I don't think he does it on purpose. He has a short attention span for anything that doesn't directly concern him. Some might call it self-centered, but I think he's just dull-witted.

"I'll bet it's a bitch trying to get anyone out to fix it today. Problems all over town. The guys down in homeowner's are goin' nuts trying to keep up with the phones this morning. Luckily, Brenda and I didn't have any trouble. Knock on wood."

He leans over and raps on the faux wood grain laminate of the bathroom door.

"Actually, Dennis, I will probably have to take off a little early this afternoon to meet the window guys at my apartment."

"So, maybe we could talk about the Klein case now."

"No problema," I say, smiling and giving him a thumbs-up. "If I could just run into the bathroom first? I'll meet you back at my desk."

"Oh right. You were just coming in weren't you? Meet ya back there."

Dennis returns my thumbs-up signal, but as with anything "hip" that Dennis tries to do, he comes off looking awkward. He thrusts his whole arm out and cocks his thumb too far to the right, like he's hitchhiking.

I have a mental picture of Dennis after hours in his suit and tie, thinning hair combed forward, stomach sucked in, trying to pick up girls at a dance club. He's married, but that only reinforces my fantasy. His wife, Brenda has come by for lunch a few times. She's a big, blond ex-cheerleader packing about seventy extra pounds, a spray-on tan and upper arms like a pair of pork roasts. I think she'd come after Dennis with a hammer if he even looked at another woman. My imaginary filmstrip usually ticks out before I see his brains splatter.

I pull open the door to the men's room and escape inside. I have maybe ten minutes before Dennis gets suspicious and sends someone in to find me. That's not nearly enough time to concoct a believable story about the non-existent research I've done on Hugh Klein. Relieving myself into the urinal, I ponder a few clumsy excuses. *I'm waiting for details from past cases to be shipped from other insurance companies. I'm having trouble getting depositions from the witnesses at the doughnut shop. The dog ate my research.* I watch the flush swirl my pee down and out into the sewer.

Dennis is playing with a Chicago Cubs' commemorative paperweight when I come back into the cubicle. In my slippers, I'm quite stealthy and he flinches a little when I suddenly appear around the corner.

"I'm back," I say, trying to sound like Arnold Schwarzenegger. Dennis doesn't get the joke. He sets down the paperweight.

"Charlie, I'm a little worried about you. I haven't seen any reports on the Klein case for a couple of weeks now. Is he giving you some trouble? Because if he is, we need to figure out what to do. I *know* you understand how important it is that we kill this claim. It's huge. Corporate's making noises about jobs riding on the outcome. I love ya like a brother, Tiger, but if *my* job's on the line, *your* job's on the line."

"Not to worry, Dennis. I'm not really having trouble, it's more like choreography."

"I'm not following you."

"Or wrestling. Maybe it's more like wrestling."

Dennis perks up when we change from dance to sports, but he still looks confused.

"You know how wrestlers circle in the ring? They're checking each other out, getting a read, trying to psych out the other guy. That's kind of how it is with me and the illustrious Mr. Klein. We're circling."

"Circling?"

I trace an imaginary orbit in the air with my index finger. Dennis sways back and forth on his feet, following my finger's path with his whole body. I'm tempted to suddenly switch to vertical undulations, but I think he'd tip over.

"He knows we don't buy his story, but he's a professional. He's moving very carefully, trying to figure out exactly how we're going to go after him. So, I'm keeping a real low profile. Watching his every move. Pretty soon, I know he's going to screw up. One wrong move, and I'll get him in a headlock."

I pantomime a strangle hold and pull my face into a grimace. Dennis stops swaying, picks up my paperweight again and tosses it from hand to hand.

"What you got so far?"

"He eats lunch every day at Nobel's Deli on 12th Street. I got the owner there keeping track of what he orders so we can follow the whole diabetic angle.'

"And?"

Dennis attempts a fancy, arcing toss of the paperweight, misses the catch and it thuds to the floor, dangerously close to my wounded feet. Reaching for it, he whacks his head on the corner of my desk.

"Geeze, are you okay?"

He straightens up, sets the paperweight back on my desk and rubs his head, which makes his hair stand up like a hamster's.

"And?" he repeats, ignoring my sympathy.

"And, he has a girlfriend."

"A girlfriend? Now, *this* could be interesting. Have you talked to her?"

"Circling, Dennis. Circling."

Talked to her? I just made her up this minute.

"I know who she is and where she works. If I spring too early, it will tip him off."

Dennis purses his lips and pushes his glasses up his nose.

"It *sounds* good, Charlie, and you know I have all the confidence in the world in you, but I gotta get something for Corporate. Fill out a 20-23 report, would ya? Give me something to send 'em."

"You got it, Big Guy." Dennis loves it when you call him Big Guy. Almost as much as I hate it when he calls me Tiger. "How about tomorrow AM?"

"How about today?"

I point at my slippers and shrug.

"I have to split to take care of the home front, remember? Tomorrow. I absolutely, positively promise you a 20-23 by tomorrow."

He reaches up and smoothes his hamster hair.

"I'm going to email corporate and tell them that."

"Go right ahead. You'll have it. I guarantee you."

Dennis leans forward and punches me in the shoulder. "I knew I could count on you, Tiger."

He disappears around the divider and down the hall. I can hear him calling out to my compadres as he goes. *Slim, BJ, Shack, Buddy,* everybody's got a nickname. I suspect most of the time he simply doesn't remember anyone's real name.

I slip on my coat. No use sitting back down. It's almost noon. I'll stay up late tonight and manufacture a few facts about Hugh Klein's imaginary girlfriend for the 20-23. It's really nothing more than a status memo. I could probably copy the stats on some starlet from a gossip column in *People* magazine and no one would be the wiser.

I wave to Helen as I pass her desk on the way to the elevator. I think she's worked on this floor since before I was born. I like her. She's old school working-girl. Always wears a dress, high heels and hose. Hair always up in a hairspray helmet. Nails always bright poppy red.

"You outta here?"

"Got an appointment, Helen. I'll be back first thing tomorrow."

"Okay. By the way, I forgot to compliment you on your footwear earlier. Looks mighty comfortable."

"You know it. Tomorrow, I'm wearing the robe."

Helen lets out an enormous laugh then makes a little snorting sound as she gasps for air on the intake.

"You're a stitch, Charlie. A stitch and a half."

The elevator opens and I step in. Helen's still laughing as the doors slide shut and I begin my descent. On the way down, I push the annoying Dennis dilemma from my mind in favor of another looming responsibility. There was a message on my answering machine this morning from Howard Stanich. I heard the ringing when I was in the shower, but in my crippled condition I knew I'd never make it to the phone in time. So, I let the machine pick up. The burglars left the answering machine. *They* probably had cell phones.

His message said he was following up on the first message he'd left about the summary report. Since I'd never returned the first message, and then there was a pause in which I imagined the annoyance on his face, he was checking back to make sure everything was okay. He wondered if there was a time that would be good for us to get together.

As much as I dislike Howard, I think he finds me twice as objectionable. But we still need each other. Kind of like the United States and China. We just need a summit meeting to lay down a few ground rules. If we can agree, in principle, not to blow each other up, everyone will be happy and we can continue to pretend to be civil and sell each other computer games and cars and flimsy T-shirts.

There are no repair vans outside the apartment yet and it's very cold inside. Lily asked me to turn off the heat until the window got fixed. The call light is blinking on the phone.

"Albert, it's Lily. The guys won't be there until around 2:00. Everything's taking longer than it should today. Sorry to make you wait. Let's not even try to get together until tomorrow or the next day. Okay with you? Call me."

I erase Lily's message and pick up the phone to call China. Or maybe I'm China.

"Nesler Pharmaceuticals," says a lilting voice I'm sure is front-desk Janet. Her voice is super cheery, as if answering phones for Nesler was just this side of euphoric.

"Howard Stanich," I say. "It's Albert Mackey returning his call."

"Certainly, Mr. Mackey. I'll connect you right away."

"Thank you, Janet."

I like to use people's names when I'm talking to them. Someone I interviewed once told me he found it incredibly annoying. That's what I like about it. It keeps folks off balance. A person instinctively responds to the sound of his own name. So, pepper a conversation with someone's name and he thinks, "hey, that's my name, that's me, that's me again." This constant disruption makes it harder to follow a train of thought, which makes it harder to lie, if you are trying to lie.

"You're . . . uh . . .you're welcome," Janet stutters.

The phone clicks and I hear the plaintive wail of Kenny G's saxophone for a few seconds.

"Albert, thank you for returning my call," Howard says on the other end of the phone. "I was beginning to worry something was wrong."

"Nothing wrong, just been busy. You know how that is, don't you?"

No answer. He's probably outraged to think anything about us could be similar.

"I was thinking," he says, finally. "Perhaps we should get together and discuss some of the more technical aspects of Michael's research. Just you and I. No need to bother Lily with the dry details."

I remember how distraught Lily was at being kept out of the loop by Michael. Howard was doing exactly the same thing, shielding her from something she was really dying to find out more about. Still, I think a meeting between just Howard and me is a good idea.

"Actually, I could come over right now if that fits into your schedule. I was supposed to meet some repair people here at the condo, but they've been delayed. Are you free?"

"Right now?"

"I know it's last minute, but I just found out myself."

"Let me juggle a couple things around and make a few calls." Howard is sputtering a bit. I can hear pages flipping. "Can you give me a half an hour?"

"Perfect. See you then."

Driving across town, there's an odd break in the clouds and bright blue patches of sky. People are out on the sidewalks, hurrying, probably figuring it will start storming again at any moment. At a light, I watch a young woman, tethered to an Irish setter, jog past in a blue warm-up suit. The sidewalk's cracked and she dodges the uneven surface; the setter matches her pace. I like animals. I don't have any. My nomadic lifestyle doesn't really lend itself to pets. One of my foster families let me get a puppy once when I was about thirteen. I think they felt sorry for me. Orphan guilt was always good for a few presents. This pup was just a humane society mutt: part lab, part collie, part whatever. I named her Billie because she was mostly white with a stubby little tail like a goat. She was a barker. The neighbors called a lot to complain, which made my foster mom get all flushed in the cheeks and slam down the phone. We tried everything to get Billie to stop. Even one of those collars that send out a shock every time the dog barks. Except Billie figured out just how loud she could bark without setting off the shock. She wasn't stupid, just annoying. I came home from school one day and Billie was gone. My foster mom said they took her out to live with some friends in the country. They gave me a turtle in a shoebox. Two months later, I went to live with another family. I wasn't stupid, just annoying. It's interesting how easily some people let go and others hang on for dear life. Take it from someone who's tried to hang on and had the rope cut. It's better to let go. Hanging on only gets you heartache ... and a nasty road rash.

I pull up in front of Nesler Pharmaceuticals and check my watch. It's been just twenty minutes since I hung up from Howard, but I like being early. It shows respect. Being late is inconsiderate and self-centered. It says you believe your time is more important than anyone else's. Being on time is considerate and shows you to be organized and efficient. Being early encompasses all the benefits of being on time and adds the extra bonus of showing the person you're coming to see that he is important enough for you to be willing to wait. Appearance is everything. I wonder what Howard will think of my slippers.

Janet looks up and smiles as I walk in. Her braids are tied together today in a loose ponytail.

"Hello, Mr. Mackey. Here for Mr. Stanich?"

"Yes, Janet. I'm a little early."

"Let me ring him for you. Coffee?"

"No thanks, I'm fine."

I take a seat. The phones ring incessantly and I watch Janet calmly punch buttons to route messages. She's wearing a headset so tiny it makes it look like she's talking to herself, like those damn cell phone headsets. I don't know how many people I've crossed the street to avoid only to realize they weren't paranoid schizophrenics, they were just chatting on their phones.

"Mr. Mackey, Mr. Stanich will be right out. Are you sure I can't get you anything?"

"Really, I'm fine. You *can* tell me how you manage to handle all those calls by yourself. Looks like air traffic control if you ask me."

"You get used to it." She laughs. The phones begin to ring again and again she juggles the barrage without breaking a sweat. "It's not as hard as it looks," she says, looking at me after the ringing stops.

"I certainly couldn't do it."

"Sure you could."

The door behind Janet opens and Howard emerges. Janet stops smiling and directs her eyes to her desk. She seems to be waiting for one or possibly both shoes to drop.

"Albert," Howard says, striding toward me.

He's wearing a deep blue suit, but is without his usual shirt and tie. Instead he has on a cream colored sweater. Very lightweight. Looks like silk. I'm sure it is.

"I'm certainly impressed by your flexibility, Howard," I say, standing to shake his hand. "I don't think there are many CEOs who could wedge in a last-minute appointment like this."

"I'm happy to do it. You actually gave me an excuse to cancel a lunch appointment I'd been dreading with one of our investors."

"Glad to be of service."

Howard notices my slippers. I jump in to defend myself.

"Ah, the slippers. Sorry about that. I had some storm damage last night. Broke a big window and managed to cut up my feet pretty good in the dark. Regular shoes were not an option today."

Howard looks concerned, and I can't help thinking he's probably less worried about my feet or my window then about the fact I've gone out in public wearing bedroom slippers.

"Well, then, let's go sit down, shall we?"

I follow Howard back towards the door.

"Did Janet offer you coffee?"

Ah ha. There's shoe number one. Janet's shoulders tense as we walk by but she doesn't look up. The phones start ringing again. I'm not about to let the other shoe drop.

"Yes she did. Twice, in fact. I turned her down flat both times, but it was very nice of her to offer, especially with the phones ringing continuously like they do."

Howard doesn't answer, but I notice the sliver of a smile on Janet's face. Howard and I continue through the door and down the corridor to his office in silence. He is several steps ahead of me the entire way.

Howard's office is as immaculate as before. I take a seat and remove a small notebook from my briefcase. With his back is to me, he thumbs through files in a drawer in his rear credenza and I notice a bald spot is forming at the top of his head. He spins back around in his chair to face me, holding several file folders.

"As I'm sure you know, Albert, there's a lot riding on the release of this new drug. You've been around the industry long enough to know how things work. We've already fielded preliminary calls from some of the big guns. If things continue going well, we're in line for a billion dollar buy-out."

Billion with a B. I try to keep my eyes from popping out of my head.

"I'll be blunt," Howard continues, holding the file folder in both hands as if ready to rip it in two. "The investors are nervous. All the press surrounding Michael's death is getting to them. They're starting to question everything, but I think your book has the potential to settle things down."

He releases his grip and sets the folder on the desk, stretching both palms across its cover. Maybe it will levitate. Howard's hands are freckled with age spots and he doesn't wear a wedding ring.

"It will get people focusing on Michael's dream again instead of agonizing about cost overruns on the lab construction. How far away are you from the final draft?"

He stares at me. His eyes are so close together I'm surprised they don't cross. How far away am I from *finishing*? What a crack up. He thinks I've started.

"I'm not ready to set up a book signing schedule, but Lily and I have made great headway. I'd say by summer, we . . . "

"Summer!" Howard spits out the word like a piece of gristle. "We can't wait until summer. There's too much on the line."

He's breathing very quickly. If he hyperventilates I won't know what to do. But as my own panic rises, Howard seems to pull himself back together.

"There are too many lives on the line is what I mean," he says. He closes his eyes and draws in a deep breath. "I apologize for that outburst. It was completely unnecessary and, I'm sure, wholly undignified. It's just that the situation I am in requires immediate attention."

A thin line of sweat glistens on Howard's upper lip. Lip sweat is tertiary level nervousness. Primary is armpit sweat, secondary is back sweat; if you get to lip sweat, you're just one misstep away from the full faucet-down-the-side-of-your-face sweat.

"Are you in danger of losing your funding?" I ask.

"I won't lie to you. I've had at least one investor threaten to pull out. I was hoping to hear your book was closer to completion. Of course I understand you have a complicated task under normal situations let alone working in the shadow of Michael's death."

I am fascinated by Howard's transformation from poodle to pit bull and back again. I'm beginning to think he's more of a chameleon than I. A clock ticks loudly from somewhere behind me.

"Tell you what, Howard, I'll pretend that outburst never happened if you agree to give me some real information about those original test participants. What do you say?"

Howard is shocked. I can tell because one eyebrow is slightly raised. He moves his hands back to the file folder on his desk.

Tick tock.

"I take it you were dissatisfied by the information I provided you in the summary report."

Tick tock.

Howard sits back in his chair. He has something for me in that folder, but he's not giving it up without a good reason. He's a shrewd man. More than that, I'm starting to believe he has a real sentimental streak when it comes to

Michael, protective even. He's old enough to have been Michael's father. Maybe there's more to the relationship than I understand.

"We're being blunt here, right Howard? Time is of the essence? Then I need something more than I could have gotten off your web site. I need real information. You said you wanted to get together today without Lily so we could go over the 'technical details.' I *have* the standard research. In order to move forward, I need to know the background, the details, the dirt."

Howard lurches forward, hands on his thighs. His eyes drill into mine.

"There is no dirt," he says, giving the "t" so much emphasis it sounds like an extra syllable.

I push it, wanting to see how far Howard will stretch before he breaks.

"There is *always* dirt."

"Not here!"

Crack. The room is silent except for the ticking clock and Howard lowers his voice.

"Not on Michael's project," he says and then he's quiet.

I lean forward and place my notebook on Howard's desk. I take a pen from my pocket and begin scribbling notes. Howard reaches forward and slides a heavy crystal pyramid out of my way. We both understand the first game is over, I've run the table and the balls have been re-racked.

"Michael came in after your early phase three testing, right?"

"Right."

"And, it was those early results that captured his interest, right?"

"Right."

"Did Michael interview the original participants?'

"A few. Not all."

"Why not all?"

Howard pulls on his ear lobe. That's called a "comfort gesture." Tugging on your ear, rubbing your nose, grabbing and holding one finger—these are all childlike gestures, things we might have done when we were young to calm ourselves in a stressful situation.

"I assume he felt it was unnecessary," Howard continues. "As you're aware, anonymity of participants is strictly enforced, however Michael was coming in as a surgeon and researcher himself, not merely an investor. We were prepared to set up interviews with everyone."

Howard twists the crystal pyramid until its base is square against his stack of file folders. As he does, the light hits it from a new angle and I catch the image of a plane etched into the surface. I stop taking notes.

"Do you fly Howard?"

"What?"

"Are you a pilot? That looks like it might be some kind of flying award."

"No, just decorative, a gift, but yes, I do fly. I've been a pilot for about ten years. It was something Michael and I shared."

"Really? Do you go up often?

"Not as often as I should. Free time is never in abundance for me, especially these days."

Howard shifts the pyramid approximately one quarter inch to the right. He must have some super-hero kind of power to see at perfect right angles. *Grid Man, able to align corners in a single bound.*

"Let's get back to our original group," I say. "Can you give me some more details about the pianist? His results seem amazing."

Howard finally opens the file in front of him, scanning through pages that look very much like the pages of a patient's medical chart. All the notations are handwritten, and even though I am very good at reading upside down, I can't decipher anything. Classic doctor illegibility. Howard shuts the folder and moves it off to the side. My pen is poised over my notebook.

"His daughter came to us," Howard begins. "She'd heard about the testing from a friend of a friend of a friend. Often times, even I don't know how all the participants come to join us. That's really Gavin's area."

So Gavin is the number one scavenger. That's very interesting. I picture a seagull with Gavin's face swooping down out of the sky, plucking old people out of their walkers.

"As I recall, this particular patient was quite advanced in his symptoms. In fact, I remember being a bit reluctant to take him. I feel our greatest potential for success lies with early intervention. But, contrary to what you may think, Mr. Mackey, I do have a heart."

Howard pauses for a moment, leans back in his chair and smiles at me. His smile is reptilian, satisfied, as if he's just swallowed something much larger than his head.

"The daughter told us her father had been a concert pianist. Not a famous solo artist but a well respected orchestral member and a teacher. I don't really follow the classical music scene. Do you?"

I think about Mia for a second but shake my head, no.

"He was very small. Barely five foot three and maybe 110 pounds soaking wet. But his hands were big. They were made for the piano. His fingers were long and thin and there was no swelling in his joints. I know that's an odd thing to remember about a patient, but of course I knew he'd been a pianist and so I took note of his hands, but more than that, every time I saw him his hands were moving. Clasping and unclasping, rubbing, clenching, twining. It was almost as if he thought he could squeeze the memory back into them."

Howard demonstrates with his own hands.

"So when you met him," I ask. "How long had it been since he'd stopped playing?"

"According to his daughter he had been able to continue to play even as other memories deteriorated, but that's normal. Alzheimer's is regressive, so our earliest learned behaviors are often the last to go."

I'm scribbling notes as Howard tells the story. I'm also thinking how horrible it would be to slip backwards like that—to unspool.

I realize Howard is still talking.

"This present to past regression is why sometimes you'll have a patient who doesn't appear to notice relatives and friends around him and can't carry on a conversation, but when the crowd gathers to leave, he'll thank them for coming. We learn the basic routines of politeness as very young children and they pop back up automatically. Our pianist had been playing since he was three or four years old. When he and his daughter came in for the interview, the majority of his symptoms were quite pronounced, but his daughter said he'd lost the ability to play only six months earlier."

"Where is he now," I ask. "I'd like to interview him and his daughter."

"I'm sorry, that's impossible."

Howard crosses his arms.

"Impossible?"

I scratch the word onto my note pad and underline it. I stop writing but don't lift my pen from the pad. Instead I lift my eyes and stare at Howard.

"Why?"

Howard shifts in his chair and smoothes an invisible wrinkle on his slacks.

"Anonymity is a requirement of the testing. It's a legal contract we have with all the participants. I could jeopardize the entire project if I were to go against it."

"Don't these people love to talk about their recoveries? At the funeral there were a lot of people who spoke about how Michael had helped them. And, of course, there were all those TV interviews Michael did."

Howard reaches up with one hand and rubs his neck. This is the choking gesture. It means there's something he'd like to say but he's keeping it in.

"I could be mistaken," he says. "But I don't recall that any of the people who spoke at Michael's funeral were our test participants. They were most likely people from his own practice or research."

"What if we had just one or two of the patients sign a release saying they waive their anonymity for this one interview? Your choice, perhaps the folks who traveled the talk show circuit with Michael and are used to the media."

I think this is a reasonable request and an innovative solution to our impasse. I'm not demanding the whole enchilada, just a small bite. He's got to give me something and he knows it.

Howard brings his hands together as if in prayer and taps them lightly against his lips. His eyes are closed. I think he's just considering my question, but if he is really praying, I hope I don't get struck by lightning.

"That's not entirely out of the question, Albert."

"Really?"

Damn. That slipped out. It's not good to sound surprised when your strategy works. I look at Howard to see if he noticed. He's still praying.

"What I mean, Howard, is anything you could arrange would be extremely helpful. I want to be able to bring the research up to the present. You know, a 'where are they now' kind of thing. Readers always want to know how the story ends."

"An interview is one thing. I don't think these people will want their lives laid open for everyone to see in a book."

"Even if they knew it could help someone else?"

"I'll look into it. That's all I can promise. There are a couple of participants who might be more willing than the others. But it will take me several days at least to see what I can come up with."

Howard stops speaking abruptly and I've been in enough conversations with him to understand this means he is done with the subject at hand. There will be no further discussion. After backing him into a corner over the test participants, I'm reluctant to push further, but I have to. I need more details than Howard is willing to divulge.

"In the meantime, if I can't talk to the participants, how about the investors?"

I think Howard has stopped breathing. His expression is frozen, his lips forming a rigid horizontal line across the bottom of his face. You'd have to slice them apart with a knife in order to allow him to speak. But that turns out not to be necessary because he suddenly forces the line into a sly smile.

"I was going to say no, but I just got a delightful idea. I would love for you talk with one of our investors. I think it might be good for everybody."

"I'm glad you agree."

Howard is positively grinning now.

"Roger Jones. You need to talk with Roger Jones. He's one of our biggest investors. Right now, he is also one of the biggest pains in the ass I have to deal with."

This is a decidedly un-Howard-like statement. Along with that goofy grin, it makes a bizarre package. It's creepin' me out.

"What's the problem with Mr. Jones?"

"He thinks we're too far off schedule. He's ready to pull out his money unless we find a way to get things back on track. He's worried Michael's accident was the death knell for the entire project. I get at least three calls a day from him, none of them pleasant."

"I'll hazard a guess he was the lunch date you cancelled for our meeting."

Howard nods.

"Jones has been in on lab construction from the very beginning," Howard continues. "He can give you his perspective on the entire project. It will give him a way to vent his frustrations, he'll stop calling me, and you'll get more information than you ever wanted. He's a talker."

Howard slides open the top drawer of his desk and removes a small pad and pen. He scribbles something and hands it to me.

"That's his direct line, rings right at his desk. He is always there. The man has no life outside of work."

"What exactly does he do?"

"Commercial real estate. Big deals. Office towers, corporate parks. He owns this development we're in."

I look at the piece of paper. It's a local number.

"He's here in town?"

"Lived here all his life. Call him. You'll like him."

"You haven't made him sound particularly likable."

"When he's not shouting and complaining, he's actually quite personable. I used to like him a lot. I'm sure once we get over this little disagreement, I'll like him again."

There is the sound of a soft chime. Must be that clock I heard earlier. Howard looks up over my head then back at me.

"I hate to cut this short, but I wasn't able to completely clear my schedule this afternoon. I'm afraid I have another meeting. Shall we schedule a new time to get together?"

I shake my head.

"Let me call Jones first. And you can follow up with the test participants. We should both have enough to keep us busy for a little while before we need to meet again."

Howard gets up and walks around to the front of his desk. He sits on the corner and crosses his arms over his silk sweater.

"You don't like me much, do you Albert?"

This catches me completely off guard. Does Howard actually care what I think about him? I pause in the middle of gathering my pen and notepad and look up. I cannot stop my face from registering surprise. It's true, I don't like

Howard much, but I didn't think it showed. I'm not used to people discovering how I really feel. I must be slipping.

"I think we got off on the wrong foot," he continues. "And I think it was probably my fault. I know I come across as a bit straight-laced. But I prefer order and predictability. Everything surrounding Michael's death has been chaotic. I'm simply not cut out to deal well with the chaos. I'm afraid it's put me on edge."

He extends one hand to me.

"I'd like to start fresh."

I drop my pad back down on the desk and accept his peace offering.

"Okay," I say. "But if we're going to bare our souls here, then I should probably fess up to being too harsh. Hazard of the trade. Sometimes I'm too cynical for my own good."

"We have a lot to gain from one another, Albert. I'd rather have you as a friend than an enemy."

Howard and I are more alike than either one of us would ever admit. He's about a hundred times smarter than me, but we both have an image to keep up. We both care about Lily and respect Michael. We are both trying very hard to make the best of a bad situation. Just because his is real and mine is imaginary doesn't make it any easier. I am not ready to go for beers with the guy, but he does seem to be sincerely apologetic about his behavior. He also has a lot of information that would be very helpful if I'm ever able to move this ridiculous project forward. He'd probably be more willing to divulge some of it if he thought of me as an ally.

"You can never have too many friends, Howard."

TEN

I am standing outside a convenience store, listening to Lily's phone ring in my ear. The break in the clouds is long gone and it's drizzling again. Voice mail picks up and I leave a short message asking her to call me. From inside the store I hear the minor chords of Indian or Persian music. There's a guy with a stringy ponytail at the counter buying a case of Pabst. He looks a little drunk already. I open the door and the volume of the music jumps. The clerk looks over at me and smiles.

"Hello and how are you today?" he says.

I nod and head back to the coolers. It's closing in on three o'clock and I haven't had any lunch. One door of the refrigerated section is devoted to an assortment of prepared foods. Microwave burritos, plastic-wrapped sandwiches, bagels and cream cheese. There's also a selection of frozen dinners that look equally unappetizing. Even fast food would be better than this, but I'm here and the food's there. I grab a couple of burritos and head for the check out.

"Hello and how are you today?" the clerk asks again.

"Good. And yourself?"

"I have been particularly well, thank you."

I wonder if this guy knows he's fulfilling my stereotype of a convenience store owner. Dark and wavy hair, a mustache, the skin around his deep-set eyes darker than the rest of his face, like two shades of melted chocolate. Warning buzzer: we're not supposed to notice skin color; everyone's the same. Bullshit. If your skin were beautifully smooth and brown wouldn't being compared to chocolate be better than being compared to gravy or mud or ... bullshit? One of the things I like about my hobby is walking a mile in someone else's loafers. We're different. We look different, we act different, some of us like mayonnaise, some of us don't. I wouldn't mind someone describing my skin as melted chocolate instead of how they usually describe it: chicken flesh, marshmallow cream, the underbelly of a trout.

The scanner beeps as it records my lunch. A group of three teenage boys clomps into the store and the clerk watches them walk into the candy aisle. Two are tall and gangly; the third is short and thick. They're all wearing matching rock band t-shirts and indolent expressions.

"You're pretty close to that big lab project, aren't you?" I ask. "You get a lot of the construction workers in here?"

"Why yes we do. Very good for business."

He smiles and drops the burritos into a paper bag, still watching the teenagers who have moved into the next aisle to read magazines.

"Young boys," the clerk calls out to the teens. "I cannot sell the magazines if they are wrinkled and covered with your greasy fingerprints. Only touch what you are planning to buy."

The kids look over at the clerk then laugh to each other, but they put the magazines back and return to the candy.

"That will be $3.19 with tax. Anything else?"

I fish a five dollar bill out of my pocket.

"Did they stop working after that guy died? You know, the doctor guy?"

He rings up my sale and counts out change.

"Oh no. They never stop working. I believe they must finish no matter what. Such a shame about the doctor. I heard he was important."

I take my paper bag off the counter and pocket the change.

"I think he was."

A pretty young woman walks in and heads for the dairy case. With a blond ponytail, tiny pink shorts and matching pink sneakers, she looks like a life-size Barbie. The boys watch her. I watch her. The clerk watches the boys.

"Always the good people die," the clerk says. "Never the bad people."

He smiles at me again.

"You know what they say," I reply. "Only the good die young."

"Billy Joel, right?"

"Yeah, Billy Joel."

"Have a nice day, sir"

I turn to head back to the car with my burritos. The Barbie girl is at the counter now with a carton of yogurt and a water. Behind her are the three boys, each holding a liter of pop and a bag of chips. I have to get out of Stereotype-Mart before a cop comes in for a doughnut.

Sitting in my car, I wonder if Billy Joel really *was* right. If so, what does that make me? I was the one who didn't die. The survivor. The one who lived to tell the tale. Like that's some sort of prize, except it's more like being condemned to stay behind and relive the story. Maybe bad people are stronger, more disease resistant, better able to suffer the slings and arrows of everyday existence. But I don't think so. I think we're at the dawn of a major good-people revolution. They're gonna rise up and smash the bejesus out of the bad, which will make us all one.

The road in front of the lab expansion project is not the shortest route home, but I'm curious to see it for myself. Lily has been promising me a tour, but other things keep getting in the way. The storm did some damage. Shards of plastic hang like black icicles from the upper floor on one side of the building. A man in striped coveralls is inside sweeping water over the edge with a giant push broom. Sweeping water. Isn't that kind of like herding cats? The far side of the building appears to be intact with windows in place and a stone façade. It's going to be an impressive structure, but it's far from finished. I can understand why Howard is starting to freak out over the whole thing.

I loop around the block and head back towards the condo. There's white panel van in my driveway with Sam's Glass Repair painted in large red letters on the back and huge racks hanging off either side. The racks are empty. My front door is open and I hear a loud whining noise as soon as I step out of the car. It sounds like one of those leaf blowers. As I start up the stairs, a guy comes out of the door with my tree limb over one shoulder. He's young, probably not more than 18, just a kid really, with thick black hair and a brick shithouse build. He stops and looks at me, balancing the huge branch like a jacket he's casually tossed over his shoulder. He's wearing jeans and a sweatshirt. The sweatshirt has the same red lettering as the van.

"Hey," he says, shouting a little over the noise and moving to one side to allow me to continue up the stairs. "This your place?"

"Yes it is."

"We're almost done. Thought I'd get this out of your way."

He hefts the branch up off his shoulder to indicate what he's talking about.

"Thanks. I appreciate that. I was pretty surprised to have that thing come through the window."

The kid shakes his head as if sharing my disbelief.

"You're not the only one. We've been all over town today fixin' stuff. But I think you win the prize for the biggest."

He shifts the weight of the branch and starts down the stairs.

"You know," I say. "I thought it was pretty strange it wasn't a pine branch that came through the window. The only thing around here is pine trees. Can't imagine where that thing came from."

The kid's forehead wrinkles into three massive skin folds.

"Who knows?" he says. "Could've been a snag. You're in a real wind tunnel here. This branch could've been stuck up in one of your trees for years. Finally got a big enough wind to bring it down, I guess."

"I guess."

"Whatdya think, someone hurled a branch through your window in the middle of a freakin' storm?"

He laughs, and I laugh too, embarrassed because that is exactly what I think. The kid clomps down the stairs, the branch bouncing a little bit against his tree trunk of a neck.

I step inside the condo. The noise is so loud I have to cover my ears to walk back to the bedroom. Two more guys are in there, neither one as large as the tree-toting kid. I can see why he was elected to carry out the branch. There's a new pane of glass covering the spot where my shower curtain was stretched this morning. One guy is cleaning the window. The other is running the source of the noise, a dusty shop vac. Vac guy notices me come in and leans down to shut off the noise. I uncover my ears, but the ringing persists.

"Didn't hear ya come in," Vac guy says. "We'll be outta your way pretty soon."

"Looks good," I say, admiring the sparkling glass.

"You lucked out. We had one pane left and it fit your window."

"Guess it was about time for a little *good* luck."

The guy cleaning the new window looks up and chuckles.

"Lucky for us too, 'cause now we're done for the day."

He swipes his rag across the window with a flourish then stuffs it in his back pocket.

"We just gotta finish vacuuming," Vac guy continues. "Sorry about the noise."

Without waiting for my consent, he flips on the machine and goes about his business. It's like being trapped in a cage with howler monkeys, but it doesn't seem to bother Vac guy or Window Cleaner guy. I escape down the hallway and into the kitchen to heat up my burritos.

The phone rings.

"Hello," I shout over the screaming vacuum.

"Albert?"

"Yeah."

"It's Lily. What on earth is that noise?"

"The repair guys are here. They're vacuuming."

Tree kid comes in and waves at me as he heads back to the bedroom.

"I can't hear you very well," Lily says. "Call me when they're done. I need to talk to you about something."

"Sure thing."

"What?"

"Nothing."

"What?"

The call clicks off and I stand there for a minute holding the phone.

The bell on the microwave signals the completion of my luncheon feast. The burritos sit side-by-side on a paper plate, oozing a thick yellow-brown slime. I'm okay with that. I'm so hungry even yellow-brown slime won't stop me.

The only time I remember being grossed out enough to lose my appetite I was about fourteen and living with the Andersons. They had a very old, very crazy grandmother named Ruth who stayed in the spare room off the kitchen. She got to make Sunday dinner every week and once in awhile she liked to set the table with some of the antique china and crystal she kept in a tall curio cabinet in her bedroom. One Sunday, she dished up some undercooked chicken and overcooked broccoli. Pretty standard fare for Grandma Ruth, however, this Sunday she'd also prepared a special cranberry juice and 7Up cocktail, which she served in some of her prehistoric crystal goblets. I took a sip and determined the drink to be the highlight of the meal, until I took a good look inside my glass. There was a large mummified fly in my cocktail, pieces of its wispy, spider-silk ropes trailing it as it floated across the pink, fizzy juice. I couldn't make it to the bathroom. I threw up on the carpet in front of Grandma Ruth's bedroom.

As I polish off the last, tasty bite of my burritos, the howler vacuum mercifully shuts off and I hear it rolling down the hallway. Vac guy appears a second later dragging the beast by its hose.

"We're all done in there," he announces. "I'm pretty sure we got all the big stuff but you might want to vacuum a couple more times in the next day or so. Sometimes glass works its way out of a rug. Want me to leave you this for a few days?"

He's pointing down at the shop vac, which is heeling at his side like an obedient dog.

"Nah, that's okay. There's one here somewhere."

The other guys come down the hallway and Tree Kid kicks the shop vac out of his way. It teeters on its metal casters, nearly tips over, and then bounces back into balance thanks to a quick jerk of the hose by Vac guy.

"Dammit, Donny," Vac guy shouts. "Could ya think for two seconds before you do something?"

Donny mumbles something that sounds like "sorry" but could have been "shithead." Vac guy is about half Donny's size with greasy hair and a pathetic mustache. If I were him, I wouldn't mess with Donny, but sometimes it's the small ones that surprise you—little terrors packing a six-inch blade.

"Thanks again," I say. "I know you've had a long day. I'd offer you a beer if I had one, but the cupboard's pretty bare right now."

"It's cool," says Window Cleaner guy, who appears to be the boss man. Maybe he's the Sam of the big red letters. He's carrying a five-gallon bucket filled with tools and caulking guns. "Work's guaranteed, so if you have any problems, give Mrs. Rudolph a call and we'll come back out. Have a good evening."

They file out the door and Donny slams it behind them. The quiet is nice but now I notice how chilly it is. The heat's still off. I walk to the thermostat on the wall and turn the furnace back on. The burritos are gurgling in my stomach. They want out.

I grab the phone handset and collapse on the couch, throwing my slippered feet up onto the coffee table. The van rumbles to life in my driveway and the guys and their howler vacuum pull out and gun it down the street.

It's already dusky outside the window. Time to pull the curtains closed and pretend there is no more outside, only inside. I could take a little nap. The last twenty-four hours haven't yielded much in the way of sleep. I tip my head back and let my eyes drift back in my head.

I hear a car pull in. It's not the bad muffler sound of Sam's repair van. I lift my head from the couch and look out the window. It's too dark to see anything except the glow of headlights. I get up and cross to the door, stepping out onto the porch to lean over the railing. There's a dark car idling in the driveway. It looks like Lily's Mercedes. I raise my hand and start down the stairs. A surprise visit from Lily? Lily in a trench coat over bra and panties? Maybe I'm still asleep and this is a dream. Don't wake up, don't wake up. But the car backs out and pulls away. Someone must have taken a wrong turn. I'm awake. I'm wide awake. Wide awake and still holding the phone handset.

I walk back inside and dial Lily's number.

ELEVEN

I catch Lily on her cell phone on the way to a yet another fundraising dinner and fill her in on my meeting with Howard. She's not very impressed, says she doesn't understand why everything Howard does takes so long. She is intrigued about me interviewing Roger Jones, calls him their biggest investor in more ways than one. The cell starts to break up but before it goes dead I think I hear her laughing.

As Howard predicted, Jones answers on the second ring. Even at 6:00 in the evening.

"Roger Jones"

"Mr. Jones, this is Albert Mackey. I got your number from Howard Stanich over at Nesler."

"What's our Howie up to?" Jones asks. His voice booms over the phone line full of good humor, as if asking about a favorite son.

Howie? Are we talking about the same person?

"He's fine. The reason I'm calling has to do with your investment in the Nesler lab project. I'm writing a biography on Michael Rudolph and Howard seems to think you're the one to give me some perspective on the project."

There's no response. Maybe he hung up.

"Mr. Jones?"

"My perspective?" Jones hurls the words through the phone then explodes with a laugh. "Well that's pretty damn interesting. I thought Howie hated me. Maybe 'hate's' too harsh a word, it's more like he'd prefer I fell off a cliff."

"Actually he spoke quite highly of you, as did Mrs. Rudolph."

"Lily?" Another high volume fast ball. I pull the phone a couple inches from my ear.

"Yes, Mrs. Rudolph is assisting me on the research for my book."

"Lily I like."

"Could you spare a little time to meet with me? I promise to keep it as short as possible. I know you're busy."

"Work day's over, Mr. Mackey." His voice is so stern and definitive, I know he must be the boss of about a hundred people.

"I understand that, I didn't mean right now," I say, already apologizing. I am the boss of nobody.

"I did."

Jones lets fly with another laugh. This guy's a real card.

"After work is actually better than during the day for this kind of thing," he continues. "I don't have anything going on tonight that can't be done tomorrow."

It's been an entire day of impromptu meetings, why stop now?

"Right now sounds good to me, Mr. Jones. Where should we meet?"

"Let's grab a drink. Do you know Tony's? It's on Second and Liberty."

"Sure, I could be there in about twenty minutes."

"I'll be there sooner, get us a table. Look for a big guy in a gray suit."

Roger Jones hangs up without saying goodbye. The room is getting a little warmer. It should be back to normal by bedtime. I cross the floor to grab my jacket, which is when I notice my briefcase, which is when I remember the 20-23 form I promised Dennis. Shit. I still need some sort of a story about Mr. Klein's nonexistent girlfriend. I reach for my coat on the back of the couch and knock a pile of papers onto the floor. The repair guys must have brought them in to cover the floor or something. They're miscellaneous sections from several weeks ago. An article at the bottom of one of the pages catches my attention, "*Local Teacher Busted as Part-time Escort.*" Reading further, it describes some lady who spent her days teaching phonics to second graders and her evenings teaching gentleman callers another kind of oral exercise. Very interesting, to say the least. Better still, perhaps something the soon-to-be girlfriend of Hugh Klein might find as an appealing pursuit. Sounds fun. The 20-23 will take thirty minutes tops to whip out when I get home, depending on how much graphic detail I want to get into. There are days when I love my job.

Tony's is one of Park Hills' oldest establishments of fine spirits, which is a nice way of saying it's been around a while and looks it. The bar itself is the best feature. Heavy, dark wood that's soft and smooth, rubbed to a gleaming finish by years of hands reaching for one more round. There are only about a dozen tables and only half of them are full. It's easy to spot Jones, but he's someone you'd be able to pick out even if the room were over flowing. His description was dead-on. He is a very big man in a very big gray suit. He might be the biggest man I've ever seen in my life, at least outside of those documentaries on the Discovery Channel about the people who get so big the fire department has to remove a wall to get them out of their bedrooms.

I approach his table and step around into his field of vision.

"Roger Jones?"

"Mr. Mackey. Glad to see you're prompt." He reaches for me with his enormous paw and gives my whole arm one single shake. "I'm not a very patient man, I'm afraid. Have a seat."

I sit and almost immediately there's a waiter at my side.

"Can I get you something?" the waiter, a slight young man with yellow hair, asks.

I glance quickly to see what Jones is drinking. A short glass with amber liquid and a few swimming ice cubes.

"Dewar's, water back."

The young man retreats to the bar. Roger Jones sloshes his drink, sending the ice cubes spinning. He looks at me through thick black-rimmed glasses. His white shirt is open at the collar, a collar that has to be at least 18½ inches. He must have them custom made. There's a tie, also loosened, in a traditional red and navy pattern. Very businesslike. No nonsense. I am fascinated by his neck. It's so fleshy it appears almost liquid. There is really no chin, the skin simply drapes from his cheeks and folds down into the shirt collar. I think this is a genetic characteristic as well as a weight problem. Some people simply lose their necks over time; perhaps this is where the phrase "head and shoulders above the rest" originated. Apart from his neck, Mr. Jones is proportionately huge. His suit coat hangs open, revealing suspenders, the fat man's friend, holding up an impressive pair of pants. Were there a belt circumnavigating his girth, it surely would be as long as I am tall.

"I've heard a little bit about your project, Mr. Mackey," Jones says. "Seems to me you were the very eloquent young man who spoke at Michael's funeral."

"Yes sir, that was me."

I feel like a peasant who's been given an audience with some enormous king, like I better impress him or "off with my head!" But I think it was the queen who said that.

"Good job," Jones says, picking up his drink again. "Very good job."

Harrah, the king is pleased!

Roger Jones continues to look at me. His eyes are not roaming across my face or body, he's staring directly at me as if downloading information from my brain and out my eyes.

"How long did you know Michael?" I ask, hoping to break the data stream. He blinks.

"Not so very long. Of course I'd known *of* him for a number of years. He's Park Hills' most famous son. You gotta be livin' under a rock to not know who he is. But I didn't really meet him officially until I got involved with the lab project."

"And how long has that been?"

"Guess it's been almost three years now."

The yellow-haired boy is back with my drink.

"Run a tab would ya, Denny?" asks Jones.

He looks at me. "You'll be wantin' more than one drink if you're going to listen to my life story."

I stutter for a few seconds. I hope he knows I'm here about Michael not him. If Jones wants to talk about Jones, I don't think I have the guts to change the subject.

"Just kiddin' around," he says. "Don't look so worried. You ask the questions and I'll answer them."

He takes a drink. I do the same.

"How did you get involved with the lab project?" I ask, trying to pull on my confidence and take back some control of the situation.

"You mean, why'd I decide to invest? Funny, I've been asking myself the very same question the last few weeks. I got some major doubts they can pull this thing off without Michael, but I'm sure Howie already told you about that."

"He mentioned you'd been concerned about the progress."

Jones laughs. Another laugh that matches his size. It tumbles out in great waves.

"Concerned? Yeah, I've been a little bit concerned. I put my money on Michael Rudolph. Somethin' tells me this dog don't hunt without him."

"You bought in purely on Michael's reputation?"

"That and Lily's persuasion, which I probably don't need to tell you can be a very powerful thing. That gal could probably tell me to cut off my own dick and I'd at least consider it for a couple minutes. You ever seen her walk out of a room?"

Roger Jones is staring through me again. I think he's scanning my brain this time, looking for evidence of whether or not I might be doing more than research with Lily.

"I'm sorry, am I offending you? I'm a crass sonofabitch sometimes. And you writer types are probably a sensitive bunch, aren't ya? All PC about women in the workplace and all. Well, screw you. I've got a ton of money and I've been, seen and done it all. Nothin' much shocks me anymore, so I prefer to cut through the bullshit and call it as I see it. Michael was one hell of a lucky bastard in the bedroom, I'll say that about him."

I have no idea where this conversation is going, but I obviously have very little to do with its direction. Somewhere along the way we'd drifted into a discussion of Lily Rudolph and what a hot chick she'd be in bed. As much as I agree with this line of thought, I feel the need to push Roger Jones back on track. If we'd ever been on track.

"What did you know about Michael's research?"

"Not too much. I don't get into all the scientific stuff. Bunch of braniac gobbledygook, but Lily did tell me some stories that were pretty amazing. Turns out one of my own employee's father was one of the original patients or whatever you call them."

"You mean a test participant? Really?"

"I don't know what you call them, but Lily told me a story about how this old guy, the employee's father, was helped by the drug they're developing."

Now *this* was interesting. Not that Roger Joneses' diatribe on the merits of Lily Rudolph's butt hadn't been interesting, but this information could actually prove helpful instead of making me slightly sweaty.

"Do you remember the story?"

Jones leans back in his chair, putting about 450 pounds of pressure on the ladder back slats.

"I do remember the story, because I thought it was such a good one. Starts out this lady's father is just a regular old guy. Retired, getting into some hobbies, enjoying those golden years they're always promising us. He's a little forgetful, but no more than the rest of us. A misplaced pair of eyeglasses, a neglected pot on the stove, his daughter's birthday. Then one day, he forgets his way home. He's out walking his dog, not more than four or five blocks from his own house, and he can't remember how to get back."

I remember Lily's story about being lost in the woods. How everything familiar can turn its back and leave you for dead.

"This seems like a pretty run of the mill story when Lily is telling me about it," Jones continues. "I mean my own uncle's in one of those Alzheimer's homes, the ones where all the hallways and sidewalks run in circles so the residents won't wander off. Anyway, Lily tells me how this poor old guy just goes down fast after that. His wife's been gone for years, and his only daughter, my employee, doesn't know what to do. She can't leave him alone. She can't afford to put him in a home. Guess I don't pay her enough."

Roger Jones gives me a conspiratorial wink and swallows another drink.

"Somehow the daughter hears about this drug study they're doing at Nesler and she gets her dad signed up for it. When the dad starts in with the treatment, he's so far gone he doesn't even know what year it is anymore. He doesn't know his daughter, he doesn't know where he is, and he thinks the nurse bringing him his medicine is his mother. Can you imagine being that messed up? Just take me out and shoot me, I say."

He shakes his head side to side, causing his neck to sway back and forth. Pudding. It kind of reminds me of pudding.

"So he's in there for about three weeks. They actually keep the patients. Is that what you said they called them, patients?"

"Participants."

"They keep the participants right there in the facility for the whole time. I guess to make sure there aren't any outside factors that could interfere with the research. So this guy's there for about three weeks and his daughter comes back to visit. She comes in, her father is sitting up in a chair, he's dressed and neat as a pin, his eyes are clear and his hands are steady. He's reading a book. He looks up when she comes in and says, 'Hello, dear, have you had lunch? They're serving fish today.' He's completely lucid. In fact, he's beyond lucid. Turns out the book he's reading is in French, a language he learned as a college student at the Sorbonne but hadn't used in probably fifty years. In three weeks. Three fuckin' weeks. Well, I heard that story, and I said, 'sign me up.'"

"Did you ever find out who the employee was?"

"Never did. I don't really care. It's an amazing story no matter who it happened to. Dontcha think?"

Amazing alright. All the stories were amazing. It was like an on/off switch. One minute they're totally out of it; next minute they're reading French novels. The cynical side of me felt "beyond belief" might be a better description. But Roger Jones is no fool, despite his crude tone and elephantine bulk. Something tells me that there's a sleek, sharp brain operating the controls.

"Where is this guy now?" I ask. I drain the last drops of my scotch and gulp down the water.

"I don't know. I assume he's back at home living his life. But, to tell you the truth, Lily never followed up on any of that. We all got so caught up in the lab construction, and then with Michael's accident ... well, I guess I just never thought about it again."

Jones signals for our waiter.

"You want another drink, Mr. Mackey? I do."

The waiter acknowledges Jones' order with a bob of his yellow head then looks at me.

"Sure. Same for me."

"And some of those fried cheese stick things, Denny," said Jones. "I love those things. You like 'em, Mackey?"

I'm starting to understand how Jones keeps his girlish figure.

"One of my favorites," I lie.

The waiter grabs our empty glasses and scuttles off to fill our order. Jones reaches up and loosens his tie a bit more. His neck sways.

"You know what boggles my mind about this whole thing, Mr. Mackey?"

I shake my head, assuming he means something about the science of neurotransmitters or brain chemistry, both of which are certainly boggling to me.

"I can't figure out what could have happened to cause Michael to crash his plane."

Wait a minute. He's cranked the wheel down another path of conversation. This guy would make an unbelievable investigator. He is driving us wherever he wants; I don't know which way we're going with this, but I'm happy to be along for the ride.

"I believe they determined it was pilot error on take off," I say. I actually don't know anything other than what was in the newspaper story. Jones is tracing the rim of his glass with his hotdog-size index finger. Around and around and around. He's thought about this whole thing more than he's letting on. It's eating at him.

"Michael wasn't the kind of guy to make mistakes," Jones says.

"Everyone makes mistakes, Mr. Jones. I bet even you have made a couple in your life."

"Geeze, I've made a shitload," he says, chuckling and slapping at his man breasts. "But I'm just a fat slob with a lucky streak when it comes to real estate. Rudolph was a perfectionist."

I starting to kind of like this guy. He's the real thing. No pretense or affectation. Doesn't seem to take himself or anyone else too seriously. He leans forward, drops his elbows on the table and wags a fat finger in my face.

"You'd have to be goddamn spot-on to come up with the theories Michael came up with. Guys like that don't make big mistakes. Not even under pressure. In fact, they're better under pressure. It just doesn't make sense to me."

Denny returns with our drinks and a sizzling platter of fried mozzarella. Jones reaches out, plucks two sticks off the tray and pops them into his mouth with a whiskey chaser. There is no visible Adam's apple to indicate consumption. The food is simply gone, like a seal slurping a sardine.

"If I didn't know better," he says, reaching for a third cheese stick. "I'd say it was something more than an accident. Problem is, everybody loved Michael. You saw the funeral. The man had no enemies. He was a god."

"Did the investigators look into anything besides pilot error?"

"Of course they did. They have to because of NTSB rules. They looked at mechanical failure, weather, even tested his blood for drugs. It was all inconclusive."

"Well I guess that answers your question," I said, grabbing one of the fast-disappearing appetizers and dunking it into a bowl of marinara. "I think FAA and NTSB rules are pretty strict about leaving no stone unturned. I'm sure they looked at every possibility."

Jones wipes the mozzarella grease from his lips with a napkin.

"Have you ever talked with Lily about it?" he asks.

I'd sooner choke to death on fried cheese than talk to Lily about Michael's death. I hate it when I can tell she's even thinking about it. It's like watching a car stall. Everything dies.

"I've actually avoided the subject," I say. "We've been concentrating on putting together the big picture of his research. I haven't wanted to bring up such a painful subject."

Roger Jones drops another morsel down his throat and smiles at me.

"You really like her, don't you?" he asks, still smiling.

"Of course I do. She's an incredible person. I like her and I admire her."

I am getting very warm. It could be the consumption of cheese sticks and scotch, but I doubt it.

"No, I mean you *really* like her, don't you?" Jones smirks at me and rolls his eyes. "Hey, I completely understand. Like I said before, that is one very pretty package."

"Michael Rudolph was my friend, Mr. Jones. Roger. It's not at all what you think."

Hot. It is getting very hot.

"Not thinking anything. Not thinking anything at all."

He is smiling. Smiling and swallowing.

"I'm probably way off base," he says, but he doesn't stop smiling. "Puttin' too much of myself into the equation. I know I couldn't be around Lily Rudolph for any length of time without turning into a drooling idiot."

I have not started drooling yet.

"But then I'm a horny old goat. You sensitive types can keep your emotions under control, can't you?"

"It's all extremely professional," I say. Do I sound whiney? I think I sound whiney and maybe a little ill-at-ease with a dash of guilt-ridden. "I don't appreciate what you're insinuating."

Roger Jones erupts in laughter and drops his arms down on the table. The plates and glasses do a little hop.

"I like you, Mackey," he says. "Don't think I trust ya, but I like ya. There's something about you that reminds me of me. A little bit of the shark. Know what I mean?"

I shake my head. I appear to have been let off the hook about Lily, but Jones has my number and he's about to dial it up.

"Sharks are quiet, stealthy, they know when to take advantage of a situation. I think there's a bit of the shark in you, Mr. Mackey. And, I like that. I like someone with a little bit of the shark. You got any more questions for me?"

I smile back at Roger Jones. I like him too. He knows there's more to my story than I'm letting on, but he isn't going to push it. I know he's way smarter than he lets on, and I'm not going to push that either.

"Are you really going to pull your money out of the lab project?" I ask.

"No," Jones answers. He sniggers under his breath. "But I like to make those geeks at Nesler nervous. They're fun to watch when they get all panicky. Their brains don't help 'em then."

I smile in agreement, imagining Howard sweating through one of his fancy silk shirts.

"Anyway, the damn thing's almost done. I may as well see it through."

The cheese sticks are gone. A few more patrons have filtered in and the tables around us are filling up.

"Have you been over to the lab construction site lately?" I ask.

"Nope. Heard there was some storm damage. Guess I ought to go over and see for myself."

"I drove by this afternoon. It doesn't look too bad."

"I'm sick and tired of the delays," Jones says, swatting the air with one hand. "You'd think we were building the friggin' Taj Mahal for how long it's taking. Maybe I'll give my pal, Gavin a call."

"VanMorten? I thought you dealt directly with Howard Stanich."

I'm surprised Jones would settle for anyone less than numero uno. Maybe the tubby guys like to stick together.

"I usually do, but Howard can be a tough fella to get a hold of sometimes. Gavin's my fallback. He's a little slow on the uptake, but he aims to please. You've met him?"

"Yes, he strikes me as an usual fit for the job."

"I'd like to say he's smarter than he looks, but what you see is probably what you get."

Yellow-haired Denny approaches our table once again.

"Anything else, gentlemen?"

"I'm good. What about you, Mackey? Can I get you anything else?"

"I'm fine, but please, let me pay. I'm asking the questions."

"Thanks for the offer, but they know me around here." He gestures at the waiter. "Denny's already put everything on my account. We're good to go."

Denny smiles and reaches for the empty cheese stick platter. Jones waits for him to clear the table and watches him walk back toward the kitchen. I think he's admiring his butt. It appears Jones is an equal opportunity butt-admirer.

"Mind if I give you a little piece of advice, Mr. Mackey?"

"Of course not."

"Keep your eyes open."

"For what?"

"For the unexpected."

"I'm not sure I understand what you mean."

He pushes back from the table and hoists himself out of the chair. It's like watching a whale breech.

"There's something going on. I can't quite put my finger on it and that pisses me off, but there's a piece missin'. That's why I've been on Howard's back. Things are draggin' on too long. I don't know if it's all because of Michael's accident or if there's something else wrong. I just don't think I have the real story."

The real story. That's what I'd asked Howard for too, and what he'd assured me I'd gotten. Maybe Roger Jones was paranoid as well as prurient, but I think he might be on to something. I wonder if he knows anything about native tree branches.

"It's been a pleasure meeting you," he says, extending his huge hand, enveloping and crushing my own. "Take my card and feel free to call if you come up with any other questions. And do me a favor; tell that twit, Stanich that if he knows what's good for him, he'll return my phone calls in a more expedient fashion."

Jones presses a business card into my hand and I automatically slip it into my coat pocket.

"Be happy to, but it might be few days before I see him again."

"That's okay. In the meantime, I think I'll take my own tour of the job site and chat with some of the guys. Maybe they can tell me more about what's going on."

"Go to the source. That's my motto."

"Good luck on this book of yours. It sounds like a big job."

"Bigger than you might imagine."

"Oh I know big," he says, laughing and pulling his jacket closed across his spacious expanse of shirt. "I know all about big."

With that, he heads for the door, still laughing. The other patrons turn their heads at the sound and stare. The door closes behind him and I realize Denny has come up behind me and is also watching Jones leave.

"Quite a guy, huh?" Denny says.

"I can honestly say I've never met anyone quite like him."

"He seems pretty harsh, but he's really a pussycat. If he likes you, he'll do whatever he can to help you."

"What if he doesn't like you?"

"I would not suggest being in that position."

TWELVE

I walk across Tony's parking lot, alone. Not getting-into-a-car-by-myself alone. That's obvious and not too distressing. Alone in the broader sense. Roger Jones, as loud and obnoxious as he is, has a circle of long-time friends. People know him. Like him. Ask him to parties. I start the engine and let it warm for a minute.

I know the people I work with, but they're only people I work with. If I had to pick one of them out of a police line-up, I'd probably fail. Phil, Todd, Karen, Sam, Sherry, Rob—their names roll off my tongue but the faces are indistinct, one morphing into the next. Belinda has blond hair and a big ass. Or is that Evelyn? Doug? They're acquaintances. They're all just acquaintances. I guess I'm more of a surface feeder, content to take a few bites off the top and leave the rest for the pearl divers, the people who can hold their breath for several minutes. I don't like it down there in the deep end.

I check the rearview mirror and back out of my parking space. Why now? Why does it matter now?

Park Hills' downtown core empties after dark. There are no clubs, few restaurants, no scene. You've got to drive to Chicago for that. After ten o'clock, only empty office towers are left to guard the sidewalks and dumpsters. You're pretty much out of luck unless you're interested in a 24-hour grocery or a check cashing store. The few people driving along the empty streets don't know me. They're probably headed home. Home sweet home. Home, home on the range. There's no place like home. I roll down the window a bit and let the cool night air hit my face. I should probably have something harder smack me in the head ... maybe knock some sense into me.

My ability to blend in has always been one of my best qualities, like the Cheshire Cat. He was cool. The way he could disappear into the background and leave only his grin. But what if he got stuck? What if one day he couldn't come back and stayed a grin forever?

I think I would make an interesting scientific test subject. Researchers are always arguing about how much of personality is genetic and how much is environmental. If, as the environmental camp asserts, personality is developed by the reactions of the people around us, then outside perceptions should be a window to our true self. If someone sees a pathetic slob and treats you like a pathetic slob, then a pathetic slob you must be.

In my case, people's perceptions are under my control. If I can convincingly portray a pathetic slob, that's who they see, that's who they believe me to be. But it's not really who I am. I've shut the window to true self and closed the blinds. How tight? I know a little of the real me bleeds through even when I'm pretending to be someone else. How secure? I've never been one alternate personality for more than a few hours at a time. I've been Albert Mackey for so long now it's starting to take more effort to switch back and forth. I'm a little worried I'll lose track of who I am and say the wrong thing. Or I'll say the right thing, but to the wrong person.

One year, I think I was fifteen or sixteen, I got a reversible t-shirt for my birthday. One side was plain green; the other side was red, brown and black stripes. It was just two t-shirts sewn together, which made it double thick and kind of hot, but I thought it was extremely cool. At the time, I believe I thought it was "bitchin'." Wear it one way on Monday, turn it inside-out on Tuesday. Two entirely different shirts in one handy package. I was eating lunch one afternoon in my bitchin' shirt and spilled burrito grease down the front of the green side. It soaked right through to the striped side and left a big stain. So you see my point, right? I made a mistake on one side and it leaked through to the other. As Charlie, I've never minded having acquaintances instead of friends. As Albert, it kind of bothers me. And then there's Lily. Roger Jones was right. I do really like her. But there's the question again. Who likes Lily, Charlie or Albert? She doesn't know Charlie.

We're co-mingling, Albert and I, blending, but not smoothly like cream in your coffee, more like oil and vinegar. Allowed to sit, we separate. Shake violently and we're mixed up for awhile. I toss my salad dressing head side-to-side and take a deep breath. The air outside the car's window is sharp and damp. It smells late. Have you ever noticed time has its own aromas? Early smells fresh and unused. Late reeks of wasted days and stale ideas.

The longer Albert is around, the more real he becomes. It's like that old kid's book, the *Velveteen Rabbit*. The toy rabbit was around so much and loved by the little boy for so long, it finally became real. If Lily loved me, would I become real or would Albert become real?

Is this what happens when you go insane?

The road stretches out in front of me. I pass under the streetlights with their comforting pools of intermittent light. One blinks out as I drive underneath. Maybe there's a metal plate in my head transmitting high frequency interference. That would explain a lot.

I stare through the windshield and see the road, but inside my head, the picture I see is Lily. Lily likes Albert, but I don't think she'd care much for Charlie. He's socially unacceptable in so very many ways: delivers eulogies for people he doesn't know, picks up strange women in unfortunate circumstances, lies about who he is and what he does. He is a snappy dresser, but that's not tipping the balance.

It's the ultimate cosmic joke. I've become my own antagonist. Damned if I do, damned if I don't.

I press down on the accelerator and the streetlights flick by like frames of a rickety filmstrip. The faster I go, the closer together they become. At sixteen frames-per-second, individual film frames coalesce into a clear picture. A moving picture. How fast is that in miles per hour? How fast do I need to go before I can see what is going to happen? I hunch over the steering wheel and focus on the end of my hood. *Faster.*

To create a believable character you must give him a flaw. My eulogy characters were all easier to accept because they were imperfect. They were scared or repentant or critical. They stammered and searched for the right word. Sometimes they cried. Badge of honor. Heart on your sleeve. *Faster.*

I'm almost home. Albert's almost home. It's Albert's condo in the pine forest with its high ceilings and new window. Albert's food. But inside is Charlie's briefcase with work that needs to be done. Work that needs to be turned in at Charlie's job in the morning. *Faster.*

The lights are surrounding me now, blurring together. They seem to be coming from all sides, bright and unrelenting. My eyes focus, and I realize the most intense lights aren't streetlights, they're headlights and they're heading right for me. Instinctively, I pull the steering wheel to the right to avoid the piercing light. It rushes by, horn blaring loud then soft. The Doppler effect.

I'm no longer on the road. The road is gone. I'm going too fast. My foot fumbles for the brake. One foot, both feet. The car is traveling forward, and I think, downward. The hood dips forward, the ground feels mushy under the tires. Sliding, sliding, and then a sudden, dull thump, jarring enough to pitch me forward into the steering wheel. Not hard enough to deploy the airbag. My head cracks against the wheel. The engine dies.

Shouldn't I burst into a ball of flame? Isn't that what happens in all the action movies? At a pivotal moment in the story, something bursts into a ball of flame, but the hero leaps free of the wreckage, in slow motion, arms and legs pinwheeling. But there is nothing. No flame. No slow motion. I am simply stopped. Stopped on the side of an embankment, up to my hubcaps in mud and muck. Thank God for so many consecutive days of rain. Saved by soggy leaves and some kind of buried, tire-stopping tree root.

I listen for sirens, for someone to call out to me, asking if I need help. But no one knows I'm down here. No one except the idiot who ran me off the road. But, did someone really run me off the road or did I cross the line and head for him? I can't remember. I listen again. The driver of the other car must have stopped. He must have seen me go flying off the road. The engine is making a clicking noise. I listen harder. A couple of crickets chirp their condolences, but there's no traffic noise rushing by from up above. Where's the other guy? What kind of lunatic would come that close to annihilation and then simply drive off? Jerk. Of course, he's probably saying the same thing. He's probably going through ten *Hail Marys* right about now, grateful he's alive.

I push the driver's door open about two inches before it sticks solidly into the mud. Great. I reach up and explore my forehead. There's a knot the size of a cantaloupe rising up across my brow and something sticky over my right eye. I lean over and tweak the rear view mirror toward my face. In the darkness, I can't make out much more than the outline of my head. Flicking on the dome light, I see there's a dandy boxer's cut across my brow bone that is bleeding ... a lot. Blotting it with my sleeves seems to make it worse and now my shirt's all bloody. The whites of my eyes have both gone red and the skin around them is already turning purple.

That cut is going to need stitches. I have to get out of the car, climb back up to the road, and find a doctor. Since I'm not Gumby, going out the door is not an option. The half-open window will have to do. This escape hatch looks much smaller than I'd like, but the window controls don't operate when the car's not running, and I don't think this car is going to be running anytime soon. I crank the key in the ignition just to test my theory. Nothing. I'm surprised the dome light works. Unlatching my seat belt, and with my back to the window, I reach up to grab the edge of the roof. I tip my head and shoulders backwards and pull. The small of my back rakes across the edge of the glass.

"Shit!" I hiss into the blackness.

With the top half of my body out and my butt balanced precariously on the edge of the window, I can lean back and see the stars in the night sky. Ordinarily a beautiful sight, right now the pin pricks of light act as illustrations for the sharp little stabs of pain shooting up my forearms as I try to heave my weight up and out the window.

"Star light, star bright, first star I see tonight. I wish I may, I wish I might, make a wish on you tonight. Get me the hell out of this car!"

One more heave, this one with an accompanying ho, and my ass bumps through the window and drops down to the door handle. I am now sitting, kind of, a fact for which my biceps are extremely grateful. I relax my arms and close my eyes. The stars of the night sky are now twinkling across the inside of my eyelids. I feel a little woozy. It probably wasn't a great idea to get into a car accident with little more than scotch and fried cheese in my stomach. This, coupled with the loss of blood and the exertion of yanking myself out the car window, is beginning to take its toll.

After a few minutes wrestling with near-nausea, I again grasp the edge of the roof and snake first one leg then the other through the window. As my left leg makes its final exit, the back of my shoe catches on the window edge. It jolts me off balance and I fling my hands off the roof, hopping madly on one leg for a few seconds until my shoe pops free and I am finally back on both feet. None of this has helped my sour stomach. I stand for a moment, my Nikes slowly sinking beneath the squishy leaves and mud, and then I vomit. A slurry of booze and cheese curds pools on the ground and drips from my chin. This is when I remember my feet are still pretty sliced up from the other night and I should not really be hopping on them. I'd scream, but if a schmuck screams in the forest and no one is there to hear it, does he make a sound?

When I suck one shoe out of the muck the puke trickles into the hole left behind. I guess, like water, puke seeks the lowest point. This would be among my lowest points. I lean back in through the car window and retrieve my note pad. It's only now, turning to the task at hand, getting the hell out of here, that I notice just how far away the road is. I'm a long way down, easily 100 feet from the top. I could continue going down, but who knows where I'd come out. Up is the only escape. The metaphor is not lost on me. Go down into the unknown darkness or straight up into the light. If my head didn't hurt so badly, it might be funny. Comical. After all, comedy is just a hop, step and a jump to the left of tragedy.

Shoving my note pad into my belt, I head up. Up and out. The ground is so saturated it's like climbing through molasses. My shoes make toilet plunger sounds. Every once in awhile there's a bush I can grab on to for a bit of extra leverage, but mostly it's just slimy, slippery shit. I don't know what time it is. I should get one of those swanky watches with a light-up dial.

If I could quit focusing on sliding back down to certain death, my next order of business would be to figure out how this all happened. Actually, I don't think I'd die if I fell. Knocked unconscious maybe, but probably not killed. However, I would have to start climbing all over again and that would make me want to die. So, it's really a wash.

Let's review the facts. I know I was going too fast. I know I wasn't paying full attention to the road. But, I'm sure I was going straight. I was staring at the hood of the car. I was an arrow. And, if someone were trying to run me off the road, wouldn't he do it from behind? He'd be following me, not hurtling at me from the opposite direction. You'd have to be nuts to come after someone from the front, like a game of chicken. What if I hadn't veered? *He* would have had to correct at the last minute. Not only nuts, you'd have to be some kind of a racecar stunt driver to pull that maneuver. It had to have been me. Didn't it? *Didn't it*?

There's the road. I've never been so glad to see crumbling asphalt. With both feet on solid ground I turn and look back down at my car. I could have, no, I should have been killed, or at least broken into several pieces. Just up the road a stand of scruffy pine trees lines the embankment. A few more feet and I'd have accordioned into them instead of driving off the edge. Good thing I already threw up.

Now what? I haven't heard or seen another car since the accident. I still need a doctor, and I have to get a tow truck to drag up what's left of my car. Better start walking. Lily's right. I really need a cell phone.

THIRTEEN

"Charlie, I'm telling you exactly what they told me. Klein is denying everything. Says he doesn't have a girlfriend, and if he did, she wouldn't be turnin' tricks on the side."

Dennis is standing at my desk. He's not leaning on anything. He is pissed.

"I don't know what to tell you, Dennis. It came from one of my most reliable sources."

My imagination is usually quite reliable. Over the years it has produced any number of credible sounding people, places and things.

"Ain't cuttin' it this time, Buddy Boy."

Buddy Boy? What the hell happened to Tiger? Clyde Fenton in accounting is Buddy Boy. I don't like the sound of this.

"We need proof. Photos, witness statements, best yet, the girl herself. Right now, all I got is your word, which is buying me a big pile of nothin' upstairs. I need more."

Dennis is staring at me. I can see his scalp where he missed a spot with his comb-over this morning.

"I think we've already talked about how important this is," Dennis continues. "I want you to verify what you've gathered so far and then get more on top of that. You have until Monday."

"That's not enough time," I blurt out. Actually it's only Thursday, under normal circumstances, a couple days plus the weekend would be plenty of time. But I have a few other irons in the fire right now.

Dennis leans on my desk, but this time it's not his normal friendly slouch, it's a two-handed forward bend over that places his face uncomfortably close to mine.

"I'm worried about you, Charlie. You don't seem yourself. You look like crap. I understand about the car accident and all, but is there something else going on I should know about?"

I roll back in my chair. What if I spilled the whole truth? It would feel so good to tell someone what's really happening. But Dennis? On the One-To-Ten Acquaintance Scale, Dennis rates about a two point five, which is better than just about everyone else, but is lame nonetheless.

"I'm sorry," I say. "I'm just a little frustrated about how tough this case has been. Klein is good, really good."

Dennis stands up again and crosses his arms.

"We knew that going in. It's why I put you on the case. We can't lose this one, Buddy Boy."

Buddy Boy. There it is again.

"Don't let me down, because if I go down..."

"I know," I interrupt. "If you go down, I go down. No one's going down, Dennis. I can get you what you need by Monday. Just let me get to work."

"Morning," Dennis says, turning to leave. "Monday *morning.*"

Well isn't this a slice of sunshine? Since I'm not really an investigative journalist or a published author, something tells me I better try to hold on to my real job. I'm going to have to call Lily with some sort of excuse why I can't see her for the next couple of days. She does know about my car accident. I got a lot of sympathy for that one, especially with the black eye and three stitches. I look like I got the shit beat out of me. All things being equal, I probably deserve to get the shit beat out of me. Perhaps I can whip up a little residual ailment.

Lily answers her cell phone on the first ring.

"Lily Rudolph."

I pinch my nostrils closed with a thumb and forefinger and lower my voice.

"Lily, it's Albert."

"You sound awful. What's wrong?"

"Woke up this morning with a head full of snot and I can hardly swallow. I must have caught a cold walking back from the accident the other night. Or maybe at the Urgent Care where they did my forehead. Those places are germ factories."

"Oh no! Is there anything I can do? Do you want me to bring you over some soup or something?"

I savor this image awhile before replying. I'm lying in bed propped up with plush pillows. Satin pillows. Lily crosses the room toward the bed carrying a steaming bowl of soup. She's wearing a red gingham apron. That's all, just an apron.

"Albert? Are you still there?"

"Huh? Sorry. I had to get a Kleenex."

"Do you need anything?"

"No. I'll be okay. I think I just need to rest. Besides, I wouldn't want you to catch this thing. Can we take a day or two off, make sure I'm not contagious?"

"Of course. Just get better. But you have to promise to call if you need anything."

"I promise."

I hang up and stare at the stack of folders on my desk. I have a craving for soup, but first things first. I flip open the top folder. Inside is a report detailing all the people we tracked down from the doughnut shop. I'd posted a sign on the cash register offering $50 to interview anyone who had been at the shop around the time of Mr. Klein's alleged tumble. It generated quite a few calls, but very little information. I was beginning to suspect a link between high doughnut consumption and low test scores. Maybe I missed something the first time through.

Most people go through life reflecting on how well everything fits together. To them, one thing leads logically to the next. I'm always looking for the anomalous, the mismatched sock. I've been thinking about what Roger Jones said. How there was something about Michael Rudolph's accident that bothered him. Something that didn't fit together.

The first interview in the folder is an inane conversation about whether adding glaze to a traditionally plain doughnut was a baking breakthrough or a travesty. The next several transcriptions aren't much better. Then we get to Marilyn Andre. Marilyn says she was seated at a table right by the door on the day in question. She actually uses the phrase, "day in question." Must be watching too many Perry Mason reruns. She claims to have seen Mr. Klein exit the shop. She saw him stop at a table opposite hers and pick up half a dozen containers of extra frosting. I read her transcription again.

"When you buy one of their cinnamon rolls, they give you extra cups of the cream cheese frosting if you want. You know what I mean. Those little plastic cups with the lids. You can have as many as you want. They keep them right there on the counter and you can just grab 'em. Personally, I think they put on plenty of frosting as it is, so I never take extra, but some people take a bunch. Anyway, these teenagers had been in earlier and they each took about four or five of those little cups. Of course they didn't use 'em all. It'd send you right into diabetic shock. So they left them behind on the table. And this guy walks by on his way out. This guy you're asking about. He walks by their table, stops, looks down at all those little cups of frosting and he takes them. Every single one. Drops 'em into his coat pocket. I thought it was kind of weird. Like picking up someone else's garbage. And he was dressed nice too. Trench coat, slacks, loafers. But then I thought, what the hey, they're just gonna throw them away anyway. Who cares?"

Thank you, Marilyn. This might be a piece of the puzzle. I'm willing to bet that cream cheese frosting, applied liberally to the bottoms of one's shoes, could compromise traction. I have a nice pair of Kenneth Cole's back at the condo. I'll just stop on the way home and pick up a can of frosting. Mr. Science in action.

Standing in line at Kroger's, I feel a little odd purchasing a single can of Duncan Hines Creamy Home-Style butter cream frosting. They didn't have cream cheese. The checker simply scans it and drops it into a bag without a second glance. I imagine she's seen just about everything come down that conveyor belt. I don't think she passes judgment or questions your choice of

Extreme Fudge Avalanche ice cream over a nice head of lettuce and some Tofurky.

My new plan is to gloss over the whole girlfriend thing with Dennis. I'll blame it on bad sources and take the hit for not verifying the information. Cut my losses and move on. If my frosting experiment turns out as expected, the next step will be to get a hold of Klein's shoes. Even if he wiped them off, there should be some residue in the stitching. I haven't figured out how I'm going to talk someone out of his shoes, especially if they're still on his feet, but I'll come up with something. I always do.

I think it's unfair how artists and writers and musicians get all the credit for being creative. As if the rest of us would be hard pressed to make our way through a coloring book let alone produce a work of inspiration. I consider my work to be very creative. It takes imagination to come up with a story that can convince a claimant I'm on his side. There's more than a little ingenuity in my ability to ask one question and get three answers. And it takes originality to tackle a challenge from a new angle. No one's going to present my work in a gallery at MoMA, but a clever solution to a tough problem is as elegant as any sculpture.

It's good to be back in the saddle again. To mix my metaphors and species, I've felt like a fish out of water pretending to be Albert: the writer, the consummate professional, the nice guy. It's wearing me out. If I can catch Klein, it'll be like the good old days. Another rock crawler uncovered and left to squirm in the sun. Dennis will be happy. He'll stop calling me Buddy Boy and leave me alone for a while. There'll be a lot of backslapping around the office. Another success for Charlie Sandors.

Because that's who I am, I'm Charlie Sandors. I'm good at what I do.

It's not completely dark when I get back to the condo with my frosting. The days are getting longer. I set the grocery sack on the counter and punch a few keys to retrieve my phone messages.

"Hi Albert, it's Lily."

You've reached Charlie, Lily, go ahead.

"You must be trying to sleep. I just wanted to check up on you and see if you're feeling any better. Give me a call later if you want a rain check on that soup offer. Bye."

I'm not sleeping, Lily. I was never sleeping. I'm wide awake and I'm playing you for a fool. Can't you see that? It won't be long before you find out exactly how big a jerk I am. I think they put lying to grieving widows right up there next to stealing candy from babies. For an encore, maybe I could kick a puppy then push an old lady down and take her purse. Why won't you stop being nice to me? I'm going to hurt you.

Beep.

"Albert, Howard Stanich here."

Howard?

"Heard you were in some sort of accident. Hope everything's okay. I wanted to follow-up on your meeting with Roger Jones. Call when you can."

Beep.

How does he know I was in an accident? He must have talked to Lily. Either that or he's watching me more closely than I thought.

Another dial tone and a beep, then nothing.

I look at the sack on the counter. Suddenly, I don't feel much like conducting my experiment. I don't feel much like Charlie. I slump down on the couch. Albert's couch. No, Lily's couch that she's letting Albert borrow.

There was another girl once. Before the funerals. Before the milk of human kindness passed its pull date. Before cynicism lodged under my fingernails. Her name was Sarah. Hell, it probably still is Sarah. We'd been thrown together in a required college English class. Her, an English major; me, hauling myself through the Business Department. She wore her long brown hair piled on her head, held in place with one, gigantic silver clip. Sarah's eyes were blue some days, green on others. We made small talk about small talk, wondering why people should have to force themselves to be interested in the weather or your new haircut or pretend people living pretend lives on a television sitcom. We laughed. One day we skipped class and drank gallons of coffee and watched a bad movie in the middle of the afternoon. Another day, her boyfriend came back to town and she introduced me as "her good friend, Charlie." The boyfriend shook my hand, hard. Sarah smiled at me. Her eyes were blue that day.

This is all getting so messy. Somewhere along the way, I started to care about Lily, worry about what happened to Michael, even fret over what might happen to Howard if his investors finally get the better of him. Normal people call this empathy. It's not an emotion I've ever traded in, but Albert seems chockfull of it. I've made too many promises to too many people on both sides of my dual life. The teeter-totter isn't going to stay in balance forever. Soon, something tells me very soon, one end is going to slam down and the other end is going to fly up and smack me in the balls.

I get up and walk to the window. Outside the residual winter daylight is disappearing. But it's not raining. Maybe a walk in the fresh air would clear my head. I can see the lake from here. Yes, a stroll around the lake would be good.

Blue Lake, although adorned with a completely uninspired name, is considered to be one of Park Hills' greatest assets. A paved path loops all the way around, nearly two miles worth. Various civic organizations have renovated flower gardens, rolling lawns and little beach areas. I've ended up here with a funeral fling or two. Very romantic, in a communing-with-nature kind of way.

My route takes off from the parking lot and through a dense stand of pines. As dusk descends into full-fledged darkness, I'm grateful for the little garden lights lining the path's edge every few feet. In the spring and summer, the lake is crawling with people right up until the gates close at midnight. But tonight, I haven't seen a soul. Probably too cold, and I imagine the rain will start up again before I make it back around. When I breathe in, I catch a watery tang in the air. I've always liked that smell. The rich, musky aroma makes everything seem satiated and healthy. I breathe in deeper. Alone in the dark, the smell is soothing.

For the first time in weeks, I felt good about work today. I forgot about Lily and Michael and Nesler Pharmaceuticals. But only for a little while, and I know a hundred breakthroughs on a hundred cases won't be enough to push them out of my head for good. I keep walking, slowly circling back to where I started.

Directly up ahead are the horseshoe courts. Tall stakes stand along one end like thin grave markers. Stone benches line the other end, empty at this hour of contestants waiting a turn to toss. Except they're not empty. Someone is sitting on one of the benches. From this distance, I can't make out much more than the slumped shape of a person. Could be a man, could be a woman. He or she is completely still. The surprise of seeing someone out here sends a jolt of adrenalin through me, but it's not fear. I'm curious to see what it is, who it is, and there's nothing menacing about the form. It's as if I'm approaching a statue.

"Hey there," I call out, stepping off the path and walking toward the figure. "Didn't think I'd see anyone else out here tonight."

No movement, not even a turn of the head.

"Are you okay?"

The light from along the path barely reaches us. I'm just a few yards away now and can tell the person on the bench is a man, an elderly man. He's wearing only a polo shirt and slacks, no coat or hat. He must be freezing. I hurry the last few feet across the wet sand of the courts.

"Sir, is everything okay? Are you hurt?"

The man finally shifts his position, tipping his head slightly to watch me jog toward him.

"Hello, Martin," he says as I reach him.

The man smiles at me. His face crinkles around the eyes. Then abruptly, his expression blanks.

"My name's not Martin, sir," I say, sitting down next to him on the bench. The concrete is cold and damp. The man's hands are clasped in his lap. "Are you waiting for someone?"

He looks down for a moment, then back up at me. His eyes roam across my face, searching. He looks away again.

"I'm cold," he says, loudly.

His pants are thin cotton, almost colorless in the dim light, and his shirt bears the embroidered crest of a local golf course. Looking down, I notice his bare feet are stuffed into ragged slippers. Hardly an appropriate outfit for the waning days of winter.

"Do you have a coat?" I ask.

He swings his head back around to stare at me.

"Martin!"

He's smiling at me again. Poor guy. He's obviously out of it. Probably wandered away from some facility.

"Yep, it's Martin," I say, joining his delusion. "Sorry I'm late."

"I'm cold!" he yells at me again.

I take off my down jacket and place it over his shoulders, gently guiding his arms into its warmth.

"I'm plenty warm. You take my coat."

It's much too big on his old man frame. He looks like a marshmallow on a stick.

"Let's head back, whatdya say?"

I stand up and hold out my arm to him. He looks up but doesn't get up.

"Where's the man?"

"He's ... uh ... he's waiting for us back at the car. He's gonna wonder what happened to us if we don't get back there pretty soon."

I move my arm closer and he grabs it with both hands. The puffy sleeves squish together as he pulls himself up.

"He knows what you did."

The poor old guy looks really worried. Worried little marshmallow.

"It's okay," I assure him, walking straight out across the grass, avoiding the mushy sand of the horseshoe courts.

We're quiet as I help him onto the path and we head back toward the parking lot. He's still holding on to my arm, but his gait is smooth and sure. Not bad for slippers. His head, which only comes up to about the top of my shoulder, is covered with thick, white hair that's been neatly trimmed. I try to remember if there are any retirement homes nearby. I imagine someone somewhere is frantic to find him.

"Martin?" he shouts suddenly, dropping my arm.

"What?" I reply, figuring it's best to continue being Martin until I can get the guy back where he belongs.

"You shouldn't have done it."

"Why not?"

"It's wrong. Everyone knows it's wrong."

"Well, then, I'm sorry."

He starts walking.

"She was only doing what she thought was best," he says.

The lights of the parking lot come into view. He doesn't speak again. We're heading across the empty lot when an old Volvo station wagon pulls in. It hugs the far sidewalk and then spots us. The headlights flash and it turns and rushes directly at us. I pull the old man behind me as the car brakes right in front of us. The driver throws open the door and leaps out. It's a woman, maybe forty or forty-five. Her long black hair is pulled into a haphazard bun and she's wearing wire-rim glasses. She looks like she's been crying. The old man turns away, as if the commotion is too much for him. The woman bolts around the front of the car.

"Dad!" she screams, running up and grabbing her father's hands in hers.

He looks confused and doesn't respond.

"Dad, it's Mary."

He turns away. The woman looks at me.

"Who are you? Where did you find him?"

I'm so stunned by the turn of events I can't answer for a moment. I'm also temporarily unsure whether to respond as Charlie or Albert. I punt.

"I was just out for a walk. He was sitting on the bench over by the horseshoe courts."

She doesn't answer. She simply pulls the man toward the Volvo. He follows obediently, and she settles him into the passenger's seat, carefully helping him out of the huge coat.

"Is this yours?" she asks, handing me back my parka.

"Yeah. He was really cold when I found him. Has he been gone a long time?"

The woman glances over her shoulder to check on her father in the car, and then turns back to me. In the stark glare from the parking lot lights, I can see the lines grooved into her forehead and around her eyes. She's too young for her face.

"He's been gone for about a year."

FOURTEEN

The woman named Mary stands with me in the parking lot. Her story tumbles out. I've seen it before when interviewing accident victims. The relief of coming through a stressful situation triggers a torrent of information, as if the person had not only been holding his breath in panic, but also his words. The ultimate exhalation is impressive.

"I'm not quite sure what happened," she says. "I had some people over. I don't usually have people over to the house, but they're old friends and they know about Dad. He'd finished dinner and I'd gotten him set up to watch his favorite TV shows. Everything was fine. He wasn't agitated. He seemed fine. After everyone left, I went back to check on him and he was gone. Just gone. His bed was still made. The light on his nightstand was on. The TV was on. We were all in the living room so I'm guessing he went out through the kitchen. There was music playing. We were laughing and talking. We were actually having a good time. I haven't had a good time in so long."

She pauses. To catch her breath maybe? She looks at me again. Really looks at me this time, and now I see embarrassment in her face. Embarrassment and maybe a little fear. Who the hell am I? To whom, exactly, is she pouring out her soul?

"It's okay," I say. "I'm just glad he's safe. Do you need any help?"

"No, thank you. Thank you for being so kind to him."

"Why did you come *here* looking for him?"

"He loves the lake. We come here almost every day, doesn't matter what the weather is. It seems to make him happy just to see it."

Of course it does. Most people think they love nature because of its beauty, and it is beautiful. The trees and water and all that are nice. Sometimes, like in the case of the Grand Canyon or the white sand beaches of Siesta Key, really, *really* nice. But what they actually love is how nature is so accepting, so nonjudgmental. You can just be yourself in nature. A tree doesn't care what kind of job you have. The flowers don't mind if you've put on a few pounds. The lake could give a rip whether or not you can remember its name—or your name. You look at nature, nature looks back at you and everybody's happy.

"I know what he means. I came down here myself tonight to clear my head. It's nice to just enjoy the quiet and the smell."

"The smell?" She looks at me quizzically.

"The water. I think the smell of the water is calming."

I take several deep breaths to show her I'm not crazy, and then realize huffing and puffing out here in the dark must look ridiculous ... and crazy.

"I guess I've never noticed the smell." She sniffs the air, probably to humor me, and smiles. When she does, I see a resemblance to the old man.

"What's wrong with him, if you don't mind me asking?"

"Alzheimer's mostly."

"Mostly?"

"There are other things. Physical things. But he's not so bad I can't still take care of him. At least I thought so until tonight. He's never done anything like this before."

It hits me then, like a baseball bat to the head. Alzheimer's patient, local guy, the right age. It couldn't be.

"Is your father part of the Nesler drug trials, the Alzheimer's drug trials?"

The woman named Mary steps backwards. She's wearing wooden soled clogs that make a *clop-clop* sound on the cement.

"Why would you ask that?" she says, her voice quiet and small. "Do you work for Nesler?"

"No. No I don't."

I'm trying not to make her nervous, yet I hear the timbre of my voice rise in both pitch and intensity. I can't believe my luck. I take a step towards her. If it weren't for those damn clogs, she'd probably take off at a dead run. But that would leave her father trapped in the parking lot with the crazy guy. She stands her ground, glances back toward her father and crosses her arms over her chest. She's wearing a brown wool coat missing two of its four buttons.

I feel gears clunking back into position. After scrapping and clawing my way into what so far has amounted to very little information, God just dropped an angel into my lap to answer a few questions, a bolt from the blue. Did you know that's a real scientific thing, not just an overused cliché? They also call it "dry lightning." Most lightning bolts carry a negative charge, but dry lightning holds a positive charge, which gives it about ten times the current. And, instead of coming straight down from inside the rain shaft of a typical thunderstorm, a bolt from the blue travels horizontally, away from the storm, sometimes several miles away. Sometimes it travels into an area with beautiful blue, sunny skies before it curves to the ground and takes out a golfer. In the insurance industry, we call that "an act of God."

I smile at Mary to try to put her at ease, but I'm so excited, the grin probably makes me look slightly demonic. Layered on top of the water-smell comment, the heavy breathing and the shouting, I'm well on my way to lunatic. I push all the air out of my lungs in one slow, continuous breath and force my voice down to a whisper.

"My name is Albert Mackey. I'm writing a biography of Michael Rudolph and I've been researching his involvement with Nesler and the drug trials. This is an incredible stroke of luck. I've been begging Nesler for information about the test participants, but I can't seem to get anything out of them."

Mary takes another step backwards. *Clop. Clop.*

"My dad was involved in the trials." She's whispering now too. "But he's not anymore."

Yep, I'm totally freaking her out. I stick my hands in my pants pockets and rock back on my heels, trying to relax my stance. Casual. Just a regular guy in an empty parking lot, asking a stranger personal questions about her family. Nonchalant.

"Was he one of the original participants?"

"Yes," she answers, still whispering, still staring at me. Deer in the headlights. She looks back again at her father. "I don't think this is something we should be talking about. I don't know you and you don't know me. We should really be going anyway. My dad's exhausted."

She turns and starts back toward the car.

"Please don't go, Mary."

She spins back around, fear flashing across her face.

"How do you know my name?"

"You said it when you ran up. You said, 'Dad, it's Mary.'"

"Oh," she sighs, looking down and twiddling one of the two remaining buttons on her coat. She is not particularly attractive. Her wire-rim glasses are thick and keep sliding down her nose, which is beginning to turn pink in the cold air. There's a cleft in her chin. She probably doesn't know this was formed when she was still in her mother's womb, when the left and right halves of her jaw bone didn't fuse properly. It's a birth defect, but people call it a dimple.

I try smiling again, without the undertones of mental illness.

"Albert Mackey," I introduce myself for the second time and offer my hand.

She looks up at me, back at her father, me, and finally takes my hand.

"Mary Anderson," she says. "And that's my father, Jake Tucker."

The first spattering of returning rain hits us. I can see the splash marks on her glasses.

"I can't help you, Albert. You seem like a very nice man, but my dad is really quite ill. I can't afford to jeopardize his medical coverage. I'm sure the people at Nesler will find you someone else to talk with. Besides, Dad wasn't one of their success stories."

I like Mary. She seems very normal, very sweet. It's my fault she's anxious, not to mention damp and cold. I'm not very sweet and certainly not very normal.

"How could talking with me possibly jeopardize your father's medical coverage?"

"It's confidential. We signed papers saying it would be confidential. If I break that promise, they'll stop paying. I don't make enough to cover it all myself."

"Who will stop paying?"

"Nesler. They pay for all Dad's medical bills, but only if everything stays confidential."

"If what stays confidential?"

She huffs at me, like an exasperated parent explaining for the fifth time that I cannot have a cookie.

"His problems. His medical problems. The drug wasn't successful on him. He didn't improve the way the others did. In fact, I think it made him worse. My father is dying."

We stand in the parking lot. Mary Anderson and me. Big, fat drops of rain are coming down now. Jake Tucker is beginning to fidget in the front seat of the Volvo. I can't think fast enough to sort everything into the proper category. Mary is scared of something. Scared of her father dying, scared of Nesler Pharmaceuticals, scared of me. Maybe all three. There's something very important here in the wet parking lot. Something I can't let go.

"I need to know more about this."

"I can't. I just told you that."

"No one will know. I won't tell anyone."

"You're writing a book!" She is shouting now. Shouting and walking backwards to her car. "No. Don't you understand? No!"

Her hand is on the door handle. She pulls open the door and the dome light illuminates her father. He is staring out the side window. Even with everything happening on the other side of the windshield, Jake Tucker is looking in the opposite direction.

"Who's Martin?" I shout before she can pull the door closed.

Through the prism of collecting raindrops on the windshield, I catch only a distorted glimpse of Mary Anderson's face. The door swings back open and she steps out. I have her attention. That's pretty obvious. But, I can't tell if she's angry or afraid.

"Your father kept calling me Martin. Who's Martin?"

Her features relax slightly and she slowly pushes the car door closed and comes back over to me. The rain is falling harder now, cats and dogs will be next, but Mary doesn't seem to mind, but her glasses are speckled with drops and it must be hard to see me.

"His best friend. Martin was his best friend," she whispers and then checks back over her shoulder, even though there's no way Jake Tucker can hear us from inside the Volvo. "They met during the initial testing phase at Nesler. Hit it off right away. They went golfing and bowling together. Watched games on the weekends. And, they came over here to the Lake a lot to play horseshoes with, as Martin called them, 'the other old geezers.' They were real good friends."

"Were? Did something happen?"

Mary glances back again. Jake is watching us now through the side window, but with an expression of complete disinterest, as if we are a particularly boring exhibit at the zoo: chatting humans in their natural habitat.

"Martin lived with his wife in one of those big retirement communities. I don't think they had any local family. He was doing really well on the drug therapy. They were planning on moving back into their own house, but before that happened, his wife died. Stroke or heart attack or something. I never did get the whole story. So, Martin decides to move out west to live with his son. He'd call Dad every once in a while, but their mental states were so different by then, I think Martin started getting a little perturbed trying to carry on a conversation. Anyway, the calls started getting fewer and farther between. I didn't know what Dad thought about it or even if he noticed. But you said he called you Martin? I guess there's some memory bouncing around in there."

I nod. Mary looks up at me. Her dark hair is cut into choppy bangs in the front, which are beginning to paste to her forehead with the weight of the rain. She smiles Jake's smile again and there is a kindness in her eyes that makes me smile back.

"Once Dad's own problems started to crash down, I forgot all about Martin. We hadn't heard from him in so long and it didn't occur to me to try to contact him. The months flew by. Dad got a little worse every day. Then, I don't know, maybe a couple weeks ago, I was looking for a roll of tape in the junk drawer and came across a picture of the two of them at the horseshoe courts. I must have made a copy for Martin at one time and then thrown it in the drawer and forgot to give it to him. Do you ever do stuff like that?"

She stops and pulls her coat tighter. I feel a little guilty that Mary Anderson is standing out here in the cold rain, but it does make a fitting backdrop for her story.

"Everyone does stuff like that," I say.

"I guess so," she continues. "I thought if I could get a hold of Martin it might be something for Dad to look forward to. I showed him the picture and asked him if he'd like to talk to Martin. I remember him looking at it for a really long time. I didn't see any recognition on his face. He finally gave it back to me and said, 'Okay.' That's all. Then he went back to the movie he was watching. It wasn't what I had hoped for, but it was better than, 'I don't know.' So I called him."

"How long ago did you say it was?" I ask.

"A few weeks. But here's the thing, I couldn't get a hold of him. I tried directory assistance. Nothing. I knew he was in California, but I couldn't quite remember the city. You can't give them a whole state to search through, especially a state as big as California. There are about a million cities in California that start with either 'Los' or 'San.'"

Mary takes off her glasses and attempts to wipe them dry on her coat. It just pushes the water around but she puts them back on anyway and squints at me through the smudgy lenses.

"I tried to let the whole thing drop, but something about the photo must have stuck with Dad, because he started asking me about Martin all the time. We'd be sitting at dinner or watching TV and he'd ask me when Martin was coming. It was like one point of light he could focus on and remember, even when everything else was dark. I finally called Nesler, but they pulled out their trusty confidentiality banner and refused to give me any information."

"Does he still ask about him?"

"Not as often, but yes, he does. I feel awful about it, but I don't know how I can tell him so he'll understand."

Suddenly, the horn on the Volvo blares. Mary Anderson and I jump and turn in unison. Jake Tucker is leaning over in the seat. The horn blares again, a long sustained note in a very uncomfortable pitch.

"Dad!" Mary shouts. "Stop that!"

Three more honks, these in quick succession.

She runs over to the car and yanks open the door. I see her lift her father's hand from the steering wheel and gently push him back over to his side of the car.

"I want to go!" Jake yells at her. "I'm hungry."

"Don't honk the horn." Mary's voice is calm but firm. "We're leaving in one minute. I promise. But we won't leave if you keep honking the horn."

"I want to go."

"One minute," she promises again, holding up her index finger.

Mary straightens and looks at me over the top of the car door. The bun at the back of her head is unraveling. She pushes her glasses back up her nose.

"That's all I can tell you, Albert. I'm sorry and I hope you understand. Good luck with the book."

She ducks back into the car and starts the engine before I can protest. Her headlights flash on and I have to turn my head to avoid the glare. When I turn back she's backing up and turning to head out of the parking lot. All that information, just driving away. Luck has swooped down, poked me with a stick and flown away.

I make a mental note of her license plate number.

FIFTEEN

"I'm sure it does sound unusual, Mr. Klein. And if I were in your shoes, no pun intended, I'd probably be wondering the same thing."

I have Hugh Klein on the phone. It's late evening but not too late for a little telemarketing. I'm calling from the condo in case Klein has caller ID. This is an incredible long shot, but the frosting test with my loafers was successful. Coating the sole didn't make the shoe banana-peel slippery, but it was definitely slick enough to fake a convincing slide. Klein has likely already mastered a Hollywood drop: lots of noise, arms flailing, no attempt to break the fall, exaggerated moaning once down. The experiment also left quite a frosting slick on my floor, which it probably would have done on the sidewalk near Klein. But I'm betting nobody noticed it in all the commotion, and the rain that day would have washed away any evidence within minutes. I figure I better try to follow through on my idea while it's fresh. Besides, it keeps me from thinking about Mary Anderson and her father.

"I really don't have time right now," says Klein, trying to gracefully back out of our conversation. I'm actually amazed how polite he is. "And, anyway, I don't think I'd be interested in your offer."

"I guarantee you'll love it, sir. I absolutely guarantee it. There's no risk and I'll come to your home or business to pick up and deliver your shoes. It's a new idea and I'm just getting started with it, but it's really catching on with the business folks like yourself."

"I don't even know if I own four pairs of dress shoes."

He's thinking about it. The door is open a crack and I'm about to shove my polished toe inside.

"A successful man like you?" I say, clucking my tongue in disbelief. "I bet if you look in your closet, you'll be surprised. There are probably shoes in there you don't wear simply because they look dull and scuffed. We can take care of that. Four for the price of two with 24-hour turnaround. Can I put you down on the schedule for tomorrow?"

"You know, what the hell. Nothing else in my life is going good right now. I may as well have shiny shoes. Put me down."

Bingo. Even I am impressed by this charade.

"You won't be sorry, Mr. Klein. I'm looking forward to a long and happy relationship between you and Shoe Fly Mobile Shoe Shine Service. Where would you like us to pick up your shoes?"

"Come by the house tomorrow morning. I'll leave them in a bag on the front steps."

"Your address?"

"3436 Autumn Ridge Drive."

"Thank you again, sir. Simply write your name and address on the bag and we'll take it from there. Your bill will be attached with your cleaned shoes. Don't hesitate to call the number on the tag if you are dissatisfied in any way, but I know you won't be. I know that, sir."

"Whatever you say, son. Good luck to you."

We hang up.

Shoe Fly Mobile Shoe Shine Service! I should get some sort of medal for this one. By making him gather up four pairs of shoes, I'm sure to get the shoes he was wearing the day of the incident. These days, who owns that many pairs of leather dress shoes? Everyone's all about business casual. It's a gamble, but I'm feeling pretty good about it. Twenty-four hours should be long enough to photograph the shoes and have the lab pull out any residue. I guess I'm going to have to actually clean them too so he doesn't get suspicious. Too bad a business like this doesn't really exist. I could use them.

It's nearly 10:00 already; time to call Dennis at home and let him know things are looking up on the Klein case. He sounds a little groggy when he picks up. Or drunk.

"Dennis it's me, Charlie."

"Goddamn, Sandors. Do you know it's 10:00?"

"Sorry; after this morning, I thought you'd want to know right away that I've caught a break on the Klein case, and I .."

"What've ya got?" he asks, interrupting my explanation. His words slur together; I'm going down on the side of drunk over groggy.

"I've still got some work to do, but I think I found a little something Klein overlooked in his set-up. Like I said Dennis, he's good, he's very good, but I'm better."

"You're killin' me. What did you figure out?"

"I'm not gonna say until it's a lock, but I should know by tomorrow. I just wanted to call and let you know I won't fall through. You seemed kind of on edge this morning."

"Ah, yeah, sorry 'bout that," he says. His voice is thick and I can tell he's working to form every syllable. "The guys upstairs are chewing my ass on this one, and you know which way the shit rolls when it starts moving."

I picture Dennis in his recliner at home, wearing boxers and a t-shirt, his comb-over still molded to the contour of his head, phone in one hand, highball in the other.

"It's okay, Dennis," I say, comforting him. You gotta love the guy, he's just so predictable. "But, to pull it off, I need to make one stop in the morning. So, I'll be in late and then downstairs in the lab most of the day. Maybe this would be a good day to go golfing."

This makes him laugh and we go back and forth for a while with golf jokes. Since this call is designed to pull Dennis off my back for awhile, I'm waiting for him to end the conversation. That's another free interview tip for you: to instill a sense of control and confidence, let the other person feel in charge; keep talking, keep the dialogue rolling, let him make the move to close.

"Well, Charlie," There it is. Curtain's coming down. "I'm sure you have a big day tomorrow, I better let you get some sleep. Go get 'em, Tiger."

Buddy Boy is gone, Tiger is back. Things *are* looking up. On the flip side, all of this also means another twenty-four hours away from Lily. Maybe I should call her and check in. She still thinks I'm deathly ill.

I dial the house phone and it rings five times. I'm getting ready to hang up when Lily answers.

"Hello?"

She sounds breathless.

"Lily, it's me. Did I wake you up?" I ask.

"Albert! I'm so glad you called."

"I'm sorry it's so late."

"It's late? What time is it?"

"Closing in on 11:00. Are you okay?"

"I'm fine. I've been working. Hey, you sound a lot better."

"Uh, yeah, Sudafed."

Crap, I forgot the stuffed up nose voice. I gotta stop embellishing my characters or I'm going to need a database to keep track of everyone and their idiosyncrasies.

"What do you mean—*working*?" I ask.

"I figured it out."

She's almost shouting now.

"Figured *what* out?"

"How to get into Michael's calendar. I figured out the password."

"You're kidding me? What was it?"

"Lilybette."

"What?"

"Lilybette. It was his pet name for me. I found it on a card taped to the inside of the desk drawer. At first I just thought it was cute. That he had my name written on his desk, like it was the next best thing to carving a heart into the top. But then I noticed there were other things written on the card. One was N4816T. That's our plane's tail number and I know Michael used the middle numbers as his ATM password. Below that was the word ALVIN. That's my old dog's name, and it's also the code I came up with for the security company. If the alarm goes off, they call here first and you have to know the code word is ALVIN to stop an automatic dispatch. There were some other ones too that didn't make any sense at all."

I was lost somewhere back at the beginning. At the Lilybette part. I found it endearing and excruciating in equal parts. The rest of the information spilling from the other end of the phone wasn't quite registering.

"That's when I figured they must *all* be passwords," Lily continues, her voice rising in pitch with each sentence. "Even Lilybette. So, I tried it in Outlook and it worked. It worked! It opened. You have to come over."

"Now?"

I can barely jam a word in. I've never heard her like this. I think we just got a major break. That or Lily has lost her marbles and gone a little heavy on the caffeine.

"Can you? I think this is important. I'm seeing the basic calendar and when I click on a date square it opens another thingy. I don't recognize any of the names. But maybe if we can figure out who they are, they can answer some of our questions about Michael's research."

"Lily, can you slow down for a minute?"

"I'm sorry. I just can't believe I figured it out. Me! Computer-illiterate me!"

"So exactly what are you seeing. What *thingy*?"

"I can't explain it very well. It's like an appointment card with a bunch of places to put information, but all the information's not there and I think some of it's in code or something."

"Is it a database?"

"I don't know. You have to come see it. Can you come see it?"

"Alright. If I promise to come over, will you stop, take a deep breath and calm down?"

"Sure! Come right now."

The phone goes dead. I stare at it in my hand. That was surreal. I'm pretty sure I called in the first place to tell Lily I wouldn't be able to see her for a couple days. Instead, now I'm supposed to drive over to her house at almost midnight. I'm just a stick in the water, bobbing along in the current; merrily, merrily, merrily, life is but a dream. Unless a beaver finds me and uses me to build a damn.

I grab a coat and head out the door, locking it behind me. As the deadbolt clicks into place, there's a sudden reflection of headlights in the living room window. I glance over my shoulder in time to watch a black BMW pull away from the curb across the street. Pretty fancy rig for this neighborhood.

Traffic is light and the drive across town to Lily's only takes about thirty minutes. The house is dark and still, but I see a glow coming from the windows of Michael's study. I remember the first time I came here, ready to cancel the farce and move on. Was it weeks ago or years ago? What exactly was it that stopped me from stopping the madness? Pity, vanity, curiosity, lust? If you create your own world and choose the folks you want to inhabit it, then, as the puppeteer, you also should be able to dictate the interactions and craft a happy ending. Somewhere along the way I'd lost control. My characters are forging ahead of their own accord. If they are real and this whole mess is really happening, then Albert must be real. If A equals B and B equals C, then A equals C. I've always wondered what happens to B in that equation. Is it some kind of algebraic exile? Apparently, nobody wants to play with B anymore. Charlie's in danger of being ditched.

I ring the doorbell and it echoes deep within the giant house. The drizzle from earlier in the evening has continued with cold stubbornness. The stone steps are like slabs of ice, chilling me from the feet up. Time churns to a halt as I wait for Lily to answer the door. Footsteps. The creak of a massive hinge. And then, here she is. Cue the violins, here she is.

"That was fast," she says.

"You said right away."

Lily's wearing a Northwestern University sweatshirt over jeans and her hair is smoothed back with a red cloth headband. She smiles and opens the door wider for me to pass. The entryway is dark, but Lily doesn't seem to notice. She closes the door, grabs my arm and hurries back toward Michael's study with me in tow. She doesn't have any shoes on.

"I still can't believe I figured this out. Aren't you impressed?"

"Completely."

"But now I'm stuck again. It's like those Russian dolls that come apart. You open one and there's another one inside of it to open."

"You got this far, we ought to be able to figure it out from here."

Her hand slides down my arm and she takes my hand in hers. Her skin is cool and soft. I feel her wedding ring slide across my palm. She pulls me into the room and over to the desk, finally releasing her grasp with a flourish, launching me into the chair in front of the computer monitor.

"Look."

I look at the monitor. There's a standard Outlook appointment window on the screen.

"I've been opening up each date that had an appointment time listed and the same box thingy comes up on each one," Lily says from over my shoulder. "Close that one and try it for yourself."

I follow her directions and close the window. Behind it is the main calendar. I slide the cursor to a date, December 3rd, and click. A new window pops up with the name *Clyde McDonald.* The date and time are listed but no location. There's also a hyperlink in the notes section.

"You're right," I say, staring at the flickering screen. "There are a few more dolls we need to open up. What happens when you click on this link?"

"What link?"

"This one."

I move the cursor to the link *s:\research\ clydemcdonald.txt.* When I click, an error message comes up telling me, *The folder or file could not be opened. Path does not exist. Make sure path is correct.*

Lily sighs. I feel her breath hit the back of my neck, hot and smelling slightly of cinnamon. "Do you know what that means?"

"I'm not sure." I click okay and the message disappears. "Have you found any names you recognize?"

"Nope. Not a one. I've been writing them down on a piece of paper."

She steps around my chair and shuffles through some loose papers on the desk, pulling out a piece of yellow notebook paper. She hands it to me. There are twelve names written in her loopy cursive.

"Eight men and four women," she says. "About the only thing I can come up with is I think they're older, at least judging by the women's names."

I glance at the paper. The first name is Myrtle Olcott. Lily's right. I doubt we've produced any new Myrtles since about 1910. There are dozens of perfectly good names no one uses anymore: Edna, Roberta, Edith, and my favorite: Thelma. On the other hand, we can probably afford to cut back on the Brittanys, Sarahs and Katies.

I continue to scan down the list, screeching to a halt at name number 11, Jake Tucker. My throat goes dry and a single gasp escapes.

"What?" Lily asks, leaning back in to see the names on the paper.

"I know this guy."

"What guy?"

"This one," I say, pointing at the paper. "Jake Tucker. I just met him earlier tonight."

"What do you mean you met him?"

"At Blue Lake."

"Blue Lake? You're sick; what were you doing at the Lake?"

"I thought a walk would help clear my head, so I went down to the lake."

"You're going to get pneumonia. What was this guy doing at the Lake?"

"He was lost. I helped him get back to the parking lot and then his daughter showed up to get him."

"How old is this guy?"

"I don't know, 85, 88, somewhere in there. He'd wandered away from his daughter's house."

I see a light bulb, and then an entire chandelier flash on over Lily's head.

"Alzheimer's?" she asks, looking at me in amazement. "He's one of them, isn't he? He's an original test participant, isn't he?"

"Yes."

"Then that must be it," she shouts, grabbing the paper out of my hand. "That's who these people are. They're original test participants. Michael was meeting with them one by one."

"Maybe," I say, although this is exactly the same thing I am thinking. "I don't know any of the other names. It could just be a coincidence."

Lily drops the paper and stares at me.

"What else could it be, Albert?" she asks, very slowly, as if I have lost my ability to reason.

"I don't know."

I lean back in the chair and close my eyes. I see Jake Tucker sitting in the Volvo, staring out through the rain splattered windshield. I see Mary Anderson's eyes pleading for understanding.

"Why are you being so weird about this?" Lily asks. "We just figured out Michael spent a huge amount of time during the last few months of his life interviewing the original test participants. He was looking for something. Don't you want to know what he was looking for?"

I open my eyes. Lily is standing over me, looking down; her eyes demand an answer. She is unusually close. Her hair falls forward creating a curtain around her face. Her breathing is a bit erratic with the excitement of our discovery. I want to reach up and touch her, rest my hand on her chest and feel it rise and fall. When I don't answer immediately, she snaps her head up and steps back, crossing her arms, camouflaging the movement of her chest.

"What is with you? This is a big deal!"

I rub my hands over my face and sit up again.

"Nothing's wrong," I say. "I know it's a big deal. I'm just trying to make sense of it all. I've had a rough night."

Lily sets the list of names back down on the desk. Her face is calm again. She probably figures since shouting isn't getting her anywhere, she'll try to talk me in off the ledge.

"Tell me about Jake Tucker," she says. Her voice is quiet, composed.

"He's dying," I answer, looking directly at her. "He has Alzheimer's and now he's dying."

She reaches up and pulls off the red headband, stretches it between her hands once, twice, three times, then loops it around one wrist.

"From the Alzheimer's?"

"I don't know. Complications. His daughter wouldn't tell me. Couldn't tell me. Said it would mean the cancellation of his medical coverage if she talked to me."

Lily crosses the room and looks out the window. She can't possibly see anything. It's too light inside and too dark outside. But still she looks.

"I couldn't get her to tell me very much," I continue. "He looked healthy enough, but that doesn't mean anything."

"Who?" Lily asks, not moving from the window, still staring into her own reflection. "Who would cancel his medical insurance?"

"Nesler. She said they were paying for all his medical bills but everything was confidential."

Lily finally turns back toward me, her hands at her hips. Her hair swirls around her shoulders. She's biting her bottom lip. If I wasn't already sitting down, my knees would buckle and topple me like two scoops of Jamoca Almond Fudge on a hot day. Wait, is she speaking again? Concentrate.

"Something's not right, Albert. Michael would never have spent so much time with all these people unless it was really important. My husband was altruistic and caring and forever curious, but he was also a perfectionist. He didn't like it when he couldn't understand something. He approached everything like a science experiment. Used to drive me crazy sometimes, but it almost always worked. He'd methodically go through all the options one at a time until he had an answer to his question. He didn't chase dead ends."

"You think he was trying to figure something out?" I'm struggling to stay in the moment but I still can't see straight. Now I'm imagining Lily eating ice cream, slowly, catching all the drips.

"I know it. I don't know what it was, but I know he was searching. Wasn't he like that in school?"

For an instant, the question throws me completely. Why would I know what he was like in school? And then, just as quickly, I remember I am supposed to be Michael's old college buddy.

"Focused is a good word. Pit bull would also be a good description."

This makes Lily smile, which I love, but she's not smiling at me, she's smiling at a memory of Michael, which I hate.

"Maybe we should get a hold of Howard and confirm these names," Lily suggests. "He might know what Michael was doing."

"I don't think so. I didn't know anything about it. I think Michael was doing this on his own."

"Why?"

"I asked Howard directly if Michael knew or had talked with the original test participants. He said Michael had maybe talked with a few, but definitely not all."

Lily tugs at the sleeve of her sweatshirt, as if she could pull out the answer like a magician's bouquet of flowers.

"Maybe these aren't all the people."

"You don't understand; the question didn't faze him. If Michael was doing such methodical interviews and Howard knew about it, he would have flinched. It would have been almost imperceptible, especially given Howard's demeanor, but believe me, I would have seen it."

"How can you be so sure?"

Poor Lily. You are so trusting, so lovely and so trusting. I'm sure because I know how *I'd* do it. Poor Lily. If you knew how much Charlie wanted to come out right now and grab you, kiss you, touch your hair, your face, every inch of your body. If you knew the turmoil right below the surface, you'd be impressed. You'd understand how I can be so sure. I know what it takes to pull one over, to throw in a pile of chips when all you're holding is a pair of threes. I know how because I've done it, because I'm doing it right now.

"I can tell when someone is *uncomfortable*," I explain. "Howard breezed through that question without the twitch of an eye. Call it journalist's intuition."

"I still think Howard's our best bet when it comes to unraveling all this," she insists. "Michael was working so closely with Nesler; I'm sure he would have let them know if he'd discovered something."

"What if it was something bad?"

Lily doesn't skip a beat.

"He would have shared that too."

"Right away?"

"What do you mean?"

"Michael was a scientist first and foremost. Didn't we just agree on that? And if his credibility was on the line, wouldn't he have wanted to prove his hypothesis before he brought it to someone else? He was a perfectionist; isn't that what you said?"

Lily doesn't answer. Shit. I've hurt her again. I shove her into remembering Michael then kick out the supports. I stink at empathy. She crosses the room to the couch and sits down hard, head in her hands.

I keep talking. I only want her to see the logic. I don't want to make her cry. Michael must have been one hell of a guy. I wonder what it would be like to have everything go right in your life, to have everybody love you, admire you, name their children after you. Maybe the universe can't keep that kind of lopsided life in balance. So much good and no bad. You're throwin' off the curve. You gotta go, make room for the rest of us average folks.

"I think Michael was doing what he did best, researching a problem to find a solution."

I get up and walk over to join her on the couch. I sit down next to her. It's a bold move, which she doesn't seem to register.

"I think we need to keep looking before we bring anything to Howard's attention. We need to know what Michael's notes mean and we need to make sure these people are really the original participants."

"How are we going to do that?"

Lily looks up at me. Her eyes are full of concern, brimming with anxiety. I put my arm around her shoulders. She tenses for an instant and then lets go. I leave my arm there as long as I dare, as long as I can. I want to cut it off and leave it there forever. I give her a squeeze and drag my protesting arm back into my lap.

"I don't know how we're going to do it." I say. "I think we're just going to keep looking. I do know Jake Tucker had a friend named Martin who was also one of the original test participants. I don't know his last name, but it's somewhere to start. Let's keep looking at the appointments and see if we can find Martin."

"It's getting awfully late," Lily says. She glances at the gold bracelet watch on her slender wrist. "It's almost 1:00. Maybe we should give it up for tonight. I don't want you to have a relapse."

"Huh?"

"I don't want your cold to get any worse."

Damn, forgot again. I make a few sniffling noises.

"We can start up again in morning," Lily says. "Can't we?"

The morning. From the back of my brain an emergency warning bell sounds. Tomorrow morning is when I'm supposed to pick up Hugh Klein's shoes. Tomorrow morning is when the guys in the lab are going to prove my icing-on-the-cake theory. Tomorrow morning is not good.

"Sure, we can look at it again in the morning," I answer, lying through my teeth. "I'll head out and we'll touch base first thing."

"Why don't you just stay here?"

This phrase is tossed out so casually I almost miss it. Stay here? She's asking me to stay the night. A heat wave rolls through my system. Maybe I do have a fever, maybe I really am sick.

"If we're just going to start first thing, and first thing is only a few hours away, it doesn't make sense for you to go all the way home. We have two perfectly good guestrooms. You can have your choice."

Of course, she's just being nice, not naughty. She is the good one. I am the evil one. I am the one who would do just about anything to touch her ass. Please, Lord, please give me strength or give me opportunity. Don't keep me here in the middle.

"I don't want to be any trouble," I say, knowing I should leave, knowing there is only so much control any man can be expected to exert. "I don't mind driving home. Really."

"You're being ridiculous. It's no trouble. Beside, this way, we can get started at the crack of dawn. What do you say? I promise to get up first and make coffee."

This is an image that sends me spinning. Lily, wearing a very short, very transparent nightshirt, in the kitchen, pouring two mugs of steaming coffee. Her hair is tousled, she is barefoot, and her toenails are painted bright red.

"I won't take no for an answer," she says. "I just know we're on to something."

Oh, I'm on to something all right. That's my problem. I'm on and I can't get off.

"If that coffee's a guarantee, then how can I say no?"

"Perfect. Come on upstairs and I'll show you the rooms."

She hops off the couch and is out the door before I've had a chance to gather my extremely rattled thoughts.

"Come on," she calls from the hallway.

I drag myself to my feet. I look at my hands. They are not shaking, but they glisten with sweat. I wipe them on my jeans once and then once again. I don't have a cold, but I am horribly sick.

SIXTEEN

I turn to look at the radio alarm clock on the nightstand for the fourteenth time in the last fifteen minutes. It is 3:03 AM. I have been awake for over two hours. Actually, I never went to sleep, so if you count yesterday, I've really been awake about eighteen, almost nineteen hours. There is a low hiss coming from the heat vent, but that's not keeping me up. There's the rain outside, clicking against the window in three-quarter time—probably a leaky gutter. But that's not keeping me up either.

The king size platform bed with its poofy goose down comforter and Egyptian cotton sheets is quite comfortable. The entire post-modern, blond-on-blond guest room is comfortable. I am the only thing hellishly uncomfortable. I don't belong here. A feather is poking out of the comforter cover right in front of my nose. I reach out to grab the pointy little end and pull. The feather pops out and I hold it between my thumb and finger, twirling it to fluff up the downy wisps. It didn't leave a hole. Of course, it's dark, there could be a tiny hole, but I don't think so. I think it's magic. It has to be magic because you can't put it back into the comforter without making a hole. It's stuck out here now with me. Can't go back. Can't sleep. I drop the feather off the edge of the bed. It takes a long time to fall.

Down the hall, at the other end of the oriental carpet runner, Lily is sleeping, probably stretched out across the bed she once shared with Michael. Or not. I've heard it can take a person months, sometimes even years after the death of a spouse to get used to sleeping alone. The surviving husband or wife will continue to sleep within the confined space of his or her original side of the bed, not venturing out, not even ruffling the covers on the other side.

I flip onto my stomach, bury my face in the pillow and breathe deeply, sucking the 400-thread-count cotton in and out my nostrils. My shoulders and neck ache, which I believe is what happens when you have a high level of stress. Stress and guilt and regret and anxiety. Toss in a little despair and that should be enough to make me blow my brains out all over these pretty white sheets.

I roll over again and stare directly at the clock. The red digits roll over to 3:04. I think this is what my physics professor in college was trying to explain to me. Time is entirely relative. It can fly by like a peregrine falcon or crawl by like a banana slug. But you can't stop it, and you can't train it to land on your arm.

3:05. I sit up. I'm wearing only boxers and the cool air in the room raises a map of goose bumps down my arms and legs. In just a few hours, I am going to have to come up with some excuse to leave. I can't let my opportunity to nail Klein fall through. He's good enough at his scam that I'm unlikely to get another chance. But what Lily and I discovered in Michael's appointment book is also crucial. We're so close. To what, I don't know, but we're close. There's no way Lily is going to let me leave without a hell of a lot of questions.

I try to picture Michael's computer calendar in my mind. It's a simple page of squares with dates. We organize our lives into these little squares, increasingly diminishing squares. One giant square for a year, each month smaller, each week smaller still, each day a bite-size chunk, each hour sliced into smidgens. When the squares get too tiny, then what? Like Michael, do we die? Experts say without some kind of organization, we'd die anyway. Our lives would be a whirlwind of millions of tiny squares, too random to fit together, too chaotic to exist. We need orderliness to survive, or at least to make it to the dentist on Thursday. The answer is there. The answer is in the order.

Why don't I just get up and have another look? There's no sleep in my future. I'm too restless, which, by definition, means without rest, without a chance in hell of settling down. I don't think they use the word "hell " in the dictionary definition, but they would if they could.

I might as well do something constructive.

My clothes are draped across a small, boxy sofa in the corner of the room. In the shadows, it resembles a squat butler waiting with my shirt and trousers over his arm. I pull on the clothes, pick up my shoes and tiptoe across the floor. I don't know that I've ever tiptoed before. I feel a little silly. But I don't know if Lily is a light sleeper and I certainly don't want her to know I'm sneaking around her house at three o'clock in the morning. A floorboard in front of the door lets out a squeak, a gargantuan squeak like the King Kong of mice. I stop, mid tiptoe, and listen for Lily to burst out of her room, demanding to know what all the commotion is about. Nothing. Maybe it wasn't quite as loud as I thought.

I push open the door and creep out. It's tempting to steal down the hallway and peek in on Lily, maybe watch her sleep. Maybe stand next to her bed and listen to her breathing. Did you know humans adjust the pace of their breathing to match the person nearest them? If you're sitting next to someone and you can hear him breathing, pretty soon you'll start breathing at the same rate. In and out, in and out, as if unison breathing will allow you to share the oxygen in the room more efficiently. I turn back around and head for the stairs, my footsteps muffled by the cushy carpet.

Michael's study is off to the right at the bottom of the stairs. The desk lamp is still on and so is the computer. The yellow of the lamp and the blue of the screen saver ought to combine to create a pool of alien green light around the chair, but it's just a warm glow. I sit myself back down in front of the monitor. The screen blinks back to Michael's Outlook calendar as soon as I move the mouse. I open another date. December 4th. The appointment window pops up. This one is for *Rory Talbot.* I add his name to our paper list, close the window and go to another date. December 8th. The familiar window opens. *Martin Stachlowski.* This must be our Martin! I add him to the list, carefully spelling the unusual last name.

Every date window has a hyperlink in its notes section. And when I try to click on it, every one gives me the same damn error message: *The folder or file could not be opened. Path does not exist. Make sure the path is correct.* What path?

Several years ago, well before I'd gone freelance, I worked on an early Internet scam. A big banking client was getting hit with a rash of credit card losses. Turns out some guy, some really smart guy, was moving stolen credit card numbers through a web site by embedding the information behind a seemingly legitimate web based business that sold three hundred varieties of hot sauce. This was before security on the web got as sophisticated as it is now. Back when it was still possible to hide chunks of data within the page coding. You could buy the hot sauce online, and I believe the guy actually went to the trouble to send it out; but if you were looking for hot credit card numbers, you could buy those too. You just needed to know which hot sauce bottle to click on and how to hack into the code to find the numbers. You were delivered that information via a phone call and an overnight envelope. The streams of information were from such disparate sources it was almost impossible to link them all back together. But the guy on the case, Stan, the guy I was training under, he was a programming genius. I actually remember the night we found it. We'd been methodically checking suspect commerce sites for about fifteen hours straight. Stan wasn't much of a talker, so that meant I'd been listening to clicking computer keys for about fifteen hours straight. My job was to keep each site live on my computer and click on whatever Stan asked me to click on to see where it took us. About 11:00, we were plodding through the *Sauce Sultan* site when I clicked on a bottle of *Dangerous Dan's Dragon Flame Habanero Sauce*. I got the cracked image icon that told me there was a broken link. I let Stan know and prepared to move on to his next request. Suddenly there was furious typing from Stan's keyboard, a strange little snorting sound, more typing, and then mild-mannered Stan leapt up from his chair, pumped his fists into the air and crowed like a rooster. Cock-a-doodle-doo! The full-on Old MacDonald. He'd found the hidden credit card numbers behind what appeared to me as a broken link. I was impressed. I'm still impressed when I think about it now. Good old Stan. I heard he retired last year and moved down to Florida. I hope he got a couple of chickens.

If Stan could do it, I can do it. If Michael was the consummate researcher everyone says he was, he'd have reported all his findings in detail. Somewhere there was a cache of notes, interviews, questions and answers, hopefully more answers than questions.

I wonder about Lily in her room upstairs, sleeping, breathing in and out. I want to discover this for her. I want her to wake up and come downstairs, preferably in that same see-through nightshirt I conjured up earlier, and I want to hand her a stack of printouts. What *I've* unearthed for her. Like a cat dropping a limp shrew at her feet, the rodent's neck bent back under its sagging body. A proud offering, a token of all I can do.

It's a little pathetic how I continue to fantasize about Lily. She hasn't given me the slightest encouragement, other than to resist throwing me out of her house on my ass. Most of my fantasies involve Lily naked; sometimes she's wearing tall white leather boots, but usually she's just naked. They're not always crude. I also imagine her reaching for me, turning to me for comfort. Asking me to hold her. Me, Charlie, or me, Albert? Funny, in my fantasies, she doesn't use my name.

Since we always crave what we can't have, my longing for Lily is guaranteed insatiable. I cannot have her. I will never be able to have her. It's like those evil toy cranes in the grocery stores. Right past the checkout, there it sits, a big glass case filled with a neon jumble of sad-eyed stuffed animals, a remote control steel claw hovering above. It should be a cinch to clamp down on their soft little heads, to lift one, two, maybe three or four out of their plush pile and deposit them into the prize chute. But it never works. You can never get a good grip. You press your nose against the glass, frantically clicking the remote control buttons while the seconds earned by your quarters tick away, watching the little creatures rise up and tumble back. Look, but don't touch.

Lily's probably used to men lusting after her. Beautiful women develop a unique force field that deflects any open-mouthed gawking and returns stinging darts of rejection directly back into the wide eyes of the gawker. I've seen it happen. Hell, I've felt it happen. Lily's made a couple of comments about quirks of Michael's that drove her crazy. He was too particular, too guarded, too busy. That's minutia. Grasping at straws. I am no Michael. For that matter, I am no Albert. I am simply Charlie. But good ol' Charlie is the one with the skills to get into this computer.

I open the main hard drive and check the capacity. The drive is nearly full but the list of files and their sizes don't match. There aren't enough files to fill a bucket let alone a giant hard drive. Where are they all hiding?

That's it! Of course that's it. What an idiot. There aren't enough files because they aren't all showing. I go back to the menu and tell the computer to *Show Hidden Files*. A huge list of additional files pops up. I begin to scroll through. My eyes run across the names, looking for patterns. I'm no programming genius. I'm not even sure exactly what I'm looking for. Still, I know it's here. I'm not Stan, but I am Stan's student and I remember my lessons. There's reason and method and a certain amount of repetition. First look for the pattern, then look for a break in the pattern. Be sensible and logical. Scroll. Search. Scroll.

When I was little, back when everyone was alive, my little sister Gina and I would play a game called Rabbit and Bear. I was Rabbit and Gina was Bear. I don't remember why we thought a rabbit and a bear would be friends. Seemed like a good idea at the time. Rabbit and Bear would go on adventures. Sometimes the adventures would take place in the closet, sometimes in the backyard, sometimes across a pile of couch cushions. In our animal kingdom, Rabbit was smarter and bigger than Bear, and so Bear was required to do whatever Rabbit ordered. One day, Rabbit ordered Bear to find a golden treasure. I think that's a common kid theme, discovering a hidden treasure that could keep you in candy and soda pop for the rest of your natural life. So Gina, aka Bear, spent the better part of an afternoon searching, truly searching, because that's the great part about being a kid; it is completely plausible there is a golden treasure buried in your backyard. So plausible, I remember pitching in to help after a while, worried the "finders keepers" rule might kick into effect if I wasn't along for the discovery phase. We found lots of shiny rocks and broken glass that came pretty close to golden treasure, but it wasn't until the end of the afternoon, when we were both getting kind of tired of the game, that we found the key. Actually, Gina found it, a rusty skeleton key. She held it out to me, gripped tight in her grimy fist, like an archeological prizefighter. When I reached for it, she yanked it back. I tried ordering her to give it to me. That didn't work. She knew what she had. Power. She sprinted into the house and hid the key in her room. I tired bribing her for it. I tried scaring her into giving it to me. I tore apart her room looking for it. But she never broke under the pressure and I never saw it again. Eventually, I forgot about it, and finally, I imagine it burned up with the house. And yet, metal doesn't burn very well, so sometimes I wonder if it ended up in the yard again. I wonder if it's still there and if I went back, could I find it?

I focus on the screen. My eyes hurt. It would help if I knew what I was looking for. Scroll. Search. Scroll. And then, there it is, my little red rooster. Cock-a-doodle-doo. A 10GB file called *personal.tc.* The biggest file in the list and the only one with the .tc extension. I immediately go back to the program files. True Crypt. Of course, hard drive encryption software. I'm losing my edge. I should have thought of that before. I'd just paid through the nose for a job seminar on encryption and the guy had called True Crypt one of the best.

I launch the program. The menu of virtual drives starts at E: and goes to Z:. I pull open the desk drawer and stare at the piece of paper Lily showed me with all the passwords. The last one on the card is written in thick black felt pen: *stc leahcim*. I open True Crypt drive S:. It asks me for the password and I type in *leahcim*, Michael spelled backwards. True Crypt responds with an error message, *Incorrect password or not a True Crypt volume*. Shit, this is getting really old. I try to remember the other tricks we learned in the seminar, the tricks that reduced the likelihood of password-cracking software discovering common words. Replace the letter "e" with the number 3 because it resembles a backwards capital "E". Replace a lower case letter "l" with the number 1 because they also look the same. I try opening the S: drive again, this time using *13ahcim*. It opens, revealing a long list of files. I go back to the appointment calendar, click an appointment, click the link and there are words on the screen. Michael's words from beyond the grave.

I should wake up Lily. But if she gets up, I won't be able to leave, and I have to leave. Later. I have to leave later. Right now, I have to read.

SEVENTEEN

I begin to read and almost immediately feel like a voyeur. These notes were not meant for anyone but Michael. At first scroll, they don't appear to be particularly personal; mostly opinions and observations, but they are still the chronicle of a stranger. Contrary to what Lily and all the others from the funeral believe, Michael was someone I'd never met. His world of wealth and science and popularity orbited completely out of range of my sorry little planet. But after all the research and the stories, I feel like I know him. I can almost hear his voice in my head, muttering to himself, typing in his thoughts, capturing them before they get away. Data. To him it would have all been data, the facts and little details that might mean something, somewhere, sometime to someone. Maybe now. What did you see, Michael? What did you want to tell us? I'm listening. Talk to me.

November 8

S could not provide original patient files, said they were with FDA for review, said he had requested their return but was still waiting. Would like data prior to interviews, but explained to S, could probably work without them. S offered again to do follow-up interviews himself and provide me with summary. Tempting. Schedule so full. No time to talk with all participants myself, but must make time. Need grant money, so need new success stories—at least three, maybe four. I know what they're looking for, who will perform under pressure. Can't rely on someone else to do selection. Can't show up on Oprah with someone who can't string two sentences together once cameras start rolling.

November 12

VM called today, confirmed he'd contacted FDA again, this time requesting copies if originals were still under review. VM helpful, but slow. Received cost-overrun report on construction. Need another $500,000 to force completion on schedule. New environmental issues. Underground tanks of some kind. Another hundred thousand or more. Authorized bank transfer. Remember to ask Lily about next fundraising dinner.

November 20

Went by Nesler to pick up file copies. Assumed they would be here by now. Nothing. Janet confused about what I wanted. Both S and VM out of town for Thanksgiving. Explained exactly what I was looking for, Janet promised to follow-up.

November 27

Janet brought file copies by house yesterday. Lily dumped them on my chair, didn't mention them until this morning. I wish she'd keep track of things better. Note from Janet saying she hoped this was what I was looking for. Included cover memo with names of all patients whose files were attached. No card or anything from S or VM, must still be out of office.

November 30

Myrtle Olcott, 79. Drove herself to office for interview. Very well-dressed. Vitals good. Only complaint was some discomfort with abdominal pump when reservoir refilled every three months. Discussed world affairs. Better versed than I on most issues. Chart notes indicate younger sister as primary caregiver. Patient indicates sister no longer sharing residence, broke hip in bad fall, admitted to local rehab facility. Patient seemed unsure of when or if sister would return. Very chatty, very confident. Resembles Aunt Bea from old Andy Griffith show. Would be good on camera.

December 3

Clyde McDonald 81. Accompanied to office by son. Answered all questions himself. Does not seem to rely on son in any way. Very interested in painting. Brought me small framed piece. Abstract. Quite well done. Claims no prior knowledge of painting or art. Spent 50 years as a plumber. From a plumber to a painter. Could be good story angle. Patient excused himself to go to restroom at which point son mentioned patient sometimes stayed up all night painting, asked if this was normal. I explained how intense brain activity can cause periodic sleeplessness, suggested he be watchful for extended hyperactivity. Patient may be too volatile for public presentation.

December 4

Rory Talbot, 68. Young but wheelchair bound and on oxygen. Resides in local assisted living community. Facility in news recently because of apparent suicide of staff member: woman, mid 50s, worked as a CMT for nearly a year on graveyard shift. Supervisor found her slumped in hallway with empty syringe. Patient filled in details not covered in newspaper. Said woman's shirt was open to the navel and syringe was hanging out of an exposed breast. Patient asked how common it was to commit suicide by cardiac injection. Told him I was not expert on suicide. Seemed morbidly fascinated by experience, probably a function of trauma. Curiosity as coping mechanism. Patient quite articulate in opinions on situation, offered several options for equally unusual terminations. Impressed with patient's level of understanding of physiology and mortality. Could be good interview with some coaching.

December 7

Iris O'Shea, 88. Moved from last known address shortly after end of testing. No forwarding address. Emergency contact number lists sister in Detroit. Disconnected. Follow-up with S and VM regarding new contact number. Status unknown.

December 8

Martin Stachlowski, 85. Relocated to son's home in Thousand Oaks, California upon death of wife. File flagged as acute Alzheimer's upon entry. Follow-up visits note immediate and drastic improvements. Letter from wife attached to chart indicates concern about personality change, says husband is moody and secretive, quick to anger when friends or family do not or cannot share new level of intellectual examination. No longer interested in favorite hobbies or pastimes. Spends almost all time in front of computer. Interesting intensity. Check California address and phone number.

December 10

Phone call from S, upset about files, said Janet should not have released them without his review. Apologized profusely, said he would have removed files of patients known to be inappropriate candidates. Asked me to return remaining files, said he would handle follow-up summaries and provide list of three patients as optimum interviews for grant application. Time and efficiency critical at this point. Agreed with S and returned all files except Martin Stachlowski, case unusual, would like to speak with son, perhaps patient also.

December 13

Contacted Don Stachlowski, Martin's son. 57-year-old accountant in Thousand Oaks. Said mother's cause of death was stroke due to infarction. Had been shocked to get call, mother had been healthy, planning trip from Illinois to California. Nesler handled all funeral arrangements, sent son cremated remains. Only son, no other family, no need for local service. Asked about any complaints from patient during last few months. None. Any chronic illnesses? None. How was father dealing with death? Didn't speak about it, but appeared to be coping well. Son spoke highly of drug testing program, said father had shown remarkable and rapid improvement. Son had enrolled Stachlowski in program. Had come out to set up everything, very impressed with Nesler. Was father's current personality unusual at all? No. Kept to himself, had developed tenacious addiction to the computer and Internet. Any close friends? None that he knew of, said father snapped at him recently about how, "some people no longer mesh with the fabric of society." Didn't know what that meant, son called him, "just another cranky old guy." Left son with my phone number. Asked him to call if father began to exhibit any unusual behavior. Reassured son it was simply in the interest of patient follow-up. Puzzled by father's personality shift. Early chart notes describe a gregarious man, a retired auto parts salesman. Very boisterous and happy, even as early dementia settled in. Liked the company of others. Played the accordion.

December 17

Revised files from S have not arrived. Taking forever. Received voice mail from Don Stachlowski, said he found something in his mother's things I might be interested in. Returned call, no answer. Fundraiser tonight for lab construction. Original investor, Roger Jones, indicated he is willing to put in additional half to three quarter million. Haven't met him, Lily says he is serious. We could use the money.

December 18

Don Stachlowski left another voice mail, going out of town for holidays with friends, but will call upon return. Mentioned finding photograph of father with another man about same age. Words "me and Jake" written on back of photograph. Son remembered question about any friends his father might have had. Maybe "Jake" was a friend.

December 20

Files arrived from S. Three patients to interview. Two women, one man. Do not recognize names or general histories from original research, but cover memo from S assures all three would make excellent subjects. Has contacted all and they are expecting my call. That makes it easy. Should be able to see them within next few days. Note to ask S whatever happened to pianist; he would make good video subject. Meeting Jones this evening to close deal on additional funding. $750,000. Jones obviously infatuated with Lily. Probably would have given full million if she held his hand and helped him sign on the dotted line.

December 27

Surprised to receive "me and Jake" photograph in the mail today from Don Stachlowski. Accompanying note contains local Park Hills phone number and short message from Don. He found photo and phone number in old address book in mother's things. Don't understand why he's so fired up about photo. First time I talked to him, got impression he hadn't bothered to open boxes his father brought with. Once you start looking, you probably can't stop. Note says friend's full name is Jake Tucker. Doesn't ring a bell. Note also mentions father's reluctance to talk about Tucker. Father increasingly irritable when asked about anything regarding testing experience, has demanded son have no further contact with me. Apologizes for having to cease communication and closes with odd mention about stress of sudden disappearance of the neighbor's dog.

January 4

Unusual coincidence. Discovered Jake Tucker's name on desk, came across old cover memo Janet prepared for original set of files. Listed all patient names. Jake Tucker's name on list. He is not one of three files S delivered for interviews. Must be something unacceptable. Still have photo and phone number from Don Stachlowski. No answer from Jake Tucker. Not even an answering machine.

January 8

Ruth Fitzgerald, 79. Interview number one. Living in nicely appointed apartment complex with six cats. Chart notes show stage two dementia prior to drug testing. Patient appears completely on track, talks virtually non-stop. Apartment filled with several sewing machines, colorful quilts are stacked on every surface. Blood pressure, normal. Heart rate, normal. Slightly overweight, but not dangerously so. No family in area. Has help for light housekeeping and some meal preparation. Complained only of allergies she says are related to the cats, claims to love cats more than hate allergies. Eager to show off quilts, which are extremely detailed and complex. No two the same. Asked how long she'd been a quilter. Said she just picked it up, not hard, works around the clock and can finish one in about a week. She insisted I take one, searched through piles and presented me with a blue, silver and white quilt with a star pattern made of hundreds of tiny interlocking squares. Would not take no for an answer. Frenetic, like a windup mouse. Too intense for TV. What was S thinking?

January 22

Other two patients selected by S are satisfactory, but not dramatic. Not nearly as high-functioning as my earlier interviews. Would rather track down patients whose original stories were more compelling. Spoke with S and VM. They are researching. Also asked S for file on Jake Tucker. Video crew wants to get started on fundraising program, calling every day, very annoying. Note to direct calls to Lily. Things are not coming together smoothly. Too busy to track down all the loose ends. S and VM distracted by lab construction. Still no answer at Jake Tucker phone number.

January 28

Surrounded by incompetents. S and VM called out of town. No explanation. Research not complete on other patient interview options. Am scheduled for back-to-back surgery tomorrow. Lily has obligated me for some abysmal dinner engagement same day. Voicemail from Don Stachlowski asking about that damn photo again. Who the hell cares?

February 3

Tired of waiting. Some things you just have to do yourself. Hacked into Nesler server and downloaded copies of patient files. Not too hard. Pretty low level security for such an important company. Perhaps I should mention vulnerability to VM next time I see him.

February 11

Cannot sleep. Re-read notes, looking for patterns. Patients are all better. Better than before. Not just halting damage, not just recovering function. Patients are smarter, producing new neurons, making new connections. Appears to be what we always wanted, a way to rewire limbic system. Not just heal, improve. This is proof that will break open funding. Indicators all go up. Their reservoirs are drained, re-filled, and their intelligence tests improve each time. It's all good, but something's out of place. Their brains are firing, but it's not controlled: it's fast, capricious, like a wildfire. They are better. But are they better than ever? If fire surrounds itself will it burn through all connections? Is it possible to get better and better and better? Where does it stop? What if it doesn't stop? Stroke? Insanity? Worse? Cannot sleep.

February 15

Reached daughter of Jake Tucker, Mary Anderson. Father diagnosed with pulmonary fibrosis. Dementia acute. Requires near constant supervision. Did not improve on drug therapy. Made appointment for interview and observation. Daughter very hesitant. Call S again for Tucker file. S confirms Tucker was negative responder, questions interview potential.

February 18

Met with Jake Tucker. Matches profile of typical early to mid-stage Alzheimer's patient. Unable to stay on track long enough to answer my questions, but upon leaving, pulled me aside and whispered in my ear that Martin Stachlowski had murdered his wife. Daughter overhead comment and apologized profusely, insisting story was latest in her father's string of paranoia. He had told mailman same story earlier that day. Her explanation makes most sense, but cannot shake intensity of father's declaration. Cannot be true, but patient certainly believes it to be true. Left another message for Martin's son.

February 21

Cannot sleep again. Something wrong. There's a pattern I missed before. The notes are random but recurring. People have died. Pets have disappeared. Homes have been destroyed. Individual situations ordinary, almost mundane, but side-by-side, results are startling. More than coincidence. People and things that were annoyances have been dispatched with exquisite design. Don't think patients have become smarter, they've become sociopathic, eliminating with horrifying precision anything and anyone they choose. Who would suspect them? Sweet Grandma and Grandpa, so happy to have their minds back. It's the perfect alibi. So smart, so very, very smart. Jake Tucker isn't crazy, maybe he's only sane one left. S needs to know. Trials have to stop.

February 22

Contacted S and VM, still out of town. Can tell they don't believe my theory. S adamant it's coincidence. Says tragedies happen within everyone's lives. Put any group of strangers together and you'll find a string of unfortunate events. Says they're just things that happen to people. I tell them about what Jake Tucker told me. S reminds me Tucker rarely coherent. Not convinced, tell S meeting is necessary to look at all remaining patients. Put every one through battery of psychological tests. Told S, will pull name and money from any further research or testing unless we follow through. S finally agrees to fly back in, but wants offsite meeting. Nervous about information leaking to investors or press. Suggests we both fly in and meet up north at Barnett to review, strategize. Seems unnecessary, S insists press are watching, dogging him for information every time he comes or goes. Have agreed to meet. S promises to take my theory seriously. Can tell he doesn't want to, thinks it will delay things. Too damn bad. My stamp of approval is all over his drug. If it's true, if this thing is causing psychoses, if I've helped create these monsters, it doesn't matter. I'll go public with it now and shut down the whole lab. S is positive it's nothing, a fluke, an oddity that can be explained away. He keeps assuring me nothing drastic will be necessary.

That's the last entry. Two days before Michael's plane plunged into the Rock River. I watch the cursor pulse on the screen at the end of his final sentence: *He keeps assuring me nothing drastic will be necessary.*

Murder is pretty drastic.

The windows behind me are brightening. Dawn. Soon I'll be into my second twenty-four hours of chaos. The light illuminates the dust swirling the air, mimicking the thoughts in my head. I need to get out of here before the sun shines. Like Count Dracula. No time to print all of Michael's entries for Lily. I close the file and the program. No time to check to see if he kept a copy of the updated patient files he'd downloaded from the Nesler server.

Just enough time to write a note. My own journal entry on a scrap of paper. I lay it carefully across the keyboard.

Lily,

Discovered something important. No time to explain. Will call you later. Don't worry.

Albert

EIGHTEEN

I spot the sack of shoes on Klein's front porch. His house sits mid-block in a quiet neighborhood of well-tended flower gardens, brick retaining walls and swept driveways. It's a two-story Tudor with a steeply raked slate roof, copper gutters and full dormers jutting out on either end. Some of those past insurance settlements have gone to good use in the home-improvement area. The front windows are still curtained against the morning light.

The car clock reads 6:02. Only dogs and crazy joggers up this early. I wonder if Lily is up and has read my note. When you tell people not to worry, that is exactly the point at which they start worrying. I should call, but there's no time to call. I have to stay focused on what's in front of me. A Kroger's plastic bag full of leather shoes.

I hop out of the car and climb the stone steps curving up to Klein's front porch. As if I've tripped an invisible guy wire, sprinklers suddenly rise from the manicured lawn and unleash a slash of water across my pants. I dodge subsequent assaults and finally reach the porch damp but not dripping. I grab the bag and turn around, hesitating a moment to plot my escape past the streams of water. I hear the door open.

"Shoe Fly?" asks a voice from behind me.

I pause, dying to answer with the obvious, "don't bother me." Instead I spin around and smile through the screen door.

"Yes, sir, Mr. Klein, sir. Here to pick up your shoes, as promised."

"I was hoping I'd catch you."

The dirty mesh of the screen door obscures his face, but I can still make out the shape of the famous Mr. Klein. He's wearing a thick, white terrycloth robe looped around a generous mid-section. His chest is thickly carpeted with dark hair. In sharp contrast, his head is bald. Not bald*ing*, completely bald, like Mr. Clean, but without the pirate earring. He pushes the door open and his features come into view. Plump cheeks, heavy dark-rimmed glasses, and gigantic eyebrows, like little whisk brooms above his eyes.

"Listen, there are five pairs in there instead of four. Can I still get the same deal?"

What a guy. Always looking for the angle.

"Five for the price of two? That's quite a discount, but if it insures you'll be a Shoe Fly repeat customer, we'll make it happen. Could you spot me a little extra time though? Say I bring everything back tomorrow afternoon instead of first thing?"

"You got a deal, young man."

He looks at me, his pupils magnified to the size of kumquats behind the heavy glasses.

"Have we met before?" he asks.

Why yes we have. I'm that nervous feeling you get that you're being followed. I'm the reason you hate to answer your phone.

"Don't think so, sir," I reply, smiling so wide it hurts. "I've only been in town here a few months. But I've got one of those faces. People are always thinking they know me. I must look like everyone's second cousin twice removed."

Klein laughs and releases the screen. It slams shut.

"Tomorrow afternoon it is," he says. "Leave 'em on the porch if I'm not here. Saturday is my day to visit my pop at the home for lunch. Salisbury steak and creamed corn." He laughs again. "Nothing soothes the soul like institutional food."

He shuts the door, but I remain staring at it. "*My pop at the home*?" Klein. Klein. There was a Klein on Michael's patient list. I'm sure of it. I don't remember the full name. James or John or Jules or something. It couldn't be the same person. That would mean my two worlds are about to collide. I believe when worlds collide there is usually a horrible explosion.

I walk back down the steps to the car, not caring when the sprinklers whack me on the backside. I needed that. Now if I could just get someone to whack me upside the head.

Pulling away from the curb, I consider driving straight to Lily's. This is too much for one small brain to handle. I'm desperate for someone to confide in. But not Lily. Not yet. She only knows one side of the story. By the time I could explain my entire parallel universe, a lot more shit would have hit the fan, and something tells me I'm up to my knees in it already.

The cards are beginning to fall into place. Not fluttering gracefully from the sky like a game of 52 Pick Up, but slapped down hard. Blackjack. House wins. Howard and Gavin know what Michael discovered and Michael is gone.

If they assume I know what Michael discovered, Albert is gone.

But not yet. Albert is not gone yet, and Charlie may be just the one to keep him around. Forgive me, Lily. Forgive me for making you worry and for stirring up this mess in the first place. But I'm here now, and maybe for once I can clean up after myself. Forgive me, Lily. Forgive me for falling in love with you. Then, forget me.

I turn the corner and head for the condo. I need a shower and a shave and a clean shirt and tie. Charlie Sandors has some work to do.

The condo is chilly when I step in. It's early, but the heat should have kicked on by now. That damn message light is blinking on the phone again. I'm sure it's Lily. I wonder how many times she's called.

Click. Beep.

"Albert? Pick up, Albert. I got your note."

Her voice is shrill, panicky. Has she been crying?

"What did you find? Don't you dare leave me in the dark. Call me back immediately."

She's upset. Deservedly so. I'd be pissed too if I'd awoken to an empty house and a mysterious note. Be patient, dear Lily. I need to do a little more digging. I promise you'll be the first to know what I discover. That is, unless I am the last to know.

There's another message.

Click. Beep.

"Sorry to bother you so early, Mr. Mackey. It's Gavin VanMorten. I know this is last minute, but I wanted to tell you Channel 2 is coming out to the lab construction site this morning. It's for their Sunrise News segment. Should happen about 7:00. Howard thought you might be interested. Again, my apologies for the early call."

Why didn't Lily tell me about this? Surely she knew. We were supposed to be working this morning. She promised to get up first and make coffee. Maybe that just meant turning on the coffeemaker as opposed to bringing me a steaming mug of coffee in bed. Maybe she planned on sneaking out before I woke up. Guess I beat her to the punch.

I glance over at the kitchen clock. 6:45. The clock is next to the sink. Over the sink is a window. The window is open. Did I leave the window open? No, it was raining when I left for Lily's. I walk into the kitchen and slide the window closed. It's big, but hardly seems big enough for anyone older than six to climb through it. I'd like to convince myself I left it open, but I can't. The paranoia is building. Being in the kitchen reminds me I haven't eaten in quite awhile. I pull open the refrigerator. Slim pickings unless I can make an entire meal out of condiments. Maybe a glass of orange juice for now. I can grab something on the way to work.

I cross into the living room and search for the remote. Fishing it out from between the sofa cushions, I scan to channel 2. An extremely happy young woman is talking about the weather in front of a big map of Illinois. I turn up the volume and head back to the bedroom to change. It's a bit gray now, but it's going to be a "super nice" day according to the happy young woman's voice. That must be official weather terminology. I peel off my clothes. Man, I am really hungry; it's giving me a little headache. Can't jump in the shower yet, though. Have to wait to see dear ol' Howard on the news.

I wander back into the living room in my boxers and stare at the TV. The weather gal is gone, replaced by two exceedingly happy anchorpersons. It doesn't seem normal to be quite so delighted at 7:00 in the morning. When the red light goes off over the camera lens, do they slump back in their chairs, full of the same despair and exhaustion the rest of us feel on the morning of a work day? I'd like to think so.

The grinning male anchor is introducing Howard's segment. The scene cuts to a woman reporter standing in front of the lab construction site. The sky is blotchy gray with clouds so low they appear to hover right over the reporter's head. If there's a breeze, it's not moving her hair, must be professionally trained hair. She's wearing a bright yellow squall jacket emblazoned with the station's logo and doesn't look quite as happy as the people back in the studio. Probably why she is just a reporter.

"Thanks, Steve. I'm here this morning with Nesler Pharmaceuticals CEO, Howard Stanich."

She steps to the left and the camera follows her, revealing Howard. He looks great. Expensive navy suit and red tie pressed to within an inch of its life. Not a hair out of place. Very impressive. He must get up every morning about 4:00 and re-iron all the clothes that have come back from the drycleaners.

There are thirty or so people in the background. It's mostly a sea of black and gray suits, with a few guys in suspenders and hard hats adding incongruous spots of red and yellow. I glimpse Lily in the front row. Then the camera zooms in on the reporter and Howard.

"Mr. Stanich. We've heard conflicting stories about how the lab expansion project has been going since the unexpected passing of Michael Rudolph. We appreciate you coming out this morning to talk with us about it."

"Thank you, Carol. I appreciate you getting up so early to stand in front of a half-finished building."

Howard chuckles and the reporter echoes with a little giggle. He looks so very sincere.

"Of course," Howard says, his serious tone returned. "These have been trying times for all of us, especially for Michael's family."

He drops his eyes momentarily at the mention of Michael's family and draws a breath. What a pro. He'd be great at eulogies.

"Those of us at Nesler who knew Michael best and worked with him day-to-day on this incredible project, well . . . we still can't quite believe he's gone."

The camera creeps back out, and I can again see the crowd and the building in the background. Lily stands at the end of the front row. She's wearing a gray pantsuit with bright gold buttons. Her hair is pulled back and dark glasses hide her eyes. It's impossible to read her expression on the little TV screen.

Damn, my head is throbbing. I really don't need a headache today.

"This lab was one of Michael's dreams," Howard continues. "Possibly his greatest dream. We are lucky he was so involved in all phases of its planning and construction. His early involvement gives us a solid framework to complete the construction exactly as he would have wanted it."

Someone in the crowd begins clapping and the others quickly pick up on this example. Howard pauses again and waits for the applause to die down. I swallow the last of my orange juice and set the glass on top of the TV.

The reporter jumps back in the conversation.

"Can you tell us when construction will be complete and when you expect to start handling patients?"

"Well, Carol, I can't give you an exact date. As anyone who has done any remodeling around their own house can attest, construction is a 'best guess' kind of game."

Laughter ripples from the peanut gallery.

"But we certainly plan to be substantially complete by this summer with the doors opening before the end of the year."

"That's quite a bit later than previously expected, isn't it?"

"Somewhat later, but we are hoping to accelerate the process where possible."

Howard should run for office. He can answer questions without providing a shred of information. It's a real skill.

The blood is pounding so hard in my temples it's getting difficult to hear the TV. I hope this doesn't go on much longer. I need to shower and get into the office. If I don't get Klein's shoes to the guys in the lab by 9:00 there's no way I'll get them back in time.

Howard is speaking again. The camera is following him as he and the reporter walk toward the lab building. The image looks a little fuzzy. Someone should tell the cameraman to check focus. I sit down on the couch. Now the picture's really blurry and the audio is all weird. I wonder why they don't cut back to the studio. I blink to clear my vision. Nothing. Maybe it's not the TV picture, maybe it's the TV. Suddenly, the entire room stretches out like a balloon, snaps back, and then flips end over end.

Fade to black.

A phone is ringing.

Someone should answer that.

Could be important.

Is it my phone?

It's cold.

I crack open my eyes. I am face down on the couch, a small puddle of drool under my chin. I'm wearing only boxers and my head feels like someone's been sitting on it. If I could just lift my head off the couch I could look around. Up. Up. Lift, up. That's not working. I'm staring at the back of the couch, at an extreme close-up of the fabric's weave, blue and green and black. Maybe I could just turn my head. Yeah, that would be good. Turn. My cheek rakes across the cushion, slowly, slowly. Cheek, chin, cheek number two, and there we have it, a new view. It's my TV. A soap opera is on with a pretty girl talking on the phone. Must have been her phone ringing, not mine. Light is flooding through the front window. My eyes dart around the rest of the room. I can actually feel them rotating in their sockets. It's not a good feeling.

I try to compartmentalize my thoughts. Where am I? Condo. What is wrong? Collapsed on couch in boxers, having trouble moving. What time is it? Don't know that one. Afternoon probably, judging by the sun. Why am I here? Million-dollar question with no clear answer at hand.

I send a command to my extremities to move me into a sitting position. This time there's a bit more cooperation and I manage to swing my feet onto the floor. Since my head weighs at least two hundred pounds, I have less success convincing my upper body to budge. Finally, my arms respond to repeated requests and push me up into a sitting postion. It's a good news, bad news thing. It's good to be upright; it's bad trying to balance my gigantic head on my tiny neck.

The pretty girl on the soap opera slams down the phone and they cut to a commercial of babies in funny hats. The last thing I remember, Howard was on TV and I was getting ready to go in to the office. Now, Howard is not on TV, babies in hats are on TV, and I'm still in my underwear. I look over at the clock on the kitchen wall. 3:15. I've been out for eight hours. What the hell happened? Shit. I've lost the whole goddamn day.

My thoughts begin to fall back into a linear path and the situation becomes clearer. Based on the sorry state of my head, I think it's safe to say I was drugged. I think I know who, but I don't know exactly why. Howard and Gavin can't possibly know what I found in Michael's computer. I'm willing to bet no one knows about his notes. But I'm sure my first instincts this morning were correct. They *believe* I know. I was writing Michael's story, right? I must know everything about him. Everything. If Michael knew all about Nesler, and I knew all about Michael, then I know all about everything. Targeted for murder by association.

But why knock me out? If you're going to go to all that trouble, why not just kill me now? I reach for the remote and silence the babies in funny hats. My orange juice glass is still sitting on top of the TV. There was something in the juice. Had to be. I didn't touch anything else. I stand up. Too quickly. A kaleidoscope of colored shards swim in front of my eyes and I almost go down again. I grab the glass and sniff. No smell. In the kitchen, I retrieve the carton from the refrigerator, open the spout and smell. Fresh oranges, nothing else.

I hurry back into the bedroom. No time for a shower, just throw on jeans and a sweater and splash a little water over my face and hair. Since it feels like bears have been living in my mouth, I do take the time to brush my teeth. I take stock in the mirror as the toothpaste foams. Presentable. Rumpled, but not scary.

I grab the bag of Klein's shoes and toss in my glass and the carton of juice. We're all going to work. 3:45. It'll take some fancy talking to get the lab guys to stay late on a Friday. I stare at the clock, trying to gauge how long they'd have to work to get everything done. Just below my line of site, invading my peripheral vision, the curtains are blowing around the kitchen window. I drop my eyes and almost drop the bag of shoes and juice. The window is open. Again.

NINETEEN

"Who wants pizza?"

I stride into the lab reception area with four steaming boxes of deep-dish sausage and pepperoni. The room is small and cluttered. Fluorescent ceiling panels throw off a hot greenish light; one tube is flickering erratically, ready to snap and die. Pizza alone won't sell my case to these guys, but hot, greasy food is a good place to start.

"Hey there, man," says Brad Trenton, the lab manager. He's sitting behind a small wooden desk piled high with multi-colored file folders. "To what do we owe the privilege of a visit into the bowels of the building by the famous Charlie Sandors?"

"Working a case, Brad," I answer, approaching the desk and laying my offering before him. He doesn't bother to move any of the folders. "Working to keep the world a safer place for righteous folks like you and me."

Brad lifts the lid on the top box and examines the contents. Nodding his satisfaction, he closes it again and looks up at me. Brad is older than me, not by much, maybe 38 or 39. I've always thought he was the polar opposite of what a scientist should look like. No pocket protector and Buddy Holly glasses for this guy: he's built like one of his own steel filing cabinets, big, square and tough. His blond hair is pulled back into a thick ponytail, revealing an angular face covered with freckles. He's a great guy, but one of these days, I think the *Baywatch* gang is going to notice he's gone missing. Even more than the surfer-dude body and good looks, it's the freckles that always knock me for a loop. It's like having Dennis the Menace explain the laws of physics to you.

"Not that I would ever question your motives, Chaz, but this pizza stinks to me like a bribe."

"You cut me to the core. A guy can't drop by with pizzas for his friends without being accused of ulterior motives?"

"No one comes down here without a damn good reason. We have no windows and no girls."

Brad's two lab techs come through a swinging door at the back of the office, most likely drawn by the smell. These guys are a much better fit for the geek role. Justin is short and round with a crew cut and very rosy cheeks, like he's always slightly embarrassed. Dave is skinny, bespectacled and has '70s helmet hair. He also has a tattoo of barbed wire around one wrist. I've never had the guts to ask him about it. There's either a whole other Dave in there somewhere, or it's simply proof he has been stupid drunk at least once in his life.

"Pizza break," Justin announces, making a bee-line for Brad's desk. "Good to see ya, Charlie. You slummin'?"

"On a mission. What's up with you guys this afternoon?"

"Up to our assholes in bloodwork," says Dave, following Justin over to the pizza.

"How'd you like a real challenge?" I ask.

"I'm going to totally regret saying this in about two minutes," says Brad. "But, tell me about it."

He grabs a pizza slice and kicks back in his chair. Dave and Justin perch behind him on a counter. The fluorescents hum and the dying tube strobes on and off over Justin's head.

"It's a two-fer," I say, trying to sound upbeat. "I'm looking for two different things. One, I've got these shoes."

"Shoes?" Justin asks through a mouthful of hot cheese.

"Shoes. Men's leather dress shoes to be exact. I need to prove the presence of buttercream frosting in the fibers of the stitching along the soles of one of these pairs of shoes."

Dave stops mid-bite.

"Why would someone have frosting on his shoes? Unless maybe you're one of those strippers who jumps outta cakes."

"That's my problem, Dave. You just gotta prove it's there."

"I can't work on something unless I know the circumstances."

"That's bullshit, you work on anonymous stuff all the time."

"Okay then, I *want* to know the circumstances," Dave admits. "Your stuff is always interesting, Charlie. What's with Frosting Man?"

"Okay. Frosting Man is a Mr. Hugh Klein, slip-and-fall artist extraordinaire. For his latest tumble, I believe Klein had a little help from some cinnamon roll frosting."

"That sounds almost plausible, but how on earth did you get him to give you his shoes?" Brad asks.

"Trade secret. Let's just say I need to return them ship-shape. Make sure you take lots of before photos of all sides and verify all your steps. I'm probably going to have to destroy all the evidence before I bring the shoes back to Mr. Klein."

"So that's riddle number one," says Justin. "What's riddle number two?"

"Much more pedestrian. I have a glass and an orange juice container I need you to check for narcotics."

"What kind?" Dave asks, his lips slick with grease.

"Any kind," I answer.

"Can you narrow it down?"

"Then I wouldn't need you, would I? And, isn't it good to be needed?"

Dave rolls his eyes and swallows the last of his pizza.

"You know, Charlie," Dave says, finally wiping the grease from his face—with his shirt, of course, not with one of the fifty napkins piled next to the pizza boxes. He misses a spot and I stare at the red splotch on his cheek while he finishes his thought. "It is Friday, and it is almost 5:00, and I can hear the call of the wild."

I think about the tattoo on Dave's wrist and briefly consider whether or not he might actually have something wild that could be calling to him. Brad interrupts my musings with his own suspicions.

"Please say you aren't going to tell us to do this for you now. We've been slammed all day."

"I never *tell* you anything, I always ask. And, I always ask politely. This time, I'm prepared to go as far as begging. This is really important. The pizzas were just for starters. I'm willing to pull out the greenbacks for this one."

I reach into my back pocket and retrieve my wallet to put my money where my mouth is. It's an empty gesture. I'm pretty sure I only have a few dollars on me. I'll have to hit the ATM at the 7-11 across the street to do the deal.

"Name your price. I'm desperate. I was planning to get everything to you this morning, honest. Things just got all messed up. Everything's messed up. I really need your help, guys."

"Whoa, Chaz, pleading does not become you," Brad says, leaning forward onto his desk and peering at me over the top of the pizza boxes. He looks serious. Well, as serious as someone can look with a face full of freckles. "Let's put this in perspective. Based on what you've described, this is a good six or seven hours of testing."

Dave moans in the background.

"Can the attitude," Brad barks.

Dave shuts up but folds his arms across the front of his lab coat and I can see the tattoo. Justin is eating his fourth slice of pizza, but who's counting?

"If we go off the clock for you, Charlie, it's not going to be cheap. Corporate has come down hard on outside work. They found out last month that a couple of the Chicago labs had full-on businesses going after hours. If we get caught, it's an automatic suspension without pay."

"No one will know," I promise.

I can sense the door of opportunity creaking open. Brad's mercenary streak is showing. He can make the other guys stay. Justin doesn't seem to give a shit. Dave'll make a stink, but he'll go along in the end.

"There is no fucking way *a single soul* can find out about this," Brad continues. "If it was anyone else, I'd say no, wouldn't even think twice. But you've always been straight with us, and there was the time you house-sat for my sister Leigh at the last minute when she flew off to the Bahamas for that quickie divorce."

I'd forgotten all about that, but Brad was right. I did stay at his sister's a couple years ago. Nice place up in the hill district. I'm pretty sure I brought one of my funeral flings there. Stacy? Lacy? No, Tracy. That was it, Tracy. Cute little Korean gal. Just lost an uncle. Amazing tits. You're backsliding, Charlie. Concentrate, goddammit.

"Fifty bucks an hour," Brad says.

I think I missed something during that stroll down daydream lane.

"Fifty?" I ask, incredulous.

"Fifty each."

Dave and Justin both look at Brad. We're all doing the mental math. Six or seven hours at $150 per hour. That's over a thousand bucks. Christ almighty, where am I going to get that kind of cash? I try not to flinch.

"Is that your final offer?" I ask.

Brad smiles. He has dimples too, did I mention that? Dimples *and* freckles. It's freakish really.

"Take it or leave it, Chaz Man. I've got my boys to think of here."

He gestures to Dave and Justin who are also smiling. I am the only one not smiling. I close up my wallet and replace it in my back pocket. Brad's smile fades a little.

"I don't have that kind of money on me."

"Of course you don't," Brad says, grinning again. "If you were carrying around that kind of folding money, I'd charge you double. We can wait until Monday. Banks are open on Monday."

"I believe you have me over the proverbial barrel."

"Don't be so negative. Remember, if it was anybody else, I wouldn't be offering at *any* price. It's a sweet deal."

"Okay, you win."

"It's win-win, Chaz. We get the dough, you get the info."

The three lab extortionists laugh at their own joke. I turn to recover the bag of stuff I'd dropped by the door when I made my grand entrance with the pizzas. I bring it back to Brad's desk and set it down at his feet. Brad pulls it up onto his lap and studies the contents.

"I'm really counting on you guys," I say. "I'm going back upstairs to do a little work while I'm waiting for the results. I'm also going to figure out how many organs I'll have to sell to raise that thousand bucks."

Brad looks up at me and those damn dimples pop back into his cheeks.

"I like you, Charlie. Don't worry, you'll get what you pay for."

With that, he grabs another piece of pizza, stands up bag-in-hand, and all three of them disappear into the lab.

I stand there next to Brad's desk for a few minutes, staring down at the decimated pizza. I should have a piece, but after our little exchange, I've lost my appetite along with over a thousand dollars. I turn and head out into the hallway towards the elevators. At quitting time on a Friday night, I wait forever for a car to come all the way down to the basement. When the arrival bell finally dings and the doors slide open to let me in, I hear footsteps running down the hall. A hand slides in at the last minute and stops the doors from closing all the way. I see a barbed wire tattoo, and as the hand pries open the doors, I see the complete Dave. He's quite winded. He leans against the doors to keep them from closing. The elevator bell rings and the doors bump against his back as they try to shimmy closed about every ten seconds. People above us want to go home.

"Glad I caught you," he says, still panting.

"Glad you didn't cut off your arm."

"The shoes. There are five pairs of shoes. Which pair has the frosting?"

"I don't know."

"We can't test them all, that'll take forever."

"That's why you're makin' the big bucks, Dave. Maybe you'll get lucky and it will be the first pair you choose."

Dave studies at me with a blank expression. For a split second I'm scared of him. He's really a lot taller than he looks in a room full of other people.

He breaks his gaze and pushes his glasses back up his nose. It's a comforting, geeky gesture that restores my confidence.

"Look at it this way," I say. "More shoes means more hours, which means more money out of my pocket and into yours."

"You know, that's really Brad's trip. I wouldn't have reamed you for that much."

"It's okay. I should be able to get reimbursed for it if everything goes as planned. So it really will be a win-win. Think you'll be able to get some evidence for me?"

"Sure. If there's something there, we'll get it. That's why we make the big bucks."

He smiles and steps away from the doors back into the hallway. I watch him squeeze into oblivion as the doors close. The car jerks and starts its ascent to the fifteenth floor.

TWENTY

No one in his right mind is going back up to work on a Friday afternoon, so I get a free ride to the top of building. The offices are quiet and most of the lights are out. Helen's reception station is neat as a pin. I've always been impressed with how organized she keeps everything. The entire staff spends all day dumping shit on her desk, but at the end of the day, every speck of paper is gone. Even her wastebasket is empty. Once, I accused her of sending everything she hadn't completed through the paper shredder at 4:55 each day. She laughed, but she never did contradict me.

I trudge back to my temporary space. I work for Dennis so much I really ought to have my own office, but rules are rules. Temps and freelancers are the office Bedouins and must camp wherever space allows. Lately that means being squeezed in between Eleanor Schumacher and Bill Langford in customer service. Bill eats lunch at his desk, so most days the entire area smells of either tuna or Cup O Noodles. Eleanor's not stinky, but she has covered every inch of her cubicle walls with snapshots of and artwork by her grandkids. She has seven and will launch into amusing anecdotes about all of them to anyone at anytime. It's best not to catch Eleanor's eye.

There's a stack of phone messages under my mouse. That's where Helen puts things if she really wants me to see them. I shuffle through them. Nothing particularly interesting. Nothing that can't wait.

I flip on the computer monitor and watch my desktop blink into view. My first order of business is to try to track down Martin's son, Don Stachlowski. Something tells me Martin and Jake are important players in this morbid game. I'd like to know if Don Stachlowski ever spoke to Michael again before his death. I remember from Michael's notes that the man lived in Thousand Oaks, California. How many Stachlowskis could possibly be there, or anywhere else for that matter? I log into the address search engine the company subscribes to. It's a Northwest firm that claims to have the most complete, most current database of phone and address records in the country, possibly the world. It's a valid claim. I've found every person I've ever searched for. It's the same company that serves major corporations, government agencies, the military, even the FBI on occasion. People would be shocked to know how quickly they can be identified. I type in Don's name and location. There are actually six Don Stachlowskis in the country, but only one in Thousand Oaks. I dial the number. It rings twice.

"Hello?"

"Mr. Stachlowski?"

"Yes?"

He sounds hesitant, probably figures I'm calling to sell him vinyl siding.

"This is Albert Mackey."

"Do I know you?" Stachlowski asks.

"No sir, I don't think so. I'm working on a project for Jake Tucker's family. I understand your father and Mr. Tucker were good friends."

"Jake Tucker? Yes, they were." His voice softens. "I didn't know him, but I do know they were friends. Is everything alright? He hasn't passed away has he?"

"No, sir, he hasn't, but he is quite ill and his daughter is trying to do some pre-planning for that eventuality. We don't think it will be long, and she's trying to pull together some loose ends while her father is able to participate."

"I'm sorry to hear he's not doing well. Are you a relative?"

"No, sir. I'm with the funeral home. We're assisting Mr. Tucker's daughter with some of the preliminaries. She's trying to create a photo collage that illustrates the highlights of her father's life. She tells me your father was a big part of Jake's life in the recent past. I was hoping you might have some photographs or mementoes—something we could use for this tribute."

"Boy, I'd love to help you, but I already gave away the only photo I had."

"You did?" I up the level of anxiety in my voice. I need to sound little more pathetic. "That's unfortunate. I don't suppose there's any way to get it back?"

"I don't think so, but," he pauses and I wait anxiously for the conversation to head in the desired direction. "Are you calling from Park Hills?"

"Yes sir, I am."

"Then, you're familiar with Michael Rudolph?"

"Of course. Everyone here in town was horribly saddened by his death."

"He's who I gave the photo to."

"Michael Rudolph?" I ask, trying to sound astonished. "Why would you have given your father's photo to Michael Rudolph?"

"Funny thing is, he called me about Jake Tucker too, not long before his accident. Out of the blue, just like you're doing now. When we first talked, I'd never heard of Jake Tucker, but I asked Dad and he remembered him. Although he didn't seem too thrilled to talk about it. Maybe they ended on a sour note, some disagreement? My dad can be pretty cantankerous. Anyway, I did a little digging through my mother's stuff and sure enough, I found a photo and a phone number."

So far this is all stuff I already know. I strain to sound interested and not push too hard. Keep focused, Charlie, don't let this one get away.

"Well, I'll be darned. Why do you suppose Michael Rudolph was calling? Was it about the testing?"

There it is. The question crawls through the phone lines from one side of the country to the other. Answer me, Don. I need an answer. Tell me what Michael said to you.

"I don't know."

Shit. Not okay. *I don't know* is not the answer we're looking for. Next contestant, please.

"Could have been," Don continues. "Dr. Rudolph and I never spoke again in person, but he did leave a message on my phone machine."

Hang on, hang on. Don't give up on the man now; he has something to say.

"A message?" I ask, prompting the story to continue more rapidly.

"It must have been three or four days before he was killed. That's kind of eerie isn't it? He called and left a message. I don't remember it all exactly, but it was about the drug program. Something about a theory he had, and he asked about flying my father back to Park Hills for some kind of special testing."

"Did you call him back?"

"I tried to, but didn't get an answer. I left him a message and then I called Nesler and let them know."

I stop breathing.

"You called Nesler?"

"Sure. They take care of all dad's medications and stuff. I figured they could explain things to Mr. Rudolph better than I could. The next day, I heard about the plane crash on the news."

"Who did you talk with at Nesler?"

"Howard Stanich. Nice man."

There's genuine warmth in his voice. He actually likes Howard.

"He was so helpful when mom passed away," Don continues. "I couldn't get away from work to help Dad take care of the details, but Howard told me not to worry. I showed up for the funeral and he'd taken care of everything, paid for everything, flowers, a little reception, everything. He's a very nice man. I owe him a lot."

No, he owes *you*, Don. You don't know it, but he owes you one father. He took yours, experimented on him, and then tossed back a completely different person. Oh, and he's probably also responsible for your mother's death. Yeah, he's a really nice guy. The world needs more people like Howard Stanich.

That phone call Don Stachlowski made to Howard must have been the proof Howard needed to confirm Michael was on the verge of revealing his drug's fatal flaw.

"So, you never heard back from Mr. Rudolph?"

"No. Howard seemed to know what I was talking about and he said he'd take care of everything. All this medical stuff is way over my head. I was more than happy to hand it off to him. But all this doesn't help get that photo for your display, does it? Maybe you could contact Mrs. Rudolph. Or, why don't you ask Howard. Have you ever spoken with him? He's very nice; I'm sure he could find out something for you."

Yes, I'm sure he could. In fact, I'm sure sweet ol' Howard's already found out more than I'd like. Let's wrap this, Don. Time to move on.

"You've been so helpful, Mr. Stachlowski. I appreciate all your time. I'll certainly see what I can do on this end to track down that photo. Thanks again."

"You're welcome. I'm sorry I couldn't do more."

"You've been extremely helpful, really."

"Please give my respects to Mr. Tucker's family. This is a rough time for them, I'm sure."

"Thank you, I'll let them know. Good night, Mr. Stachlowski."

"Good night," he pauses. "I'm sorry, I've forgotten your name."

I pause for an instant. Will he call Howard again? At this point, it probably doesn't matter.

"Mackey. Albert Mackey."

"Good night, Mr. Mackey."

The call disconnects. Was I wrong to not make up a new name? If Howard's watching me as closely as I think he is, he's seen me come and go. There are dozens of businesses in this building, but with a little bit of persistence, he could rule them out one by one until he realized there was no Albert Mackey anywhere. No Albert Mackey, but another gentleman who bears a striking resemblance. I may not have blended yet in Howard's mind, but things are starting to run together. There's not much time.

I stand up and look over the top of my cubicle. The only windows in this area are along one wall at the far end of the floor. As the light outside fades away, they begin to look like a row of symmetrical black squares, like minimalist artwork. I leave my desk and weave around the other empty nests until I reach the windows. I stare out into the squares of other office towers. Somewhere on the other side of the city, Lily is wondering what happened to me. To Albert. Right now, I would give anything, everything to take it all back. To rewind all the way back to the morning the obituary appeared in the paper. I would read the story of Michael's death, shake my head in pity, and turn the page.

Behind me, I hear a phone ringing. It's got to be a direct call. Outside calls go to the switchboard answering service after hours. I sprint back to my desk. It's my phone all right. I grab it on the seventh ring.

"Sandors," I hiss into the phone, out of breath.

"Hey, Chaz, I've been ringing forever," says Brad, his voice a husky chuckle. "Were ya in the can?"

"Uh, copy machine," I answer, although I don't know why I care if Brad knows I was just staring out the window. "I was using the copy machine."

"Right," he says, stretching out the 'i' for several seconds. "Anyway, I wanted to let you know we're going into overdrive on this. Dave's come up with the prefect test for the frosting, but it's a three-step proof. It'll take him until almost midnight."

The implied message behind Brad's information is *ka-ching*! I try to ignore it.

"What about the orange juice?"

"Justin's working on that one. He'll probably be done sooner than Dave, but not by much. As you recall, you didn't give us a lot to go on."

"And what exactly are *you* doing for your fifty bucks, Brad?"

"Supervising. Someone's got to make sure everything is done right. And, I'm also talking to you."

I picture the dimple pressed against the mouthpiece of the phone at the other end, because Brad must be smiling. Grinning even. A freckle-laced cavern imbedded in his cheek.

"I'll be back down there around midnight, Brad."

This time it's my turn to draw out the vowel for a few seconds before biting his name closed with a hard consonant.

"We'll be here," he promises, sweet as pie, and hangs up.

7:00. Time to find Mr. Klein's father. I grab the yellow pages from under my desk and flip through to the Retirement section. Park Hills has an even dozen facilities. I pick up the phone and practice my delivery prior to dialing.

I'm calling with a lab report for Mr. Klein. I apologize for the delay. The cover sheet on the file shows we were supposed to contact Mr. Klein this morning. Apparently, his report was overlooked. The rest of the staff has left for the night and I'm trying to locate Mr. Klein. I'd hate for him to have to wait all weekend for his results.

The first three homes are cordial but confused. None show a Mr. Klein as a resident. I apologize profusely each time and continue dialing.

"Good evening, Grace Fountains, may I help you?"

The voice on the other end of the phone is young and sweet. I launch into my prepared speech.

"Jonah Klein?" The sweet young voice asks. "He's in our Alzheimer's Care Unit. I can't imagine they left instructions for you to contact Jonah. He couldn't possibly understand a lab report. Perhaps you meant to call his son, Hugh?"

"That must be the other number here in the file. I am so sorry to have bothered you."

"No bother at all."

I hang up and write my second piece of information on a scrap of paper. Jonah Klein, Grace Fountains.

Assignment number three requires a DMV search. It's been over 24 hours, but I can still remember the license plate number of Mary Anderson's Volvo. I type it in to the database and within a few seconds I have the information I need, the street address of Mary Anderson and her father, Mr. Jake Tucker. It's not too far from downtown. I can drop over for a little visit and be back at the lab well before midnight. I could call first, but I'd rather only explain myself once. I doubt Mary will be happy to hear from me in any shape or form, but if I'm standing on her front porch, I think she's too polite to slam the door in my face.

I shut down the computer and grab my coat from the back of the chair. A piece of paper flies from one of the pockets and lands at my feet. I stoop over to pick it up. It's Roger Jones' business card. I look at it, turn it over. On the back a number is scrawled in pencil. I recognize it as Lily's private cell phone number. I smile. Hope he wrote that down somewhere else or he'll be sorry when he realizes this particular card is gone.

I slide it back into my pocket. I want to call Lily. What would it hurt if I just took a minute to let her know I'm okay, that I'm working on something important and I'll tell her all about it soon? I could also tell her how much I wish I could be the person she believes me to be. I could tell her I've never met anyone before who's made me want to be real.

Real? *Real what?* I'd laugh if someone said that to me.

But Lily wouldn't laugh. She'd look at me with her sad eyes, take both my hands in hers, purse her lips into a little half smile, and sigh. It would be a long, heartfelt sigh. I would then melt into a puddle of Jello at her feet. I think I would enjoy being Jello, occupying that magical state between liquid and solid.

I can't call Lily. Not until I'm sure about everything. If I can prove to her what really happened to Michael, maybe my own pitiful story won't seem quite so ridiculous. I'll still be a lying sonofabitch, but I'll be a lying sonofabitch who uncovered a scandal and brought her husband's killers to justice. How could you not love that?

TWENTY ONE

Mary Anderson's house is in a 1960s subdivision just fifteen minutes from the center of town. The low-slung ranch style homes are comfortably worn around the edges. Number 2717 sits in the middle of the block. I recognize the Volvo parked in the driveway. There's a short hedge along both sides of a walkway leading from the street to a set of three crumbling steps covered in worn Astroturf. The hedge has been recently trimmed into a neat box shape, but the rest of the landscaping is wildly out of control, nearly obliterating the front windows and encroaching onto the porch.

I press the doorbell and wait. A porch light goes on over my head and Mary opens the door. She's wearing a simple white blouse and black stretch pants. In the space of a few seconds her face transitions from puzzlement to recognition to horror. She must be too stunned to shut the door.

"Hello, Mary."

"What are you doing here?"

"I don't suppose you'd believe I was just in the neighborhood?

My banal attempt at levity falls flat. With a thud.

"Why did you come here?"

Her voice sounds so tragic. I should just leave. I've screwed up enough lives as it is. Did I really need to drive all the way over here, looking for someone else to terrorize?

"I wanted to make sure your father was okay?"

A lame excuse. A flimsy reason. Typical Charlie. Play on her sympathies and make her feel sorry for you. It's all about you.

"How did know where we lived?" she asks; her voice a little shaky. "We're not in the phone book."

"It's my day job," I say, matter-of-factly. "I can find just about anybody."

"Are you a cop or something? I thought you said you were a writer."

The fear is edging out of her voice now. She's getting angry.

"I'm not a cop. I need to talk to you."

"We went through this before. I can't talk to you, whoever you are."

Enough. Chatting politely through the screen is getting me nowhere and I have a deadline to meet. Dead line. The point at which your chances run out. I raise my chin and stare through the screen at Mary.

"I'm working with Lily Rudolph to try to find out what really happened to her husband. I don't think his death was an accident and I think you might be able to help us."

She looks stunned again and stutters a bit through her next words.

"Michael Rudolph? Why on earth would I know anything about Michael Rudolph's death? I don't really travel in those circles."

"Your father was one of the original Nesler test participants. The majority of the other originals are dead. I think Michael Rudolph found out what was happening to them and wanted to put a stop to it. But someone put a stop to him first."

Mary's eyes slowly close behind her glasses. They remain closed so long it makes it awkward to continue to look at her. Finally, she exhales a single, long breath and opens her eyes again. She's not looking at me, she's looking over my shoulder into the street. Without saying a word, she steps back and holds open the screen for me to come in.

Inside, there's no hall or entryway. We've stepped right in the living room. It's a little sparse on furniture, but tidy. A large blue couch dominates the floor, flanked by twin end tables with matching lamps. A vintage La-Z-Boy sits at an angle to the couch. There's a chunky wooden coffee table holding the week's TV Guide section, a water bottle and some pill containers. A television balances on a rickety pedestal at the far end of the room.

"Can I get you a cup of coffee or something?" Mary asks.

"Thanks, I'd like that. I'm looking at a long night. A little coffee would probably do me good."

"Cream and sugar?"

"Cream. Or milk. Whatever you have."

"Have a seat," Mary instructs, gesturing toward the La-Z-Boy.

She disappears down a little hallway into what must be her kitchen, leaving me alone with the discount furniture. I select the blue couch over the recliner.

As a child, at my very first foster home, I had a rather unfortunate recliner incident. The family's bio-son, that's what they have you call the *real* children, was about my age and he and I were playing astronaut on his dad's recliner. I was the astronaut and he was Mission Control. I'd lean all the way back and then count down from ten to one. On one, he'd push with all his might on the footrest and the chair would snap back into its original position. That was blast off. We'd done it about a gazillion times without any problems. But at gazillion and one, something in the footrest gave way. It cinched closed with a metallic twang, pinning my left arm between the back and the seat. The son yelped and ran out of the room. I yelped and tried to run, but was firmly clamped in the jaws of the chair. It was a good ten minutes before the kid came back with his dad to release me. By then I was starting to lose feeling in my fingers. I think we both got in trouble, and the chair never really worked right after that.

I slip off my coat, toss it over the arm of the blue couch and pick up the TV Guide. It's open to a half-done crossword puzzle. Five down is an 11-letter word for lacking feeling or tact. Starts with an "I". Oh, oh, I know this one. Mary comes into the room with two cups of coffee.

"Insensitive," I say, holding up the crossword.

"Huh?"

"Five down. The answer is . . . insensitive."

She smiles and sets the cups on the table then sits down in the La-Z-Boy.

"Do you like crosswords?" I ask, realizing she must think I'm an *insensitive* idiot.

"They're supposed to keep your brain healthy," Mary says. "It's Albert, right?"

"No, it's Charlie. I probably told you it was Albert when we met at the lake, but my real name is Charlie. Charlie Sandors."

Mary tilts her head to one side. Her hair is down tonight, falling below her shoulders. Without rain slicking it to her head, I see it's thick and actually quite a pretty auburn color.

"Why would you give me a fake name? You *are* a cop aren't you, or maybe one of those private detectives?"

I push up the sleeves of my sweater and lean forward, my elbows on my thighs, my hands clasped in front of me, praying Mary will take me seriously.

"Nothing quite that glamorous. I'm an insurance investigator, but that's got nothing to do with why I'm here. Through a string of bizarre circumstances, the majority of which you'd never believe even if I took the time to tell you, I'm in the position of trying to solve what I think is a murder and a cover-up."

Mary reaches out for her cup of coffee with both hands. I expect incredulity or at least basic skepticism, but Mary shows no astonishment at all. She appears to accept my explanation at face value. She settles back into the recliner—must have never been trapped in one.

"If I was smart, Mr. Sandors, I'd ask you to leave now," she says, so quietly I have to lean forward even more to hear her. "But I'm not too smart and I'm very tired . . . and for some insane reason, I think I might believe you. I've wondered for a long time if anyone would ever ask any questions. If anyone would ever care what happened to these people."

She sets down her coffee cup without having taken a drink.

"But our society doesn't like to be bothered by people who've outlived their usefulness. If they die, so much the better, right? Fewer old fogies queuing up at the buffet line. Fewer cars with their turn signals stuck on for miles. Fewer people who remember what it was like before televisions and cell phones and computers and all the other gizmos that occupy our world. Fewer people who understand what life's really about."

I'm quiet for a minute, not sure if there's more to Mary's sermon. But she appears to be done.

"You're right," I say. She gets it. She understands something is wrong. "Most people wouldn't notice, but Michael Rudolph wasn't most people. You and he actually have more in common than you think, at least philosophically."

Mary smiles and removes her glasses, wiping the lenses on a corner of her blouse.

"I don't really know a lot of details about the Nesler project. Dad never told me anything about it, and now he can't remember."

"Who was your contact at Nesler?"

"Gavin VanMorten."

"What about Howard Stanich?"

"I know the name. Isn't he Gavin's boss?"

"Yes, and he's really the one in charge of the project. Are you sure you never talked with him?"

Mary looks up at the ceiling, searching along the plaster cracks for the answer.

"Maybe once," she says, looking at me again. "He's the one who called to ask about my father's funeral arrangements."

"Did he think your father was dead?"

She laughs. One short burst.

"No, he knew Dad wasn't dead, but he also knew he was quite ill. He wanted me to know Nesler would handle all the arrangements for a cremation. I thought it was odd at the time, but I guess I figured it was some kind of corporate policy or something."

"How long ago was it?"

"When he called? I don't remember for sure. A couple of months maybe."

Two months would put the call right before Michael's accident. Exactly the same time Don Stachlowski said Howard had called him.

"Do you remember anything else about the conversation?" I ask.

"He asked me about Michael Rudolph."

"What about him?"

"If he had called me."

"Had he?"

"Yes."

My voice escalates in speed and volume.

"Why didn't you tell me that before? You made it sound like you barely knew who he was."

I know I'm speaking louder than necessary in the tiny room, but I can't help it.

"What did Michael call you about?"

Mary presses her back into the recliner, trying to move away from me. Before she can answer, a crash from the kitchen interrupts us. Mary jumps up and runs out of the room. I follow.

Jake Tucker stands at the counter. He's wearing striped pajamas and the same slippers he had on when I first came across him at the horseshoe courts. Remnants of a coffee cup lay at his feet. Spilled coffee forms a lake on the counter and dribbles over the edge onto Jake's slippers. He looks confused and worried. Mary approaches him quietly. She takes his hand and guides him backwards away from the mess and into a chair at their kitchen table. He doesn't resist.

"It's okay, Dad," Mary says. "Let's get this cleaned up, shall we?"

Mary grabs several towels from a drawer and soaks up the coffee lake. I bend down to gather the cup shards. Neither of us says a word while we pick up the mess. Jake drums his fingers on the table. Mary tosses the dirty towels into the sink and turns to her father.

"Dad, do you want me to make you another cup of coffee?"

He doesn't answer.

"Or some milk? How about a glass a milk and a Little Debbie? Does that sound good?"

The drumming stops for a second. Jake must be trying to process the question. He starts drumming again without responding.

"Yep, that sounds good to me too," says Mary. "Charlie, do you want a cake?"

I glance around the tiny kitchen. There's avocado green wallpaper with white daisies, an ancient dishwasher, the kind you have to hook up onto the faucet, and real linoleum on the floor. It reminds me of my grandmother's kitchen in Evanston. I take a seat at the table next to Jake.

"That'd be good," I say. "Let's eat cake."

Jake looks at me as if he's just noticed I'm with them in the room. He smiles, undaunted by the fact a strange man is suddenly sitting next to him. He extends his hand to me. I shake it. Then he turns away from me and continues drumming on the table. Mary stands behind us pulling glasses from a cupboard.

"He likes to shake hands," she says. "He won't remember you were here after you go, but while you're here, he'll probably shake your hand three or four times. Just play along, if you don't mind."

"Of course," I say.

She crosses to the refrigerator and gathers a carton of milk and a cardboard box of Little Debbie Devil Square cakes. She brings everything to the table and sits down with us. Shaking the last two cellophane-wrapped packages from the box, she slides one over to her father and opens the other one herself. There are two chocolate squares in each package.

"Do you mind sharing?" she asks. "Dad likes to open them himself and I usually let him eat both."

She hands me a cake. Jake wrestles with the cellophane seal, frowning in concentration. He finally opens the package and grins as he pulls out a chocolate square and takes a big bite.

"I'm sorry I shouted at you like that," I say, picking up my cake and inspecting its waxy finish. "It's been an amazing twenty-four hours. I'm trying to tie up too many things at once, but I really don't have a choice. There's not much time."

"Not much time for what?"

"I just have a lot to do tonight," I answer, minimizing my real concern: not much time for me to remain alive and breathing.

"I should have told you about Michael Rudolph right from the start," Mary says, sounding a little guilty. "But I didn't know if I could trust you. You have to admit you're a strange person to have popped out of nowhere."

I nod in agreement. She doesn't know the half of it, but I'd say her description is dead on. I'm a very strange person and I have materialized in her life like some kind of wacky street magician's trick.

"Michael Rudolph called me sometime around the middle of February," Mary continues. "He wanted to know about Dad's condition. He asked me a lot of questions about his health, when he started to decline, what type of symptoms he had."

"Did he tell you *why* he wanted to know all this?"

"He said he thought there might be a side effect of the drug that was causing serious problems. He wanted to meet my father and examine him."

"He called just the one time?"

"Just once. That Howard guy from Nesler called right after that, and then there was the plane crash."

"So, you told Howard about Michael's call?" I ask, my tone heading back up again in volume.

"Sure I did. Why wouldn't I?" Mary says, a bit defensively. She's picking the chocolate coating off her cake with her fingernail. "I figured he knew about it already anyway. That's when he told me about the confidentiality agreement. He sounded like he was okay that I'd talked with Michael, but there was no doubt I shouldn't say anything to anyone else."

"Did he threaten you?" I force my voice to soften. I need Mary to trust me, to confide in me.

"Not in so many words, but he made it clear I should stop talking if I wanted my father's medical bills to continue to be paid."

Jake polishes off the last bite of his first cake and takes a swig of milk. He turns to me with a look of surprise. I have apparently dropped from the sky and landed at his table. He offers to shake my hand. We shake and he starts in on cake number two. Mary sighs. But it's not impatience, just quiet and familiar.

"I told you. He's actually a little quiet tonight. That whole mess with the coffee probably scared him."

"Nobody from Nesler ever called you back?"

"Nope. Fine with me too. I don't want to talk with them."

"Would you call them tonight if I asked you?"

Mary gasps, which makes Jake drop his cake into his milk. He puts his whole hand into his glass to fish out the remains.

"What? Why?" Mary asks, frightened, looking at me now with the same concern that was on her face when she first opened the front door.

"I think it's time to draw Howard out into the light," I explain. "I want him to know how close I am to exposing him."

"I don't understand."

"I want you to call Howard tonight and tell him about my visit."

She shakes her head in protest, which causes her glasses to slip down her nose. She pushes them back up and stares right at me.

"That would be dangerous for both of us."

"Not if you time it right," I say. "Wait about an hour after I leave. I'll give you Howard's cell phone number. He always has his cell phone."

"He'll wonder how I got it," Mary says, refusing the idea before I can even explain it.

"He'll be too surprised to hear from you to even ask. But if he does, tell him Gavin gave it to you. It'll take him awhile to figure out that's not true. Tell him Albert Mackey stopped by your house this evening and was asking you a bunch of questions about side effects and Michael and Martin Stachlowski."

I'm speaking very quickly, as if the faster I can deliver the request, the more likely it is she'll accept it. But, I know it's a long shot. If I were Mary, I wouldn't do it. If I were Mary, I would have shoved me off the front porch into the neatly trimmed hedge.

"What's Martin got to do with it?" she asks, confused at the new page in my already complex story.

"Michael called Martin's son, Don about the same time he called you. Howard knows it because Don called and told him."

I stop, realizing that trying to explain everything is a waste of what little time I have.

"Look," I say, letting all the frustration bleed into my voice. Not caring anymore if Mary sees and hears the urgency—the fear. "You don't have to understand everything. You know I'm right. You've known for a long time there's something wrong with the testing. All you have to do is call. I'll do the rest. Just call and tell Howard I seem to know an awful lot about a lot of stuff."

"He's going to be so mad."

"Exactly. That's what we want."

"I don't want that."

Mary crosses her arms and glares at me. Her Devil Square sits on the table in front of her surrounded by frosting crumbs. Jake is looking at it.

"Please, Mary. He won't be mad at you. I promise. You're just the messenger. Tell him you wouldn't answer any of my questions, you were scared, you told me to go away and never bother you again." I pause. "I'm sure those are all the things you wish you'd said when I showed up at your door."

I try to smile at her. I need her to help me. If I can coax Howard out into the open, I know I can get him to talk about Michael. Especially if he thinks he still has one up on me.

Mary is not smiling back. Jake's hand darts out and snatches her Devil Square. I pass him mine.

"Thank you," he says, grinning at me. At least someone is happy I'm here.

Jake's sudden participation in the conversation seems to bring Mary out of her funk. She looks at her father, happily consuming his cakes, and then turns back at me. She drops her hands into her lap and sighs. It's the same long, resigned sigh I heard before and in it there is sorrow and heartache and regret.

"Tell me exactly what you want me to say," she says.

I give her a detailed script to repeat to Howard. I remind her again to say it was *Albert* who was here, not Charlie. If Howard hasn't yet figured out we're one and the same, I'd like to keep up the charade just a little bit longer. I explain she should tell Howard I said I was going out to Nesler headquarters, that I was going to try to get into the building. I need Howard and Gavin as far away from the lab as possible. It won't take them long to figure out the diversion, but I don't need long.

"Will I see you again?" Mary asks.

"Probably not," I answer, honestly and a little sadly. "I'm not sure how this is all going to turn out, but I doubt it will be good."

Mary looks down at her milk glass.

"Take care of Jake, okay?" I say, struggling to hold on to my smile.

At the mention of his name, Jake looks up. There's a chocolate ring around his lips. He extends his hand to me once again.

"Pleased to meet you," he says.

I take his hand, this time in both of mine, and hold on.

"Pleased to meet you," I answer.

He tugs against my grip, wanting his hand back so he can continue with his Devil Squares. I reluctantly let go. When I look back at Mary, I see tears on her cheek.

"I'll do it just like you said." She's speaking so quietly again I almost can't hear her. But I appreciate it. I'm glad someone finally knows what I'm doing and doesn't think I'm completely insane.

I push back from the table and get up to leave. Jake doesn't offer his hand again, which must be my final cue to be on my way. Mary follows me back to the front door and lets me out, her face barely visible in the dim porch light as she holds open the screen door.

"You're doing a good thing," she says.

"Maybe I am, Mary. And, maybe, I'm doing a really stupid thing."

TWENTY TWO

It's almost 10:30 when I pull away from Mary's house. She has to play her part well to convince Howard to come after me, but I actually think she can do it. She's been pretending for months that everything with her father is 'okay'; it should be easy for her to finally dump on Howard and tell him there is a problem he might want to look into.

I should have time to swing by the condo and check my messages before I go back to meet Brad and the boys. Traffic is light in the waning hours of a Tuesday night. Except for the stop lights, there's nothing and no one to slow me down. I turn the corner onto my street and my headlights sweep across the condo's driveway. Lily's car is parked there. There's a light on in the living room. She's waiting for me. I resist the temptation to step on the gas and race out of the neighborhood. The opposite side of the street is empty but for one lone car, a black BMW. Its parking lights are on low. I slowly press down on the accelerator and drop my head as I drive past both cars.

At the end of the block, I turn right and head down toward the Blue Lake parking lot. If the BMW recognized me, he could already be following. I continue past the entrance to the park and drive instead onto a nearby side street. This street is crowded with cars along both sides. I jimmy in between a giant pick-up and a jacked-up Monte Carlo and kill the engine.

I crawl across the seat and slowly open the passenger's side door, half stepping, half rolling out of the car and into the shadows along the sidewalk. It's close enough to the lake that the trees and bushes surrounding the houses blend into the densely forested perimeter of the park. Between the moonlight and the street light, I have just enough illumination to run along the edge of the lawns, stopping every few minutes to listen for an approaching car or a barking dog. I pause in front of a small bungalow near the very end of the street, just a few yards from the entrance of the park. The house was probably once very lovely, perhaps even a summer lake retreat for city escapees. But the streets around here have gone downhill in the last ten or twenty years. Too close to the action now, too much traffic, too much noise for any civilized souls. They're mostly rentals now, rundown and shabby with cars parked on the lawns and sofas on the front porches. Even in the dim light, I can tell this little place is crumbling in on itself, going back into the earth.

I listen again for tell-tale sounds. Car? Dog? The last thing I want to do is run into a snarling pit bull guarding someone's backyard marijuana patch. I look over my shoulder. Nothing there, no one. I step into the yard and start walking toward the forest just beyond its boundaries. Running now, but carefully, skirting dropped bicycles, abandoned lawn chairs, and a single cowboy boot. The lights are out inside the house, but I'm not taking any chances. Quiet, must be very, very quiet. My foot kicks a discarded gas can buried in the tall grass. I freeze, offending foot in mid air, and suck in my breath. I wait for the lights to flick on inside the house. Still dark. From the far end of the neighborhood, a dog barks. Once, twice, three times, and then he too goes silent. I drop my foot, let out my breath and continue the last few feet into the safety of the forest.

I should be able to run under the cover of the trees all the way around to the back of the condo. In the summer, the park's maintenance crew does a good job of keeping the underbrush to a minimum, but it's still pre-season and winter's foliage has reclaimed a good deal of the forest floor. Ferns and ivy slap at the bottom of my pants. My shoes are heavy with mud and dead leaves. Scurrying noises to my left and right signal the presence of nocturnal wildlife distressed by the lummox crashing through their habitat.

This is way more of a cardio workout than I'm used to. If it weren't for the adrenalin coursing through my veins, I'm sure my heart would have burst inside my chest quite a while ago. I'm not sure exactly where I am. The smell of the lake is everywhere, moist and rich, but I think I'm still quite a ways up from the shore, from the circling pathway, from Jake and Martin's horseshoe courts. I have to stop for just a minute to catch my breath and remember what the hell I'm doing.

I picture Lily sitting on my couch. I wonder if she checked my messages. There are likely to only be messages from her, so that won't help her curiosity. The condo is a mess. I ran out in such a hurry this afternoon, I left clothes all over the bedroom and dishes in the sink in the kitchen. I don't suppose she cares. I do suppose she wonders what's happened to me, where I was when she woke up to an empty house, why I left her such a strange note, how I seem to have vanished into thin air. Does she know someone is watching her, or more to the point, watching her and waiting for me?

Up ahead I can see the trees begin to thin out. There's a light high above. Too yellow to be the moon, it has to be the security spotlight behind the condo. It has to be because I don't think I have the stamina, emotional or physical, to go much farther. I start running again. My shoes are heavy. My heart is heavier.

I come out from under the trees and there it is. The back of the condo rising up on its stilts, the new bedroom window glinting a little in the light. There is no clear line of sight from the front of the house to the back. I'm sure there is no way whoever is in that black BMW can see me back here. The security flood is clamped to the back of the condo like a giant bird of prey and lights up the entire backyard. I bend over and survey the ground for something to throw at the window. Sticks, stones. What's that old kid's rhyme? *Sticks and stones can break my bones, but words will never hurt me.* At this point, if I could take back my words on that rainy February day at St. Mark's Cathedral, I'd willingly endure a hail of sticks and stones. But I'm afraid all I have now to save me are my words.

There's nothing around here but leaves and pine needles. I look up at the window a story and a half above my head. I wonder how they got that branch through my window in the storm? No normal human could hurl something that size that far. Must've been like the window repair kid said; must have been an old snag. Maybe I'm paranoid. What if Howard and Gavin have nothing to do with Michael's death? Lily trusts them. Regular people seem to like them. They're fine, upstanding citizens and I'm a kook who goes to strangers' funerals. Who would you believe?

I shuffle forward a little, kicking through the leaves, looking for anything I can throw. Pine cones. Under the fir tree just below the window are dozens of pine cones. They look like little hand grenades. Perfect.

I could be wrong about everything. I could be sneaking through the woods like some deranged commando for nothing. I could be, but it doesn't really matter anymore. I believe I know the truth, and even though the truth has never been my strong suit, I think I know it when I see it. Lily deserves to know the truth, about me, about Michael, about how I feel about her.

I grab a handful of pine cone grenades and launch them up at the bedroom window. The first one falls pitifully short, but the next two hit their marks. I collect more and continue the barrage. At best, they're probably making a dull thump of a sound. Lily is likely in the living room, not the bedroom. My only chance is repetitiveness. If she hears enough dull thumps, she has to come back to the bedroom to investigate.

My arm hurts from throwing, but at least I've hit the window more times than I've missed. All close-at-hand pine cones are gone, forcing me to run back and forth between the forest and my launching site.

Come on, Lily, for chrissakes. Do you have the stereo turned up full blast or something? But there's no light, no face at the window. I'm running out of ammo.

I tilt the face of my watch toward the security light and check the time. 11:10. Shit. I have to get back to the lab. Those guys are not going to wait around for me at this time of night. I have two more pine cones in my hand. I hurl one and then the other in rapid succession. They both hit dead center of the window. A few seconds later the light goes on in the bedroom. That's it. Come to the window, Lily.

I see her outline through the glass. I wave both my hands over my head. The floodlight is too bright to make out her expression, but I imagine it is one of shock and surprise. Like a bad silent film actor, I make elaborate shushing gestures, holding my fingers to my lips and shaking my head. I see the side vent window crank open. It's a narrow pane, meant only to facilitate air circulation, but Lily manages to snake her head and one shoulder through the opening.

"Albert?"

I shake my head side to side more violently and cover my mouth with my hand.

"What are you doing?"

I jump up and down, slicing the air with my arms, trying every motion I can think of to shut her up. I point to the back door that leads into the garage. She looks at me then pulls her head back inside. I wait. Please, Lily. Please understand. You have to come out the back. You can't come out the front or the BMW will see you. I run up and stand right outside the small door. It has a heavy deadbolt latch that requires a separate key. What if she doesn't have the key? I wait.

There's a knock on the inside of the door. I knock back. I hear the deadbolt click and Lily yanks open the door. She is standing just inside. The fluorescent tubes in the garage are still flickering and their light is dim. I reach around the door jamb and slap off the switches before they can glow into full bloom.

"What the hell are you doing, Albert?" Lily asks. Her voice is a snake-like hiss.

I step inside the garage and carefully close the door behind me. The only light now is a thin line seeping in where the garage door and the concrete don't quite meet. I can't see Lily very well, but I reach out and grasp for her hand. Finding it, I pull her toward me and wrap my arms around her. She doesn't resist, but her body goes rigid underneath my hug. I let go and she steps away.

"Where have you been?" she asks. "What is going on? Have you gone completely insane?"

"Not completely," I answer. "But I'm well on my way. Someone is watching the condo. That's why I had to get you to come out back. There's a black BMW parked out front. I've seen it here before."

"It probably belongs to one of the neighbors. You're scaring me, Albert. Why did you leave this morning?"

"My name isn't Albert, it's Charlie."

The revelation comes out painlessly, in a rush of words. *Sticks and stones can break my bones, but words can never hurt me.* Like hell they can't.

"What are you talking about?"

"My name is Charlie Sandors. I'm not a writer, I'm just a guy. A guy who likes to go to funerals. I didn't know your husband and I'm not writing a book."

Lily is silent.

"I'm sorry. I never meant it to go this far. I never meant to hurt you."

"I don't understand."

Her voice is very small, monotone.

"I was just pretending. It's my hobby. I go to funerals and deliver eulogies for people I don't know. It's always just been for fun. I didn't mean for this to happen."

This isn't going well. I'm going too fast. I'm screwing up. Wrong, past tense, I've already really screwed up.

"Who are you?" Lily asks, still carefully, quietly forming each word.

"I told you. My name is Charlie Sandors. I'm not a lunatic or a rapist or anything. I'm not going to hurt you."

"Why would you do this?"

"I don't know. You were so happy. It made you so happy that I was doing this book. I couldn't bear to tell you the truth."

"So why are you telling me now?"

"Because I've found out things you need to know. I've gotten myself in too deep to walk away."

Lily steps backwards and stumbles. I reach out to grab her hand and keep her from falling, but she slaps it away. She moves further back into the shadows.

"I care about you too much," I say. "I can't walk away from you."

My eyes have adjusted to the darkness and I can see Lily standing in front of me. She's holding her head in her hands. I'm making her head hurt. I'm pushing her brain to accept the unacceptable. She's holding her head so it won't explode.

"Michael was murdered, Lily. I'm sure of it."

She doubles over. Those words hurt; they physically hurt her. A scream sticks in her throat.

"Why are you doing this?" She chokes out her words between gasps of air. It's as if something is strangling her from the inside. As if she can't quite catch her breath. "Why are you saying these things?"

"I'm not just saying things. It's the truth. Howard and Gavin murdered your husband because he found out their drug was changing people, altering their brains beyond control."

My words are coming more smoothly now. Once past that initial confession, the truth just spills out over the dam. I couldn't stop now even if I wanted do. A flash flood of disclosure.

"They were getting better and smarter," I continue. "There's no doubt about that, but at some point they began to crossover from intelligence to insanity. They were systematically doing away with anyone they didn't like. Some of them started small, maybe a barking dog in the neighborhood suddenly disappeared, but pretty soon, they moved up the food chain."

"*You* are insane," Lily says, her voice rings with disbelief and what else—disgust maybe? "They couldn't get away with something like that."

"Why not? People get away with all kinds of stuff every day. Murder's a bigger risk than walking out of Wal-Mart with a CD in your belt, but if you're smart enough, you can do it. You can do it and cover it up. And who's going to suspect sweet little grandpa or grandma?"

Lily's breathing has quieted. She's standing straight but her arms are wrapped protectively around her stomach. I might deliver another sucker punch of a revelation at any moment.

"How do you know all this?" she asks. "If you're just some guy, how come you know what happened?"

"I may have started out lying about all this writer stuff, but after a while, I really *was* working for you. I was researching and investigating and I'm good at that. It's what I really do. It's my job."

"What? You're a private eye or something, Charlie? Charlie Chan?

I smile. That was good. Even with her world tumbling down around her ears, she can still make a joke.

"No, I'm not a private investigator. I'm an insurance investigator. Same idea but with a better suit and regular hours."

I smile again, at my own joke this time. Lily is not amused.

"I still don't understand how you came up with such an unbelievable theory," she says.

"I cracked Michael's notes. That's what I found this morning on his computer. That's why I left in such a hurry."

Lily steps toward me. Her dark hair falls loose around her face, framing her so she blends right into the blackness.

"You mean the notes that went with his schedule?"

"Yes. There were entries on almost every day. Just like we'd thought there would be."

"What did they say?"

A lock of hair has fallen across her face. She is so beautiful. I reach out and gently brush it to one side. She flinches and her hand flies up to the spot I've touched. I pull my hand away, but not too quickly. She looks at me, still touching the side of her head. Is that anger in her eyes? No, she's not angry with me. Not yet at least.

"Michael would have made a pretty good P.I. himself," I say, finally answering her question. "He was tracking down the original test participants, interviewing them. He uncovered the pattern. Taken individually, the instances just look like tragic accidents, but together, they are a rather deadly string of coincidences. "

"How was Nesler keeping it from him?"

"Not everybody went completely off the deep end. They were feeding Michael the normal ones and keeping the others out of sight. He wasn't supposed to see the rotten apples just the red, shiny ones on top."

Lily steps away from me, walking forward in the dark until her outstretched hand touches the wall of the garage. She turns and leans against the wall. My pupils have adjusted to the lack of light and I can see Lily's head is tipped back. She is staring up at the ceiling. Just staring. Did you know someone with a wandering eye can still see out of his roving eye? The eye itself hasn't stopped working; the brain simply stops accepting its signals. Back when the bad eye first stepped out of line and started sending conflicting signals to the brain, causing double vision, the brain just said," *Fuck this, I'm not working that hard to keep you two apart, I'll just ignore you and rely on the other guy.*" So the bad eye is still looking around at stuff, but the brain doesn't care. The bad eye is seeing all kinds of cool stuff the brain never even knows about.

Lily stops staring at the ceiling and looks at me.

"And Howard found out?" she asks. "He found out Michael knew what was really going on?"

"Michael told him."

"He told him? Why?

Her voice is so tiny, almost childlike. I'm systematically crushing her world.

"I don't think Michael suspected it was a cover-up. I think he trusted Howard and Gavin almost to the end. Otherwise, I don't think he would have agreed to meet them."

"Meet them? What do you mean, meet them?"

"That's why he went to that airport. To meet Howard and Gavin. He believed he was bringing them information they needed to know about. They were going to discuss what should be done. Michael had already told them he wasn't comfortable being associated with the drug in its current state. They knew he was ready to pull out."

"If Michael pulled out they would have lost everything."

"Exactly."

Lily returns her gaze to the ceiling. What's up there? I stare up into the darkness, seeing nothing but the outline of the garage door opener. Maybe she's looking to God to bail her out of this mess.

"All this was in his notes?" she asks, still looking at God.

"Not everything. I'm coming to some of my own conclusions, but I think there's enough evidence to support them. And, I think I can find the rest of the evidence I need to convince the authorities."

Outside a car engine roars to life. Lily and I both jump. She runs back over to where I'm standing. I recognize the low purr of an expensive transmission gliding into gear. The BMW is on the move. I grab Lily's shoulders and hold her still until the sound fades into the distance.

"What time is it?" I ask, shaking her a little.

She squirms under my grasp but doesn't break free. She presses the dial of her watch and it begins to glow.

"About 11:30. Why?"

Mary did it. She pulled it off. Her timing was perfect. If my instincts are right, Gavin was sitting in that BMW. Mary got a hold of Howard, and now Howard has just contacted Gavin. If this works the way it's supposed to, both of them should be on their way to Nesler.

I let go of Lily's shoulders but hold her in my gaze.

"Do you think you can trust me?" I ask.

She's looking right at me. The fear, the confusion in her eyes before is gone now. She studies my face, her lips pressed together in a pout, as if scanning for some clue to who I am, a star-shaped mole on the side of my cheek that marks me as trustworthy, some sign that will explain the unexplainable.

"I don't know."

"Fair enough," I say. "Do you think you could give me the benefit of the doubt?"

"Maybe."

"Good enough. You need to come with me to the lab site."

"It's the middle of the night. No one will be there."

"You have an access key don't you? From all those media tours you're always giving?"

"For the interior doors, yes, but I don't think I can get into the main building."

"Leave that to me."

"Why do you want to go to the lab?"

"I'm betting it's where Howard stashed the original patient files. Howard would keep a paper trail. He may not have confessions of guilt, but I'm betting he has notes about anything unusual that's happened in the patients' lives. Between those files and Michael's computer diary, we should have everything we need."

"Need for what?"

"To show Michael was murdered and Nesler's drug is a disaster."

Lily falls silent again. Has she forgotten for a minute that this is about Michael being murdered? Let me slap you in the face again, Lily. Words hurt like hell.

"Come with me," I say, very softly. I reach out and touch her face, sliding my hand down to cup her chin. The way you would a child you were trying to comfort. "I know I'm not who you thought I was. I lied about that. But I've never lied about wanting to help you."

She looks at me. She doesn't pull away from my hand. Instead, she tips her head toward it, resting in my palm. Her eyes are as dark and calm as the very first day I saw them, looking at me down a row of mourners in a pew. Lovely and gracious, even under such unfortunate circumstances.

"Come with me?"

She nods and I drop my hand.

"I think Michael would have liked you," she says.

"I doubt that."

"Then I'll like you for him."

TWENTY THREE

Lily's car, a sleek black Mercedes sedan with a gleaming front grille and twin spoke wheels, is not your typical stealth-mobile. I thought we might be more inconspicuous in an economy model and suggested stealing a car, but Lily thought that would be wrong. Life and death versus right and wrong? It seems to pale in comparison. But that's just me. So, we're heading off to confront two murderers in the comfort and luxury of heated leather seats.

Even with Howard and Gavin going by Nesler first, time is not on our side. Especially since we have a stop to make. We drive down the ramp into my office tower's underground parking lot and come to a stop at the security bar. She looks at me questioningly.

"Security bar," I say.

"I know what it is, Albert."

"Charlie."

"I know what it is," she says again, staring at me and speaking very slowly, as if I might not speak the same language and need extra time to translate her words from English into Idiot. "How do you open it?"

"Oh. Sorry."

I fumble for my wallet, pull out my card key and hand it to Lily. She takes it, snatches it really, and eases the car forward to the employee card-reader box that stands guard on a thick yellow post. There's a click and a whirr and the bar lifts up to let us pass. Lily tosses the card back on my lap and drives through.

"Where should we park?" she asks.

"Over there," I say, pointing across the lot to an elevator with an enormous orange "G" painted on its door. "Park in the far corner next to the elevator. I have to go down one floor."

Lily carefully follows the directional arrows, circling around to the other side of the building. She could just drive straight across; there's no one else parked anywhere. But that would be *wrong*. I'm not sure about Justin and Dave, but I know Brad drives a Corvette. No Corvette. No nothing. Maybe the lab's assigned spots are up higher. My spot is up on the fourth level. Maybe this is visitor parking. I've never been a visitor here. Dammit, I hope they haven't left without us. I check my watch. 11:51. Cuttin' it crazy close.

We park right next to the elevator. I jump out before Lily has a chance to turn off the engine.

"You wait here," I say, ready to slam the door in her face.

"No way," she shouts

She grabs her keys out of the ignition and hops out.

"You're not ditchin' me again."

She stands at her open door, looking across at me. Her mouth firm, her brow furrowed, but her eyes bright. She's enjoying this. Maybe I was wrong. Maybe I'm not the only crazy one. Or, more likely, maybe she's humoring me, stringing me along until she can alert the authorities. It's like those old suspense movies where they keep the killer talking on the phone, unburdening his soul, while a S.W.A.T. team the size of Texas is climbing in through the windows of his hideout.

"Suit yourself," I say, "but these guys haven't seen a woman all day. I can't guarantee your safety."

We slam our car doors in unison.

"I can take care of myself. I've managed to keep *you* in check all these weeks, haven't I?"

She's still looking at me over the top of the car. I realize she's known all along. I am a pathetic slob. A transparent, lecherous pathetic slob.

"That obvious?" I ask.

She drops her keys in her purse and walks around to the front of the car.

"Pretty obvious. I thought it was sweet."

Oh. That hurt. The only thing worse than sweet would have been cute. Both these adjectives describe a guy you are about to dump on his cute, sweet little head.

"You know," she continues, "if you would stop trying to second-guess what people thought about you for a minute, you might just be able to accept the truth."

"The truth? What do you mean?"

She steps forward and presses the elevator call button.

"You're a nice guy," she answers. "If you gave them more of a chance, people might actually like you."

I walk over to her. We stand side by side, staring at the lighted numbers above the door as they count down from fifteen to one. Fifteen is my floor. I wonder why the car was all the way up there. Howard? *Ten, nine, eight.* He couldn't possibly have figured it out yet. *Seven, six, five.* I have a sick feeling in my stomach. *Four, three, two.* I grab Lily, yank her away from the front of the elevator doors and slam us both against the brick wall. *One, ding.* The doors glide open. Nothing. No gun shot. No one rushes out.

"What the hell did you do that for?" Lily shouts, rubbing her shoulder with one hand and shoving me with the other.

Ding. The doors slide closed again without us inside.

"I'm sorry. I thought there might have been someone on the elevator."

"Next time, just tell me to move, okay? That was some kind of Stallone stunt move."

"I'm sorry."

"It's okay. You just scared me."

"That's because I'm scared."

Lily turns to me. She's still rubbing her shoulder. Then, in one fluid movement, she reaches up with both hands, slides them around my head and guides my face down to hers. She kisses me, hard and full, her fingers comb through my hair and grasp at the back of my neck. This is no sympathy kiss. My arms instinctively wrap around her, running first up and then down to the small of her back. I press her body into mine. Hold her. Kiss her back as strong and deep as she is kissing me. Forever. Let me stay like this forever. But she is the first to pull away. She looks down and pushes against my chest. I allow her to move back but keep my hands around her waist. Finally, she looks up at me. Her eyes are soft, black velvet, glistening at the edges. With what? Is it just moisture ... or tears? Is she cold ... or undeniably miserable?

"That was probably a really stupid thing to do," she says. "I'm not sorry right now, but I will be in a few seconds when I catch my breath."

"Don't be sorry."

She twists free of my hands and turns back to face the elevator.

"There's too much happening all of a sudden," she says without turning around to face me. "I'm losing focus. I'm probably also losing my mind, but I'm trying to ignore that."

"I'm the one who should be sorry," I say, coming up beside her. "This whole thing is my fault. I should have left well enough alone." I pick at the bottom of my sweater, looking for a thread to pull, one pull and it all unravels, like in the cartoons. "Let sleeping dogs lie, right? But I couldn't do that. I had to kick the goddamn dog."

I lean over to push the call button The elevator had simply risen to the main floor, so on this second try, it arrives much more quickly.

"I changed my mind," I say, turning to her. "You can't come."

Lily whips her head around and stares at me in disbelief.

"What do you mean, I can't come."

"They can't see you with me. You are not part of Charlie Sandors' life"

"So, introduce me. How hard is that?

The elevator doors start to close again. I instinctively jump forward and brace a foot against one side to keep them open. This wide open stance reminds me of how Superman stands: feet planted, fists on hips, cape furling. Superman knows to always stand into the wind to get the best cape furl. I know imagining myself in Superman's costume is not helping the immediate situation in any way, but as usual, I can't help it. I look at Lily. She's waiting for me to answer her question. She is not Lois Lane.

"I won't need to introduce you," I say, letting my hands fall limp at my sides. "They'll recognize you. Everyone knows the famously beautiful Lily Rudolf."

Lily sneers at the compliment.

"So they'll be *thrilled* to meet me, so what?"

"Think about it for a minute. Why would the famously beautiful Lily Rudolph be tagging along with the prominent nobody Charlie Sandors as he arrives to pick up a few illegal lab results at midnight in an otherwise empty building? Something tells me we'd have some 'splaining to do and I don't want to do any 'splaining."

Lily doesn't answer. She simply crosses her arms and stares.

"It will just take minute," I insist.

"Okay," she says. "I know you're right, but I don't like it. I'll wait here, but if you're not back in ten minutes, I'm coming down anyway."

I release my foot doorstop and step all the way inside the car, then spin to face the closing doors. I call this move *elevator ballet*: step, pirouette and stand, arms down, head back, eyes up toward the flashing lights of the ascending or descending floors. Watch for it next time you're in an elevator. It's really quite graceful, especially if several people get on at once.

I drop one floor and step out onto the shiny linoleum of the lab hallway. In the distance are the strains of Led Zeppelin guitar riffs. They haven't left yet. I jog down the hall and turn into the reception area. It's dark and quiet. A few pizza boxes are still stacked on Brad's desk. It smells like stale grease. A sliver of light bleeds out from the sides and bottom of the swinging door into the lab.

"Hey guys," I shout. "I'm here. Can I come on back?"

Someone turns down Zeppelin and Justin pops his round head through the door.

"Hey, Charlie," he says, pushing the door open and wagging a finger in my direction. "We almost gave up on you. Actually, Dave almost gave up on you, but he's still kinda pissed about the whole staying late thing."

I pass through the door into the fluorescent brightness of the lab. Dave stands at a back counter slowing putting Mr. Klein's shoes back into their bag. Justin's right. He does look pissed. Brad sits on a tall stool in the middle of room, a boom box at his elbow, smiling and slapping his thigh in time to the drum solo.

"Mr. Sandors," Brad says, standing up. He grasps the lapels of his lab coat and looks me over like a major general surveying a rather disheveled private. "We were beginning to worry about you."

"If you're finished ridiculing," I say, crossing the room in three quick strides, "I'd appreciate just picking up the results and getting out of here. I'm sure you're ready to split, and I have somewhere I'm supposed to be."

"At midnight?" asks Brad, dropping the authoritarian act and leaning toward me with a sly wink. "You have an appointment at midnight?"

"It's a long story."

There is a part of me that wants to brag about having just locked lips, in the garage one floor above, with the famously beautiful Lily Rudolph. But they'd never believe me. In fact, the ensuing laughter would be loud and long, and eventually, I'd have to punch Brad in his pretty-boy face to get him to shut up. At which point, he'd pummel me until Dave and Justin took pity and pulled him off. I'd lie in a quivering heap on the floor of the lab while the three of them stood over me. Finally, Justin would spit on me and Dave would drop the bag of shoes on my head. No, I don't think I'll mention the part about Lily.

"We've all been up a lot longer than we'd like already," I say. "I promise to fill you in one of these days."

"Your call, Chaz." Brad shrugs it off. "I'm not trying to be nosy. I have the reports right here."

He turns and picks up a thin file folder. The fluorescents bleach out his freckles, making him look almost serious. Almost.

"We should take a few minutes to go through the highlights," he says, holding the folder against his chest, his biceps impressive even through the lab coat. "You can call me Monday morning if you have any questions about the details."

"I hate to be rude, Bradley, but I really do need to leave. I'm sure you've all gone to a tremendous amount of work and I couldn't be more grateful. But I know you understand how important it is that I simply must take the results and go."

I extend my arm in Brad's direction, hand up, palm open.

"Such a sincere request, Chaz. How can I refuse? But remember, I won't be around this weekend so don't try calling me to decipher results."

"Fine, fine."

He hands me the folder and my fingers close around its spine. I draw it in to my chest and wrap my arm around it to protect the precious cargo inside. Dave strolls forward and hands me the bag of shoes.

"It was the Oxfords," he says. "And only the left shoe, not the right. That probably means he's right-handed. He stood on his right leg and smeared the frosting on the bottom of his left shoe."

"You guys are the best," I say, grabbing the bag. The juice glass clinks at the bottom. "I'll see you Monday with the money. First thing, I promise."

I turn to leave and am almost through the swinging door when Brad calls after me.

"Remember. None of us were ever here tonight. Those results aren't admissible with a standard report. I'll never admit they came from my lab."

I catch the door with my free hand and hold it open. But I don't turn around. I let his words bounce off the back of my head.

"If you decide any of this is worth pursuing," Brad continues. "You'll have to do an official 40-24 request and we'll rebuild everything. We won't need any of the evidence back. We can use the same information, probably just copy it right over from the original. But it has to be on a corporate form to make it valid and you have to have it notarized. Justin here's a notary."

The sleazy sonofabitch. He'll get paid twice for this, once by me and once by corporate to do it on the up and up. I'm gonna get stuck with the bill for tonight. If I turn around now, I know they'll be a smirk on that freckled face. So I don't. I simply step through and release the door. It swings in and out, sending diminishing flashes of light into the dark reception area. Stupid, creepy lab rats. But it doesn't matter. I got what I needed.

The elevator arrives and I ride back up to the main garage level. I open the folder. The results are handwritten on graph paper. Not that you could really call it handwriting. Most of the sheets contain nothing but random calculations and scratchy notes. There are a few spectrometer print-outs stapled to the first page and in the very back of the folder are several sheets of paper with Polaroid photos of shoes glued to them. Shit, maybe I should have let the asshole explain this mess.

A blast of cool air blows into the elevator as the doors open onto the garage. Lily stands exactly where I left her. I half expected her to have disappeared. To where, I don't know. It just would have been more in keeping with the evening so far.

"Well?" she says, walking towards me.

But before I can answer, Lily's cell phone screams, splitting the stillness of the empty garage. Either that or I just screamed.

"Don't answer it," I shout.

"Why not?"

"Who would call you at this time of night?"

"Under normal circumstances, no one. That's why it's probably important."

"Let it go to voicemail."

The shrill ringing echoes off the empty walls as if 1000 phones demand our attention.

"What if someone's in trouble?" she asks.

"Who?"

"I don't know who."

"We're the ones in trouble, Lily. Don't answer it."

On the sixth ring the phone falls silent but the sound reverberates for several seconds. A pulsating beep reminds us a voicemail is waiting.

"Okay, now check it. Check your voicemail."

Lily puts the phone to her ear and listens to the new message. I try to watch her eyes.

"Who is it?"

She drops her head and waves her hand to shush me. When she finally lowers the phone and looks up at me, I see the fear immediately.

"It was Howard," she says. "He was looking for you, for Albert. What should I do?"

I never expected Howard to call Lily. But why wouldn't he? She's the only other person who knows Albert. He's doing exactly what I want him to do. He's sweating through his monogrammed shirt right about now.

"Nothing," I answer. "I doubt he really thought you'd pick up. I'm his target not you."

Lily stares at the small cell phone in her hand as if it might have something more to say. Now that would be an invention, wouldn't it? A cell phone that produced running commentary on all your calls, like carrying around your best friend in your pocket. *Don't call back that idiot, he's just out to get you.* But Lily's cell phone doesn't speak. Lily does.

She wraps her hand around the cell phone and clutches it to her chest. Her eyes are filled with tears

"Why did he do it, Charlie? Michael was such a good person. Everybody loved Michael."

She used my name. She didn't hesitate or stumble. She used my real name.

"There's no way to explain it we would understand. Money, pride, heat of the moment. Why do we make any of the decisions we do? Most likely, because we're afraid and don't see any other way out."

Lily looks away and slowly slides the phone back into her pocket.

"What now?" she asks.

"The lab site. We have to get into the lab and find the original files. And we have to do it before Howard gets there and destroys them completely, which I'm sure he now wishes he'd done a long time ago."

I wish I could be a fly on the wall in Howard's office right now. Not that Howard would ever allow there to be a fly on the wall in his office, but if one could sneak in unnoticed, I'd like to be that fly. I'd like to see him now. Is he angry, remorseful, scared? All three? None of the above? I always hated that option on the multiple choice tests. None of the above? As if I didn't already have hundreds of useful facts rattling around in my brain, now I was supposed to absorb three additional false statements and cross-check them against the true data. Lily interrupts my internal tirade. My thoughts are wandering again, I'm pretty sure that means I'd prefer to not focus on the task at hand.

"Why are you so sure the files are there?" she asks.

"Howard's not the throw-away type. He's too anal. Look at how he dresses. On his worst day, he still looks better than me dressed to the nines. He's a perfectionist, a note-taker, a list-maker. He tidies things away, but they're never completely out of reach. I bet he has a file cabinet full of cancelled checks from the seventies."

"You're just guessing."

"Yeah, I'm just guessing. But I'm a good guesser. Comes with the territory."

"What if you're not right?"

"What if I am?"

TWENTY FOUR

"Don't drive all the way up to it," I tell Lily as the lab site looms into view. "Just park here."

"We're over a block away. I thought you were in a hurry."

"I am not in a hurry for Howard to spot your car. Just park."

Lily pulls over. Her tires scratch against the curb. In the distance, the heavy machinery surrounding the construction site slumbers in the darkness. Cranes and cats, in the shadows they begin to resemble the animals their names imply, hydraulic arms and necks curled under them as they sleep. Lily reaches into the back seat and grabs a bright yellow sweater.

"Are you going to wear that?" I ask.

"It's cold."

"You could also wear a flashing light on your head."

"What?"

"Don't you have anything a little bit darker? I was hoping to be inconspicuous. That sweater does not say, 'sneaking into a building'. It says, 'hey over here, I'm over here'."

"Very funny. I left all my camo gear at home. It's dark and I'm cold; stop worrying."

I watch in silence as Lily puts on the sweater. She flips her hair out from under the collar and it settles around her shoulders in dark, silky waves. I reach across and slide my hand through her hair and around her neck. I can feel the thin gold chain of the locket she always wears. She doesn't resist as I pull her toward me. Her head tilts back, her lips part, inviting me. This kiss is better than the first. Maybe I'm just more prepared for the delicious softness of her mouth, the sensuous stroke of her tongue. Maybe not. I lean into her, my hands exploring her body, landing first on her breasts, full and warm, then her waist, her thighs, her ass. Searching every inch, memorizing the curves. Her hands are on my shoulders, running up and down my back. And then they stop. Now they're pushing, No! Don't push me away. I press closer. Don't stop. I love you. You know that. You must know that by now. Please don't.

"Charlie," she whispers, still pushing. "Please don't."

As if reading my thoughts. As if seeing right through me. And would that be so hard? My breath comes out in jagged gasps, but I try to relax, try to sit back into my own seat.

"I'm sorry," I say. "I wasn't thinking. When I'm around you I have a hard time thinking."

"None of it makes any sense anymore," she says. "I've given up on thinking."

I reach for the door handle to get out, put my hand right on it, but then my reflexes seize. I stare at the window. Not *out* the window. At the glass itself, at its smeary, thick surface. Glass is not a complete solid. Gravity pulls at it like saltwater taffy, and after a hundred years or so, gravity starts to win. That's why windows in very old houses always seem rippled and distorted, like you're looking out at the world through a fun house mirror. Of course, this window probably isn't moving. It's some high-tech, crash-proof safety glass, not real glass. Not real sinking glass.

"I love you, Lily."

The words jump out, making a little puff of condensation on the window. They're not in my head anymore, they've escaped, and like all pent-up prisoners happy to be free, they shout and bounce off the walls and call attention to themselves. I can't control them anymore, and so they repeat themselves.

"I love you so much."

"Don't say that, Charlie," Lily whispers. "You don't mean it. Everything's too crazy."

No more happy words. My declaration thuds to the floor, twitching, writhing.

"What do you expect me to say?" she continues, grinding my pitiful, dying words into the carpet. "I don't even know who you are. I feel like those people you read about who find out as adults that their sisters are really their mothers. I shouldn't have kissed you. I don't know why I did. I obviously didn't stop you."

Silence. Heavy steel plates of silence. The car is shrinking, closing in on us. Then, her hand is on my back, a small circle of warm pressure. It stops the car from crushing us.

"I'm sorry," she says, quietly, comforting me, arousing me. "I'm so confused. I need some time."

"How much?" I ask, turning back around.

Her hand drops away from my back.

"What?"

"How much time do you need?"

I lean toward her again, touching her knee.

"I don't know. I can't tell you that."

She looks up at me finally and the emotion in her eyes is bottomless. There's a sadness there that's so deep, I know if I could reach through it would go all the way to her soul and beyond. Like the ocean or an ice crevasse or space, like getting sucked out of the airlock into the black void of the universe.

"Do you hate me?" I ask, afraid of her answer.

She places her hand over mine, holding it against her leg. I try to slide up her thigh but her hand stops me.

"Of course I don't hate you."

"You're so sure you don't hate me. Why can't you be sure you don't love me?"

"It's not the same."

"They're our most intense emotions. Love and hate. Why would one be so much harder to discern than the other?"

"Stop it, Charlie. Just stop it. I cannot deal with this right now."

Her voice chokes off as her head falls forward. Well, that was effective. I've made her cry. Pathetic oaf.

"I'm sorry. Please don't cry. I'll stop."

"I do care about you," she says. "I'm just not sure who you are."

She looks up at me. Her eyes are glazed over with tears. Some have spilled down her cheeks.

"Me either. I don't know who I am. Nobody does. Do you really know who you are?"

"No."

I wipe away a single tear and brush her hair back behind her ear.

"We have work to do," I say.

I reach again for the door handle, and this time I open the door and step out in the damp, early morning air. She follows out her side. We both look toward the construction site and start walking.

I detail my plan for Lily.

"Anything Howard has brought over here is most likely to be in the finished part, where the offices are. But that's also going to be the hardest part to get into. So, we're going to go in through the lab, the unfinished part."

"Phase Two."

"That's my whole plan. I don't have a Phase Two."

"No, that's what they call the lab construction, Phase Two. I don't know my way around in there as well as I do in Phase One. Plus, the keys I have are only for inside of Phase One."

"Don't worry, we'll find a way in. Do you know if they have a security guard on site?"

"I don't think so. Probably just one of those services that drives by every so often and checks on things."

A chain link fence rings the perimeter of the site. Signs are posted every few feet warning us not to trespass, reminding us to Keep Back, and advertising the names of the architectural firm and the bank responsible for the fence and everything inside it. During the day, flaggers keep everyone away, but after-hours a few brave neighbors reclaim the curb for their cars, betting they can be gone before the tow trucks can catch them in the morning. Here at the edge, streetlights illuminate the scene, but on the other side it fades from dim to dark to invisible. I lead Lily along the fence, looking for a gate. There should be two gates, a main one for the union guys, another for sub-contractors and deliveries. We want the second gate, the B Gate; it should be easier to get through.

Without warning, or simply because I'm focused on seeing rather than hearing, headlights sweep around the far corner. I grab Lily's arm and dive towards one of the parked cars, pulling her down with me into the dirt along the curb. On the way down, my head hits the car's rearview mirror and I swallow an expletive as we land with a sickening thump. Lily moans. The car drives past very slowly, the light intensifying. It must be the security patrol. They have a spotlight that lights up the fence line from the car's window. Guy doesn't have to get out and get all chilly, just sets down his travel mug and points the light around for a little while. Looks official enough. The car pulls past and idles for a minute just a few feet in front of us. The light arcs to the left then back to the right. It falls across the hood of our hideout and I suddenly see my hands and Lily's head. I release all the air from my chest, hoping it will flatten me further into the dirt. Then the light cuts off and the car pulls away.

Neither of us moves until the engine is no longer audible. I get up first and help Lily to her feet. Her yellow sweater is caked with dirt and debris. She swabs at the side of her mouth with her sleeve.

"Are you okay?" I ask, rubbing my head.

"I think I cut my lip. Is it swollen?"

I reach out and gently touch the corner of her mouth. She flinches.

"Sorry. Right there. There's a little cut right there."

"Great."

"The mouth heals fast."

She explores the cut with her own finger and looks at me with a raised eyebrow.

"Spoken like someone who gets slugged in the mouth a lot."

"Not really. Once or twice, but I remember how much it hurt. Everything else okay?"

"I think so. How about you?"

"I whacked my head on the mirror."

Lily grimaces. "We should hurry and get inside. I don't want to do that again."

"The car stopped up there and was shining the light back and forth. I bet that's the main gate."

I jog back over to the fence and see it almost immediately. Four of the chain link panels overlap and an imposing padlock secures their position.

"This is the main entrance alright," I call over my shoulder. "The other gate should be just a little bit farther down."

Lily jogs up beside me. She's still holding her sleeve to her chin.

"Why doesn't everybody go through the same gate?"

"Union rules," I explain, still walking, running my hand along the bumpity-bump of the chain link. "The second gate is like the servants' entrance. Guess it makes the union guys feel more important."

"How do you know so much about construction sites?"

"My dad was an electrician."

"Is he retired now?"

"Dead."

"I'm sorry."

I'm several steps ahead of her before I notice she's stopped. I turn and motion for her to hurry and follow.

"It's okay," I say. "He didn't die yesterday or anything. He's been dead for years. It's old news, really."

"I'm still sorry," she says, catching up again and touching me on the elbow. "What about your mom?"

Now I stop. She runs into my shoulder. I turn abruptly and stare into her sympathetic eyes. I don't need to add pitiful to my already pathetic list of qualities.

"Before you exhaust yourself with a rundown of my existing relatives, let me save you the trouble." I slap both hands on my chest. "It's only me. There's no one else but me. Okay?"

"Okay." Her voice is just a peep.

"Come on. I think I see the gate."

Up ahead, the straight line of the fence is again interrupted, but instead of metal panels meshed together, there's a sheet of plywood anchored in place. A giant "B" is spray-painted in surveyor's orange on the wood's knotty surface. Fist-sized holes are drilled in each edge and a length of heavy chain weaves through the links and around the board's middle, dissecting the "B" in half. A smaller padlock closes the circle but doesn't draw it taut. I reach out and rattle the chain. Lily shushes me.

"We're going to have to make a little noise to get inside the fence."

"It's locked," she says, pointing out the obvious.

"I see that. But whoever locked it wasn't trying very hard. We can squeeze in through the bottom."

Lily looks down where the plywood rests against dirt. The edge is ragged from being drug open and shut every day. Splinters of ply have curled up from the bottom and cracked off like peeling skin.

"Where?"

"It's just plywood and the chain is loose. I'll pull it back and you can crawl through. Then, you hold it open from the inside and I'll shimmy in after you."

She looks doubtful, an emotion accentuated by her rapidly swelling lip.

"You can stay here," I offer. "Give me your keys and wait over by that car."

"Pull it open," she says, squaring her hands on her hips. "I did not come this far to sit by myself in the cold next to some beat-up Toyota." She repeats her demand. "Go on. Pull it open."

I bend down and curl my fingers around the side of the board. It moves easily at first but reaches the end of its flexibility rather quickly. The triangle of open space is big enough for a terrier to wiggle through but is not going to accommodate Lily. I walk my hands higher up the side for better leverage and pull back harder, driving several splinters into my palm. The triangle opens up a few more inches.

"I don't think I can fit through there," Lily says.

"You won't know if you don't try."

Lily kneels and considers the opening. She pokes her head through, pulls it back, then tests the roughness of the plywood with one tentative finger.

"You need to try *now*," I grunt out the last word, straining to keep the opening as wide as possible. "This hurts."

She stretches out in the dirt on her side, hands and arms close to her body, and undulates into the opening like an escaping seal.

"Push out on the chain link as you go through."

"It's too tight," she hisses.

I lift one leg and kick it against the chain link panel. The metal crashes and clatters violently. Lily cries out. I'm not sure if it's pain or fear. If anyone is here and hasn't noticed us yet, this ought to get their attention.

"Damn it, Charlie! What the hell did you do that for?"

But the jolt gives her plenty enough room to snake through the rest of the way. She's in.

"Hold it for me. Push against it."

Lily positions herself against the plywood, arms straight, legs braced. I slowly let go, transferring the resistance. The opening retracts.

"Push harder."

"I am pushing harder."

Her elbows buckle and the panel clangs back into its original position.

"Shit!" She whines from the other side of the plywood. "Let me try again."

"No," I say, frustrated with how hard this is, how long it is taking. "Find something to pry it open with. Something that will give you some leverage."

"Like what?"

She steps around and peers out at me. Her fingers lace through the weave of the fence.

"You look like a prisoner," I say. "But I'm not sure which of is in and which of us is out." I cover the tips of her fingers with my palms. The criss-cross of the metal feels rough but cool.

"I'm in," she says.

She flexes her fingers. The light scratch of her nails sends an electric jolt through my arms, down to my knees and back up into my crotch. That's the kind of electrical circuitry my dad never had the chance to teach me about.

She smiles at me, but with her swollen lip, it's more of a smirk. She is so beautiful. Bits of sawdust tangle in her hair, two buttons are gone from her filthy sweater. So beautiful.

"What am I supposed to find?" she asks.

I force myself to look past her.

"I can't see very well. Is there any lumber? You need a 2x4, something long and skinny."

She turns away from the fence and disappears into the shadows, returning in a few minutes with a length of rebar.

"How about this?" she holds it aloft like a spear. "There's a whole pile of these pole thingys."

"That'll work. Shove it in between the plywood and the fence and push out. Like a lever."

Lily follows my instructions, creating an opening I crawl through with relative ease. I stand up and survey the yard. The building itself is only about 100 feet away. Tarp-shrouded piles of materials dot the landscape, probably more pole thingys.

"We've lost a lot of time. Let's go."

I grab Lily's hand and we hurry toward the building. My eyes adjust to the diminishing light. When I was little, my dad would bring me to his job sites every so often. Things were more easy-going back then, not so many rules and regulations, everyone looking over their shoulders for a liability claim. He'd just plop a hard hat on my head and I'd follow him all over. He'd let me carry spools of wire or I'd just sit and watch him work. I used to like to play with those bright-colored wire caps, sticking them on the ends of my fingers the way some kids do with black olives. Monster claws I called them. I wonder what he'd think of me now. I'm sure I didn't turn out the way he'd imagined. A white collar instead of blue to start with. No wife, no kids, no bass boat. Then there's the whole lying-about-who-I-am issue. It's like the motorcycle hellion whose kid's a nuclear physicist. The banker's boy who chooses French romanticism over fiduciary responsibility. Things rarely turn out as planned.

Lily and I reach the perimeter walls of the lab. The upper levels are only framed and still open to the weather, but the first floor is nearly done. I run my hand over the smooth stone surface.

"Pretty fancy."

"The first floor walls are faced in granite."

"There must be an opening somewhere. You've seen the plans. Where are the most windows?"

"This is the back. There's supposed to be an emergency exit somewhere. But the only side with windows is the front."

"Then we've got to go around front."

We run, hugging the side of the building like urban commandos. The front of the structure faces the main boulevard. There's no traffic at this hour but we are well within view of anyone who might happen by. If time is still ticking by as I originally anticipated, I expect at least two someones to happen by at any minute.

The light from the street is brighter on this side, casting a shadow through the chain link, projecting a diamond pattern across the front of the building. Lily was right. There's a main entrance with an arched canopy and on either side are openings for three large windows. No glass yet. Each of the empty squares is covered in plywood.

"We need something to punch out the plywood. Something like the rebar you had before would be great."

"The what?"

"The pole thingy."

"Are you making fun of me?" Lily asks, punching me in the shoulder.

"No, no, not at all. 'Pole thingy' is much more descriptive and probably a better name."

She punches me again.

We scour the ground nearby for anything useful. A few scattered scraps of lumber, an empty nail box, a plastic tarp. Nothing substantial.

Lily walks up to one of the window openings and pushes against the plywood. It flexes inward then pops back into place.

"It's not very sturdy," she says, pressing on it again.

She turns her back to the opening. I expect her to walk away and continue to help me look for a battering ram. Instead, she spins and plants a horse kick smack dab in the middle of the plywood panel. It crashes in on itself, landing flat against the cement floor. I stare in disbelief.

"TaeKwon-Do, "she says calmly, stepping through the opening and dusting off her pants. "It probably just had a couple little nails holding it in place."

I follow her through in stunned silence, making a mental note to not get on her bad side.

We stop and listen for approaching footsteps. Even more than the earlier crash of the gate, we both instinctively know this latest disturbance ought to bring running anyone in the near vicinity. There's nothing. No traffic outside, no one moving inside, only our breathing, which seems about as loud as an idling steam engine, but is probably not quite that noisy.

"Now where?" Lily asks.

"The offices. Where are they from here?"

"They face Alder Street. We have to go that way."

Lily points into the distance. Light spills in our open window hole and sneaks through various chinks in the other boarded-up ones. There are also gaps in the tarps protecting the upper level framing. It's enough to see. I grab Lily's hand and start to run. The interior of the lab is a vast open canvas interrupted only by periodic columns and piles of lumber and insulation.

I head for the darkest corner, figuring the entrance to the offices would be at the back of the lab rather than the front. Black sheeting is suspended across the far back corner creating a plastic curtain. Behind it is a doorway. A locked doorway.

"Try one of your keys."

Lily digs in her pants and pulls out her key ring. She jams first one and then another key into the lock. Neither work. She jiggles the door handle.

"No way I can kick this thing down. It's solid."

"Shit."

"Now what?"

"Shit."

"You said that already," she says, impatiently, still rattling the door.

"Crap."

I slap the black plastic out of the way and stare back into the cavern that will soon be a bustling lab. I'm sure there's another door somewhere, and I'm also sure it's locked just like this one.

"We could break the lock," Lily suggests.

"That'll take too long."

"Then what do we do? We're stuck."

"Give me a minute to think before you give up, would you?"

I look around again. We can't go through. We can't go around. What's left? I tilt my head back.

"Up," I say.

Lily follows my gaze up the wall. The cement terminates at about eight feet. Above it is open metal framing. No sheetrock. If we can get up there, we can climb through to the other side.

"How high can you jump?" I ask, keeping my voice deadpan, not taking my eyes from the top of the wall.

"Are you nuts?" Lily barks, stomping her feet in time with her words.

"Just kidding," I say, smiling down at her. She punches me. That shoulder is getting sore. "No jumping. We can ride up."

Rubbing my bruised pec, I point to a scissors lift parked on the other side of the plastic sheeting.

"You know how to work that thing?" Lily asks.

"Can't be that hard. Come on."

We climb up onto the lift platform. A key dangles from a small control panel with two levers, forward/reverse and up/down. There are arrows and pictures too, in case I'm confused by the words alone. I turn the key and the small motor rumbles to life. Once again, we are making more noise than a barrel of monkeys while having less fun. I push the lever forward and the tires slowly roll toward the wall.

"Is this all the faster it goes?" Lily asks.

"We're only going a few feet."

We bump to a stop against the wall and I push the up lever. The platform unfolds. There's a chunking sound as the supports lock into position every few feet. Lily grabs hold of the rail. We reach the limit of the lift about a foot below the top of the wall.

"Fourth floor, ladies lingerie and gloves," I say, releasing the lever and killing the motor.

"Aren't you ever too scared to make a joke?"

I sigh and sweep a clump of hair out of my eyes. Cynicism can be a pain in the ass. People think you don't take anything seriously. On the contrary, the cynic is usually the most serious one of the bunch. He's not swayed by polite conversation or the masquerade of good manners. By making light and poking fun, he dulls the truth he sees more plainly than those around him.

"Here's a secret," I explain. "The funnier I get, the more frightened I am. Once we make it into the offices, I'll be a laugh a minute."

I climb up onto the railing of the lift and peer over the top of the wall.

"There's a stair landing just a few feet down on the other side," I report back to Lily. "We can climb through and jump down to it, which is great news since I was not looking forward to my original plan of jumping down to the floor and breaking both my legs."

"You scared again?"

"Yes I am, but I'll go first."

I grab a metal stud and hoist myself onto the top ledge of the wall. Squatting there like a gargoyle, I try to judge the exact distance to the landing. It's not too far, but it's also not a straight leap down. The stairs are off to the right. I launch myself from the wall in what I hope is a diagonal trajectory and thud onto the landing in a graceless heap. Lily's head pokes up over the top of the wall.

"You okay?"

"Piece of cake," I say, scrambling to my feet and dusting myself off. Both my shins are vibrating, like someone's rubbing sand paper up and down them. "Your turn."

Lily follows my lead, except instead of tumbling down like a clod, she lands on her feet, elegantly, effortlessly, like a cat.

Things on this side of the wall are in the last stages of work, but there's still a long way to go. No wonder the investors were getting pissed. The cement floors are unfinished. Tools and torches and welding tanks line the stairs down to the bottom floor. Must be building some kind of fancy railing. Lily and I run down the stairs.

"I recognize where we are now," Lily says. "Follow me."

She takes off down a hallway. I follow, dodging paint buckets and carpet supplies. Lily stops in front of a door, yanks the keys out of her pocket and opens the lock. Inside is a roomy office with a large desk and several filing cabinets. She flips on the light; I immediately flip it off.

"No lights," I hiss, holding my hand over the switch in case she tries again. "We don't need to advertise where we are."

"We won't be able to find anything without the lights."

I dig around in my pocket, searching for the "hey-stupid-you-forgot-to-turn-on-the porch-light-again" squeeze light I keep on my key chain. "We can use this," I say, pointing at Lily and squeezing it on. She flinches.

"Sorry."

I sweep the room with my tiny beam. Three tall file cabinets are lined up in the corner. Thank you, Howard, for being such a tidy sonofabitch. The cabinet drawers are labeled alphabetically. We'll have to think like Howard. "P" for patient? "M" for Michael? "D" for dead? Lily pulls open a drawer.

"Shine that thing over here," she orders.

"What are you doing?"

"Looking," she explains in a clipped voice, over-stating the obvious. "Which is what you should be doing."

"We can't just look through everything; it'll take too long."

"Not as long as standing there." She waves me over. "Move closer with the light."

"Shit, nothing but financial statements," she says, slamming the first drawer and yanking open another. "Are you really sure they're here?" She glances up at me. I relax my grip on the light and it blinks out. Lily blends into the darkness.

It's quiet in the dark, but it's a loud quiet. Maybe it's because you've stripped away one of the senses, allowing the other four to pick up the slack. Touch, taste and smell are there for you, but it's hearing that really steps up to the plate. If you're quiet long enough, you start to notice the rumblings, the noises of the dark. The tick of a clock, a scurrying creature, the shattering of glass. Something always pierces the silence.

"Turn it back on, Charlie."

"What?"

"Turn on the light," Lily whispers, obviously annoyed to be standing in the dark. "We have to keep looking."

"Sorry." I squeeze and shine the light across the folders in the drawer. "See anything that looks familiar?"

"I don't exactly know what I'm looking for so, no, nothing looks like anything." She drops down to her butt on the floor. "You're right. This is going to take too long."

Lily drops her head into her hands. My fingers are cramping from squeezing the light. We're searching in all the obvious places, which is obviously wrong. We've forgotten the crucial question. What would Howard do? We can't think like ourselves; we have to figure out what Howard would do if he were trying to hide something.

"What would Howard do? I ask out loud, excited at the revelation. "Where would you put the files if you were Howard?"

Lily lifts her head up and stares right into the little light.

"Not in a file cabinet," she blurts out and jumps back to her feet, immediately understanding. "Of course! Not in a file cabinet. Something else, like a briefcase or a box."

She grabs the light out of my hand and searches the other corners of the room. Nothing. She falls to her knees and aims the light under the furniture. It sweeps along a small conference table, a credenza, the enormous desk. I see the beam hesitate.

"What? What do you see?"

Lily's head disappears under the desk. The light goes out and I hear a heavy object thunk onto the desk.

"You hold the light," she says, pressing it back into my palm. "It's one of those portable file boxes."

I turn the light on the plastic box Lily has found. She snaps open the lid and rifles through the folders inside.

"This is it, I think this is it. Look."

She pulls out a folder and opens it on the desk. Two metal tongs at the top hold a thick sheaf of papers. I train the light on the folder and Lily flips the pages. They're notes, mostly handwritten, each page with a date stamp. Halfway through is something that looks like a copy of a police report.

"Stop. What's that?"

Lily flips back to the page and we read along together. *Last seen at 7:00 pm on April 20th driving east on Marshall in a blue Buick Regal with Illinois plates. Wearing a tan pantsuit and light green car coat. No note or phone call left behind. No previous episodes of wandering off. Car answering the above description found approximately 45 miles out of town along the golf course maintenance access road, engine running, doors open, no sign of anyone, not even a footprint in the dirt.* It appears to be some kind of missing person report and goes on for a couple pages. I glance at the folder's tab, Mildred Everhouse.

"That name," I say, repeating it under my breath. "I'm sure I recognize that name."

The entire room begins to glow, but it's not from the thrill of discovery. The squeak of brakes causes us both to turn toward the window. The glow recedes, followed by the slam of one car door, then another.

"Time's up," I hiss. I grab Mildred's file, jam it back into the box and slam the lid. "Let's go."

"Is it Howard?" Lily asks, following me out of the room.

"It's not the Good Humor Man."

"You're scared again, right?"

"Right."

TWENTY FIVE

"Head back to the stairs." I push Lily in front of me and give her the file box.

"What are you doing?"

"I'll be right behind you. I think the gentlemanly thing to do at this point is position myself between you and the two guys who are trying to kill you."

"They're trying to kill you."

"Run," I say, pushing her again. "Shut up and run."

The file box bumps against Lily's leg as she takes off down the hall. Behind us I can hear Howard and Gavin. Lights flip on as they close the distance. Lily hits the back hallway and sprints for the stairs. We might just make it. I glance backwards to check on our pursuers, breaking the first rule of escape, "Never, ever look back."

"Charlie, hurry," Lily calls. She's not bothering to whisper anymore. Her voice is loud, shrill.

I turn around just in time to see, but not avoid, a roll of carpet pad. My foot clips the top of the obstacle and throws me off balance. I'm down. Almost to the freakin' stairs and I'm down. I hear Lily scream. The hallway lights flash on over my head and I scramble to my feet as Howard and Gavin round the corner.

"Stay where you are," Gavin shouts, raising his arm level with my head. He's wearing a short black pea coat that makes his bulky frame look even heavier than usual. At the end of his arm is his hand. In his hand is a gun. A gun is pointing at me. How bizarre. A gun is pointing at *me*. I was right. All along I was right. However, being right about someone wanting to kill you is not the winning ticket. This is one of those times when being right is horribly wrong.

A true child of the cinema, I instinctively raise my hands over my head. "Don't shoot."

"Charlie!" Lily, half way up the stairs, is shouting again.

Gavin raises his gun higher, following Lily's voice. Howard steps forward. He's wearing a full-length camel trench coat. If I was a betting man, I'd bet cashmere. Dressed to kill, as usual. His arms are down at his side, but I can see he is also holding a gun. The only hints that this evening has involved more than a jaunt to the theater are the unkempt nature of his hair and his shirt collar hanging open.

"Charlie?" Howard asks, slowly approaching me. "Where's Charlie? Who else is here with us?"

Gavin's eyes sweep the hallway, but his gun remains aimed up at Lily.

"I'm Charlie."

"No, you're Albert."

"I made him up."

"Who?" Howard reaches up with his free hand to smooth his hair, but instead it pushes up, wilder than before, like a rooster's comb.

"Albert. I made up Albert."

"Why would you do that?"

It's a valid question, and really, the crux of why I'm here right now. Here, in a half finished hallway, chatting with two people holding guns. I actually can't believe I'm still alive and breathing let alone chatting. Maybe if we keep chatting, it will delay or even defer the inevitable. But the question hovers. And when someone with a gun asks you a question, it is not polite to keep him waiting for the answer.

"It's my hobby," I say, hoping to sound casual. As if my hobby might be cooking or fly tying, like a normal person. A normal person you wouldn't want to shoot.

"Making up people is your hobby?"

"Giving eulogies is my hobby . . . at funerals . . . for people I don't know."

I open my mouth to continue justifying the whole idea, but it always sounds so stupid when I try to explain it to someone. So, I stop.

"That's it. That's why,"

Howard stares at me. Blankly at first, and then he smiles. A dry, thin-lipped smile that reminds me of cracked wood.

"Wait. That whole story was made up? There was no book? You made all that up?"

Howard laughs. A raspy, coughing sound that splinters his wooden smile. "You didn't even know Michael?"

"I didn't then, but I do now. I know about everything now."

"What the hell are you talking about?"

Howard's smile vanishes and he raises his gun. His hand is steady, his eyes are so cold, so penetrating, they drill into my skull, making two symmetrical holes directly above the bridge of my nose. I don't dare reach up to touch my forehead to feel if they're really there, to see if there's air escaping. I don't dare move, but I can keep talking.

"I know what Michael knew," I say, speaking directly into the gun, not caring anymore, daring him to shut me up for good. "Your original test patients suffered an unfortunate side effect. That is if you can classify murderous sociopathic behavior as a side effect. I know and Lily knows and other people are going to know."

Without another word, Howard squeezes the trigger and the wall behind me explodes. I cover my head.

"Howard! No!" Lily shrieks from the stairway. "Oh my god."

"Shut up, Lily," Howard says, turning to look at her for the first time, waving the gun from her to me and back again, gesturing with it like a laser pointer. "I didn't kill him. I just wanted him to stop talking."

"Why'd you do it Howard, why did you kill Michael?" Lily asks, backing up the stairs. "Isn't your job finding ways to cure people? Aren't you supposed to protect life?"

Howard laughs again and, pointing the gun up at her, making a small circle with the barrel as if tracing the outline of her face, caressing the shape.

"Where did you get that sugar-coated version of reality, Mrs. Rudolph?" he asks, sweetly. "You really should stop reading your own press releases. I did what I had to do to save myself and my company. I did what anyone would have done."

"Murder?" I shout. "*Anyone* would have resorted to murder?" I drop my arms to emphasize the insanity of this explanation. They've been up over my head for so long, I've lost the feeling in my fingers. They begin to tingle back to life as the blood returns. "You can't possibly believe that—"

"Gavin," Howard interrupts. "He's talking again."

Gavin swings his arm around and fires. A bullet ricochets off the stairs. I stop talking. Lily drops to her knees. She is still holding the file box in one hand.

"As I was saying," Howard continues, his tone as calm and informational as it was the day he gave us the tour of Nesler, "Michael stopped believing in what we'd created. He thought there was something wrong with the drug. But you want to know the only thing wrong? Michael loved those crazy old people. That's where the real problem lay."

"Tell me what happened," Lily pleads from her position on the stairway. "Tell me exactly what happened."

Howard moves closer to the stairs and places one Italian loafer on the bottom step.

"Did you know love is based almost entirely on trust? If you have any trust, you can be fooled."

Howard is looking directly at Lily. His eyes, his whole face really, is composed, serene. A tranquil businessman with a small revolver and a bland expression—it's more terrifying than a raving lunatic coming after you with an ax.

"You can be fooled into believing anything," Howard continues. "Michael wanted to believe we were going to fix things. That's why he came out to the airport to meet us that afternoon. We were going to figure out how to fix things before the media got hold of the story. We were going to make it all better and save his precious patients."

"But how? How did you do it?" Lily's voice is barely audible.

"With a little something in his coffee. Not exactly innovative, I realize, but highly effective. No nasty after-taste, no annoying residue in the blood stream, no reason to suspect anything other than a tragic accident."

Lily's head falls forward. She must be crying, but she doesn't look up. I'm so sorry, Lily. You don't deserve any of this. You should be at a country club somewhere playing tennis, getting your nails done, complaining about how hard it is to find good help. Please look at me. Look at me one last time, see me for the fool I am. Just look at me.

Everybody look at me! I turn back to Howard and yell.

"*This* isn't going to look like an accident!"

I want Howard's attention. Stop focusing on her, you asshole. I'm the one who dredged up this corpse from the river. I'm the one who figured it out. It's me you want.

"If you take us out, Howard, it's going to look like exactly what it is—cold-blooded murder."

"Actually, I was thinking murder-suicide," says Howard, quietly, in direct contrast to my screaming. He finally turns to look at me and smiles. "Unrequited love, extreme jealousy, an ill-fated affair gone horribly wrong. There are any number of people who've observed you and Lily together, Albert."

"Charlie."

"I don't much care who you are." The conciliatory tone is gone. The veneer of consummate professionalism is warping and pulling away from the core. The rotten, evil core. He spits his words at me. "I only know it won't be hard to come up with a story to explain the heartbreaking consequences of your actions."

"No one will believe you," Lily says, standing bolt upright again. "Charlie, catch."

She hurls the file box towards me, and in the same moment bends down and begins pushing and throwing everything off the stairs. Torches, hose reels and buckets of tools smash to the cement. Anything she can get her hands on goes flying. Not everything makes it all the way down. A drill hits the railing, shattering its plastic handle. A box of nails busts open and rains steel needles as it spins end over end. I reach up and miss the file box as it sails over my head.

Howard and Gavin freeze, watching the unexpected commotion with shocked expressions, as if not quite sure where to direct their attention or their weapons. I drop and lunge for the file box, crawling to where it's slid to a stop behind a pillar. I lift up my prize and turn around to show Lily. She's run to the very top of the stairs now, directly behind a welding cart. A large green oxygen tank and smaller red acetylene tank are strapped together on the front of the dolly. Her arms flex.

"Lily! Not that. Don't push that!"

There are gun shots. And screaming, lots of screaming. Are we all screaming? The cart rolls off the top step. It balances for a moment, but only a moment. And in that moment, I see Lily turn to look at me and I freeze the action. She's shouting something, but her words are frozen too. It won't hold. The instant is gone. I watch the wheels of the cart catch the corners of the steps, bouncing the heavy tanks like bottles of soda. The strap gives way and both tanks pitch forward, tumbling down the stairs. The regulator valve snaps off the oxygen first and above the crashing of steel on cement I hear the gas escape. The red tank hits the stairs. One step and its valve is gone. Second step and everything is gone. A single crashing boom reverberates and the explosion rips open in fury. Flames sweep out in all directions, reaching for anything, everything. Something slams against the side of my neck and tears through the flesh of my cheek. As I'm thrown backwards, I see Lily jump up. Too high. She's jumping too high. No one can jump that high.

"Lily!"

My face is burning. Fluorescent lights detonate over my head. Fire. Everywhere. Chewing its way through the piles of lumber, leaping over walls, licking up insulation . . . and people. Fire craves people. I grab the box and run. Run away.

I'm not sure which way is out. The building is a maze. All I can do is run away from the heat. I bump into walls in the dark. Doors are locked. Windows shatter in the distance. Maybe the sound is only in my head. Maybe I'm ten years old again and the fireman will come to get me. I clutch the box to my chest and run. My escape route intersects with another hallway. The smoke is less dense here, or it could only seem that way. Smoke is what kills you; that's what they say. And they always know. They always know what to tell you. Keep running. Just keep running. I should try to find Lily. I should stay and wait for her. But she's not coming. No one's coming. So I run. Out of the flames. Out.

A door comes into view through the smoke at the end of the hall. A heavy door with a bright red crash bar and a yellow caution sign: "Do not open. Alarm will sound." I barrel through it into the parking lot. The promised alarm shrieks, a tenor scream over the bass notes of the continued explosions. Keep running. Just keep running. Hugging the box. Across the empty parking lot. Into the street. Under a stand of fir trees marking the entrance of someone's driveway. There are houses all along this side of the street facing the construction site. Lights begin to snap on. People come out, pulling their robes over nightgowns and boxers.

Only then do I turn. I turn around and look back at the building. A building on fire never looks like it does in the cartoons, with neat little blooms of red and orange leaping out each window. It's haphazard and disorganized, like some great, hulking monster trying to shake free of the swarming flames and smoke. The black, spiraling, billowing smoke.

Sirens peal in the distance. The cool air stings the side of my face. I reach up to touch it and recoil from the feel of a wet, sticky substance where my skin should be. The file box sits at my feet, perhaps the only thing from the building that remains whole and unchanged. I drop to the ground next to it under the trees. Fire engines scream into view. There's a crowd now. The TV crews can't be far behind. I watch the fire writhing under the assault of the water hoses, not willing to release the building, not ready to return to the depths of hell.

Lily's in there. Lily's in there with Howard and Gavin and I'm out here with a plastic box of files. How did it come to this? An ambulance pulls up next to the fire trucks. No one's left, boys. Turn off your lights. Don't bother.

The tears are sudden and unfamiliar. I don't know how to stop them or why I should even try. I picture Lily's face. I conjure her up and invite her to sit next to me under the trees. It's safe here under the trees. No one can see us. We'll just sit and watch the building burn, you and I. And, I'll tell you more about who I really am. Do you remember I told you I loved you? Can you answer me now? Can you hear me? I'm so sorry.

The crowd pushes closer to the fence, angling for a better view. A woman wearing a fluffy pink bathrobe and enormous slippers in the shape of a laughing pig stops in front of my hiding place. I can only see her from the knees down, so the piggy slippers are particularly impressive. She's holding a little girl's hand. The little girl is in yellow pajamas and her slippers have giant plastic puppy heads on them. She's rubbing her eyes, and I imagine her pink, fluffy Mommy has drug her out of a deep sleep to see the spectacle happening right across the street. As they stand there, the little girl turns and sees me. She doesn't yell or jump or even tug at Fluffy Mommy to let her know. She doesn't seem to think it's odd that there's a strange, sad man sitting under the trees. She squats down just a little to get a better look at me, and waves. I wave back. Then Fluffy Mommy yanks her arm and their piggy and puppy slippers scuff off down the sidewalk.

I crawl out from the under the trees and start walking in the opposite direction. Nobody else notices the sobbing, disheveled man with the bleeding face carrying a box down the sidewalk. He doesn't really exist.

Don't worry, Lily. I'll finish things myself. I'll take it from here.

TWENTY SIX

I surprise myself, remembering how to hotwire a car. One of the bio-kids in a foster family I lived with as a teen was a late-stage juvenile delinquent. I acquired quite a few handy skills from him. Besides hotwiring, I can pick a simple lock, roll a joint with one hand and juggle. Of course, juggling is legal, but it's also weird. The media circus around the lab explosion is so raucous no one gives me a second glance when I cruise past in Lily's Mercedes.

Back at the condo, it's peaceful inside, nothing out of place, nothing to indicate a tragedy. Just quiet rooms waiting for someone to come home. I stand in the bathroom. My face looks worse than I'd imagined from the pain. There's a slash of raw skin about four inches long snaking down the side of my right cheek, like the trail of a blow torch.

It will take the police a while to figure out who was inside the lab, but I really shouldn't waste any time. I peel off my shirt. It reeks of smoke. I ball it up and throw it at my reflection in the mirror, hitting myself in the nose. It leaves a black smoke smudge as it slides down the mirror. Smoke and mirrors. I laugh at my own joke. But that's all it used to be. Just a distraction, a hobby. Everything but real. I yank open the medicine cabinet and rifle for something to clean and cover my wound.

I wonder if trauma victims normally want to take a shower. Maybe that's part of the shock. Once I snap to and realize just how much shit has hit the fan, I probably won't be able to function at all. They'll find me in about a week or so, sitting in a chair by the window like Norman Bates, rocking back and forth and stinking to high heaven.

The water feels like ten thousand needles stitching across my face. I tell myself it's good for me, it will help scour out the wound. I also scream like a little girl every time I duck under the shower head.

Clean, dressed and bandaged, I stand in the living room looking at the file box sitting on the polished oak coffee table. I reach down and flip open its battered top. Names stare up at me from the folder tabs, as if wondering what took me so long to get here. "Welcome to our world," they say. "Stay awhile. Have a cookie."

I pull a few from the box and open them on my lap.

Avery DeLong. There's a letter on fancy stationery. An embossed and foiled logo reads: *Livery Hills Jewelers*. Seems Mr. DeLong ordered a very expensive watch, but the watch had gone missing shortly after he'd come in to accept delivery and order engraving. The store was respectfully wondering if Mr. DeLong had inadvertently taken the watch at some point in the transaction as it had disappeared from the engraver's service box on the counter. The letter mentioned numerous unanswered phone messages. There's a handwritten note at the bottom of the page. The impeccable penmanship must be Howard's: *Watch returned with personal explanation of patient's new medication and interaction with an OTC decongestant. Store will not press charges. No dosage adjustment, observation required.*

Jonah Klein. Well, well . . . Hugh's father. A piece of notebook paper with a phone message taped to the top lays on a thick stack of more formal-looking reports. The message is from Hugh to Howard, and says simply, "fourth fire." Underneath, there's a list of four dates and four places. I'm guessing here, but I'd say the senior Mr. Klein was setting fires, and based on the addresses listed, I'd say he had very good taste in property values. *Dosage checked and augmented. Relocate to Grace Fountains, locked ward. Removal an option. Son paid in full.* Paid in full? Good ol' Hugh, not afraid to make a few bucks off his old man.

Myrtle Harris. The first paper in her folder is typed, a police report of some sort. *Andy Harris, 78, found dead in the bottom on his fishing boat on Blue Lake. Apparent heart attack.* A note was clipped to the report in the same precise writing. *Relocated to Bloomington. Removal scheduled for month five.*

I guess Howard *was* keeping his promise to Michel in the strictest sense of the word. He *was* taking care of the problem. Step out of line a little and they'll smooth it over with a medical excuse. Step out of line a lot and you get a new address. Step over the line completely, and you get "removed" from the situation. Problem over.

I stuff the folders back in the box. My briefcase with the lab results and insurance reports is still on the couch where I tossed it. I pull out a pad of paper, scribble the access route to Michael's computer notes and shove that in the box as well. I force the lid closed and shake my head at how much evidence is trapped inside. All the ducks are ready to be put into their rows.

The clock in the kitchen is inching toward a decent hour when my neighbors will wake up, flip on the news and spill coffee down the front of their nightshirts at the pictures of the smoldering remains of the lab and the news that bodies have been found inside. I'd best be going.

I dash off another note, this one to Dennis.

Sorry to drop and run, Dennis. Called out of town on an emergency investigation, but I'm sure the attached lab reports and case notes will be enough to get Klein. Draper can take it from here. Just for fun, tell him to ask Klein how his father is doing. No charge for this one, since I can't be here in person to roll the slime bucket and finish all that paperwork we love so much. I'll catch ya next time around. I'm sure I'll be back this way sooner than we think. There's always another rock crawler to ruin, right, Big Guy? Best, Charlie.

Justin's chemical report on my orange juice goes down the toilet. No need to prove someone was trying to kill me anymore. No need to prove anything anymore. In fact, it's a little unnerving how few loose ends there are to tie up. Dennis and a job well done, *check.* Landlord, keep the deposit, *check.* Bank account closed, forgo complimentary pen, *check.* A couple suitcases full of shirts and slacks, my toothbrush, an extra roll of bandages and ointment, *check.* Charlie's ready to roll, and just like that, Albert never happened. I guess some people aren't meant to make a mark. Maybe God puts some people on earth as placeholders—we're just here to save a spot until someone more important comes along. Watching, waiting, keeping their chair warm.

Lily would have noticed I was gone. She would have cared. She's the only one who really noticed Albert showed up in the first place. I don't count Howard and Gavin. To them, Albert was just something stuck to their shoe, an annoyance they desperately wanted to wipe off. Wipe out. Rub out. I was important to Lily. Even when she found out Albert was a sham, she saw me, the real me. She made me important. In order to wake up tomorrow morning, I have to believe I mattered to her. I reach into my briefcase and pull out one more piece of paper.

I stare at the blank sheet, forcing back the tears.

Lily Rudolph wore a gold locket around her neck. I don't know what was inside that locket, maybe a tiny photograph, maybe a lock of hair, maybe nothing. She never opened it for me. But Lily opened her life to so many people. She was the human face, the beautiful human face of Michael's research. She could open your eyes to what needed to be done. She could open your heart to understand the suffering of others. She could get you to open your wallets in order to find solutions for that suffering. When she smiled, there wasn't anything you wouldn't do. But there was another side to Lily, a side she kept locked, a side that worried she didn't really measure up to what everyone thought of her. You never saw that. No one saw that. But maybe because no one ever looked. How often do we simply take the word of others, accept the first impression as the whole person? It's easier that way. But the truth isn't easy. Reality isn't easy. Think about yourselves. Which parts are public and which are private? Lily Rudolph the Media Portrait was beautiful and self-assured, a polished surface. I feel very lucky to have had the opportunity to see a few of the reflections within that shiny surface. They were beautiful too, but in a different way. Cloudy and a little tarnished, like a silver spoon left too long at the bottom of a drawer or a secret key you find buried in the backyard. What you see is not always what you get. What you imagine is what you receive. Lily loved Michael. She loved all of you. She loved the idea of making a difference. She hated anyone who could be purposefully cruel. I won't just miss her. I will miss a piece of my life. A little piece I'll keep locked away, because all of us deserve to keep a little part of ourselves to ourselves. We don't ever have to open the locket.

I fold the eulogy and slip it into an envelope. As I look around the condo one last time, I see Lily in the chair, laughing and kicking off her shoes. Now she's holding a mug of coffee and staring, but not at me. Not at me. Click off the lights, pull the door closed and the movie clips stop. The morning air is fresh and damp with moisture rising off the lake. I breath in its smell one last time, slam my suitcases into the trunk of Lily's car and throw the file box and assorted envelopes on the front seat. If I hurry, I can deliver my packages like some demented Santa Claus and be gone before the ashes have fully cooled.

My old apartment is cold and silent except for the whirring of the tiny refrigerator. I drop a letter to my landlord and the keys on the kitchen counter. The next loser who rents the place can have my Tupperware and the ugly towels. Bank's not open, so I pull out the maximum from the ATM and slide a letter into the deposit lockbox, instructing them to hold my statements until further notice. As if they care what happens to my few dollars. I'm a record number in a database somewhere. Probably India.

The insurance office tower is also closed up tight. Glass double doors reveal an empty front lobby, no security guard at the information desk. I never noticed how big that damn desk is. It must look smaller during the day with all the people around it. The thing is like five feet tall and at least twice that long, all twisting steel, glass and stone. It's like the entrance to a tomb, or maybe one of those theme park adventure rides. *Welcome to Business Land. Please keep your wing tips and briefcases inside the car at all times. For your own safety, do not throw up your hands during the Stock Plunge.*

I unlock the doors, duck in, and lock them again behind me. A quick glance left to right for the roaming guard, some tubby guy named Herb if memory serves, and I zip across the marble floor to the main bank of elevators. Three doors open simultaneously when I push the call button and three bells chime, certainly loud enough to bring Herb running, or at least lumbering from his hiding place. I jump in the nearest car and punch the close button, once, twice, three times. Another bell as the doors finally shut. Stupid safety warnings.

It seems like I was here days ago, not hours. Just twenty-some hours ago, I woke up in Lily's guest room. I knew then the day ahead was going to be rough, but somehow, even I couldn't have imagined this level of death and destruction. Why couldn't I have gotten a flat tire? That would have been perfect. Fate's way of keeping me safe and sound in Lily's driveway. Fate must have overslept or maybe he was busy screwing up someone else's life, but he sure let me down.

My floor is dark, and I keep it that way as I walk to the back and dump the investigation folder, office keys and my security badge on Dennis' desk. There's a bit of morning light stabbing through the cracks in the blinds and I can see my smiling face on the badge. Charlie Sandors: he looks like a nice enough guy. I hear the elevator ding on the other side of the floor. Herbie, with his too-tight polyester pants, must be quicker than I remember. I exit Dennis' office and slip around the corner to the stairwell. No bell on this door, just a silly picture of a stick man racing down the stairs, chased by a bouncing ball of flame. The knob gives a near silent click as it shuts and I copy the stick man's form as I escape down fifteen flights to the street.

The parking lot of the main police station is full of squad cars and television vans with their satellite dishes cranked up into the sky. I stop a block away and scan for a possible drop point. I can't walk in the front door. I imagine they usually ask questions when you stop by with a box full of evidence. All my notes, my research on Michael, Howard's original patient reports, everything I could think of is crammed in there with the files. The top barely latches. It will be frustrating for them to search for Albert Mackey, that writer-guy from the funeral, who everyone will recall but no one will be able to quite describe or locate or really remember in any detail. The poor detective assigned to call all the medical journals to look for a technical writer named Mackey. That'll be a fun job, like a little phone scavenger hunt. What a shame he'll come away empty-handed. No prize for you, officer. You're looking for air.

I watch a patrol car pull in to the lot. The driver rolls down his window and leans out to talk to another officer who's walking by. He parks next to a row of shrubs and heads across the lot for the station. His window is still down.

I get out with the box and stroll down the sidewalk. I hear the TV reporters delivering their stand-ups from various points around the parking lot. "A local tragedy . . . Still waiting for answers . . . Investigation continues . . . Back to you, Mike . . . " There's no one near the car with the open window. I lean against the door for a minute and then toss the box through the window onto the front seat and continue walking.

"Whoa, dude, what happened to you?"

The voice comes from my right, my bandage side. I swing around and spot a shaggy-haired kid in a red flannel shirt. He's perched on the bumper of one of the TV vans, munching a doughnut. His upper lip is covered with a light dusting of powdered sugar.

"What?"

"Your face? What happened to your face? It looks nasty."

I reach up and touch the bandage. The top part along my cheekbone is wet and squishy. There must be something gross oozing through.

"Infection," I say. "Car wreck. Glass."

Good lord, I sound like an imbecile.

"Bummer, man," the kid says, accepting my monosyllabic answers at face value. "Are you from one of the stations?"

"No, I, uh, I live around the corner," I say, gesturing behind me in the general direction of my car. "I was just wondering what all the commotion was."

"That big lab project blew up during the night," the kid says, waving his arms in the air, little bits of doughnut flying. "Big ass explosion, I guess. Sounds like there were people inside."

"That's awful."

"Brings out us news ghouls though, doesn't it? Nothing like a little death and destruction to boost ratings." He chuckles and reaches into a grease-stained bag at his feet to pull out a doughnut and holds it out to me. "Want a doughnut? I got a whole bag."

I realize with a rush of saliva that I haven't eaten anything in a very long time. I accept the doughnut and the kid smiles.

"Must be kind of a drag living so close to a police station," he says, finishing the last couple bites of his doughnut and reaching into the bag for another. "Sirens all night long."

"It's not so bad," I say. Little puffs of powdered sugar punctuating my consonants. "You get used to it."

"Guess so. Does it hurt?"

He's looking at me. I think he's looking at me—his hair is so long it falls almost down to his nose. He must see me, and the rest of the world, through a perpetual hair curtain. Better than rose-colored glasses, I suppose.

"The noise?"

"No," he whines. "Your face, does it still hurt?"

"A little."

"You're going to have a hellacious scar, man."

I swallow the last bite of doughnut and lick the sugar off my fingers.

"Probably. Always wear your seatbelt. That's the moral to this story."

"Trevor!" A woman's voice shouts from around the front of the van.

"Gotta go," says the kid. "That's Amanda, our star reporter. She gets nervous when the camera's off for too long."

"Thanks for the doughnut."

"Sure thing. Nice talkin' to ya."

He disappears around the side of the van and I make a run for the sidewalk. Activity's picking up everywhere. I gotta get out of Dodge.

My last stop is Mary Anderson's house. There's a light on in the kitchen and the morning newspaper lies rolled up in the middle of the lawn. The grass is damp as I cross to pick up the paper. No fire headline here. I bet newspaper people hate it when big stuff happens after the printing deadline. I slip Lily's eulogy under the rubber band where I know Mary will see it right away and lean the paper against the screen door. She'll know what to do. She'll help me say goodbye, because I didn't get to do that.

It's 7:45 when I hit the freeway and blend into rush hour traffic. The lab explosion is all over the radio news.

"Fire investigators are still combing through what's left of the Nesler lab site. We've received word they have located human remains, but the bodies are badly burned and positive identification is not yet available. However, the latest report we received, just about an hour ago from fire investigators, is that one man, Gavin VanMorten, an employee of Nesler Pharmaceuticals, was pulled out alive. His condition is extremely grave. We're told he is comatose with second and third-degree burns over 90% of his body. We don't know his current condition, but we do know the police are holding out hope he might regain some ability to communicate. I have Police Commissioner Holgate here with me for just a few minutes. Chief Holgate, what is happening right now with the investigation?"

"It's still very early, Carol, we're just starting to put all the pieces together."

"We've heard both Lily Rudolph, whose foundation owns the lab, and Howard Stanich, CEO of Nesler, are missing. Is that true?"

"We've been unable to contact either Mrs. Rudolph or Mr. Stanich. The fact that Mr. VanMorten, an employee of Nesler, was pulled out indicates other Nesler people might have been inside the building when it exploded. We also know Mrs. Rudolph's car is missing, but friends and family have no ideas where or why she would be gone."

"So are you saying you think the remains you've found are Lily Rudolph and Howard Stanich?"

"I can't confirm that, but it is certainly a very real possibility at this point."

"Thank you for your time, Chief Holgate. As many of our listeners know, Michael Rudolph, Lily's husband, was recently killed in a tragic plane crash. The Rudolph Foundation was underwriting the lab construction and the assumption being heard out here is that Lily was meeting with VanMorten and Stanich on some sort of lab business when the explosion occurred. No one is sure why the meeting was taking place at such a late hour, but there are so many unanswered questions this morning. It will be days before we fully understand the true story behind this tragedy."

I turn down the radio. I can make it to Chicago in three hours. At some point they'll discover Lily's car in the train-station parking lot. By then, I'll be gone. The true story will be gone. The TV kid was right: death and destruction rarely brings out the best in people.

TWENTY SEVEN

The locals in the small coffee shop are complaining about the weather. *Coldest spring on record*, according to the man in the wool shirt and red suspenders. He tells the pretty blond waitress he'd bet his left nut there'll be another snowstorm before the week's out. That sounds like an awfully serious gamble and makes me glad I'm wearing a hat.

I turn the page of my newspaper and continue searching. Years of big butts have worn permanent indentations in the booth's brown plastic bench and I have to keep shifting my position to keep from rolling into one. After three weeks, it's getting difficult to find much information about Park Hills in the Chicago paper. But there's not a hell of a lot of news options here and I feel pretty lucky to have snagged a *Tribune*. I'm in a tiny town by the name of Vicksburg, Vermont. It's what the tourist brochures describe as "quaint," which means there aren't a lot of extras. You got your coffee shop, gas station/grocery/deli, antique store, couple of churches, a school, and the Tall Timber Motor Lodge where I've been staying. That pretty much covers the bases I guess; anything more would be frivolous.

There it is, finally, on page twenty-three. Coverage has been slinking from the front page, every day a little farther, backing away from the spotlight, soon it should be able to turn and run out of sight altogether.

Witness Death Halts Nesler Trial. Death? I scan the article. The earlier reports had been much more action-packed. The initial story about the lab explosion had made the front page all over Illinois, even got a hit on CNN and Fox News. The story stayed hot for days as they broke open the whole conspiracy behind the Nesler testing. I especially liked it when they found the notes and the files, from an *anonymous source*, and began identifying all the original patients. There were interviews with medical specialists, even a picture of Mary Anderson and her father. I must admit I was a little upset there hadn't been more coverage of the *anonymous source*. It was as if he'd never existed. As if.

I hadn't been able to find any mention of Lily's funeral, but I have a picture of it in my mind. There are huge stands of flowers: roses, ivy and lily of the valley. All the beautiful people are there again in the pews. Mary delivers my eulogy herself, even though she's scared. She cries at the end. The beautiful people wait in silence until she finishes crying and then look down at their empty laps.

It was easy to disappear. Ridiculously easy, really. But evaporating is one thing, forgetting is another. Forgetting is ridiculous to the point of absurd. Kurt Vonnegut absurd. A parking place in front of a trendy restaurant absurd. When I close my eyes, I see Lily fly up through the flames. When I open my eyes, I see her in Michael's study, framed in the window, hair falling forward. There's really no break. Awake, asleep, staring into a cup of coffee, I can always see. The most forgetting will allow you is to open a compartment in your brain where you can deposit the images for short periods of time. But the compartment is small and the latch is weak and before long, the images sneak out again and settle in behind your eyes.

Witness Death Halts Nesler Trial. Gavin finally gave out. Never spoke another word. I'm the only one who knows the last thing he said was, "Stay where you are." Sorry, Gavin. No one stays in one place for long. I guess it's hard to have a trial without someone to prosecute. Really no use sending a dead guy to jail; he'd just take up space. The article says his remains will be shipped back to his family. Touching.

I have to make one call. Not really returning to the scene of the crime. I prefer to tell myself I was the one who helped stop the boulder from crushing more victims, not the one who pushed it off the cliff in the first place. But I needed to know more than what the newspapers were telling me. What is it the therapists call it? Closure? I needed closure.

Mary answers the phone on third ring.

"Hello."

"Mary? It's Charlie."

Silence.

"Charlie Sandors," I explain.

"Where did you go?"

Her voice is thin and hoarse.

"I had to leave, Mary."

"Where are you?"

"It doesn't matter. How are you? How's Jake?"

I picture Mary sitting at her kitchen table, her glasses sliding down her nose.

"We're okay. All the commotion's been a little hard on Dad. He doesn't understand what's going on. To tell you the truth, I don't either."

As usual, I'm making Mary's life miserable. But just once more, just one more time and I'll leave you alone.

"Did you get the eulogy?"

"Yes."

"And you delivered it?"

"Yes."

I want to ask her what people thought. I want to know if she got the inflection right, the pauses, the tone. How did the crowd react? What did they say afterwards?

"Who did you say it was from?"

"I didn't say and no one asked."

No one asked? No one cared. Just another collection of words. Nice words about a nice lady. How nice. People don't listen. They hear, but they don't listen.

"What about the other patients?" I ask, changing the subject. "What have you heard?"

The line goes quiet. Did I lose the connection? Reception up here in the mountains is pretty sketchy sometimes.

"Why are you calling me, Charlie?" Her voice is still barely above a whisper. "Shouldn't you call the police and tell them what you know?"

Ah. Reception is fine. Communication is sketchy.

"I can't call the police. There's nothing to tell them anyway. I left them with everything."

"I figured that was you."

"Did they ask you about me?"

"No. They didn't know you'd ever met me."

I wonder how long they tried to find Albert Mackey before he became a file folder of dead end notes in a box, sealed and date stamped and archived.

"And you didn't volunteer any information?"

"No."

"Thank you."

"There are some things that are meant to be private."

She'd understood the eulogy. I knew she would. That's why I'd left it for her. I wonder if Jake is there at the table with her, watching her talk, watching a fly crawl across the counter.

"So have you heard anything?" I ask again.

"They're going to rebuild the lab. The Foundation has promised that. And they've located all the original patients who are still alive and brought them back to Park Hills. There's a new program, but it's based more on Michael's original theories and less on the drug and stem cell therapy."

There's a pause as my unspoken question hovers.

"Dad's not part of it," she answers my thought. "He's not healthy enough. At least not right now. Maybe later."

We both know *maybe later* doesn't exist for Jake. Maybe today, maybe tomorrow is the best we can hope for.

"It's really calmed down a lot," Mary says. "The media stuff. The phone stopped ringing a week or so ago. Do you know someone from *People* magazine called me right after it happened? Can you believe that?"

"I saw a picture of you and Jake in the *Chicago Tribune*."

"Really?"

"Uh huh."

We're dwindling. Soon the conversation will resort to the weather.

"Mary, I'm sorry if I hurt you in any way. I didn't . . . "

"No," she says, interrupting. "I think we did the right thing. I think we made a difference."

"I hope so."

"Will I hear from you again?"

"No. You're rid of me for good. I promise."

"Then take care of yourself."

"You do the same, Mary. You do the same."

When I hang up the phone, I imagine Mary on the other end doing the same thing. *Click.* Done. Turn and walk forward. Always walk forward.

The tiny Lutheran church with the white spire is barely a quarter full for the funeral. Snow falls lightly outside the windows. Maybe the weather has kept people away. Or maybe there just weren't a lot of people to come. As the short service comes to a close, a slightly built man stands and walks to the front of the chapel. He bears the leathery scar of a burn victim across one cheek. He walks up the aisle; the small crowd stares and whispers. No one seems to recognize him. He hears them wondering. This happens all the time. It's part of the game. Charlie Sandors turns to face them, smiles sadly, and adjusts the microphone to speak.

"Gavin VanMorten was a man who loved whales."

The End

About the Author

LIZ MCKINNEY-JOHNSON spent the majority of her professional life as an award-winning marketing copywriter and creative director, running her own agency for most her career. There she honed the ability to wade through piles of client-provided data, unearth the one or two pieces of information a normal person might actually find interesting, then craft that discovery into an attention-grabbing message. It's a skill that translates well to plot and character development. As does the field itself, since most advertising is about 98% fiction.

More from The Eulogist

As a purchaser of this book, I would like to personally thank you and offer you a bonus. If you can take the time to write a review, please email **admin@theeulogist.com** with a copy of what you wrote, where it was posted and when. Be sure to use your primary email and include your name.

Once every three months, your name will be entered into a drawing for a **$100 Amazon Gift Card**. Use it to buy more books . . . or whatever captures your imagination.

I will also add your name to my email list so you can be among the first to know when additional titles will be released.

You can contact me through theeulogist.com, which is also where you can follow *Charlie's Latest Thoughts* – random musings on the people and places he encounters on his daily travels.

www.ingramcontent.com/pod-product-compliance
Lightning Source LLC
Chambersburg PA
CBHW051228260626
47162CB00002B/318

* 9 7 8 0 9 8 9 0 6 8 1 3 0 *